THE
WORMING
OF
AMERICA
OR,
AN ANSWER TO THE
ARRAIGNMENT
OF
WOMEN

THE WORMING of AMERICA or
An Answer to the Arraignment of Women

ISBN 978-1-7321669-0-5
First edition

www.free-gracepress.com

THE WORMING OF AMERICA

OR AN

TO THE

ARRAIGNMENT

OF

WOMEN

By

AUTUMN LEAF

Printed in the year, of the
Free-Grace Controversy,

Boston
1650

Contents

ILLUSTRATIONS

INTRODUCTION

Like all good Awakenings and revolutions, the Great Awakening and the American Revolution started with a good conversation. But when and with whom did that good conversation start? New England Transcendentalism started somewhere, but where and how? The seed of Civil Disobedience was planted by someone in Massachusetts, but by who and why? Mahatma Gandhi and Martin Luther King must have relied on someone with strong shoulders to bring down the English Empire in India and segregated America, but who?

It certainly was not the royal Puritans of Boston and Connecticut, but it was the Separatists of northern England. They carried the torch of the *"Good ole cause"* across the Atlantic and formed Providence, Rhode Island; Exeter, New Hampshire; Plymouth, Massachusetts; and Southampton, New York. Judeo-Christian historians will say the American War for Independence in 1776 wasn't class warfare, but the English Civil War was and the French Revolution certainly was... so why not in America also?

The American Separatists weren't scared of fighting for an Enlightened Commonwealth. Patriots, men like Thomas Paine with his *Common Sense* pamphlet lit the spark that ignited the American Revolution. So what happened to this American fire, what happened to the First Amendment in America that forbids our government and its taxes from favoring or establishing any religion? What happened to the founding fathers' advice to exclude all religion from our commonwealth for the common man? What happened to the Declaration of Independence from royal monarchs, standing-armies, and financial debt in America? Why did American politicians violate the distribution of wealth revolution and the commonwealth war for independence? And why did the royal enemy of the Separatists — the religious Puritans or the Judeo-Christian fascists of Boston in 1650 — come to rule both political parties in America 2018.

Here within *The Worming of America* those questions and philosophical questions from the English Civil War in 1640 are asked once again. Is life for the royal "*haves,*" or, is life for the commonwealth — "*the have-nots?*" Questions about debt... is America still a colony for the Bank of England and the Queen via the Federal Reserve? Is America still a colony, a dumb soldier (a Gomer Pyle) for English imperialism and its Empire? Is America a control-fraud democracy? These almost four-hundred-year-old English and American questions sting today in 2018 just as sharply as they did in 1650. Perhaps their attack is even more crippling today because these unanswered questions have been purposely buried by religious politicians in both American political parties. Embarrassing American questions about our standing-armies' war crimes against humanity and critical questions about the rights and freedoms of women — all go unanswered in 2018. These American questions about the truth and treachery are infected wounds that are still festering — a prisoner's dilemma. These questions of authority, these lesions are a social gangrene and were brought over from England's and Europe's civil wars. These sad questions are not in the spirit of America, and their existence is America's failure.

Free-Grace Press, in good-faith to our founding fathers and to our future, is proud to re-publish Autumn Leaf's, *The Worming of America, or an Answer to The Arraignment of Women,* which is a post-modern historical-fiction study or play on questions of debt, sin, and freedom. As the publisher who found this pamphlet / novel, we have included all 28 original drawings and the following two letters as a Foreword and a Preface. The letters were picked out of many anonymous notes and letters left behind with the novel for the last 368 years. Front letters in this printing encapsulate an anonymous female (Genealogist X) as the Foreword and then a male's (Professor X) opinion of the novel in the Preface.

In the polemic spirit of Jane Anger's _The Protection for Women_ we publish _The Worming of America_ as a rebuttal to Joseph Swetnam's novel published in 1615 titled, _The Arraignment of Lewd, Idle, Forward, and Unconstant Women: or the Vanity of Them. Choose You Whether: With a Commendation of Wise, Virtuous and Honest Women: Pleasant For Married Men, Profitable For Young Men, and Hurtful to None._

Our author and illustrator Autumn Leaf, in the spring of 1650 Boston, shares her thoughts, pain, and drawings with you the reader for over four hours on the morning of June 1st. Autumn Leaf is a daughter of _"The good ole cause"_ — the eternal war between _the haves_ and _the have nots,_ as she writes and draws out her case. Autumn's claim, as it's been with all civilizations in time, is the malicious and willful betrayal of the common man and their family by politicians and high priests who have enriched themselves well before their citizens and parishioners. Autumn's religious and civil reformation case is not brought forward as her mentors brought theirs: from within the church court, out of cozy academia, or from comfy castles in England and Europe. No, Autumn Leaf moves beyond Giordano Bruno, Martin Luther, and William Blake, as her struggle takes place during the "Monstrous birth" of American imperialism in 1650 Boston.

Autumn Leaf has written a tragic-comedy: in one large part, it is a treatise to our English thinking soul, and in another smaller part, she has created a theater of the absurd. The satirical prose is in the languid and serious style of Virginia Woolf woven together with dialogue and descriptions reminiscent of Flannery O'Connor and Walt Whitman. _The Worming of America_ is a journey / inspection of fourteen children possibly representing the cardinal sins of America. Female and male white greed, gluttony, wrath, and envy are given a fair chance and asked to explain their "good-work." Male and female lust, sloth, and pride as our American children, are asked to explain their *good-work* in a simple, wooden, elemental classroom. As the readers, we move through an Awakening of *Might*, or perhaps an Awakening of *Nothing*? Our American journey will be filled with ups and downs / twists and turns — where our own ideas of civilization, religion, sin, debt, and humanity are questioned. Asian, Egyptian, Sumerian, Pagan, Christian mystic, and American Indian ideologies and philosophies — purposely buried to this very day by religious fascists — are now exhumed into the light.

On top of this literary triumph, *The Worming of America* is not just for the literate, but for the illiterate. Non-English readers are not excluded either, as all of Autumn Leaf's original illustrations are included in this printing and they alone express and describe the novel in an universal visual language. The sun will shine tomorrow even as you read or look into this dark comedy, and for better or worse the truth will be felt and laid bare in the American sunlight. Not because we live within our Fathers' *Age of Reason*, no... quite the opposite, as our author Autumn leaf writes. *The Worming of America* will be heard in 2018 and beyond because America now lives in the age of treason.

FOREWORD

Dear Reader,

As a genealogist and amateur historian, I travel to many small towns and former towns now in ruins to dig around in courthouses and old church baptismal records. Some of these places are so much from a former time that they don't have accommodations for an out-of-towner with a notebook and a lot of questions. So I have equipped my little car with all I need to camp out. I literally travel back in time to do my work.

This past summer I gained access to an old family farm on Shelter Island, New York. Taxes and upkeep had rendered the large compound too expensive to keep up, even by the well-heeled family who had commissioned my investigations. The family heirs, fighting amongst themselves, would be junking the home's contents in preparation for selling it to the highest bidder.

The family lawyer sent me a house key and leave to carry away anything that might help me describe the foundation of their family and, in turn, American history. The current large Victorian farmhouse with numerous agricultural out-buildings and barns stands like an understated manor. A pasture rambles down to a boathouse and dock on the bay, the design of an enlightened and gothic America long gone. These bedrooms and parlors were the regal comforts of _Great Gatsby_ "summer folk" who had enjoyed this place for their at-ease periods in their self-important lives. Chipped blue china, warped old portraits, maps on the walls, a trestle table on a long, screened porch — all these suggested stories. But my quest was in the dark and dusty library, at the backs of closets, in the attic — places things might have been hidden by those who had secrets. My client is separated by generations from those secrets, but curious about the past of their prominent forbears, whose history you likely know.

As the hired genealogist I found some things that well satisfied the family lawyer on-the-record, but other finds that I presented off-the-record, and the family will likely keep these very quiet. What I found was an old pamphlet — a novel or diary — from 1650, dedicated to Mary Dyer: a founder of Quakerism in America. Mary is to have rumored to have stayed on this Shelter Island property before she left to fight the Puritans in Boston in the spring of 1650. This novel undermines the accepted history of my client's family (and American history) so thoroughly that they would certainly not want the book to come to light — and that is their privilege.

So after I write what follows here I will leave this novel with my bookmarks and comments just as others have done for the last three hundred and thirty-seven years. I will continue on my travels, but beforehand I will secrete a copy of this book in another place where it will be discovered and brought to light later — for it should come to light — but not at my direct responsibility. I have a duty to my employer and to my own family. So, what can I say about this book?

The Worming of America, or, an Answer to The Arraignment of Women is a complex novel — or is it just an astounding diary of 1650? It has multiple layers reminiscent of a sonata or multi-movement symphonic work. The authorship and voice belong to Susan Hutchinson, the daughter of Anne Hutchinson, who was banished from the Boston colony for not respecting her Elders in 1640. Anne Hutchinson was later massacred with most of her family by the Lenape Indians in New Netherland, but Susan her daughter was spared. She was spared by the Indians, but taken hostage, and they changed her name to "Autumn Leaf" in the five years she lived with them. This novel takes place in the spring of 1650, a few weeks after Autumn's ransom was paid by her Boston relatives and she returned to Boston civilization from New Netherland, which today is New York City.

The book carries us through a brief morning with Autumn Leaf walking to school through the Boston streets, then interacting with her teacher and classmates in school, then all of them go to the hanging of Mary Dyer. Mary was a Quaker heretic who had been befriended by Anne Hutchinson in earlier years and, it seems, set up correspondence with Autumn Leaf in the woods of New Netherland.

Autumn's bitter, critical, and widely-sweeping view of her surroundings, her history, and her fellow townspeople has the tone of philosophy, not history. Autumn is the heroine who embodies these ideas, finding comrades in Mary Dyer and perhaps, partially, in her schoolteacher, "Ms." Appleton. The book is puzzling in a post-modern sense — it is full of modern questions and references and is not strictly true to its own historical context. Time collapses and layers itself with the reinforced themes that a musical work might have.

It's fascinating that in this particular morning in mid-17th-century Boston we can explore world history, really, and the ongoing tensions among those of differing political, religious, and ethical persuasions, just as we do here today in 1987. The story follows several themes that interweave like music. We have the morning at school, the series of Mary Dyer's letters to Autumn, and Autumn's history with the Lenape. Beyond that personal experience we have a larger story: we learn of the local history of Boston's relationship with numerous other Indian tribes, the "homeroom inspection" of Boston's children, Mary Dyer's own drama of dissent, and the large ongoing tension of the English Civil War.

That war in Autumn Leaf's eyes was a short-lived war of *"the have-nots"* against *"the haves,"* or the common man against the royal monarchy, in which the royal Crown fell and then rose once again ten years later.

In this novel Autumn Leaf incisively observes the Boston streets of 1650, painting a picture for us that we will not soon forget. She also explains her time with the Lenape from an analytic, outsider's perspective from close quarters, giving insight there that most Bostonians of her time would never have. The collection of sinful students in the school represents every possible perversion of Boston culture of the time (and of our time). They are all unpleasant children in one way or another, as could be expected representing the seven deadly sins as is rumored and talked about in the many notes and letters stuffed into this old pamphlet.

If I did have a demand, as a woman, I would ask Autumn the narrator, "Why are all the heroes heroines? Does no man qualify for enlightenment?"

Overall, the complex structure is intriguing, but it is tricky the way it all fits together. A reader who can follow the narrative should feel proud of having worked out the puzzle of it. Everything Autumn tells us comes through her gimlet eye into her vulnerable mind, as I see it. She saw her family slaughtered and then was herself taken captive for years. Was she enlightened by the Lenape or is she suffering Stockholm Syndrome? Is Boston an enlightened education or more of an incarceration for her?

In some ways the voice is amazingly beautiful, and sometimes the language is so dense and intricate it's difficult to follow. The rough sexual language and profanity are jarring and certainly not what I would expect in a 17th-century Boston girl's diary! But her voice is clear and her quiet dislocation with "Nothing," in Autumn's words, is so raw and fresh that I must quietly leave this work somewhere it may be found by others.

I will never see Boston's early days... or America's latter days... in quite the same way.

Genealogist X

Shelter Island, New York

Summer of 1987

PREFACE

To My Dearest [Xxxxx],

During this early spring of 2004 I paid a visit to our ivy league college president. She has a picture of a pupa alongside another picture of a beautiful caterpillar. The caption reads, "Don't quit until the miracle happens." As tenured professors, we are encouraged to view our students as unrealized miracles. We nod in agreement about educational miracles and privately joke of spending childhood vacations lighting caterpillars on fire. If given a choice, would this caterpillar remain like most of us — rooted in fear and fixed in place? Reading *The Worming of America* has changed me. Be forewarned.

I would never have addressed this free-grace controversy debated throughout this book if it weren't for you who found it in the attic of your friend's house. Everything has been happening so quickly with us since you enrolled in my American Poetry class. I am not sure what's going on except that you look beautiful wearing my shirts after your visits to my townhouse. I know you forced your way into my heart, but I wasn't sure exactly why. Were you looking for a good grade, help with your senior thesis paper? Then, you laid these *Worming of America, or, an Answer to The Arraignment of Women* pages on my lap, much like a cat who lays a dead bird at her masters' feet. Your gift was a demand for a book review if our liaisons were to continue. I would never read any old book found in a New England attic not reviewed by one of my ivy classmates, but like the furry caterpillar, what choice did I really have now with you?

The book is the story of a morning in 1650 through the eyes of unforgivingly critical Autumn Leaf. She is the daughter of Anne Hutchinson, who was banished by the Puritans from the colonies for her religious beliefs. Anne and her family was subsequently killed by Indians as she wandered south into Dutch territory which today is New York. Her daughter Susan, or Autumn Leaf, was taken prisoner and lived with the local indigenous tribe before she returned to civilization. Naturally, Anne's daughter would have trouble accepting a society that treated her mother so unfairly. Autumn Leaf's morning culminates with a class trip to view the hanging of Mary Dyer, another religious deviant who sympathized with Anne Hutchinson's idea of free-grace.

I found this book most unsettling. Spun around and dizzy like a child on a summer day, I found myself swirling in the images. As you know, I constantly ask my literature and poetry students to explore and question structure and prose, but when I see this authentically achieved on the page, I am puzzled, irritated, and threatened if the work is not championed by the ivy-league and it's wanna-be henchman writing the newspaper and magazine literary reviews.

I wonder is there anything this writer respects or holds dear? It is certainly not the Bible, the Elders of England, Europe, or America. I am perplexed, not knowing which direction the attack is coming from. All things explode at the cellular level. I never knew what was coming around the next corner as I read. Sometimes I found myself pleasantly surprised, others times shocked and repulsed. I like the author to give me a secret nudge so I know the meaning of their ambiguity. Here I am only left stroking my beard until I turn that critical eye toward my own existence, which then seems intentional.

As you know, my dear [Xxxxxx], I do go to church and have gone my whole life. And you, my only love, you refuse to attend. You dismiss me saying, "I have better things to do like laundry and sleep. Just read that *Worm-book*, my little Professor, and explain the free-grace controversy to me!"

I then felt fraudulent kneeling and chewing on the stale cardboard flesh of God in church, I washed the wine across my lips and sat hunched and frozen in the pew. I ached with the thought of my lover not letting me touch her body until I gave her my review of this free-grace controversy. I started freezing up intellectually like a child.

I am a professional middle-aged married man with a family, but really just a hedonistic boy — a hypocrite. I am a respected college professor who lives for the attention of college girls, yet every week I go back to church or synagogue with my family and throw my life up to some emasculated man hiding behind a man-made invention. In my first Jewish marriage and family I said my "Afternoon Prayer," now in my second Christian marriage and family I say my "Hail Marys" and go home to my hypocritical family all over again. No matter who I pray and talk to, I pray and pray, getting older and older, talking and talking... and God... and my prayers to him... only feel like they are fading away — as death slides in.

As with my religious experiences, I like my reading experiences prepared and on my own terms. The worst reading is to have prose with no answers, no expected rhythm, or an unorthodox measure, yet ambiguity and unanswered questioning drives the pulse of this work. Autumn Leaf jumps around within philosophy, history, and ethics not using *haiku* but *haibun* with a metafiction prose. The prosimetrum meter becomes not just an expressive tool, a "mathesis" style, but all together — a mathemaku style. This metafiction and mathemaku style is not a just post-modern and hyper-modern style, but a meta-modern style.

The novel is a true historical-fiction novel, but not a true historical fiction novel. Correct or incorrect is not the issue, but our life and soul is the issue. The novel adopts no standard form, moving itself toward a vibrant individual style and freedom. As I read about the "homeroom inspection" I feel as if I was there in that 1650 Boston classroom looking towards Autumn Leaf with pleading eyes saying, "Save me. SAVE ME!" And all, she says is, "It's free and right in front of you. It's all free."

I think yes, but ask Autumn, "Why can't I unbind myself?" But Autumn wouldn't answer. My questions went to the brave Mary Dyer, but she said nothing either. I asked God to free me and I was free in my imagination, but very alone on my floor crying, for I was not familiar with freedom. In the orthodox ivy league, we abolish style and freedom even though we all know freedom is evolution and style is the man.

But my dear [Xxxxx], here within *The Worming of America* beware, the female author has style and she evolves with us. Once we the reader get ahold of the structure it shifts again. I wanted to dismiss this work as polemic, anti-religious, and anti-social, but as time moves on, moral and stylistic points I cannot forget or escape are solidifying all around me. I feel used and exhausted, but illuminated.

It was then that I saw, like a diamond through the brain, the answers you sought in my review of this book. I now send this brief review to you now, as my love for *The Worming of America* has taught me not to ask so many silly questions.

That's because after realizing our salvation is always free and not based on material works, I got off my floor and cried to myself. I asked in the dark of my study, "God, are you here now?" A soothing flow of free-grace warmth came down upon me — I was "Awakened." My next thought was, "God, have you been watching me this whole time?" There was no answer, no warmth... just cold silence, more of Autumn's "Nothing." I then realized I didn't need an answer from God and that was the point. I was free now... graceful... I suppose, light, but kind of sad. Sad because I finally realized my "good-work" floats in the air alone. All of my life's material goods, power, and petitions to the Lord are bundled up and sitting in a dusty bin, under a desk in a cold and lonely mail room. The mail-man never comes.

I eagerly await your love and attention again, [Xxxxxx], although for some reason I'm sure my review and answers to this free-grace controversy will disappoint you. Everyone's free-grace or Awakening is unique, unusual, and disruptive because selflessness goes against our individual grain poet-ically. And for those self-realization reasons, for those poetic reasons, I doubt I will ever hear from you, or see you again.

I wish you the best. I wish you free-grace!

Sincerely,

Professor X

Spring Semester, 2004

CHAPTER I

Not a Mayflower, but a Lioness — Crowns for Kids

NOT A MAYFLOWER, BUT A LIONESS

he misty red brick maze of Beacon Hill, Boston, burns like a dark and rosy fire here in 1650. My mouth is still dry and pasty like the breakfast biscuit I just ate. I stumble out of my aunt's house and walk down the street to school. It's a little after 5:30 a.m. in the morning as I try to catch my breath in this grey, foggy, early sunrise. My heart is racing as I duck inside a carriage-house doorway the shape of an acorn. I'm on Charles Street and I can relax a moment in this cozy keyhole alcove. Inside this blind-spot, I close my eyes. It smells like wet bricks, a horse stable, and slow fires smoldering. It's quiet.... Far off I can hear busy blue-jays or maybe cat-birds squawk, twit, and fighting for their own morning biscuit. My goodwill churns now, my harmony rolls, and I exhale slowly. Relaxed, my eyes still closed: it's calm here, a cease-fire for just a fleeting moment.

My eyes are still lightly closed, fluttering... I feel Nothing, but something. I breathe slowly, listening to my heart — gradually, purposefully sensing and feeling my breath. Inhale, exhale — inhale, exhale... it's graceful here as I transpire into a meditative recess. The grey light dissipates with flecked reds, greens, and yellows. Multiple colors give way to different shapes of blue rising and falling in my consciousness — a child's thought: an affection and excitement about Nothing. I've learned to heed, I've learned to merge and yield hitherto. It's respectful and thoughtful here, and, most of all — kind.

From somewhere far off two mourning doves sing me a two-step triplet in the hollows of drab Boston with their sunny wooden flutes: "CooOOoo-woo-woo-wooooo.... CooOOoo-woo-woo-wooooo.... I blow a kiss of gratitude for their language and whisper, "*C'est Magnifique.*"

I suppose I've come and I'm going to this smart twilight... not a day too soon. My life is a respite within oblivion, an Awakening within oblivion, and is similar to a clean and cold pillow turned over during a long slumber after a tiresome journey. My slumber is driven with a warm sub-consciousness now and a new, dark, positive energy. I am alone, but not alone — someone or something is holding my hand.

I listen to the watery earth spin and it ratchets me up. I think about opening my eyes and the sleaze of society oozes back into my spirit and I shudder down. "Uugghhh!" I exclaim out loud, thinking of the Boston civilization I live in. Methinks me not humane — methinks me not human... I tell myself, spin little girl, spin, spin! Trying to get in sync with my Puritan society. The floating, tilted, and rolling Puritan world. I glance quickly down Charles Street toward the ominous Church of England, now franchised to America as the Church of Boston. It's drowning in a red-tide of bricks both horizontal and vertical. The clumsy crimson brick sidewalk and road are a bumpy, lumpy, and busy red graph that melts into towering townhouses. Under this red matrix, bricks fight clear-cut trees and amputated American roots that will not give up. The roots still smell like lush brown mud and green piney saplings snapping with antiseptic turpentine on a spring day.

And here I am — a female façade, a flower in a rock-garden desert. And if I drop the façade, society will drop me from the nearest tree with their Boston ballet or perhaps a burning at their stake. But beforehand, *they*, the "Divine" Boston Elect and Elders will hang me neatly, draw me correctly, and quarter me precisely a witch or a whore, but most likely both.

My head and body parts will be scattered about the countryside, yet the Elders are only two-thirds right in accusing me of being an anarchist and an adulteress. Dear reader, pray, I'm also an artist as I write, draw you pictures, and share a June morning with you this fine spring day in 1650.

My name.... I have no name, when someone says *her*... I turn to face them. My name used to be Susan Hutchinson. I'm the red-headed daughter of the first American libertarian, Anne Hutchinson. I still go by my American Indian name, Autumn Leaf. I'm eighteen years old — a Briton gone "Native."

It's a fogged-in spring morning here in Boston, New England. The mist is vaporous and nebulous. It could be six a.m. in the morning or almost six p.m. in the evening as grey-devils billow and scurry about. I spent five years (since I was twelve years old) living in the New Netherland woods with the Lenape Indians. It's been ten years since I lived here within Boston's "Civilization." My family and I were found guilty of not respecting the Boston Puritan Elders and Elect in 1640. We were banished and excommunicated from the Boston Church and the Massachusetts State to the woods of America and America ate my family alive.

The freshly stoked morning fires on Beacon Hill piddle smoke out of the fine marble, brick, and fieldstone chimneys hosting a dance with the grey-lady mist of the Atlantic Ocean. The grey dew from the Charles River is tidy, pale, and briny. The chimneys burn a sweet and sunny New England incense. Perhaps some barky Swampscott pine or a Lexington locust log smolders gently, cradled in the large and proud fireplaces of Beacon Hill. After this rest, I will weave onto Pinckney Street, down to Willow Street and along the Boston Common up onto State Street. Yes, that's correct: these Puritans actually named a street after the "State." On the State Street hill our three buildings look like close friends sitting for a painting of themselves they have commissioned to celebrate *their hill*. They sit side by side as if having a lively conversation. Our small, tidy, red cedar clapboard schoolhouse symbolically sits to the left of the grand and large white-steeple church which proudly sits in the center of this Puritan *hill*. On the right side of the hill, the brown oil-stained and sunburned building houses both the jailhouse and the State House. The State House is dirty and rowdy at all times of the day and night with bankers, jailers, criminals, and their politician lawyers. Deals get done and deals get undone as these white-devils slither like a lynch mob. The State House is not a meeting-house, but a merry-go-round house. The State House acts like an oil on a rusty bolt, and it is a good friend, a pub, and/or a conduit to the other buildings busy educating souls and saving souls. The two choices for a white-devil in training is clear and on both sides of their white-steeple church: a well-groomed and spotless education or a greasy incarceration.

The slender and shadowy streets of Beacon Hill are the off-red color of a female cardinal — enveloped and shrouded in wet, smoky air. These streets are built with blood-red bricks and the foul slop from our English ships' bilge. It is an oily and thick slop from bathing humans and fighting rats topped with a scum rainbow and fat, healthy fleas jumping, swimming about. Fleas walk on this water like prophets, like magicians, shamans, and wizards.

This bilge-blood grounds and adheres nicely to the cobblestone grout on Beacon Hill. That's because it's built upon the Biblical "Hill," as royalist Mansard roofs rise three and four stories, connecting into handsome townhouses aligned perfectly and morally. Narrow and tight streets block the sun, and the architecture foreshadows the crowded and mad human race to the townhouse on the Park with a view to the southwest. My ankles and feet are in pain, I'm uncomfortable in my new priggish Boston shoes. I'm a wobbling sad clown in my high-heeled boots on these lumpy and bumpy cobblestone streets. I'm dreaming of my Lenape moccasins, especially after I reluctantly surrendered them to Aunt Alexandra a few weeks ago. The iridescent cobblestones are the shape of Marblehead fieldstones or American turtle shells: Indian Turtle Gods perhaps balance the Beacon Hill world on its back? The round, solid rocks are grey-green, tan, and brown granite. These stately homes and carriage houses are cut and hammered by disciplined blacksmiths and carpenters with exceedingly straight squares and well-proportioned relationships.

Each brick home is divided symmetrically by black eyelash shutters and shades that strategically enclose the American castle's royal scheme. White curtains billow in the townhouse windows as alleyway winds disturb the dreary overcast sky. Unseen black and steely cannons swing three hundred and sixty degrees within Beacon Hill forts like those on battleship galleons. As I walk on, blinds blink with shifty eyes, opening and closing in the murky grey-green shadows of morning on Spruce Street. Glooms with running mascara follow me and then disappear when I turn back to face them. I pause, I listen like an Indian.... I think this is silence... as I hear the clumsy Puritans scuttle away, tripping over themselves in their castle caves — hiding in their own homes. "Alas!" they cry as they whisper and hiss at me from murder holes when I turn about. Nay, I walk on undeterred, homeless, and examined on Charles Street — dancing with my shadows — dancing for myself. Looking for Willow Street, I pass along on Spruce Street with curtain walls and heavy black doors made for a King. Doors more like draw-bridges with fanned and crowned transoms that poison America with a "New London" architecture. Golden brass knockers sing and trumpet within a web of black iron, spiked fencing, and gates that look like lonely spears, missing... not in spirit, the macabre English fruit of someone's head on a spike.

My female life, my prophesized prospect as an Abrahamic

woman, an Abe-Babe: draped, wigged, and/or just made impossible — a fairy-tale porno. There I'll be: a woman burning, again hiding in alleyways and jumping through doggy-hoops, doing tricks for everyone in the Common — around the world. Here I am: an Abe-Babe, a perfumed and polished poodle, playing parlor-school games with friends, family, and society. I feel sick thinking these words, distempered, a creature hated by the Boston sun. I am a virgin control-fraud in an enlightened costume of grotesque proportions. I'm sweltering uncomfortably beneath my woolen navy-blue coif. I'm fashionably incarcerated in my whale-bone corset. I am pale and frantic, shaking under my dark auburn petticoat and apron dyed a cherry brown with an ox's blood. I abhor society, I'm afraid of society because it takes away my life — my breath. I hope to change society, and as such — I'm more in love with, or should I say, I'm more in respect of my life. I respect my breath.

Still standing within my alcove, listening to my lungs and larynx, I think I hear a voice or some people talking. I peek out onto Charles Street and there are three ladies in front of the Church of Boston. I think how uncomfortable I would feel if I went into *their* church, there I'd be: a siren in a myth or a hag of delusion. Nay, my church is in the dirt, my church is the salty sea-spray on the beach that mists and fogs water into a garden — this garden I tend is in my mind and my church is in this mud.

I relax again and remember pleasantly living in the woods with the Indian terrorists for five years. I'm lost about why our Judeo-Christian civilization still, even after the Reformation, suppresses femininity with no guilt. I against I, women against men — the heroic arraignment of women continues! I'm still dumbstruck with the "Human-Race" and its finish line. I'm still wondering who's in this *human-race* and where the beginning and/or finish line is. What happened with our English Enlightenment, our English Civil War, and our Glorious Revolution? What happened to the enlightened common man? The common woman? What happened to the commonwealth and, more important — common sense? I live in America not during the age of reason, but during the age of treason.

I am not ashamed of these beliefs — I'm free. Five years ago, after struggling to live with the Lenape Indians for a year or so, I also surrendered. Perhaps it was my sister-clan whispering and berating me under their breath during the beginning of my Indian captivity. The Indian woman and other children would cackle and peck at me, calling me "Walofang" (White-Devil) under their breath instead of Autumn Leaf. It became "Walofang this" in the daytime and "Walofang that" in the nighttime, just as with the bully children on Boston and Rhode Island playgrounds during my earlier childhood. Any civilization's children are always scheming, always taunting, malicious, and cruel, forcing you to submit, to succumb, to obey, not to their unique children's playground tribe, but to their parents' religious tribe. These playgrounds' whispers, screams, buzz, and glares haunt, trouble and scar every child, and every adult around the world, including myself! Haunted to this very day — no matter our age we remember being hurt — we remember survival of the fittest on the playground. These sufferings under no circumstances evolve, age, heal, or draw close to a finish line this animalistic race, this human-race.

Henceforth, I will stop engaging in combat with my white-devil female origins. I stopped struggling with myself and washed off my make-up, my facade, and my Judeo-Christian Elder approach to life. I unchained my second "X." I removed the black chains from my silent sister X and became not a second sex, or the *Other*, but I became myself — a whole. I breathed for the first time in my life. Relentlessly joyful. I happily lost my shit in the woods.

This genetic admission, and my ancestral confession, opened up my Awakening to my potential. My potential was crushed in between Puritanical tribes and Indian tribes, but, thanks to my Maker or Creator — I was able to dwell in my bitchy mother's free-grace. The more the Puritans in Boston or the Indians in the woods tried to sell me their "Tribe" with their "Truth," the more I felt the savage honesty and inner light of free-grace.

I know my mother would be happy with this libertarian education or Awakening of mine as the free-grace ideology that she brought to America quickly died. The mournful death of free-grace came about after my goofy grandfather back in England (while on house arrest!) taught my mother thoroughly about religion, ideology, and philosophy. Grandpa Frank, an English Separatist and preacher, raised and taught Annie like a boy so she lived like a man. My mother's education was achieved in the best of health for both student and teacher, for both daughter and father. Grandpa Frank then trimmed Annie's sails for America — not on the *Mayflower*, but on the *Lioness*.

I figure I should see what the church ladies are up to so I slowly peek out onto Charles Street. With a fright, my reflective and happy morning ends and I'm running again.

The Boston Governor, Minister Winthrop, deliberately turns the brick corner a few blocks in front of me, catches my eye, and is now briskly walking towards me. "Clippity-clop, clippity-clop, clippity-clop" go his knee-high fine leather boots made for riding ass and kicking ass. Winthrop is a vicious and nagging knife in the back one can never pull out. I shuffle out of my doorway alcove and pretend to be straightening a flower in the planter box. The minister wears one of many long black cassocks welded right, and he floats like a black iron maiden with his Puritan high-hat downcast. Winthrop is a dark-ages phantom from the Spanish Inquisition here on these somber and smoky streets of Beacon Hill. His brittle brown eyes are twitching scorpion tails filled with toxins. Minister Winthrop's high-born eyebrows, nose line, and eyelashes are fragile sticks, painted and high-lighted with brownish lamp oil. The Zion gypsy sows and grows to his sullen chin a dirt-bag's white-devil goatee that partially hides his vindictive and incredulous mouth. He has a medicinal body-lotion smell about him, like that of an arthritic old lady. The minister's bird-like face is lop-sided with a larger lazy eye and a smaller lizard eye. The minister's dead eye isn't dead — it sees more than his good reptilian eye, in order to steer himself through the many forks in the road. The Minister believes that one's thoughts, decisions, and actions cause only death and hell or death and heaven. Hell has an extremely large door one can easily just fall through, but on the other side of the forked road — the door to heaven is more a pin-hole and Winthrop is its gate-keeper.

For the Minister, or the Governor, as he wears both hats like a Cheshire cat, death is always a threat or a reward and always dependent upon the Elders' and Elect's mood. Withstanding this lifeless, fragile soul, Minister Winthrop's face is propped and swaddled comfortably in a large white ruff made of the finest Chantilly lace. The lace is also embroidered, web-like, on his cuffs that show off and accentuate his ladylike claws and manners. These drooling lace accessories in certain lights elevated the Divine spinster out of his dungeon-dog social status. Winthrop leashes his own mind and soul to the inquisitors' dungeon floor because a dog without an owner and/or slavery and incarceration feels better to him than happiness. Pain is home for the religious dog.

The Minister sees me sailing along on the white-cap chop of my own sunny world and dictates to me in a hushed authoritative voice, "Wouldst have time to smell the roses, Ms. Hutchinson? Pleaseth me and walk like thou hast a purpose!"

The Minister trails and follows me like the smoke and ashy stench from my burnt-out homestead back in New Netherland six years ago. Smoky ashen death is still stuck in my hair even after I shaved my head numerous times. My hair,

Minister Winthrop

like fire, grew back, and still no matter which way I turn I smell a smoldering murder in the woods. I turn left, then I turn right and my hair brushes my cheeks and I still smell my home and family burning. The smell is singed into my skin, it leaps off my lips — death was seared into my soul at twelve years old. Winthrop is a walking death accessory; he is my lonely blackened chimney still standing where my home used to be — a monument as the charred floor to my home smolders like burnt-out logs in a vacant fire-pit. The Minister then surprisingly picks another more manipulative yet kinder voice from his stacked audio deck and speaks louder up ahead, past me, to the church-ladies that litigate downwind and out of sight.

"Prithee, my dear ladies, for I tarry; I will warm the church for our morning prayer in just a moment."

The loyalist-ladies are titillated by the thought of warmth and look from afar like chirping and flapping hungry baby sparrows in a nest. The Minster will more than warm his congregation of chick-a-dees this morning. The Minister is a balanced control-fraud. He is sin — the black yin female; the minister is also the savior — the white yang man. The Minister is arsonist and fireman; Winthrop plays both sides of the bet. He is buyer and seller — the Governor is mortgager and mortgagee. The Minister is both a good cop and a bad cop working a tithe and a conviction. Winthrop is the up-early dirty-bird dropping worms to the ladies who lunch. And much more important, as the self-destructive Abrahamic customer is always right within rising religions, capitalism on-the-go, and rising tides, is that Abe-Babe customers and parishioners are turned on and/or Awakened by praying for their own pain — but more likely praying for others' pain. These religionists pray and crave to be crucified or scorched alive a high priest, a prophet / poet, and/or a savior or saint in their tribe's "Holy-War." A *holy war*, which is just as futile as any war, but suppos-edly this *holy war* is for the afterlife. The war for the answer to the afterlife... the holy war should be called the "Answer War." The war in which no one on earth can answer or be vilified for — till it's too late.... The *holy war* and/or *answer war* should really be called the, "I Don't Know, So I Will Kill You War." The war and murder occur in spite of and because of the bread and circus. The juggling act with an English flute or a Jew's harp is accompanied by an assassination here and a *coup d'état* there — and because of this the religious Abe-Babe customer loses their insurance policy. The Jew and the Catholic slowly drown a sinner, floating in the ocean sky grasping for anything that can existentially float... anything — and uninsured.

Desperate, itchy, with absolute liability, in duress and on the hook — Abe-Babe consumers are turned-on! They are aroused and stimulated by being lied to, suckered, winged, branded, draped, wigged, seared, fried, and clubbed, and withstanding commonsense, Big-Abe and his Babes get off existentially with a religious bribe that perpetuates a "Forgiveness" control-fraud. These capitalist customers gain rank in their religious standing-army corporations by lying and deceiving others about Abe — who everyone is talking about because, of course... Abe gets paid and Abe gets the babes!

I straighten up consciously and try to play my good schoolgirl part, looking down, — never being so brash as to eyeball the man, and say only, "Of course, dear Minister, I was just helping out a wilted flower."

Before I finished that sentence, an evil look was launched from an old woman inside the townhouse. With a scrunched-up face that looked like a dried white apricot, she drew the curtain closed in front of this flowerbox I was fixing and slammed the inside shutters. I suddenly realize asking questions about the white man, the monarchy, the royalty, the Elect and the Elders' power is not a healthy hobby for a passionate pilgrim here in America. Questions in America are unsaid, unspoken, scorned, locked out, shut out, drawn and despised; questions are buried in the flower box, but answers are grown in the garden.

The Minister, or maybe more the Governor, turns to me again, and in a hushed sly tone says, "Let it die, you fool, let it die," as he passes me in a brisk manner, squinting his eyes as if to induce a Catholic inquisition on me and the flower.

"Let it die," he concludes, as if the flower deserves to die painfully. A colorful flower crucified or burned at the stake fills Winthrop's heart and body with blood. Winthrop and those like him — the rabbis, the priests, and the lawyers of every religious government and corporation — all put forth the same high-treason proposition that "Questions are the root of all evil." In these control-fraud civilizations, any fool who asks a question will have his or her head put on a spike. The Christian Zionist's "Divinity" (substitute Divinity with abstract, unanswerable, and unprovable religion) spawns the devilish children called "Divine Love, Divine Laws, and Divine Court... that of course trusts in, prays, and/or worships a Divine God. My mother questioned the Puritans' religious love, law, and God with her free-grace controversy, and it landed her symbolic head on one of those Boston spikes. This is a "New" England education, same as the "Old" England education... kissing the rod. We are bred and polished to accept punishment submissively, to love our abusive master with a whip. We are the loyalist subjects only educated in order to pay the tax, and only cultivated to kiss an Elder's abstract and personal God's rod.

This common-sense awareness highlights, colors, and sharpens my view on these prison-ship streets. Majestic affects, royal illuminations, and Divine advantages barely made it over the surly Atlantic Ocean to an American atmosphere and time zone. Regardless, royal foundations swirl and simmer unabated in America even though King Charles may have lost his head in England.

The good minister Winthrop plays his part in a colony

gone wild. He rushes ahead and quickly huddles with his loyalist spinsters, who do a double-take, gawking and muttering when they see me coming towards them. These vinegar tasters, like three poodles in tutus made of feathery lace with matching parasols dance at their doggy park. Mrs. Radcliffe, Ms. Vassar, and Mrs. Holyoke are all there, smacking / licking their lips, snacking on each other's misery with fascist doctrines, but calling there doctrine a religion.

And here I go down my path, on my way — the red-headed step-child whose family was banished by the Minister and the Town Council over the free-grace controversy. These Beacon Hill rubberneckers know my family was then slaughtered by the Lenape terrorists in New Netherland. I was captured and "Adopted" as a slave by these Indian terrorists. I lived with the enemy for five years in the woods and I did not necessarily need or want to come back to Boston.

Minister Winthrop and his horrid harem of ladies lick their lips and flutter about. The royalist loyalist faggot-mob meditates out loud so I can hear them gossiping about me in front of *their* sour church.

Mrs. Radcliffe — a legalist, aghast, bitter, and aloof, says, "How in God's good world would anyone turn away from our civil society? We should create laws to stop her!"

Mrs. Holyoke, an asexual fat little Buddha, in an acrimonious missionary tone scolds me: "What virtues does this child have? Does the pain and suffering of living with those primates in the woods ease her suffering?"

Ms. Vassar, kind of clueless, natural, vulnerable, and slightly salacious, says, "Why would that cute, saucy and sweet little red-head want to stay in the woods with all those big strong wild men?"

These politically-correct crème-de-la-crème ladies are tortured and terrorized with my lack of social respect for them. My disrespect is not just for them, but for our parents, our Elect, and our Elders. My disrespect is for all authority posing as a false God. My only respect is for nature, and the mystery of my Maker, whom no one in this world knows. And it is my reverence, it is our human reverence, for this most important human mystery I call Nothing (that we all share) is where we all meet, naked — spiritually and emotionally, we can reconcile.

In contrast, my biological disrespect for my mother and father is hereditary. Dishonoring Elders is the same crime my mother was charged with by the Massachusetts Town Council. Big-Daddy Winthrop was both judge and juror at my mother's trial. He was both Moses and Bloody Mary, leading a mob to burn my mother. These politically-correct sociopaths are petrified, policed, and taught in practice by psychopaths to never to think or speak such a healthy and common sense thought as that the Bible is an old ruse — a capitalist man-made invention.

The Minister, the good shepherd, tries to herd his lazy loiterers into their church. "Come now, ladies, nothing to see here, nothing but a dead flower." They drag their feet and shimmy towards the large church doors, nervously looking over their shoulders at me with manic eyes.

Abrahamic laws of heresy, blasphemy, and/or damnation corral your imagination as a child until the day you die. But beforehand the rabbi, the priest, parents, and civilization break the child like a horse. The Jewish child, the Catholic child, and the Muslim child with Abe-Babe parents is saddled, blinded, bridled, ridden like a horse, jockeyed like a stallion with a parental bit in its mouth and a parent's whip slapping its ass. The Minister and his pledging sorority sisters will always hate or despise me, the eternal child, because they despise themselves. All is vanity, all is low self-esteem for religionists and courtiers with their priest-craft and King-craft. Hitherto, I felt sad and ashamed for the Minister and his marmalade ladies because hate is the only thing that enlivens their jelly-fish souls. Hate is the morale, welfare, and recreation for the Abe-Babe standing-army. Jews and Catholics prophesize that it's love that turns them on, but it's really hate that gets them off. Dread, anxiety, and loathing animate their low self-esteem and fear into "Loving" and "Lawful" social pursuits. It's not that I miss the preacher's tea party or the sorority sister's social with envy, or even that I pity the preacher and his flock from a martyr's position. It's because little Ms. Vassar and Company look so wounded, fearful, and so deeply pegged and nailed down as they unsuccessfully strive to appear the opposite — that is, free and luxurious: physically, spiritually, and financially.

As I approach, Ms. Vassar arduously puckers her lips, practically blowing me a kiss. Mrs. Radcliffe is so prickly that she unconsciously bares her teeth and growls during her attempt to smile.

Mrs. Radcliffe is speechless and incoherent, a stuttering shrew, and starts to wish me "Good morning," tipping her wide-brimmed Sunday hat forward, but it tilts and starts to fall.

A kind breeze starts a hat juggling act with her hat, as Mrs. Radcliffe's colorless eyes start flying round and round like a spinning wheel shuttle. She grabs for the straw hat and so does Ms. Vassar and they play a kind of merry widow patty-cake with the hat for a few moments. Mrs. Holyoke steps back and watches in condescending glee at the tennis match, which ends quickly with Mrs. Radcliffe's hat falling into a dirty puddle. Their jealous eyes and manic mouths never stop gambling, never stop spinning a yarn. Multiple choice hysterical women: Eve or Mary? Mary or Eve? A clean whore or perhaps a dirty whore are the two choices in a woman's Abe-Babe life. A virgin mother, a sorrowful mother, a *mater dolorosa* — a debauched mother, or a whore mother — is your feminine multiple-choice or bi-polar choice life. With the latter being physically impossible, there isn't much of a choice for a sorrowful Abe-Babe.

These orthodox women are fashionably frantic, cursed, and inherently malformed. They are narcissistic, unborn, unexamined, leaden ladies cat-fighting to not just kiss the rod, but bullying, bickering, and buggering viciously to get fucked by the rod. Mary is joylessly impaled and impregnated and Eve is crucified to her swinging garden gate.

The Minister reaches down and picks up Mrs. Radcliffe's hat as it drips slowly. He holds it away from his clean and pressed dark robe as if it is a dead rodent.

I am thinking it funny again, me being bullied here in 1650 Boston by these American royalist loyalists when it has been rumored that King Charles — whose royal name smears and sullies this American street and its nearby river — is probably still running from the rowdy rabble back home in England. On second thought, King Charles's head is probably rolling through Parliament right now, and contrary to this, here in America the rabble's royal ass-kissing is an American currency on the rise!

All the same, I turned away from this *civilization*, I went native, and then I was branded a terrorist. Besides going native-terrorist, I'm a multi-generational blasphemous heretic. I am a Protestant's preacher's daughter, for whom, of course, our mortal enemy is the co-mingling of church and state and/or synagogue and state. My Protestant or protestor pedigree goes back to northern England, the Reformation, the Protectorate, and the English Commonwealth. My enemy is the religious minglers, networkers, and *friends* of standing-armies. My nemesis is the Catholic apostles of pump and Jewish disciples of dump selling pump-and-dump Divine indulgences to benefit their control-frauds of love, law, and God.

These unbalanced religionists, these orthodox soul murderers, compel me back to the Indian forests, filling me with a desire to hunt, to live, to stalk the woods. I follow the deer path through the wood thicket and here I find balance.

It's where I'd rather be compared to smiling and curtsying to my neighbors in Boston in a holy hurry on their way to where? Mecca? Mt. Zion? The Common? Some Nirvana? Or perhaps they're just sliding on down to the swampy and slinky Fens? Coveting, drooling, stealing, and killing their way to their religious confessionals. Bostonians begging, buggering, praying and absolutely always paying for forgiveness. The wizard Elect of Boston, Jerusalem, or Oz "Talk" to their white-devil fairy-tale Gods behind the religious curtain, selling penance and Divine indulgences to their addicted sinners. This moral sell out in the name of our human race is promptly done in the morning confessional, so by the afternoon the pumpers and dumpers can punctually continue to rape and pillage with a "Divine" and clean conscience.

Is this human race my race? Nay, my life is in New Netherland along the morning shore with my bare feet in the low-tide clay and my body in the sunshine. I inhale the sweet-grass air, the green mania, and many salty seas converging into one river. Here with green briars and pitch pines at this sandy dawn on the tranquil Long Island Sound — otherwise known as the "Devil's Belt," I sit across from the rising sun behind the glacier spit known as Long Island. This sunrise is the one and only "Holy" miracle on earth that no one witnesses, that everyone in America misses every day. Here at Hell's Gate, with my Six Nations wampum belt, the Sound and the Atlantic ebb and flow and this is where I go when I close my eyes. I will take my pen and ink, and with a smidge of dirt here or there, I will draw you a picture for you dear reader, so you will see the simplicity. This is my keel — this is my Creator. The teal-colored water glass is ferocious lava and has the viscosity of electricity. I respect the hot morning star sun rising now in the east and it heats me as the rush of the Atlantic's smarmy and salty water in front of me

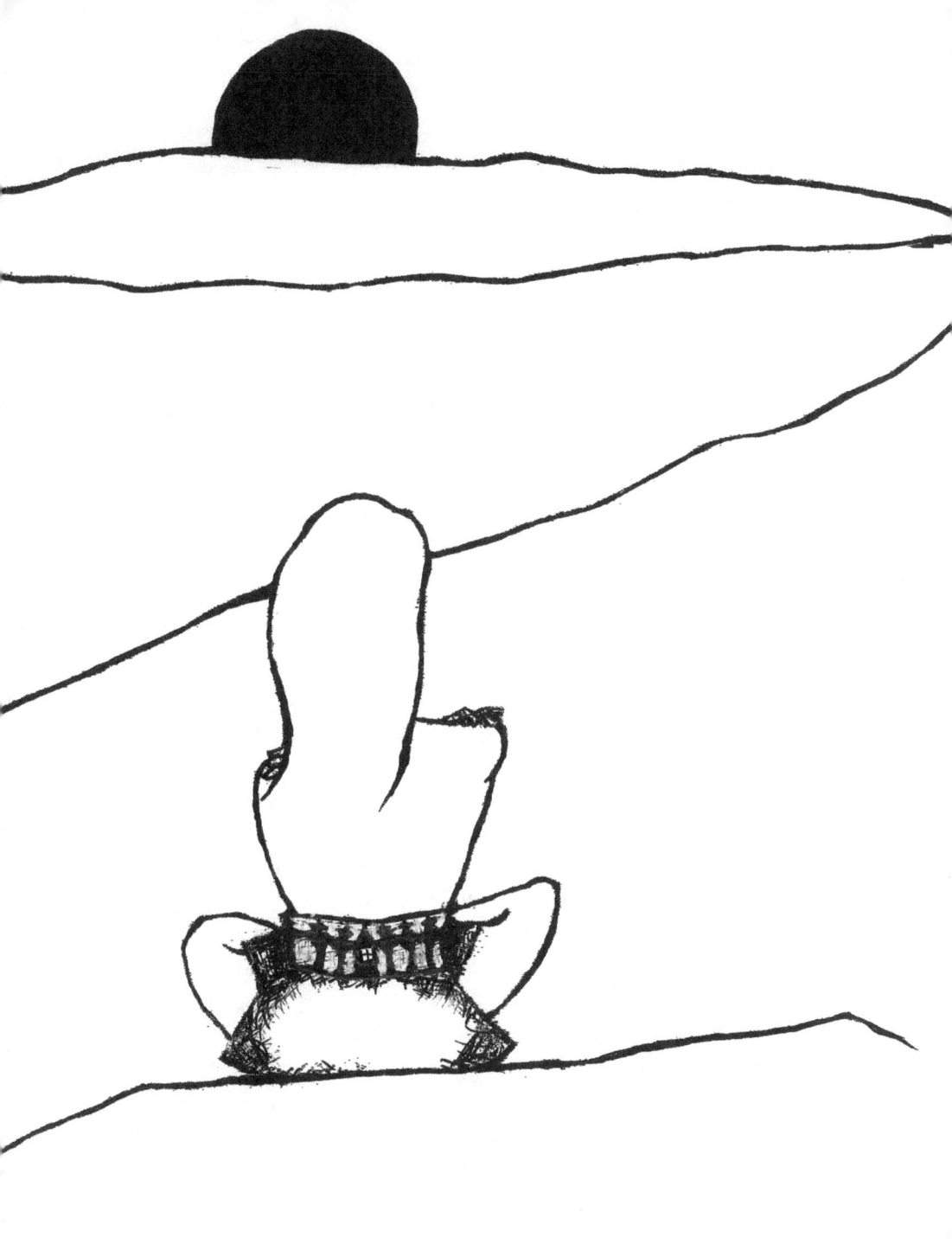

Autumn Leaf at Sunrise

mixes with the mountain water from New England's rivers. It all races like mad... down to Manna-hatta.

There was inner peace for me living as an Indian, scouting along the thorny wood with my mind whistling and floating along with birdcalls and other animals hunting for food. I understood clearly who my enemy was. There was dignity and harmony, even though I, a "Savage," was hungry and lean with no material possessions. Here in Judeo-Christian America, everyone is my enemy. Here in Boston, I walk to school now to be educated with my enemies. If I'm honest, my church, synagogue, and/or tribe is filled with my enemies. I break bread, pray, and sleep with my enemy. Everyone is the enemy or witness on Charles Street, in the "New Jerusalem" of the week, tithing and fornicating the new hee-haw Yahweh employee / convert of the month — on the soap-box / altar of the year.

I'm still walking towards Minister Winthrop and his church ladies as I think how the ladies resemble my Aunt Alexandra. Aunt Ally, as I call her, is a haughty woman more English than American who has bumbled her way through life on inheritances and coy nonchalance by greasing all moral problems with her ideology that "It's all for the best." Every predestiny calamity from spilt milk to spilt blood is covered with Aunt Ally's trickle-down chorus. The maudlin choir members moan and drone in pain because they're selling and singing poison through their nose: "It's aaalll for the beeesst." Emotionally delusional women marching in reverse like my Aunt Ally make my hands sweat and my mouth go dry. I walk on towards the Church of Boston as I lick my lips, whetting my appetite for a fight.

My aunt has paid dearly for me to fight for this "Good ole cause," walking these Boston colony streets with fine clothes from mother London's haberdasheries. Aunt Ally seems to enjoy paying ingeniously, deeply, and poetically for me. I'm a shopping-for-salvation trophy and/or a bill — a tithe to "Divine love," a cross-to-bear of gift-love for patriarchal "Aunties." So, now henceforth Aunt Ally will be keeping an eye on Annie's little girl: me — a little object A, forever more a pariah's daughter — not just a threat, but a patriarchal hobby — a power-trip, an ego trip, a signifier, a get out-of-hell (get-out-of-your-own-mind) hobby.

Aunt Ally and I were shopping just the other day, and we ran into Mrs. Randison and her son Lawrence. We were down by the dock shopping for food and house-goods. The rough smell of slaughtered tuna and shellfish was rank and livid. Many other shoppers mingled about. Merchants hawked goods from spices to fabric, and their cries mixed well with those of the large white seagulls swooping and squawking above. Local Indians quietly sold vegetables the colors of American rainbows that grey and decrepit Europeans can only dream of.

In the midst of this busy market, after only a few weeks in Boston, I ran straight into Lawrence Randison — a kissing-cousin from long ago. I could tell it was Lawrence by his gait — on his toes, head held high, walking softly like a monkey-cat on the prowl playing peek-a-boo with his prey. He didn't see me and my Aunt behind him, so I meowed softly like a tomcat into the wind at my back, "Nice sword, soldier."

Lawrence heard my cry and froze in mid-step. He turned around in a flash, smiled, and said nothing besides looking into my eyes with volumes of quiet and complex delight.

Mrs. Randison, who was standing next to her son, turned around blushing and said to my Aunt in a condescending tone, "Oh, weellll, look who it is. Why, little old Susan Huchinson... and she looks so charming in her new clothes, yet I pray and hope she mendeth from those Indian woods and grows quieter."

Then, turning to Lawrence she instructed him: "Lad, you keep your mouth shut and merry on down the road."

Sister X, Aunt Ally, Mrs. Randison, and others keep me impressed, imprisoned, and manipulated, so civilization's tar-and-feathering of my witchy mother can be socially, legally, and religiously swept away — a sacrifice to their fabled Jewish and Catholic god plagiarized from an Egyptian and Sumerian god. The white-devil male and female society Attacked, Divided, and then Starved my family, waiting to Profit (ADSP), but orthodox Aunt Ally just says, "It's all for the best!" Nevertheless, I'm Autumn Leaf, a grain of opal sand on the lonely winter beach blowing in the wind that will infect and mature to a black pearl in the spring.

My Aunt Ally questioned out loud to Mrs. Randison with genuine surprise, "Susan quieter?"

Aunt Ally looked deep into my eyes, smiled a "Yeah-right; never" smile to me, and then, keeping her eyes locked on mine, said with an energized smirk to Mrs. Randison, "Yeah, quieter.... My little Susan will be joining the monastery any day now!"

I suddenly picture myself a dirty Eve trying to get back into the Jewish and Christian garden only if I shut-up and then I laugh to myself with that quiet garden thought, because there is no such thing as a quiet garden.... No garden party for me; I am dirty-whore Profit: born only from Attacking, Dividing, and Starving. I am an orphan floating and paying for someone else's crime. I'm dirty-whore truth. I'm dead, but brilliant. I am a red autumn leaf that's held on way too long, still on fire and still alive, against a December blue sky, a leaf that appears out of the corner of your eye, a streak, a red feather, an auburn thought, a yellow memory and/or a scarlet flash flickering and floating against the bright indigo winter sky. Autumn Leaf is floating and flying, just for a fleeting moment; now don't blink, for it's a morose and shy, yet victorious moment.

My mother and our family were left socially and spiritually abandoned, divorced, crucified, branded, forsaken, and, most important — to blame. How can I escape her sin that is now my sin? How do I escape my parents' sin? Their original sin? My ancestral debt is a crime against humanity. My original sin is a control-fraud. Punching up at my oppressor with their pillow over my face, how do I rise above parental debt? Spiritual debt? Societal debt and/or student debt? How do I float above the savage Catholic inquisitor and the merciless Jewish debt collector?

Do I negotiate with society; do I act my life away? Am I a reasonable citizen or an unreasonable citizen? Am I the second sex? The "Other?" Do I option-trade my soul? Play derivatives with the white-devil wizard behind the debt-traders curtain? Do I follow society playing Blind Man's Bluff in the money-changer's dark pool? Do I litigate and fornicate in the judge's chambers with the other courtiers and Cavaliers? Do I postulate the priest? Do I titillate the rabbi in his rectory? I'd be stepping on my neighbor, tithing, bribing, and extorting my way through life, paying high interest on borrowed time. I'd be a service oriented citizen in the white-devil Empire pissing and shitting my way through life, leaving nothing except ruins. As reasonable citizens we are a tribe of parasites — happy, lucky, and excited to pay taxes, bribes, and/or pay-to-play scams. We are useless water bags scheming and toiling our way to a heavenly Oz, not for religion's sake or humanity's sake, and not even for the Empire's sake. We are reasonable (meaning we lie to ourselves) because you and I know we are lazy, rotten, and doing something very bad. We are taking the easy road and screwing over the next generation as reasonable citizens.

We just want to be cheats — we just want to sneak a peek behind the existential curtain before we religiously commit, before we pray — before we pay. Reasonable cheats cannot help themselves; it is the selfish gene, it is the low self-esteem gene — we yearn and dream to cheat. Before we bury our spouse and children in debt, before we give away our children and ten percent of our income, we want inside information on the "God" trade. Before we pay for "Divine love," before we pay for the "Law" and before we pay for "God," we want inside information — a service plan with a guarantee — but there is no existential plan or celestial warranty. Our whole life... our whole religious and spiritual life becomes an exposed control-fraud — a selfish gene merry-go-round, yet we still run off the cliff with the herd, dragging our children towards a mandate of heaven. The herd or pride pray, sell, and pay for questionable "Love, Laws, and Gods" that "Our" tribe is the *"Right"* tribe. We continue to pay and pray or pay-to-play that our religion is the *right* religion, and that *our* tribe is the true master of the universe.

On the other praying hand, on our civilization's guiding-light excuse — the selfish gene is always praying and paying for an upgraded life in the here and now. The ancestral sin and original sin excuse — which is not original at all — is that your parents, family, and/or friends in the past have paid, prayed, and/or played for not really their God's "might," but Thor's *might*. That's not really important for Abe and his Babes praying within duress loaded up with the biggest hammer, which is when and where they feel their might... so it must be "Right."

Back on Charles Street, the Minster eyes me up and down, still holding Mrs. Radcliffe's hat by its tail as if it is a dead varmint. The fog and spring bustle of Beacon Hill blows a tumbleweed of twigs and leaves into a sudden twister that smells like low-tide. The New England bluster swells up like a little grey dust-devil on the cobblestone and then scurries away.

I'm about to greet the Minister and his marmalades but instead I sing-song quietly, in a barely audible decibel within the morning mist, "Marco? Maarrccoo? Maaarrccoo?"

The Minister and his heckle-jeckle flock can perhaps hear my false-flag falsetto. I can smell their dead-grandma blue hair as they pant and sweat out expensive perfumes. They chirp frantically not to themselves but more to the blue-jays and catbirds. Mrs. Radcliffe says, "Did Ms. Leaf say something? Is Autumn putting a spell on us?"

Ms. Holyoke says, "That Autumn is a bitter wind."

Ms. Vassar quietly laughs to herself and then sings playfully, softly, and seductively to me — clearly in the moment, in the game, in the race: "Pooolllloooo...."

I remember as a child when we played "Marco-Polo" in the green shallows of Mt. Hope Bay in my Rhode Island summertime. Burly and brawny low-tides and afternoons that smelt like the ocean's finest condensation sparkled in the sunlight sea-spray and were always painted with a holy and golden Rembrandt ochre — a honey mustard that is smooth and saturating with its honeycomb light. Within this busy-as-a-bee New England late afternoon, we happily drowned and danced the Blind Man's Bluff. That light and those afternoons seemed to last centuries as the snapping turtles nibbled on our toes. We screamed the blind question, "Marco?" pleading, swimming, and hunting blind.

The hunted — floating like scared sitting ducks — evasively answered with a bluff, "Polo...." Maybe treading water, but most likely drowning slowly and never getting away! A lose-lose game for us blind white-devils that we couldn't stop playing even after the turtles were stuffed from eating our tiny toes.

Here on Charles Street shall I play this pump-and-dump game — this blind and bluff competition? Nay, I shall ebb and flow like water has since the beginning. I will have to *be*, as opposed to *not being*, as they say down by the Thames. I will have to adapt or do. I will have to adapt or die, as my brother Charles writes. I will be an American social ladder-climber — I will be a Yankee doodle-dandy! I don't have perfumed politics, I'm shorting Divinity, I have very little breasts to speak of, but I do have a very nice muffin ass.

I pass Minister Winthrop and his flock without acknowledging my Marco bluff. I look deep into all their eyes. They are all sorority girls, posing and parroting a pea-hen posse, and then I wish them "A cheery good morning to you fine citizens." They seem lost, speechless, smoked out.

I pass along a few more paces and say out loud softly and deeply from within my chest, from my diaphragm and in a deeper octave, so the minister and his missy marmalades can hear me again, "Pollo... Poollloo... Poolllllooo...."

Behind me I can hear Ms. Radcliffe, the blind bird pecking, "Polo? What does that mean? Are we blind or is Autumn blind? Ms. Radcliffe continues, "And Ms. Vassar, what part do you play in this riddle?

Mrs. Radcliffe, evasive, drowning, and bitter, concludes, "What a little Indian savage — just like her mother! Just like that bitch Mary Dyer!"

I walk quickly down Beacon Street, past Joy Street, along Court Street up to State Street along the Boston Common. I'm approaching my school now where I'm in my last year. I start to think about Ms. Radcliffe's "Just like that bitch Mary Dyer" comment, as it's rumored Mary Dyer, my surrogate mother, was captured by the Elders, Elect, and magistrates a few days ago here in Boston. This is the first I've heard about Mary Dyer since I received her last letter three months ago from some misfit place she called "Shelter Island." Mary wrote that it was somewhere near the east end of Long Island and that she and other Quakers were hiding out seeking "Shelter from Boston's bloody laws."

Mary's letters, like thoughts, feel like high-level silver clouds — clouds, like pirates floating and hiding out as blue-eyed snowbirds, tanned and dangerous on a trade-wind cirrus cloud. A silver lining of a cloudy rain for a golden hellion in a wooden nook, next to a granite cranny. These clouds, like thoughts, move fast there on Long Island: where, my Creator drew a glacial melt with water, a coast, and stepping stones as the tides go out once a day, but the island fever makes it feel like twice. Mary's letters are sandy blue outwash forever facing south — a lighthouse to sail to through the Devil's reef! This letter was the last of five letters from Mary Dyer that I hold dear and close to me.

To this day and every day, Mary's letters travel with me in my deer-skin pouch I have slipped into my notebook. I made the envelope in New Netherland with my Indian sister-clan. The pouch or soft envelope is a deerskin dyed cranberry brown. In the forwarding address area, I sewed a tranquil landscape of hunter greens mixed with sky-blue and water-blue wampum shells that weaves my twilight. Scattered in the clouds are orange and pink sherbet sparkles — shells reflecting the sun on wet clouds. It is an icy crepuscular world I'm mailing myself to with my deer-skin envelope. There is no return address for *her*; I will not be returning as I cannot conform to the religious regulations within white-devil civilization. The blue-green envelope made of muddy leather holds Mary's letters in a respectful and well-worn fashion. Our sister world is tied shut with a silvery strand of leather tied around the old seashell home of a snail — truly a humane hide!

Mary's first letter to me describes Boston ten years ago, right after my mother and our family had been banished from Boston and we left for Providence, Rhode Island. I was ten years old and Boston civilization was on a Puritan warpath, so when Mary Dyer walked out of my mother's trial, arm in arm with her — the Town Fathers went after Mary Dyer with a vengeance. These Boston Elect, Elders, and, in turn, society turned Mary Dyer into a monster bitch!

In this first letter, Mary Dyer describes how Minister Winthrop and the Boston mob dug up Mary's stillborn miscarriage from three months prior in order to prove Mary's "Monstrous deed." The Minister preached that evil thoughts and questions for the Elect and Elders are the root of all evil and that "Mary Dyer having monstrous thoughts begets monstrous births."

That is copious ancestral debt or original sin / debt laid on an innocent child and her mother. Mary was pretty close to being burned at the stake back then in Boston so she bolted to Providence, which was quickly becoming quite a little misfit island in its own right. Before she left Boston, Mary heard that Minister Winthrop described her exhumed still-born child to his God-fearing Christian parishioners on a sunny Sunday on Charles Street as "A most hideous creature, a woman, a fish, a bird, and a beast all woven together." He continued, "This unearthed monster, like Mary Dyer, is in every tree of knowledge tempting you good Christians with the devil's fruit of an answered question. Pray dear parishioners you dare not to know the devil's truth. Pray you do not dare to be different and ask why! Pray the monster does not drink your blood and steal your soul by welcoming you into his garden of earthly knowledge and earthly delights. Pray thee!"

That was seven years ago in 1643, but white-devils don't forget their power or their mistakes. Not killing Mary Dyer was a Boston Puritan mistake, but Mary's family and its wealth were keeping her alive then and just as recently as a year ago. That was when Mary was almost executed with two other Quakers who were hanged, drawn, and quartered in front of her. If Mary has been caught by the Christian Zionists here in the spring of 1650 she might have pushed her luck a little too far and gotten exactly what she wanted.

Mary finished this first letter as always in a crass, creative, and funny way:

> *I imagine this Boston mob of fools hailing the good Minister Winthrop as their savior and toll booth to 'God' will build a school or Town called, 'Winthrop' and be happy killing each other with kindness as smile fuckers. Imagine studying for a higher education in a school building called Winthrop, or fancy yourself walking down Main Street in a Town called Winthrop? Honestly, what would-you or could-you say to your classmate or neighbor? Mischief?*

The Monster

Mischief? Oh, my dear God... mischeif! MISCHIEF!!!
Over, and over, and over, and over, and over, and over...
infinitely... and eternally — mischief.

I imagine this funny Winthrop Town as I feel the leathery envelope of Mary's letters in my notebook. I rub my hand delicately along the small, glassy wampum shells sewn into the leather hide. It's a smooth, cool, cloud in the sky — a simple mathematical castle; nonetheless my letter envelope is earthbound with me. I look up towards my school and it becomes a blur. All I can think about is "The monster — a hideous creature, a woman, a fish, a bird, and a beast all woven together." I'm thinking now... maybe I don't want to change civilization... I think maybe... maybe, I want to be the Monster!

I refocus and see my school on the hill is buzzing with activity as fourteen teen-agers mill about, seven young women and seven young men slowly nudging, jostling, moving into — moving out of, prodding, and slowly conforming into a small schoolhouse box on the hill. It is a Boston education of dress rehearsals, entrances, exits, drama, exams, inspections, and social games. I have been having a hard time catching up with my reading, writing, and arithmetic; there was no need for these three-R games in the woods with the Indians.

CROWNS FOR KIDS

Boston society can be compared to the woods of New Netherland, the woods where I was almost relieved to watch the terrorist Indians slaughter my white-devil family. My patriarchal family was consummated on the control-frauds of love, law, God, and marriage, which binds and starves love itself and only seeks to build-out the "Law" and profit. The morning after the Abrahamic honeymoon was over, my family was eviscerated with imperialism, veiled as spousal need-love or parental gift-love. The final chapter of the patriarchy corporation is "Bankrupt" or "Divorced." Divorced is more like a Motion unanswered or ignored by the Bankruptcy Court. Divorced is a spiritual bankruptcy that never ends.

I think to myself about the hollow control-fraud of patriarchy back here in Boston's civil society. Infertile mothers as the imperialist, limp-dick Big-Daddies as the bad-boy patriarch; MILF as the privateer. Big-Daddy is now Limpy the Lima Bean, a caterer-waiter on a sunset sail de-crumbing patriarchy as the cabin-boy cuckold. The English and American imperialists' reckless child abuse of trading children as a commodity or a colony is the Achilles heel of humanity. The smoking gun for these unconscious patriarchal bonobos is the divorce, embargo, or bankruptcy: a shake-down of the family, the colony, the child, or the corporation. The bankrupt divorce is a moral and psychological defeat that infects and defects the family, the colony, corporation, and all its investors and shareholders.

Patriarchy is a control-fraud tort that really is a love-fraud or marriage-fraud as it creates a debt-cloud, an emotional dark cloud and a tort claim with absolute liability over all investors, shareholders and creditors involved. This low-level divorce cloud on your title blocks the warm sun of sub-conscious truth and the cool moon of conscious reflection. The bankruptcy trustee orders a forensic audit, but the accountant detectives will never find the true numbers, emotions, or the real books. The cooked-book family-plan or the family pain will be exorcised only when the divorced are conscious again, which will most likely be never. Never is a good mathematical answer from all level-headed accountants. Never will the divorced or bankrupt feel sovereignty or grace. Perhaps down the road a cloudy debtor, a disgruntled colony, an abused child, or a sullen lover will become elegant, handsome, or graceful again? Nay! Never again will the divorced children, parents, and grandparents with a whipping-boy feel the sunny debt-free grace or beauty of sovereignty.

Never will ultra-violet rays thaw these bred-for-religion children, these bred-for-cash children. The sun will never grow or shine on the "For the children" children. The Abe-Babe bankrupt parents will never feel any warmth or camaraderie on cold, elderly, and demented days at the nursing home as — *for the children* parents. Kindness and cordiality will not be shared by the — *for the children* lawyers, tribes, and politicians. And especially there will be no warm justifications, pardons or vindication for the — *for the children* religions.

All are guilty in the Abrahamic cash-for-kids Ponzi scheme, and all parental jockeys involved will always be dejected, flickering, and anxious. Grandparents, parents, and children will be desperate souls on borrowed time, a wasted life in the dark looking back at a luminescent life as our voice dims to dead air. This disquietude or loss of quiet enjoyment for the child is a crime against humanity.

This tort claim will viciously scratch and rattle in our English mind like scoring glass, like shattering glass, and then punitive damages... multiplying, multiplying beyond a debt you can spiritually afford. It will eat us from the inside out, until these unborn claims are heard. Regardless, breeding pumpers and dumpers — still disheartened and unconscious — pass their religious debt along because they are lazy and treasonous. It's easier to abuse and jockey along being *reasonable*, but that is exactly what the royal police state want you to think, as questions to the Elders and the Elect — are *unreasonable*. I, like all divorced children, am religiously and emotionally abused. We are black lights — a cold body in a spiritual sense, a dumped child that never heals and never forgets. Children unable to think or glow — never solid or fluorescent on any wavelength.

My religious and perverted family started to fall apart in Boston and then again in Providence, Rhode Island, because of my parents' patriarchal marriage games. The Indians were fighting the Dutch in New Netherland, but it didn't matter; my family and I were English, and not Dutch. The English and Dutch are both divorced and bankrupt white-devils competing for the penthouse in their Zion Inferno. The American Indian savage understands this white-devil decree without speaking English or Dutch. The Indians read only our faces; they see only our fragile, sleazy, fat, and frantic facade. The Indians look at our hornet eyes darting side-to-side nervously, up and down, over there, at our time piece or clock, desperately searching for something to sting, something to kill in order to live. The Indian savages are afraid of us... they are terror-stricken and extremely frightened; and justifiably so.... By and by, dear reader, I pray — I pray so am I.

CHAPTER 2

Living with the Terrorist —
Happiness — Made in London

LIVING WITH THE TERRORIST

t is probably around 6:00 a.m., and I have to be in class at 6:30. I look out over the Boston Common to my right and see a few folks milling around the pond feeding the ducks breadcrumbs. It must be boring and nice — humbling, to waddle along, a ducky commoner.

I swallow hard on this thought because boring is something I cannot be. I remember Mary Dyer always left me as a child with her exuberant warning, "Never be boring!" Being an untraveled nine- or ten-year-old in provincial Boston and Providence allowed me to not even understand how boring I already was. I don't think the majority of humans are filled with my quiet desperation — lonely folks sidelined, and okay with waiting for trickle-down crumbs. We are all quacking, and pooping along, feeding-off other Shakers, Quakers, and poopers around the pond.

Back in 1643, after my family received the Boston Court's decree banishing us from Boston, the seclusion of social and political divorce really set in. For my family and me, it was being the outcast, the bankrupt, the loser, the divorced that hurled our imaginations and life into a downward spiral. Out of control and desperate is how my family members met

34

their death. Frantic for patriarchal acceptance, divorced and starved, they met their Maker at the hands of a tried and true English imperialist strategy. My family was Attacked, Divided, and Starved, and others Profited (ADSP).

After the massacre of my family, I was the lone survivor and prisoner of war in New Netherland. I resisted little, as I suppose I was in shock. The Lenape Indian chief called me "My daughter from the Turtle God" (Ne-Chan Keshel-meng) and I was *adopted* and enslaved by the Lenape Indians and started working with the women of the tribe. This was good enough, as my Providence young-women's chores were similar.

However, the Lenape sister-clan power was not achieved amid fashionable women whispering and cat-fighting like those on Charles Street. Heretofore and surprisingly so with the Indians, female power was not achieved at the end of a white man's misogynist whip, nor at the edge of a terrorist's blade. I thought Indian women were just housekeepers and breeders in their savage pygmy civilization. Then I realized a few months into my terrorist vacation that the Indian men unquestionably tiptoed around the women of the tribe. Specifically, dainty and delightful was the male Indian, walking on eggs around the full moon, when we... when the women bled, when we all bled.

Before the full-moon dance there would always be important seasonal meetings that the Elder women in the sister-clan would set and lead. Their female Indian eyes glimmered like black crystal diamonds in a certain light; but then with a passing thought, within a side-glance, their eyes were cosmic black-holes into another universe. Indian eyes were usually clear, organic, deep, and precious as livid black water rushing beneath the frozen white winter snow. Black raven water and white positive ice: the same material, two forms: one frozen white, the other a black female sip of liquid life — water, that unbeknownst to most, is seventy percent of the world and of our bodies.

The sister-clan would sauna, bathe, and preen each other like diligent monkeys as we stayed silent in our sweat lodge, perspiring water and drinking this black raven water during the long-frozen winters of my New Netherland — my New Nothing Land. Every pore of affection was open, and we said and felt nothing, yet we were so complete — saying nothing. Primal, complete — so whole, and with warmth I've never felt with other white-devil women. Water refreshes our souls, our toes, and everything in between with just a tiny puddle in my hand. A messy slurp or maybe an icy sip as my face touches the earth's clean blood. The Indian women with their chests and chins held high had clean water blood rushing through their bodies as they transcended into birds of prey at these monthly meetings.

Wise owls and harrier hawks swooped in, wrapped beautifully in brown feathers and white-speckled animal skins. The Indian sister-clan kept astronomically and spiritually above it all. Above it all, from their feminine nest, their airy superiority was based on being a creator, not a God, but a Goddess.

The Indian women left our straw-and-mud longhouse withdrawn, with a sense of calm completion on their brows; the men scurried around like anxious ants or worry-wart buggers, looking for their ant-hill home which had just been kicked away. Subsequently, men bang the drum.

I remember like yesterday the feeling of the drum and my heart starts to race. The drum loud, hollow-skinned bass within a wooden shell, feels like rolling gentle thunder in my chest and forehead. The men bang the drum song till the thundering beat is their home. The beat echos and reverberates. The men yell and hum in unison with the beat until they sing.

My body vibrated along with the drum and their songs.

"Yeaaah! All, all, yeah, yeah. Ruff! Ruff! Hunnhhuh, huu-unnh" would be accentuated with high-noted, "Wooww! Yeaaah! All, all, yeeeaaah! Yeeeaaah! Aaaarrroow yeaa!"

Unconsciously, as I write this dear reader, goose bumps rise on me like a chill. The hair on my neck and face tingles, my eyes swell, my skin is on fire, and my palms become sweaty. This was the sound that ended my family. This is the song of America.

High pitched, "Yeaaah! All, all, yeah! Yeah! Ruff! Ruff" low, warm, and in the dirt, "Hunnhhuh, huuunnh." In the sky, an eagle is shot, a warrior is pierced through his eye with an arrow. Listen to the arrow hit, slice, and fall. Listen to his tribe carry him to the next world. "Yeaaah! All, all, yeeeaaah! Yeeeaaah! Aaaarrroow yeaa!"

Interspersed and synchronized warriors yell and yodel like dogs and wolves in a feeding frenzy of war. Vocal warriors catch an enemy's knife in their gut, or an ax head-on, and then sing themselves into their new spiritual world trium-phantly: "Yeeeaaahhhaaaweellallahalalala!"

The skinned-drum thunder is an atomic bass, a parallel beat to my heart, an enormous rhythmic earthquake.

"Crung, crung, ung. Crum, ung, drum, drum um, um." They scream, "Yeaaah! All, all, yeah! Yeah! Ruff! Ruff! Hnunnnhhuuh." The drums ring and roll the earth: "Crung, crung, ung." The screams, "Ahhhaaawllllallala!" The drums, "Crung ung, ung."

I was on the verge of blubbering and bawling, heart in my throat, mind racing, sweating — freaking!

Yells and howls of men caught in bear-traps become beau-tiful harmonies. A chorus of men march and dance in their own fire — burning, driving, getting hotter with thunder clap rhythms and echos of the tribe dying and dancing!

"Yeaaahhhaawlllllallallalala — Yeeeeeaaaaaahhhhha-aaa aawlllllallallalalalalalala!"

Wild jackals and hyenas seemed to fight in ecstasy: clenched with locked jaws on each other's bloody throats, screaming, rattling, hugging for a noble death in each other's arms. The women smiled and chanted along. My sister-clan, the Indian red queens, nodded, singing to each other in high-pitched falsettos that wavered exquisitely like bees as they eat a dead caterpillar. Shrieks and screeches of instigation were inter-mixed with goddess cries of joy on another successful dance.

The Lenape's primal majesty continued as the men beat the wooden bass drum till it reverberated along the valleys and hills of a New Nothing, until the beats' deep shadows and orange fire flashes echoed away into the dawn. The fearful shadows flickered in the forest, creating shadow monsters that were set free into Nothing, shadows and men running like wild imps into the purple Appalachian darkness.

"Crung, crung, ung, Drum, dung, drum, drum um, um..." now mixed with high toned women warrior "Yeaasahhhss! All, all, yeah! Yeah! Ruff! Ruff! Hunnhhuh, crung, crung, ung..." And then again shattered with "Yeaaahhhaaawlllllallal! — Crung, ung, ung, ung, drum, drum, drum!" A shattering Lenape song, see-saw talking to the American night: "Yeaaahhhaaawlllllallal! — Crung, ung, ung, ung, drum, drum, drum!"

The fire-shadow beat had a life of its own: "Crung crum, drum, um, o, o, m, um, um, drum, um."

The savage beat married my own heartbeat, going faster and faster — I was again part of it now! Within the shadow, within the thunder, dizzy, I felt my heart beat with the terrorist in the woods. I was transcended — Awakened, and it was horrible. The men tried to control the shadows with the beats and the beats with the shadows. The men in vain tried to control the beat, they beat the beat, but then the shadowy beat turned on them and our world was not our world. The shadows of thunder grew louder and deeper — the shadows chased and cornered the men into the shadows — the shadows beat the men!

"Crung, crum, crum, drum, um, drum, drum, crung drum, drum, um, um, drum."

The sound suffocated me. I tried to leave. I was losing control, but my sister-clan sat me down abruptly and snickered at my weak ovaries and mind without saying a word. Dealing with me — Walofang — was beneath my sister-clan. I was considered part of the Chief's slaves and not his harem, a Walofang whore and treated as such.

The men yelled, growled, and sang in a talkative harmony. The Indians were soldiers of the earth, dancing with feathered streamers. The shadow-bass became murkier and the men lost their own creation — now a shadowy beat again. The painted men ran lost into the woods — some never came back; others came back as zombies. Other warriors, stealthy and political, danced close to the fire and focused one eye on the women. Other men ran up the large maple on a low-hanging branch, perched themselves there and yodeled like a family of wild turkeys in a tree. The masked men ran over each other, men hopped in place, the brilliantly feathered men ran into each other, and then fought each other in and around the flames. The fire raged and the women became warmhearted, sincere, and genuine.

All men bang the drum — the men keep the beat — and now the beat was keeping the men. The beat became a bigger, prouder home. The men banged the drum softly now, catching their breath. Men yelled and yodeled for mommy... men cried to their wives. Men barked and whined about their children, wives, and enemies. Men cried and danced for revenge.

"Yeaaah! All, all, yeah! Yeah! Ruff! Ruff! Hunnhhuh,

huuunnh, Aaaarrroow! Yea! Yeaaah! All, all, yeah! Yeah! Ruff! Ruff! — YEEAAAHH!"

Men cried to a feminine Goddess, who said, "Fuck you, sucker-boy, you are done." The men danced in rapid, violent, and brutal positions. They danced into a mangle of colored feathers, spears, skin, and firelight. The men danced remorselessly and dissolved like dust and smoke into the night.

All men bang the drum louder. Men keep the beat loudest. These men in front of me, these mere boys with burning torches, had elaborately feathered headdresses and painted masks. These men were screaming, writhing, and dying in the dark. These men dance as disturbed electrified children during this full-moon dance. These men are no different than the men I know in Boston and London. Men dance for the woman's entertainment. The peacocks dance for the peahens, imagining green and blue iridescent eyespots aglow from friends and fans we do not have. English and American men dance with a hero's tale and/or an elephant dance — whatever makes today's fashionable woman boil, giggle, steam, and/or whistle about. Perchance today a fox-trot strut or a loon's laugh will catch the women's fancy, get the women's devotion and/or our creative evolution, right? These savage Indian men, just like Englishmen and American men, dance in vain for the sanctity of their life.

Meanwhile my sister-clan transcended dreamlike into lady raptors and women kites floating slowly together in the whip-poor-will darkness — these happy and camouflaged male ghosts of the night sang to the woods slowly that the party was just starting:

"Whiiiippperwwwilll... Whiiiippperwwwilll... Whiiiippperwwwilll....

Whiiiippperwwwilll... Whiiiippperwwwilll... whiiiippperwwwilll...."

I look into the darkness of the dangerous woods and the flute of a man-child skips along:

"Whiiiippperwwwillll... Whiiiippperwwwilll... Whiiiippperwwwillll...."

It is the male might that is right in the night. Mr. Whippoorwill doesn't just sing: "Whiiiippperwwwillll... Whiiiippperwwwilll... Whiiiippperwwwillll.... He's really singing, "Testosterone, Testosterone, Testosterone," like a hopeful child, like a hopeful boy — unending and beautiful.

"Whiiiippperwwwillll... Whiiiippperwwwilll... Whiiiippperwwwillll...."

I think to myself, what am I scared of if the dark woods sings that song? I continued to look into the black Nothing night, listening to chromosome Y singing, priming, jacking, and revving it up. Steady-Eddy with the brown feathers sere-naded the female moon and I was frozen as his hope of some-thing and not Nothing was actually a lively conversation about evolution.

"Whiiiippperwwwillll... Whiiiippperwwwilll... Whiiiippperwwwillll....

Whiiiippperwwwillll... Whiiiippperwwwillll. Whiiiippperwwwilll...."

Then my night-bird sisters became red-tailed hawks, silent as lavender powder from a butterfly's wings, looping in circles above as the whip-poor-will boys played below. I was on fire.... These female night vultures passed their peace pipe wrapped in grizzly bear capes and osprey-feath-ered shawls. My sister-clan laughed at its pudgy pigeon men waddling around pecking at each other. The men are grey, awkward, mindless, drunk dirty-birds flopping and danc-ing in circles. They dance around the fire as their loin cloths and feathers melt into black smoke that rises into the moon-light. My sister-clan seemed to rise with the hot golden red embers floating up towards the blue and black night sky, as they congratulated themselves as royal queens. These laughing owls and bubbly buzzards leisurely discussed which man they would devour next and who would clean the man's carcass. These feminine meat-eaters and these sexy man-eaters, these silent hunters, cleaned the man down to the bone, down to the spine with razor-sharp talons to hold, curved beaks to peck, night vision to always see, and atonal hearing to always hear. To hear before the wave, to hear the bow stretch in the woods, to feel the drafting air before the arrow flies.

This matriarchal hierarchy I noticed more and more. The women Elders of the tribe and their parents were cared for by all the males in the tribe. The different fathers of the mother's child did not get involved in the parenting of the child. The mother's brothers raised the child as their child or, more correctly, as the women's child, and then the tribe's child. The male Lenape warrior was a stay-at-home dad on diaper duty. The Indian men paid their respects daily to the women and their parents in a doleful and dutiful way. Ironically, sometimes the American Indian civilization is not far off from the English civilization.

HAPPINESS

My clan mother was part of the Digging clan and her name was Gela, which means "Happiness." Gela, Happy, or Hap, as her sisters sometimes called her, flowed as a sable heron in her stalky, sultry moves. Gela was about five feet six inches and more a dark muscular horse then a woman. Happy was all eyes and easily spooked with a red copper skin that glowed and blended perfectly with her horse's auburn and chocolate markings. Gela smelt like a warm and well-organized barn and riding her horse bareback was pure *happiness*. Gela became invisible within the gallop and trot with the horse's long black mane. Happiness ran as one, lost within the dark horse's shadow, streaked tail, and mane. Gela found happiness somewhere within this stampede of wild horses and the dusty winds along the sandy and rocky beach.

Happy had a pronounced, amusing presence with kind-hearted chestnut eyes on your first impression. Happy was a flowering, white, silhouetted dogwood tree on a moonlit night. She was full of breath and glowed with life, sashaying with herself — not always the strongest, or brightest, but with a friendly, pinky constitution. Happy was always sought and/or missed by the sister-clan. On the other side of the Happy coin was Hap: a burden with large ears riding a jackass. Somewhere in between these two Happy and Hap thoughts, I suppose, is happiness.

As with most people who tell you they're happy, Gela visualized herself as happy, but Happy was partly a sad Lenape bimbo. Beyond Indian common sense or happiness there was nothing except a cold Indian stare of arrogance and/or ignorance. Regardless, most of the time Happy talked in a radiant manner and moved with a silver stream gait. Be it the gift of her Indian turtle God that Happy was to be a wild horse in her next life, well, then, her sexy and strong long black hair in this life would suffice as her sultry mane in the next.

Happiness the emotion was a core foundation for the Indian terrorist. Can you, dear reader, imagine a tribe, or a perhaps even a Nation or Country, could be founded on the pursuit of happiness? A nation based on life, on life with no debt and happiness? How silly a thought! I cannot remember the last time I was truly happy.... As a child, I suppose — that's sad... distressing. Nonetheless, happiness in America still seems possible. Happiness is a haunting thought that is at home here in the American sun. Innate happiness or liberty is believable in America and that is what drove my mother and Mary Dyer towards their free-grace.

Gela managed the tribal farming as we planted the "Three Sisters" (corn, beans, and squash) season to season, not year

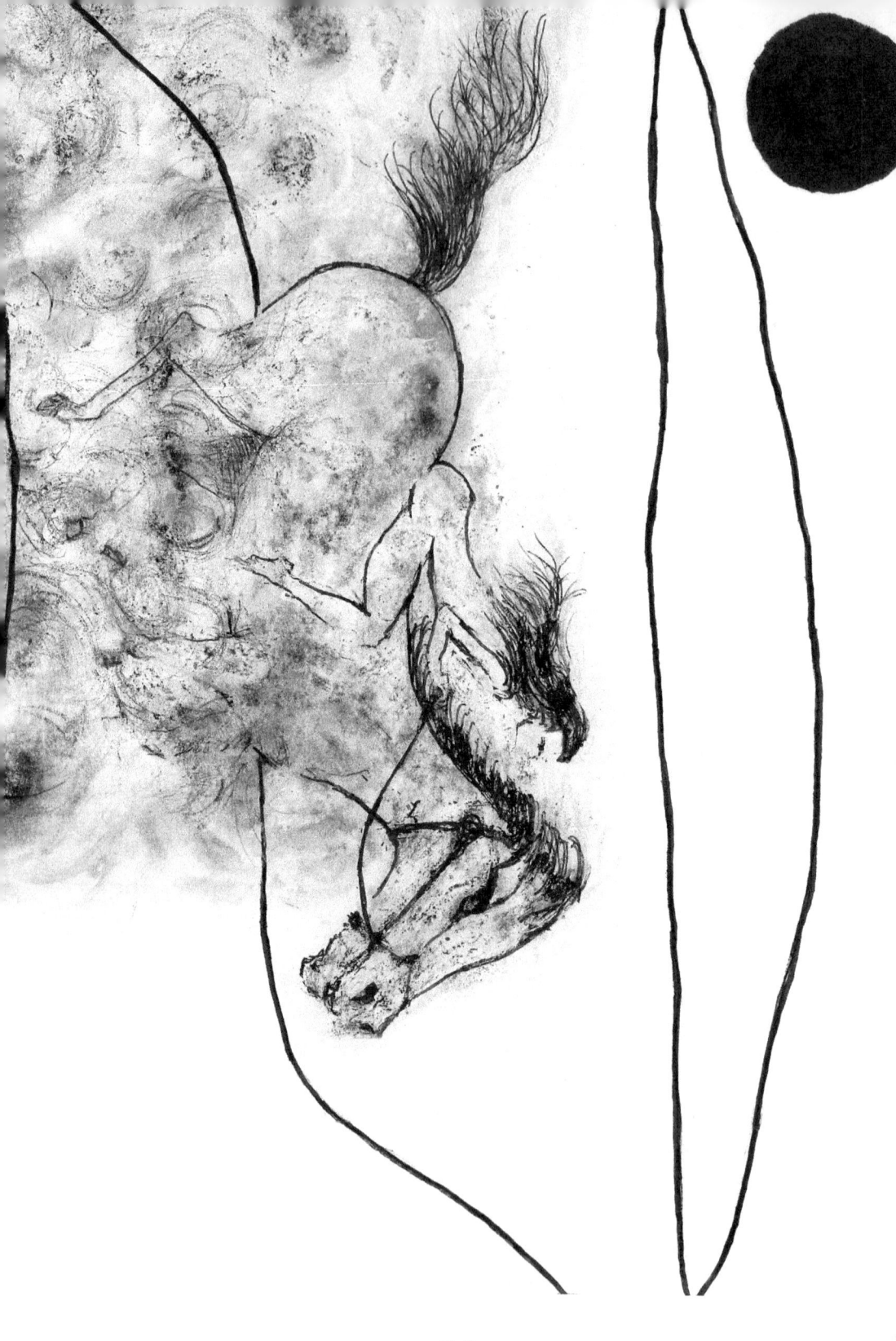

Gela

after year. The American Indian women also had sole owner-ship and responsibility of the Indian Nation's nomadic lands and would lead and govern the Indian men with their hunt-ing and gathering schedule. The Lenape women reigned with a feminine and creator touch over all government decisions of their Indian Nation.

As a white-devil orphan, I silently learned about this Indian life and thought I'd compare it to the common man or common woman in the English and Dutch white-devil civilization I had just been abducted from. The common man, much less a common woman, still had NO legal right to own property in England or America. The Englishmen and Dutchmen I left behind are still indentured servants to their countries' royal families and the bourgeois loyalists who leg-islate and police the middle and lower-class rabble for them. The courtier's liege is their life. These wounded peons are proud feudal serfs or suburban pygmies who live and die try-ing unsuccessfully to curry favor from the royal courts, mag-istrates, bailiffs, and/or janitors.

I remember as a child in Rhode Island playing with a neighbor's child whose family had recently defected from the Hartford, Connecticut, colony. The Hartford colony was run by the son of Governor and Minister Winthrop, so this Puritanical child was the typical loyalist-royalist even though his parents had recently dissented from their royalist ways. His royal full name was Rupert Jackson or Sir Jackson. What a self-important name; Sir Jackass was more appropriate and whispered more than not.

Sir Jackson was capped with short brown hair like that of a horse-hair scrub-brush. His pink cheeks and a wicked tongue with rosy lips made him look almost feminine. Jackson had the energy of the fittest, and his sky-blue eyes changed with the sun. He smelt like a bar of soap in his double-vested blue blazer doublet and trunks that matched his twinkling eyes.

Sir Jackass was a bright, mischievous, bushy-tailed royal bull in hiding.

And just as the Jesuits say, "Give me a child until seven and I will give you a Catholic," the nine-year-old little Sir Jackass, the precocious royal cunt from Connecticut, was forever the Puritan cop. Despite his parents' changes in religion, his earlier upbringing made Sir Jackass the Puritan police on our Providence playground.

Sir Jackass, whose birthday was every day, went around whispering, stalking, preaching, and grinding our Puritan guilt by saying, "I know what you're thinking... I know what you want...." He was a fat bluebird squawking and pecking away, a laughing blue snake — snickering, giggling, deriding and scorning you after it has bitten you and injected its poison. Sir Jackson would then snap his constricted victims with his white linen hanky embroidered with an eloquent red capital T and black J for his bloody and deadly namesake. For us guilt-ridden Judeo-Christian children, "Our want" was off limits, especially to an ass-sniffing Puritan in disguise pretending to be at one with Providence. Sir Jackass would suck the dirty end of his hanky so his rat-tail whip was wet and sounded like a clap or snap when he cracked his whip. Sir Jackass wasn't just a slap in the face, but a perversion of society. In between snapping the boys and girls he didn't like (which was everybody), Sir Nasty would steal kisses from the cute highbrow girls, always kicking sand in our faces with his monkey-shit exit sing-song: "I know what you want, I know what you want, I know what you want."

Most children were happy to hear from their parents, "Little Sir Jackson plays too rough, you stay away from him," but our mothers and even our fathers encouraged us to play with the Puritan anarchist. Not just because he was royal and free by birth, but, more important, cute and charming. Unbeknownst to us children at the time was that our parasitical parents knew that false images from our Elected and royal networks with the Elders is evolution.

Because of my family's Separatist heritage, Sir Jackass stayed away from me and from our irrevocable ideological differences. There were also unspoken physical fears from Sir Jackass's eyes as the Hutchinsons were known to go Viking on royalist poodles when pushed. He would stare and smirk at me, mouthing the words, "I know what you want," but I knew what the bastard really wanted and it was blood for blood's sake.

The following May Day as we twirled beneath the May pole, Sir Jackass tried to steal a kiss. With one hand, I held the May pole streamer, the other on my hip as we skipped: "Too-da-le, too-da-la" — up and over, "Too-da-le, too-da-la" — down and under, "Too-da-le-la, too-da-le-la." Other classmates held the pole as we wove a rainbow braid underneath the returning spring sun.

Red, blue, yellow, and green streamers floated above our heads with spastic children running amok. They ran and grew like spritely green sprouts of tulips in the sun as dirty brown snow packs still hid in the shade. Our May Day was a psychedelic rattan dance that interlaced Chinese handcuffs as its center spine while a dancing dragon chased its tail with spring fever. During the chaos of our celebration, I saw Sir Jackass the Puritanical pervert coming towards me, so I grabbed that hanky out of his hand and stuck it in his puckered pie-hole mouth. Sir Jackass's diarrhea of the mouth was silenced for a moment as the May Day celebration laughed in horrendous joy. This was the birth of a new American jackass, a muzzled Christian Zionist without a woeful hanky.

Sir Jackass and his loyalist white-devil fraternity of slave-lites in America, England, and Europe have no human rights — no civil rights. And certainly, there is no humanity for the common man in England's and Europe's colonies in Africa, Asia, the Caribbean and here in America. These Englishmen?

These Europeans? These indentured servants? These emasculated men? Maybe eunuchs? These humans? Sub-humans? These *Sir Jackasses* have no human rights compared to the American Indian nirvana of living free at Hell's Gate.

Perhaps the American Indian abyss in New Netherland I was living in was my murdered mother's nirvana. I lived, worked, and broke bread with her Indian murderers and I knew how heartily my mother would laugh at these cosmic American events. We had to leave northern England for the Netherlands with a huff, then we had to leave Boston with a banishing puff. And, of course, our Hutchinson house in Providence got blown down; it blew away along with fairy tales and apologies from wolves posing as red-queen grandmas.

I have to declare that, of all the Englishman's colony experiments in "Democracy and Freedom" fronting for imperialism and capitalism, Providence, Rhode Island, was the most noble and the highest bar my tribe has reached. Roger Williams and the rest of the Baptists in Providence deserve all the credit, but so does my grandfather's and then my mother's Separatist protest. Their respect, devotion, and obsession for true freedom and the "Good ole cause" is the fight of the "Haves" against the "Have-nots." Free-grace similarly punches-up against abstract religious Abe-Babe domination. Free-grace is for those who don't want to be bought, bred, and/or sold into the materialist / religionist world. The *good ole cause* and free-grace are not just for Protestants, Baptists, Separatists, Shakers or Quakers — they're for all those who want happiness and liberty now.

For my family, Mary Dyer, and myself, this has been a long protestor's or Protestant road and it ultimately killed my mother and our family. My Luddite grandfather back in St. Bott's Stone and my bitchy mother "Evolved" at the expense of seven of their children being butchered, massacred, and slaughtered because they both ventured too far into breaking the State for the common man. This Divine intervention,

Awakening, and/or Divine fruit of their Protestant life was my pure and savage vacation with the Lenape Indians. I was now living in a clean matriarchal society and I truly felt the sun and earth; the only real creators in my life, and this spiritually opened me up. I became Awakened. Happiness, my Lenape sister, kept my chin up and Annie, my deceased mum, kept my spirits up with warm breezy sunshine that sparkled off the glittering water every day. Free-grace sparkling... even on the cloudiest and snowiest days of winter under three feet of snow — shimmering! Alternatively, Anne Hutchinson's politics of freedom was brought to me not by my mother, but by the terrorists she was trying to sanctify and save from patriarchal incarceration and damnation. The American Indian providence was in their nomadic fire, which was their temporary autonomous zone. My mother did not realize that earthly Indian truth until it was too late.

MADE IN LONDON

I can remember like a moment ago, when I was thirteen years old walking in the New Netherland woods, climbing around the large split rock and then hearing the Indian's war-cries, yelps, and hollering coming from our homestead.

"Yeaaah, all! All, yeah, yeah, ruff! Ruff! Aaaarrroow yea!" Multilayered guttural and high pitched boys with axes and war paint yelling: "Yeaaah, all! All, yeah, yeah, ruff! Ruff! Aaaarrroow yeah!"

It was a humid summer afternoon, frustratingly warm and grey. The air was wet with a greenish mist, thick as pea soup. It could have been 7:30 in the morning or 3:30 in the afternoon — as the air was so wet and thick with pollen. It was that dreary, hazy, hot, and humid northeastern American weather that makes you want to hide and skulk around. The dogged humidity is a wall of black mold in your face that makes you gag with a sore throat and the flu as memorabilia. Nauseous people in their dead homes with their cat-pee rugs rejoice in this stench as the insects grow larger by the second. The claustrophobia sets in as creepers, buzzers, and crawlers crawl, fly, and slither much more quickly in this slimy weather.

I feel like a horse locked in in a stall on a hot day. I wish I had a long tail for all the flies and mosquitos that hover in the back of my ear, buzzing in my blind spot. The buzzing parasites are in the back of my head, where I will never even see them. I can only hear it eternally: "BuzzzzzZZZZzzzzz.... BuuuzzzzZZZzzz.... BuzzzzzZZZZzzzzz...." Why do these godforsaken parasites torture a handicapped horse like me in its locked stall? I suppose because the fly has might... and might in a hot barn for a fly makes right.

In this tropical humidity watery vines suffocate trees and houses in a day as you hear the grasses, botany, and animals hunting and marching. Barely breathable, with no breeze, no wind, and the good-works of nature are choking me with climbing sprouts and the wet, thick air. Bloodsuckers, carnivores, parasites, and viruses are writhing faster than a moment ago! Within this summer greenhouse, the mosquitos, spiders, cicadas, and bedbugs are breeding, strengthening, and gaining fervor, speed, and longevity. Red itchy rashes scratch and ooze with no breeze — no relief from this hot and heavy cicada song. The summer scabie heat becomes a grinding toothache that crawls under my skin. This grey summer sounds and feels like a rattlesnake, slithering and circling out of sight.

The Indians screamed, "Yeeeaaahhhaaawllllallallalalala!" and it seemed in perfect harmony with the world.

The forest leaves drip with oily sebum sap, drizzling and oozing juices from an unforeseen force of life — an action with no action. The mosquitos, cockroaches, and leeches in this *Nothing* but *something* weather have a unique advantage in eating you alive. Nature or Nothing is buzzing, climbing,

growing, slithering, breeding, and dying into a claustrophobic, ancient, and steely quietude of waiting. The bloodsuckers
and cockroaches gaze at us as we are in the wrong, that we are
the *Other*. I'm waiting in a hot waiting room in the summertime in a dead office for a meeting or a marriage that has not
been scheduled. There are reptilian receptionists leading me
along as the oxygen dissipates. I feel stuck with someone else's
life to lead — I'm poisoned, sleepless, and being eaten alive. I
am an unwilling host with someone else's larvae in my belly; I
am parasitized by my sister X — I am woman.

My family's logical pleas for help and mercy were mixed
with shrill, high-octave screams foretelling a gruesome end
and not the answer they were hoping for. Ed took it like a soldier, Faith like a rabid dog at an outdoor café birthday party
gone terrorist, and Bridget like a saint. I'm embarrassed and
ashamed to have witnessed this slaughter. I'm dirty, disgraced,
and divorced from humanity. It was all a fog until I focused on
two elaborately colored and feathered Lenape warriors dragging my mother through her garden kicking and screaming.
To see the violent terrorist or the Biblical ax dropped on a
loved one is an abomination of an education within a civil
society. I continued to tunnel in on my mother's native pest
problem in her garden as other brothers and sisters were still
on the cutting blocks elsewhere, for English scalps and their
hollow hearts were an Indian commodity and delicacy.

I focused in on my mother's burgundy cloak and her black
clog uprooting green spinach, and when her clog passed in
the air, it matched in perfect complementary harmony the
red and yellow Lenape warrior headdress. As all things rose
to this color-theory synchronicity, this feathery convergence,
the earth stopped spinning with me for a few moments before
the Indians splayed my mother across, and upon, our white
picket fence. For that moment, there was a cease-fire — this
was the *real*; this was the *Other* being murdered by *Nothing.*
Then I woke up and my neighbors proceeded to cut my mother

open and carve her up like a pig on a post. The Indians yelped and danced around in the grey leaden watery mist dripping with my mother's red blood, singing.

"Yeeaahhhaawllallalla! Yeeeaaaa! Yeeeaaa! Yeeaahhhaawllallalla!"

This shocking contrast threw me into another world. I felt a left brain to the right brain road-show — my tiny life flashed in front of me in a milli-second, I felt light and faint. Methought, this is to be.

Before my mother's head rolled through her garden, I'm sure she thought an Indian tomahawk smashed her skull. For a fleeting moment, Annie, my mum, must have smiled before the second terrorist chop came from what she saw out of the corner of her crushed and bloody eye: a shiny English axe embossed with "Made in London."

The English ax was in the hand of the Lenape terrorist and it was coming down towards the nape of her neck, and it surgically took off my English mother's head. The loyalist-royalist English were giving away their Iron Dome axes to the Lenape, Sunni, and Shawnee. Or were the Americans giving arms to the Seneca and the Shia? I can never keep track, as it's always tribal warfare with American guns and English royalty. Whether the Shia and Seneca are on our side today, or whether the Sunni and the Shawnee are on our side tomorrow, no one profits except the arms dealer.

These dealers were stoking tribal and political warfare while English and Dutch imperialists waited in the smoky wings to pick over the half-dead fruit in occupied America. The English — okay with collateral damage and friendly fire, traded financial and physical ax-options, hoping and hedging that the "Made in London" ax would end up lodged squarely in the Dutchman's blockhead. What a tragic comedy that must have been for my mother to realize that her death was a successful English trade-war hit. The counterinsurgent direct hit that flip-flops between collateral damage and creative destruction.... Regardless, some English or American dandy will then write my mother's free-grace story into a play and all of Britannia and America will chuckle. English-thinking souls laugh heartily as they are chit-chatting about wagging tits, tongues, and torture, with tea, coffee, and cookies. It's in our insipid wanna-be royal blood. Just as the Aesop scorpion sinks his own boat drowning because it's in his nature, we the white-devil dip our cookie in our tea or coffee and drown our soul.

An English mistake? Not an honest question; but it is the perfect oxymoron, and not just because the local non-friend-lies can't tell the difference between an English limey and a Dutch square-head white-devil, but because my mother, or pure womanhood, unapologetically realized Roger Williams's Providence was still a Boston-lite town, a misogynist-lite town in one hand, and in the other hand, Providence was lying to itself, portraying and branding the lie that the Providence colony is a democracy with justice, freedom, and a common-wealth government protecting the common man.

The disingenuous royal trait or courtier character of the Englishman is a shame, but for the new American woman in Providence, an English dandy, a coxcomb jackanape is a joke — a miscarriage of a man. My cheeky mother with the ovaries of an orangutan rightfully said, "Fuck 'em!" and went further into American womanhood. Annie left those blue dogs count-ing their beans and chewing on their bones in Providence. Annie went further into anarchy, adultery, and the arts. Annie went further into her free-grace Awakening; she went further into the woods of America.

An English mistake: an oxymoron, or more correctly an "Alpha-moron" — lives large in the new "Occupied-zone," the new "New Colony for Democracy," the new "New Israel." The lawyerly apostles with their fashionable liturgies and their policing deacons pump-and-dump the lower- and middle-class meek until this rabble, until these un-fashionable wheels, wobble off their axle. Behind the upper-middle-class loyalists, the ugly lower- and middle-class mob becomes undone. The servants and varlets drop an axle on their cart, yellow sparks explode as rims of steel gouge the stone road as the wheel rolls off the highway, speeding through the weeds and over a guardrail into the Appalachian hollows — the ugly, the forgotten, the unfashionable thrown into the forlorn nether of the night.

For the English, who really have no sense of selfless humor — an economic downturn or a great recession here or a commodity divestment there is English humor. English royalty, going back to the Jews' King David, are reaping Profits from Biblical collateral damage. These Abe-Bros are the Catholics, the Muslims, and the Jewish bastards fighting it out not for the Empire's sake or Abraham's sake, but for an Abe-Babe's sake. Abe-Bros killing for Abe-Babes. Abe-Bros selling and financing axes and guns to them all according to Scripture in their Bro-Bible. Their world that revolves around Attacking, Dividing, Starving, and then Profiting from our neighbors and children (ADSP).

I'm sure my mother was humbled, casual, gracious, and American enough to laugh out loud at her British Tomahawk missile death. I'm sure Anne Hutchinson, my dead mother, entered with miraculous mordancy the implicit and inaudible supranatural world, laughing out loud right in front of her Maker, laughing with good nature at the simplicity of it all, laughing at... and with, her Creator — which Americans seem born to.

CHAPTER 3

Wampy — Free Grace — The Neg-Am Jam

WAMPY

'm now up at the corner of State and Joy Street, at the top of the Common, and I look up to see my friend William Demopheare waving to me. I can see my friend William Demopheare up at the schoolhouse, but I suddenly get a strong whiff of rural America. I look down at my Aunt Ally's new white boots she bought me and I see a blob of horseshit stuck to my heel. I start scraping my white boot on the cobblestone curb, waving to William. He has the same tall and wiry build as my old Indian Chief, Wampage. Nothing else is the same, yet they're both kind of eternal boys deep in their faces and hearts. Wampage knew about this weakness and/or strength, but William does not. I turn around and look down to the Common parkland and I try to figure out which way the wind is blowing. I see the grey, green, and brown swirl of colonial America on a peninsula surrounded by wings of blue water that looks like a struggling caterpillar, like a cocooned butterfly, yellow like sandy straw and green like clover, trying to escape its past. For Americans chrysalis is horseshit on our boot, and America is a butterfly learning to fly.

Wampage, chief of the Lenape Indians, stopped his warriors from killing me that grim day in New Netherland, 1643, and confiscated my sweet muffin-ass because he thought that I reminded him of his daughter, who was killed by the block-headed Dutch a year earlier. Therein lies the politically correct option, but as most experienced women would understand, I think my cran-apple ass saved my sister-ass down there at split rock. Chief Wampage was enthralled with and amazed at my red hair, thus my Indian name, which he gave me — Autumn Leaf.

Wampage managed his clout under the wary eyes of the sister-clan mothers. He was a balanced buffoon and an agile fighter with an innate sense of manipulation and leverage. His masculine power was strangely similar to that of the English and Dutch white-devils who seem born to bully. Wampage stood about five feet, six inches tall and was built like a meaningful, but insignificant, wooden gate. His skin color was a dull rusty brown and he smelt like dry, depleted, brown dirt. Wampage always wore his feathery headdress, which made Wampy (as the sister-clan called him behind his back) look like a jovial Asian man with a good hand playing mahjong. Around his neck were yellow and peach scallop shells strung together, holding a bear claw in the center. This gave Wampy more of a Polynesian visage, as his eyes were plowed together along his furrowed brow. Wampy seemed to not stop thinking about his own nobility or maybe he was thinking about being Lenape playboy of the month.

For me — an eighteen-year old woman, or a woman of any age, I suppose — a nice ass is wampum gold. Tight, playful butts are always few and far between — whether in an Israel kibbutz, at the London Company's holiday party, or in an American teepee. A nice monkey-ass on a woman, or a man, trumps all bonobos.

Wampy, as my sister-clan rolled its eyes and looked askance, would babble on about me and his lost Indian daughter that their Turtle God had returned when he enslaved me. Wampy, after a few more shots of rum in our longhouse, would slowly dance and sing like that mourning dove I heard earlier.

Wampy

Instead of, "CooOOoo-woo-woo-wooooo," Wampy, with grey, white, and black feathers from large seagulls on his arms and legs and a grey wolf's pelt over his head and draped down his back, would dance slowly and sing, "Nichenooo-OOO-ooo, Nichenooo-OOO-ooo" while stalking, dancing, and circling around me like a hungry wolf, "NichenoooOOOooo — NichenoooOOOooo!"

It didn't matter that Chief Wampage was singing and speaking his Algonquin Indian language because the Chief had no clothes. Was this the old way? The new way? The Wu-way? It was all those and more — just another little dicky, cock-a-doodle doo way! The Wampy way? Yes, to all four questions, and specifically yes to the Wampy-way! He was a lost dog, just like the rest of the men I've met, using puppy-talk, baby-talk, and/or mommy-talk to get down my petticoat. My clan-sisters communicated this acknowledgment to me through their faces and eyes and never through their spoken language. Wampy took great pride in scalping and killing my mother and claiming me as a white-devil party-favor. I was Wampy's white-devil strawberry shortcake sundae, all day, and every day, deep in his wolf den.

Wampy also took my mother's name as a war trophy and paraded around New Netherland belching his "Yangeez Aanguage" or, English language, with his botched and stunted primate mispronunciation of "Anne Hutchinson."

Wampy would terrorize white-devil towns in Connecticut or New Netherland by burping and blurting staccato style out of his mouth, "Hi, I'm Uuun Huckson. How do you do?"

He would walk around and say proudly, "Howdy, I'm Uuun Huckson. Hello, I'm Uuun Huckson. Me Uuun Huckson, nice day today?"

Dutch and English white-devils or Walofangs walking hand in hand in Hartford would scurry away quickly, as no one wanted to deal with the native town drunk and/or Chief

Wampy — the Special-Ed terrorist. Wampy didn't realize that my mother was banished and scorned from white-devil society as a serpent spreading an ideological plague.

Wampy's "Hello, I'm Uuun Hucksen" birthday party for one with a shit-eating grin was as ridiculous as if a white-devil English town drunk went into a Lenape Indian camp and proudly started introducing himself by saying, "Hello, my name is Mr. Small Pox," and, "Hello, me Mr. Small Pox, nice weather we're having?"

Wampy also spun and spammed the dream-catcher spider web lie that he trapped my mother's soul in the Indians' spirit world with his warrior cannibalism when he ate my mother's still-beating heart after they chopped her head off. Chewing on that thought, I have to advocate and imagine that my mother was spiritually wrapped much tighter than most. So, for her to be transcendentally trapped in the Indian spiritual world by Wampy seems like a cheap and easy feather in his cap. Anne Hutchinson would not go down without a fight, whether eaten physically or trapped metaphysically by Wampy or any other white-devil wanna-be wanker cannibal with tartar sauce on his face. My mother had legally and lovingly outmaneuvered Governor Winthrop and the treacherous Reverend Cotton in Boston, yet she was still sent down the Connecticut River with the trash into the Long Island Sound — down below the Devil's Belt. So, I'm sure Annie has lots of spiritual balancing work to do in the after-life, as I don't think enemies die in the spiritual world. My mother, I'm proud to say, had many enemies, and Wampy surely wasn't one of them.

FREE-GRACE

My mother's free-grace controversy is still a communicable disease in the English-speaking soul, an infectious virus on our conscience, a nagging truth that still haunts all white-devils who hold their Bible, or their flag, too close to their hearts, and not to their minds. These Judeo-Christian bastards deal in the trickle-down currency of Divine indulgences and it shows so blatantly in our laws and their depraved power. Mary Dyer's possible execution today at 9:00 am is testimony to the overbearing power of the Puritan State. I sit in my dark classroom with an orthodox education being taught nothing except to accept orthodox executions, *it's all for the best* incarcerations, and incessant investigations triggering constant paranoia, ceaseless angst, and perpetual dread. There is no oxygen to breathe in my Boston classroom....

In contrast to Puritan servitude and bondage, free-grace rests on a *laissez-faire* or hands-off approach. I realize there is no power within free-grace. There is no loss; there is no profit. There is no "Leverage" or "Angle" with free-grace. There are no tongues to spill silly words like these that I write down on this paper. There are no words, no materialism, and no idolatry so, therefore, there is no war. Free-grace is new spirituality. It is intangible, indescribable, and beyond words because there is no price or debt for free-grace. There is no immunity or cure. After your free-grace Awakening there is no turning back because you've self-actualized.

Begrudgingly, we must realize the leverage and debt (our gift-love and need-love) we have over others — this golden calf that we milk so well, only incarcerates and disgraces ourselves. As Plato said, "Your love is the son of poverty."

Plato wasn't philosophizing about the number of crowns in our purse; he was talking about our depraved love and how... like a parasitic virus, our perverted love breeds and births our souls' emptiness and bankruptcy. Plato knew our souls have absolute liability when we have lied to ourselves and, more important — lied to others our whole life and we knew better. We knew that, honestly, nothing matters, but some of us play the Jewish and Catholic games and by playing the cash-for-kids lottery, we spiritually lost everything — including our souls. And at this exact same time of losing everything we became absolutely liable for everything the Catholic pumpers and Jewish dumpers have schemed and executed in history. We are Resurrection-Ready, but guilty by association.

We try to negotiate a plea-bargain for a lesser crime, but then realize we have to give up the white-devil drugs of need-love and gift-love as part of our parole, so we then decide to risk it all at trial. The hero or heroine in our head declares: *there has to be justice*, and our delusion soothes us, but not for long. We still wonder — is life really: lie or die? Wondering whether to lie or die, we think there has to be a middle ground, a safe space, a time-out, and we believe in our new, but really old, child's heart. This heart of ours from a sunny Saturday morning long ago, a beach day or maybe a snow day with grand plans when we all danced "Saturday, Saturday, Saturday" on this young and innocent "Day Off." The morning of a *Day Off* is a morning within free-grace.

A morning on a day off... when this free-grace thought, when it finally breaks through in a free-grace moment, when someone reaches out to you, or perhaps on your death bed, you feel tranquil and more relaxed than you have in years because now you're ready to die and you're not worried about your guilt-ridden heaven-or-hell trial. You've realized suddenly it's all so obvious! Oh... great, Nothing.... Just like I always supposed — Nothing as God. Nothing as God-love. You laugh and cry simultaneously at the misanthropic white-devil bullshit that flushed your entire life down the toilet. Or maybe you still have a free-grace chance. You can escape a brainwashed and unnatural woman, praying for royal love, law, and God, but your key to this Garden of Civilization is a "Royal Man." So rather than praying to our Maker or Creator, women pray to a false god / *a royal man*.

Therefore, some of us, having been praying to man-made inventions and false gods... for the last five years, ten years, twenty, forty, fifty years... or perchance a life time? Rest easy, pilgrim, because if you die tomorrow within free-grace, your Awakening will be yours forever because your self-reliant Awakening starts with you, and not with a *royal man*.

Just the thought of no more religious smears and slanders brings oxygen to my blood, to my brain. Surrendering to the truth or your imagined "Creator" or "Maker" sounds to me like a pope-party or rabbi-rendezvous in the confessional you've never had and always wanted.

I remember telling my mother my truth in our Providence house towards the end of our lives together. I was about twelve or thirteen and, with no doubt, then or now, I said, "Mom, your truth is selfish gift-love. You love in bad faith because you love only to receive. Your children and I — our family has suffered because of your neurosis for your gifting, for your breeding, for your motherhood: for growing your cock while you powder your nose in London shop windows and complain about the water temperature in Southampton."

My possessive red-queen Momma with knee-jerk debt prose jabbed back like a banker and/or a collection agency hounding an account in arrears: "If it wasn't for me you wouldn't even be here."

What could I say, dear reader? We've all been here... regardless, I took a new positive direction when discussing parental debt. I easily leap-frogged over the obvious suicidal brat retort that I have no God-love or Maker-love — that I'm not happy to be alive; because I am happy to be alive. Truly self-aware, I went for the repo-mom jugular — I went for the truth and confessed.

"Thanks for telling the truth, Mum, but you know what? Your debt killed me before I was born and now your entreaties of sentiment have reawakened that debt. Your love for your children is perverted affection and whorish."

This free-grace refusal to pay parental debt, this

free-grace clean slate, this original sin release, this surrendering to your pre-natal debt, sheds and pulls off your social facade or mask. Free-grace is a parental Reformation when you say like Martin Luther himself, "Here I stand. I can do no other." Free-grace strips your emotional greasy-gizzard chicken-shit skin off your biped, sub-human soul. Naked and faceless, free-grace supplants the subhuman needs for love as you surrender to the sun and to the night that have seen and heard every single lie from your deceitful tongue. Free-grace is an executioner who lets you go. Free-grace is an ashes-to-ashes surrender. Free-grace is a cheap, quick, and easy x-ray of your soul, revealing once again (surprise-surprise) that synchronicity and balance is the key. Here I stand and from where I've come, I shall return. I cannot be the Other.

My mother stuttered, questioning me: "A, a, a, who, whor, whore, a whore?! But I love you all so much!"

Free-grace is the turtle-spirit light-force, or honesty, of not caring about material delights and completely becoming one with the earth and your God or Maker. With natural zeal, you fall deeply and end-over-end in "Love," or in "Respect" for the only natural truth — your miraculous fragile and short life. Free-grace is this spiritual surrendering or Awakening of free-grace evolution. Instead of a covenant of material works (debt), you focus on a covenant of graceful spiritual works (growth).

Free-grace exists outside the subliminal outline of our shallow existence within Nothing. It lies beyond the blind contour line where your positive life or positive space (what's good in you) becomes subordinate to your negative life or your negative proof (what's bad in you). The negative proof Judeo-Christian life disgraces humans from the moment of their conception with ancestral debt — an Abe-Babe double-negative.

Looking cock-eyed through your left-brain, free-grace lights-up the right side of your brain. It is a light, guttural sense, and intellectually arousing. Free-grace is transcendental; it's another language on a different plane. Free-grace is opposed to being defined by the Jewish and Catholic negative life. Within this Neg-Am Jam life my sovereign spirit, my existence, is defined and also incarcerated by my family's original sin, by my ancestral debt — I was born to owe.

I answered my mother, "Exactly! Your love sucks, it *neeeedddsss,* it *gggiifttsss* with strings attached. You don't love or respect children — you indebt us. Your false-God makes us subjects — we become stepping-stones, cheap labor, or a colony-child indebted to you. Your false-Goddess of motherhood shrouds and conceals your failed patriarchal life."

My mother raged against me: "You ungrateful little bitch — I knew I should have dumped your little ginger ass overboard years ago. When we were sailing to America people were dropping like flies on the *Lioness* and you would not have been missed or lost. I came so damn close on one of those dark and stormy Atlantic Ocean nights. We were all alone on the rolling top-deck because you wouldn't stop crying down below in our shared cabin." In baby talk my mother mimicked and murdered my soul and said, "Suzie always whining, Suzie always wetting her pants, Suzie wanting to go home, and Suzie always complaining.... I imagined your white coddling blanket sinking into the sea and thought no God would doubt me here — you are just another wave in the sea, just another tear in the ocean."

Neg-Am Jam

William up at the schoolhouse sees me staring out to space and yells down, waving his hand to come along. "Let's go, you shaking and quaking Indian. You're going be late!"

I hold up my finger to William, suggesting I need a

moment. William holds out the palms of his hands like Jesus Christ in many European paintings, insinuating compassion and openness, but when real Christians do it, it looks like, "What do you want? You're annoying me." I can't tell the difference between empathy and irritation with most Christians, but I usually assume correctly they're angry and depressed, and I think I know why.

The Neg-Am Jam, Divinity, the NAJ life, the *invisible hand*, royalty, and/or the *Word of God* — all perpetuate the negative amortized life of doing everything for an abstract entity. Something your parents, your Elders, and/or the Elect believe in. This empire life in debt and thus getting nowhere is a human's nightmare. On the other hand, the Neg-Am Jam at the executive emperor level — doing nothing, and earning everything is a money-changer's dream come true! On yet another invisible NAJ hand — actually a squid tentacle, the Elect and Elders governing the Neg-Am Jam municipality collecting fractional interest and unearned income is a white-devil heaven on earth. The Abrahamic fruit of dead-beat sons and mathematical magic-shows swirl around the Neg-Am Jam and the crowns-for-kids scam. The NAJ life is based on moral and financial enforcement and not on an education.

The Jewish and Catholic life is based on the demeaning enforcement of the woman and child rather than encouraging an education or enlightenment of the child and woman. The "No questions life!" The "No-life," for which some men, women, and children not of *good birth* cannot "Do" with "Them." Cannot "Do" "There." These freaks with no arts also cannot "Do" "Then." Furthermore, these low-class humans, and thus their simpleton children, cannot "Do" understanding "How," and absolutely the mob, the masses, or the multitude, cannot absolutely not "Do," comprehending "Why."

The feminine alternatives to the Neg-Am Jam rules for *Mary* or *Eve* in regard to who, where, when, how, and why they are allowed to live is religiously policed and war-mongered.

Eve and *Mary* live within a profitable paradox, within a white-devil dollhouse with financial monopolies and control-frauds. Women must spiritually and physically lower themselves into sub-humans in order to just to stay alive. *Mary* or *Eve* must inflate and deflate *need-love* needing and *gift-love* giving on a sliding-scale in order to seduce the male seducer — who seduces no more. The floating margin of Judeo-Christian love is turned upside down and there is no profit, art, children, and/or evolution.

Bribery, extortion, and murder of one's neighbor is a normal day in this *New Jerusalem* or this *New England.* The NAJ life is accompanied with the Biblical ax in the new colony called *New Resurrection Ready.* The *New Resurrection Ready* rejuvenates the Jewish moneychangers and invigorates the Catholic cunts, enabling financial indulgences and profit from their negative life and negative space. Free-grace is an Awakening from this malaise that enlightens the woman and the child first because they are the most severely incarcerated, retarded, and damaged. Nevertheless, women and children are also the brightest and sharpest and they will lead us out of this Dark Age.

My mother continued ranting her hateful truth: "Oh, poor little Suzie... I gave you life and raised you the best I could. You were so cute and I just wanted to eat you up, but you were always so damn ungrateful. I even thought about selling you, but no; I kept your sorry ass and taught you the ways of the modern world and you still aren't happy."

I said, "I can be happy, Mom; just get off my back — get a hobby, get a life!"

My mother blubbered charging at me, "God damn it, I brought you into this world and I'm gonna take you out!" She scratched at my eyes and face as we violently fell backwards. We wrestled for a moment and then my mother's hate flipped back to her love. She smoothly caressed my face, and was almost cradling me. Then suddenly, like a deranged lover, her hands moved down hard and fast around my throat as her hate boiled up and she tried to strangle me. We rolled around a bit till I easily broke the aging woman's grip. Even though my mother has been dead six years, every hour, on the hour, I can still feel lulled by my mother's hands and her perverted love caressing my face lightly like a whispering snake. Then, suddenly, life is shattered and stifled — my mother strikes like a boa constrictor, squeezing my throat, choking the life out of me, garroting the good out of me, and then ceremoniously ingesting my dead body as if her love is infanticide or cannibalism.

In contrast to this feminine zombie formalism, free-grace is a mathesis currency based not just on astrological economics, but on ideological and moral value rather than negative value, or debt. This positive free-grace light is a new sun or a new currency compared to the Judeo-Christian trickle-down double-negative clouds that shade the *No Life*. This trickle-down double-negative life with abstract scheming for constant social war is self-deceiving debt for 99% of humanity. For the other 1% (the moneychangers with handmaids and handy men), the zombie religions are violent and formal child's play in the sand-box world. Religions with debt and negativity will be outlawed someday in an enlightened English-speaking commonwealth.

Still wobbling from my mother's attack, I slowly got back up and swung around so that I faced her. She slowly got to her knees and put out her hand, expecting me to help her up. I laughed, looking down at her, then slapped my mother hard in the face and watched her fall back slightly, concluding, "That's your tear in the ocean, bitch."

My mother, with a red face, glared at me brazenly, so I back-handed her, knocking her back to the floor. I concluded by proposing a free-grace question: "How does debtless providence taste now, you fat, crazy hag?" This is my parental Reformation.

Abraham and his attention-deficit and disorder sons throw sand and bully each other while screaming, child-like, "I'm better than you! Big Daddy loves me the most, so I should be in control." Abraham is a dead-beat dad, a bonobo breeding with parasites because he has nothing better to do. Abraham and his three sons are now all blind within their sand-box shit-storm. They are all jacked up with new prescriptions of Scriptures called "A letter from Paul to America, translated by the Roman Roxies," shouting, "Join me or die!" as the world slowly goes blind. This Abe-Babe scene is too disgusting and insidious to be anything but the creation of a white-devil man, a Neg-Am Jam man who believes nature, children, and free-spirits are subordinate and in moral, physical, and financial debt to a Big-Daddy in the sky.

My mother was still confused metaphysically more than physically. She was unable to rise, as she had not surrendered to need-love gravity or admitted the negative space around us was possibly positive space. My mother was chewing on a dislodged tooth, drooled a bit of spittle, a bit of blood, and then said in a garbled voice, "I, I, I, lo, lov, lov, love yo, yo, you," spluttering out a bloody tooth on the floor.

Free-grace is a neutralizer. It's as if a parent, beggar, or tax collector guided by their selfish genes asked a victim for some need-love in order to possibly "Help" or to "Borrow" or to "Collect" ten crowns. Instead you just hum in a solfeggio frequency — an elongated Gregorian chant of *Do, Re, Me, Fa, So, La, Ti*, or maybe just a long *Dooooo*? And then suddenly that parent or neighbor doesn't want that *help* or those ten crowns anymore. Free-grace is common-sense telepathy with a sense of humor. Free-grace is the *Word* of God that everyone knows, but is too much a coward to talk about because the *Word* is the earth all around us. Nature as Scripture is so simple and has made fools of civilizations' Elect and Elders for the last sixteen hundred and fifty years. No one wants to be a sad joke, so we should tend our garden, and a free-grace Awakening is a rude plow that will unearth the gluttons and sin within our society. My free-grace garden is so undemanding, hence humane, and exquisite that the parent leveraging, the pauper supplicating, or the bureaucrat stockpiling forgets what he or she asked for and just walks away in a free-grace fog. Unbeknownst to these predators, we the debtors answered and quenched their thirst for free-grace as opposed to their usual sub-human surrogate activities like parenting, begging, or shopping. This is free-grace.

CHAPTER 4

William Demopheare — Ms. Appleton — A Boston Education; or I'm Better Than You

WILLIAM DEMOPHEARE

see William Demopheare still waving in front of the schoolhouse, drifting about as my other classmates slowly filter through the small single door in this colonial landscape. Away from built-up Beacon Hill, Boston in 1650 is just a pine-barren English garrison stuck on a sandy green peninsula outlined by a marsh of eel grass. The Atlantic sea-spray wind off the harbor never stops howling and the earth is a sandy loam blanketed beneath air filled with intertidal effervescent fauna and flora. Olive and emerald vines bubble up to the sun as transient snow birds in constant migration shriek in shrill tones about their adventures. Green sea-grass carpets expand hither and thither while wild scrub brush and plump bayberry battle the four hard northeast seasons on a Baja peninsula. As the honeysuckle perfumes the spring, osprey tidy up for their summer vacation nests as they screech at their neighbors. The air smells like baked clams as the hickory smoke from the mill seasons our city on the hill.

There exist only three buildings on this high desert of gothic America. In the center is the Church of Boston — tall, lean, and mean. It is armored in old cedar shakes seasoned with salty algebraic authority. Its steeple reaches to the heavens while inside the congregation conspires within the bowels of our nightmares. Parishioners pray, "We the people," excluding everyone not under their little steeple.

On the right is the first building erected in the Judeo-Christian colonies, and that is our prison. The red-cedar shingle facade says "Town Hall," but behind this Dutch facade is a square bureaucratic box with numerous graphs, charts, and cells for empirically incarcerating life. This suntanned and greasy building is for those who don't believe and behave in accordance with Moses, Jesus, and/or our Elect.

To the left is my gable-roofed schoolhouse, short and squat, wrapped in white-cedar clapboard. All the buildings are sided or shingled with wood from the local forests. America has old-growth heartwoods and hardwoods that the English and European carpenters have not seen for centuries. Rough-sawn wood the color of apple cider with the aroma of a wise woman wrapped these three buildings nailed by carpenter ministers with hard provincial disciplines who spread *God's word* architecturally and silently with a level, a saw, nails, a hammer, wood, and a sanding block. The carpentry sermon continues quietly at night, showing off their grand plan. At night, when no light is the best light, Boston is silhouetted as a small triangular schoolhouse or a smaller church next to a larger triangular church talking to a higher God. Next to these obvious architectural relatives sits the fair and square Town Hall box, a prison squared: talking to the earth. All three are sitting, silently and patiently waiting for a Revelation on *their* hill.

William and his family moved here in 1640 from England and they have given a breath of fresh air and fresh opportunity to Puritan New England. The Demopheares, with their hands in their pockets, evolved along with the third big wave of Hartford, Connecticut, Puritans trying to escape the Church of England and the Bank of England. The Demopheares

The Hill

were the rising upper middle class, who are always either fence-watchers or fence-sitters with this "Good ole fight." These ladder-climbing Philistines don't flow like water — they flow like money. America's great rural days of having only independent entrepreneurs, adventurers, and farmers at the General Store are long gone; the *nouveau riche* rabble — who always enthusiastically play their part in the newest Ponzi scheme and/or war — have arrived.

William's sandy brown and black hair and eyes are those of a nervous calico cat in the attic. His burly eyebrows and wild hair with spider webs belie root-cellar clutter. His snubbed nose, dead-angel eyes, and motor mouth counter his frightened and fashionable actions. William is too much, too cute, too perfect. William is maybe a friend, certainly cut from a similar bolt of fabric, but different. A middle child — a middle-man — a Billy.... Billy usually smelt like perfumed body-powder, and was more a friend to my Aunt Ally, or those church ladies I crossed earlier, than to me.

William's fashion is crisp, but droops by lunchtime. William, always pleasing to please, and today with a hunter-green duck-cloth jacket and matching sprite pants, skips along. William's light-blue-and-jade striped arms are accessorized with a small jewel-encrusted buckle that lures you closer and repels you at the same time. William, just like a half-dead grandma in her lonely castle, is bejeweled with golden rings, necklaces with rubies, and a red-queen's crown encrusted with diamonds. Black plague blankets swaddle queeny William with his dead grandma eyes, waiting for a kiss in his emotional wheelchair.

William's maternal seniority is complimented, and almost eclipsed, by his bright, white ruff. William's ruff has the body and soul of a scruffy white-tailed deer quickly running away. Billy's ruff bouncing through the dark woods: William, or more specifically Billy, is a bouncy cute thing and enjoys having a bull's eye target on his white fluffy bum.

William Demopheare

The other boys in town still make fun of William even though he will inherit a lot of money from his family business. When he was a child, his mother used to powder his bum so much that the powder would be all over his britches. Puffs of perfumed powder would plume up as the other boys stomped on his ass. The other boys would sing aloud, "Billy butt-puff! Billy butt-puff! Billy butt-puff!" It would make William cry for days, for weeks — for a lifetime.

Billy, both the perfect empress and the perfect emperor beneath his padded shoulders, is every mother's dream: a sexy son she can fuck with when she's bored with Big-Daddy. William the altar boy, the bar mitzvah boy, the frat-boy; too perfect, lighting fires to smell the burn. Damaged family jewels — a pull in the weave, a genetic mistake, a frayed edge, and, most important — parasite friendly! And these boys run their entire life... nevertheless, a fashionable woman's dream! William, a man child in the making, a stylish ladies' aspiration — a good-looking numb-nut.

William and I both have a French test later, which I'm not prepared for, but I'm sure William already bought the answers from a classmate. William reminds me in a coy manner and says, "*Bonjour Madame, tu es superbe ce matin.*" (You look beautiful this morning) I say, "*Merci, Monsieur, merci.*"

William says, "*Tu as l'air triste? Seules les femmes et les veuves sont tristes. Les jeunes femmes sont heureuses! Pourquoi n'es-tu pas heureux?*" (You look sad? Only wives and widows are sad. Young ladies are happy! Why are you not happy?")

I say, "*Je ne suis triste et je passe le long chemin à la maison.*" (I was born sad and I'm passing on the long way home.)

I think about French small talk as friends and family have thrown me emotional bread crumbs, taken some trite political chances and well calculated loss-of-face to waddle along with me — Autumn Leaf, the free-spirit, the black-duckling, the witch. Some are aunts or uncles or distant cousins who turned a blind eye as my mother and our family were put on trial and banished by both the church and the state for disrespecting the state and its Elect. In the face of the state and church's economic and spiritual leverage friends and family all said, "Sorry about the *good ole fight*, but we have to protect our family." The royal condemnation of my mother and my family's free-grace beliefs was a warning shot across the bow of American freedom and independence. This British royalist loyalist threat was not answered and probably will not be answered by brave men for maybe twenty years. Maybe in 1670 the common man will stop being abused by a monarchy and their King Debt? Maybe fifty years from now, in 1700? Maybe, say, in a hundred years from now, in 1750, there will be a Great Awakening that my mother started in 1640, and it lights a fire or a guiding light. Maybe a hundred and twenty-five years or so? Say, in 1775 or 1776? Perhaps not till 1776, one hundred and twenty-six years from this day in 1650, will my mother's feminine free-grace be carried by a brave American man. The American man is now and forevermore a limp-dick until he is violent for his civil rights and the good ole cause. The American man now is nothing but an English eunuch muffin, a demented and depraved colony-child subject — a couturier, a loyalist hipster, a wanna-be royal dog chasing his metro-sexual tail in a doggy park.

I can still hear my mother's letter going off on William's father ten years ago when he wrote her from England asking about coming to America and begging for a Sponsor Letter from the Hutchinson family business. My mum, Annie, wrote back:

> *Dear Mr. Demopheare,*
>
> *I'm not sure if you are ready for America. You are a Grandee royalist who claims to be a Separatist and a Protestant. You are neither, but a weak-kneed and weak-hearted subject. An English loyalist boy, a tea-boy, a whipping-boy with no balls dreaming of an English loyalist*

lady with no ovaries. Now listen to me love, you need to be forewarned: the English garden you enjoy dancing in does not exist in America.

The disrespect for royalists was deep for me mum. She continued:

You asexual loyalists are too selfish and corrupt to stand-up to the royal English forked-tongue lawyers and their Armageddon-Ready Courts. You English politicians with your Biblical Laws and your monarchical police mix church / synagogue and state, dependent upon the day's Catholic or Jewish fairy-tale holidays. Your Church of England's fairy-tale bank holidays pay handsomely compared to the Bank of England's usual imperialism, corruption, and blackmail.

Regardless of that letter, or maybe because of that challenging letter, William Demopheare and his family journeyed to America. They come from the same Northern English Town near St. Bott's Stone where I was born. I deeply trust William's spontaneity, his child-like quirks, because it's all manically imprisoned within his parentally-guided monotony. As most Englishmen are, William is in over his head here in the vast American wilderness. William, with striped underwear and doe-like eyes, understands how the priests, rabbis, and lawyers of the English and European royal courts have woven together love, law, God, and standing-armies. Yet William (Bill with little will) gets off on how these bourgeois bureaucrats support all their Divine indulgences. Billy "Understands" (but he really doesn't understand) the taxes on our souls that he and we cannot pay. Billy the Philistine has no vision, yet he seeks power through debates with no teeth. Politically, he is a toothless, gummy blue-dog democrat running to and fro among fashionable false-flags. Shadow to shadow, Billy is gumming-on and licking-up scraps of small-talk from the gutter and calling it a political position.

Despite the electoral consequences, William continues to patronize the warm, blind, and fishy world of religious shadow theater. William is a puppet of the church and synagogue — a geisha girl performing in a kabuki dance with a liberal Judah. William is a fair young man masked as a female Onna playing a male samurai high priest. William Demopheare, the American synagogue Shogun, has the skill of kanji, and our conversations are adorable — alternating between a catty smirk, a spear, and a smudge of humor to take the edge off our corrupted American love, law, and God.

William and I walk into the dark walnut wainscoted classroom that smells like wood oil, dust, and rulers cracked on knuckles. The floor creaks like we are at a square dance at the local meetinghouse as my classmates and I shuffle to our seats. William and I sit in the rear of the classroom near the only two windows. William had a busy weekend, I know, with building his parents' homestead out towards Cambridge. William and I attended the Church of Boston/England with the other hypocrites of America yesterday. William calls it "The Protestant church with Roman Catholic robes." We often laugh about the popery who-do / we-do heavenly bells, the community cannibalism, the destruction of femininity, and the overall frankincense voodoo.

Despite the drudgery of church with my Aunt Ally and all the congregation yesterday, it was a brash, blustery, and sunny spring Sunday morning — bright and fresh as clean and folded laundry. At Sunday mass I saw William rolling his eyes during the "Sign of peace." William and the congregation were nervously hiding the fact that they are still Roman fascists still seeking revenge, seeking Caesar. William and all the people under this royal steeple are posing as Protestants but they're really in love with absolute power / fascism. William and the religious mob shake hands, and hug and kiss each other like politicians trolling for votes.

William said to me, "Peace be with you," and shook my

hand, but William's eyes and the eyes of the mob in this Roman circus really said, "To hell with you — vote for me — I will control you." After church I had to take a bath and I threw away my aunt's Sunday dress, as my soul was smeared; I was ideologically molested and then financially and philosophically pick-pocketed. The Lenape moon dance and Wampy in his wolf den was much more fun — an enlightenment, not a debt.

After we settle into our school desks, William says, carefully leaning back over his shoulder, "I heard they caught Mary Dyer again."

I look out the windows and around at the class settling in to our school day and say, "I know. I heard the same."

William and the parishioners at the Church of Boston yesterday look at me as my classmates do here in school. I feel that these ass-sniffing Mr. and Mrs. Marmalades of society just goad me or prey on me for information so they can spin a finer loyalist yarn around my neck. I'm Autumn Leaf, a yarn-bomb, a genetic repatriation here at school and at church. I'm a flayed lab frog or a skinned Mexican cat to be dissected, examined, and/or crucified every other day. Unless of course I'm speaking French to William during French class, as we look out the window and talk about the arts, the weather, and happiness... which I suppose French people aspire to.

William says quickly and confidently, not thinking, "They'll hang her this time!"

His tone hints he was thinking about or talking to someone else; perhaps he parroted one of his many dominant brothers. William tries to conceal his cocky street slang and inches backwards. "I mean... I hope, I hope they don't do anything bad to her...."

On second thought William realizes he is talking about my second mom, my kindred spirit, my sister X, and my mentor. William's look of a friend went to that of a sub-par con man just doing his job.

William tries to back-fill his long-con, fishing for a char-itable handout like a sad, sneaky dog in the rain, and says, "Well? Well? What do you want me to say?" He shrugs his shoulders awkwardly as if I have to accept his lame, bullshit behavior and performance.

Gimpy and bruised men being lame... reasonable men being reasonable. I suddenly think of the con-man politician Mary Dyer described as the new Governor in Providence around 1644. The story was in Mary's second letter to me as she wrote she was about to leave — fed up with "The American Con." I think Mary was also having to help her royal friends back in England keep their heads as *the good ole cause* was now the "*New*" English religion. Mary and her husband were also supposed to change the Charter for Providence in London as the insipid blue-dog Democrats there were sabotaging them-selves with infighting. My mother and our family had left Providence a year earlier for the same political reasons. Mary wrote that one day her future became "Explicit" as she was leaving her children at school. She had to return unexpect-edly to talk to the schoolteacher and overheard her children being persecuted by the other classmates for her political work. Mary described them as "Nasty assassins singing out of tune like little hornets on a hot day making honey."

Mary the Monster, Mary the Monster, where are you now? Where are you now?

Hanging with Annie? Hanging with Henry?

Away, away, away! Away, away, away!

I pray not rolling in the hay-ay? Rolling in the hay-ay!

Away, away, away! Away, away, away!

Mary the Monster, Mary the Monster, where are you now? Where are you now?

Burying your bastard? Burying your whore?

Away, away, away! Away, away, away!
Burying your monster? Burying your monster?
Away! Away! Away! — Away! Away! Away!"

Mary wrote that "I now agree with the children and I'm going *away*." She decided to leave all her own children in Providence with her servants, but before leaving for London Mary wrote in her letter:

Nothing I can do here in Providence — my children must fend for themselves, so I might as well be doing something valuable for my world — for my bigger family, for my human family. It will be more important than hugging my children when they get their asses kicked every other day. And then what am I supposed to do after their Mary Dyer mommy beat-down? Lie to my children and say "It's all for the best"? Life is not for the best! Life is what you fight for and children need to fight for themselves.

Mary signed this second letter before leaving Providence, Rhode Island.

Providence — Not for the Best!
Mary Dyer

William tried to bury his social crime against me, but instead hung himself up by trying to slip in some status-quo sympathy I hear from all cowards: "Susan, maybe it's for the best."

Before answering William's manhood question of, "What do you want me to say?" I think to myself... if I lose Mary to a Puritan execution or sacrifice, I'll be lost in America.... I am disoriented there for a second or two, but then good with going solo, I suddenly realize that I have just been found

—Awakened…. I swallow the bloody, metallic, and acidic saliva in my mouth and say, "*Merci, Billy, Que sera, sera.* (Thank you, Billy, what will be, will be.)

I think how the French language, and this cowardly excuse for a civilization living depressed, is so easily translatable. The English, with their *It's all for the best*, or the French with *What will be, will be*, are hand-cuffs on the mind for the neutered and spayed. For the English, it's a proud delusional charge, but the French throw it out like a sneaky curve-ball with a time extension. This combined with the heroic and Germanic Dutch claptrap I had to endure from Jan Throgg makes me tri-lingual. Jan was the Dutch broker who was my New Netherland hostage negotiator / broker with my Lenape Indian captors and/or *adopted* family. The Indians didn't appreciate the white-devil Dutch clap-trap either and had endured years of their block-head betrayals. The Dutchies' back-handed atrocities with insurances, options, treaties, and guarantees were always followed with hanky-panky politics and limp-wristed military maneuvers. The Dutchman plays second fiddle to the Englishman's military / economic / social science of Attack, Divide, Starve, and Profit, or ADSP. This forked-tongue science that even America now terrorizes with doesn't need to be taught in their schools or churches, as it is innately borne in the white-devil.

I look in front of me at William Demopheare who is a happy-go-cheeky fella who lazily dreams his father's Grandee dreams for America. I imagine William in his New Model standing-army uniform with General Grandee, the commander in chief of the English Crown is incognito, giving pep talks about the commonwealth's "Good ole cause." With his officers, sherry in fine crystal glasses, and some delicate French cheese on silver platters at the Cambridge Officers' club. General Grandee explains how they can "Contain the situation" with the signing of the *Cambridge Agreement.* Of course, beforehand, these Puritan officers officially ordered and forbade their sweat-hog sergeants down in Dorchester and around the Massachusetts State from speaking the words "Class warfare."

Grandee Demopheare imagines a civil war re-match for the English Empire — a rugby scrum for the eternal battle of *the haves* and *the have-nots*. At Oxford University in the gymnasium's wrestling ring he pictures Jacob, representing the royalist Tory Republicans on one side and the commonwealth on the other. The angelic common man Sir Cromwell will win temporarily during this civil war tussle and declare that royal property is now the commonwealth's property. And then the commonwealth in a referendum will veto the common man, and say, "We want *to have* now, forget *the have nothing* bullshit. Common man, you are a fallen angel, a dirty man — a devil!" The commonwealth declares, "We are nothing more than a gross domestic product. We are the property of the Divine English Crown, the Colony, and the Corporation: our children and our crops are not our children and food, we are subordinate to the corporation's profit — the Crown and her Empire owns us."

General Grandee imagines and hopes this frat-boy scrum at Oxford University will be similarly played out at Harvard University in America. In England, King Charles, or Sir Israel now, wrestles with Sir Cromwell, but in America I don't have to imagine an oily wrestle on a sandy beach. I witnessed the greatest grapple in America: it was man versus woman and it was between Sir Winthrop and my mother, Anne Hutchinson. This ivy league combat sport is a battle of the Skulls versus the Bones on a dark, sweaty mat. These Senators are Romans-in-training and preparing for their Congressional and Parliamentarian consummations. This is not scholastic wrestling, but professional wrestling, with civil-right half-Nelsons, libertine arm-locks, and commonwealth pile-drivers.

I remember when my mother wrestled with God... Annie yelled to the Boston Court, Sir Winthrop, America, and the world while pegging and pinning Winthrop hard to the mat with no remorse and with a gladiator's victorious glee, "This, dear Sir... this is a royal rendezvous!"

Ms. Appleton

In our classroom William, charmingly yet in a doltish way greets our homeroom teacher. "Howdy, Ms. Appleton, a beautiful morning here in Boston!"

Ms. Skyler Appleton retorts, "'Howdy' is low-class Americana, William. Don't be such a ham." She continues to slowly walk the desk aisles (four by four), looking all of us sixteen students up and down.

William, now Bill with less and less will, apologizes profusely, back-peddling as usual. "I'm sorry, Ms. Appleton, I was just playing — just trying to be funny."

Ms. Appleton stops in her tracks. William's small testicles stop squeaking. Ms. Appleton does not turn around to face Billy the beggar from Boston. She politely confiscates a piece of Billy's throat and fledgling manhood. In a dead-serious silence that she allows to echo and bounce around the wooden classroom, she places her index finger on her lips, insinuating silence is best. I will enjoy, or shall I say my ink will enjoy drawing out Ms. Appleton's eyes and lips. Ms. Appleton continues to walk the classroom aisle, not annoyed or distracted, just present and curious.

Ms. Skyler Appleton is not young, but she looks younger. She is stern, sophisticated, and beautiful to some, but untrustworthy, fragile, and socially scorned by others. Emotionally, Skyler Appleton, or Miss A, as we sometimes call her, is a hungry nun fashioned as a humble nun — a *Mary*. Ms. Appleton, with a swanky silk-and-wool tweed skirt and poncho the color of rye and wheat, knows how to separate not just humanity's chaff but its swag, and its shake. Of course, any person with common sense should always assume the antonym of another's fashion or words, so I deeply respect Skyler Appleton (a hungry nun) as I respect Mary Dyer (a prophetess) because both are Puritan double-agents — religious adulteresses.

Ms. Appleton has green iridescent eyes that are filled with indignation and tenderness — it looks as if some gentle earthly strength were needed constantly to keep her keel balanced. Her druid deep-forest eyes — one a fish, one a young lady, lead the way as her marbled chestnut hair is wound tight up on top of her feline head. Ms. Appleton's silky auburn hair matches her deep-set Scottish freckles perfectly. Ms. Appleton's small mouth on top of her Tudor neck gives the impression her mouth is bound or conscripted. Her face and mouth seem sewn shut as a geisha's tiny foot is broken and bound shut with a girly bowtie. She has a deeply hidden leer, and below her whitewashed make-up there is even a subtle grin which makes her pain unfair and unbearable.

Feminine patriarchal pain is an orange, red, and yellow flame that flickers and fusses like a funeral pyre in the wind. It is a formal funeral fire of Ms. Appleton's unsaid words and her broken life fired in a *raku* kiln. The cremation ceremony is performed with stoneware tea bowls as feminine thoughts and lives are thrown in to the burning fire. Women reduced to abstract shapes, femininity oxidized to a texture, and colors — crackle-glazed under the heat of a sadomasochistic funeral fire.

Ms. Appleton says, "Good morning, class. I hope everyone had a nice weekend planting their spring gardens. We have a busy week here, so I hope everyone got plenty of rest because every day is a garden to tend!"

While talking and lecturing, Ms. Appleton darts her dark eyes about and she clenches her fists and then relaxes her hands as if she is debating whether to punch one of us or at least punch something. One of her eyes seems to be more feline and triangular and the other deep and soulful, like that

Ms. Appleton

of a sad puppy. Ms. Appleton's voluptuous and disciplined dark ginger body beneath her grey woolen cape conceals everything, but hides nothing. She stands and smells like fine ale, but I imagined she tastes and feels more like cold root beer on a sunny afternoon. Her prematurely-grey-streaked hair is the veined colors of hay, silver barn wood, and its original chestnut. Her hair is sometimes woven tightly into a bun on top of her head, and on other days her hair is loosely woven into a French braid at the nape of her neck. Ms. Appleton with matching French cuffs is more relaxed here and seems more Parisian on these days – *a Marianne*. She has a black leather Sheffield belt on her hip, and a dark, finely woven choker around her neck, sectioned, strengthened, and building her into a lady who is viciously aware. She is present — 24 / 7 / 365 — poised and vigilant with a sense of fatal humor and enduring style. Ms. Appleton is always on edge, on that sea cliff looking out into the twinkling horizon and the misty sea breeze: rocking, surfing, and always sharpening her view and her voice, not for others, but for herself. She stands each day to teach our Boston class what is possibly right and what is possibly wrong. Skyler Appleton was born to burn or be burned; she chose to be burned slowly in Boston and is trying to teach us children something before she floats away.

Ms. Appleton's embroidered choker is woven with miraculous stitches of wampum shell flecks the color of green limy seaweed, sunset reds, and cobalt blues interlaced in an Elizabethan floral design. It reminds me of my Lenape belt but is woven by the local Pequots and has more of sophisticated art or higher spirit. Her choker, which she wears every day, has a silver capital "A" needled delicately into the center of the design. The silver "A" amongst the colorful wampum flowers sits over her throat. Ms. Appleton is a hot red-and-orange ember floating into the cold, navy blue night of New England, sailing into the American sky, unfettered, glowing and majestic.

Ms. Appleton continues her metaphysical inspection of us students, pacing the other side of the classroom, when Minister Winthrop, like a black cloud, suddenly floats into the classroom and hands Ms. Appleton a scrolled announcement.

She un-scrolls the paper, reads it calmly, and then hands it back to the minister and says, "I will see you at 9:00 a.m., good Minister."

Minister Winthrop is now Governor Winthrop — he swirls around, allowing his skirt-like cassock to float while scanning the class with his ghost-like cockroach gaze.

As the Governor is leaving, he ceremoniously stops to dust and polish the golden face of our colony's new long-case floor clock or grandfather clock at the front of the classroom, by the door. It was a gift to America from Cambridge University and the Fellows of the Royal Society (FRS) and is inscribed with a profound note upon a brass plate on the inside of its long, narrow, and black case:

Dear America,

Please protect and keep our royal time! Improve our royal knowledge for the King and wait for your redeemer — for he liveth!"

Fellows of the Royal Society of London

Every morning, Governor Grandee Winthrop would come in and polish and keep his Roman-enumerated golden "Time." For Winthrop, the bourgeois bureaucrat was keeping the gears and pendulum moving, and it is a Divine magic that only he — and he alone — could wind and govern. Governor Winthrop kept *time* and he did *time* with his funny music box. The clock is not the shape of a white-devil grandfather, but that of a grand lady — his *time* is a large Negress at attention with large black boots and an even larger black bonnet. The

Puritan's *time* is encased within the blackened ebony wood with brass Elizabethan charm and the face of strict discipline. The clock stands taller than the Governor — it overshadows him and is filled with gears, pulleys, bells, and chimes that he respects. The black Roman numbers on its round white face are bulbous and round and interlaced with black spider webs. Working together on the face of Puritan *time* are two sculpted black spears moving slowly with that spider web strength that doubles as the black hands of this *time*. Dainty grandmas had obviously hammered this steel since antiquity to be so righteous and timely — but beware, for these black queen hands of time are in cahoots with these Roman numbers. These astronomical wizards and witches are weaving circles within circles and weights within weights. Winthrop's Puritan *time* is an evil magic that makes an evil music!

Every morning after facing his Puritan *time*, the Governor turns around silently as the *Cambridge Chimes* strike the half hour of 6:30 a.m. The Puritan's time and the lullaby see-saw: "Tick-tock, tick-tock, tick-tock... E, G#, F#, B — E, F#, G#, E... tick-tock, tick-tock, tick-tock" is cute, but unnatural, and annoying. I'm coming from the naturally musical American woods with the natural Indian world and their musical dances, drum-songs, and their moonlight nocturnes that sound natural and humane. The Puritan *time* and/or music — E, G#, F#, B — E, F#, G#, E sounds unnatural, like a sad march, a childish ding-dong rhyme that is both a foreboding nursery rhyme and a child's restrictive rhyme.

The Minister turns back to the class with an afterthought about his *time* before he disappears out the door. He says in a raspy scolding voice, "Do you hear that tick-tock, tick-tock, children? It is the Monster I've described on Sunday mornings in the past, when God speaks through me, and he says, 'Beware the Monster, children. Beware the Monster!' The Monster is also a snake in every tree and in every question! Can you hear her hissing? Can you hear her slithering towards you? Tick-tock, tick-tock, tick-tock.... The Monster, like a vampire, skulks around in the evil world, biting and sucking the blood of those who question the Elders and Elect! Beware your questions, dear children! Beware the Monster!"

The class buzzes into a frenzy as Governor Winthrop exits the classroom like smoke drafting up a dirty chimney. Everyone is whispering that this scrolled announcement has to be the Mary Dyer Execution Order! My classmates look about, and the looks of pride, gluttony, wrath, lust, sloth, envy, and greed compete for attention. All I can hear is tick-tock, tick-tock, tick-tock. Ms. Appleton has walked the high priest out politely and still has her back to us by the door. She seems to be hiding something and is either crying or laughing.

Laura Kraven, says out loud with a nasally honky-tonk tone, "Lord praise the King! It's about time we get some law and order around here!"

Elizabeth Winterest scolds her and speaks from her spine: "Doff your pygmy laws, varlet — back in London you would be in the Tower waiting for the gallows pole!"

Harold Answhich said in a helpful lawyerly way, "Pray thee, dear Elizabeth, but actually colonial law is much more —"

But he was cut off by Brad Pining, who says, "In an hour, who cares? Our mutton-chop lunch will taste just as good if not better with a side of blood. Dear classmates, please remember Thor's advice: might is always right!"

Ms. Appleton's high-strung constitution couldn't always differentiate between comedy and tragedy, so I think she was both laughing and crying at the door. Tragedy and comedy are the same emotion and release the same feelings of fear, joy, and anarchy in these demented *Mary-Eves*. There is no female foundation in Ms. Appleton's thesis, there is no black and white in her intellectual capacity: it is muted and mottled scraps of grey.

Like a third-rate actress, Ms. Appleton turns around after

a long moment and tragically expresses herself in a languid way, with no tears but with a contorted face, looking down and saying desperately, "Okay, children, just another Monday morning here in Boston.... It's all for the be, be, bess... it's, it's always... always..., it's... always...."

I believe Ms. Appleton was working as a Christian missionary a few years ago in South Boston with the Pequot Indians, but something happened between her and the local preacher. Skyler Appleton was branded and blamed, just as my mother was, "Not fit, not pure enough, and/or, not holy, not Divine enough." Ms. Skyler Appleton was not negative enough, even though she continued to fashion herself rejected and undesirable — a humble nun, a humble *Mary*, not a disobedient *Eve* — which is what she was.

Ms. Appleton quietly questioned to herself the Neg-Am Jam life. She was not negative enough for the double-negative royal mission of wife-whore Eve or mother-virgin Mary. Like all virgin / whore rejects who cannot marry and are not in touch with their sister X, Skyler Appleton is a dead body, demoted to a fat-ankle schoolmarm. Ms. Appleton is an iron maiden — an angry librarian, a social worker whose spiritual sisters of art, sex, and anarchy were black-chained shut with Puritan chainmail.

A BOSTON EDUCATION; OR I'M BETTER THAN YOU

Ms. Appleton says, "Quiet down, children, we have a lot of work to do. Please calm down... we don't need your sorry jest!"

As New England children, we are talked to like mentally handicapped people and told by our fathers, the Town Fathers, the Town Selectmen, the Elders and Elect that the "A" on Ms. Appleton's choker is for her last name: Appleton. But unknown to the Elders, the Elect, the ministers, and the magistrates, is that being a good father is succumbing to the red-queen parasite that will eventually kill them. The fashionable father is a willing-and-able host to this female parasite that stalls evolution and stupefies the truth.

Being good or fashionable will get you prematurely killed as the steady Big-Daddy within patriarchy. Men are not the variable X — men are the known Y; women are the unknown. And Big Daddy will die because good fathers are just obedient, speechless, clueless, and clumsy jackasses for their red-queeny wives. Big-Daddy wanna-be's are the constant male X and/or perhaps the selfish gene. Men within marriage, like the King on the chess board, forget about manhood / the game and are overjoyed with husbandry and alliances as they politely mask their own self-aware mommy issues. The King and his men move in baby steps and are usually quite content as a mule or stepping-stone actor in their queen's hypergamy-whammy life. The red-queen moves in any direction at any speed.

Our Boston Elders and fathers, and all married men who move one square at a time with no life of their own, speak with a look of faux horror on their faces, trying to explain that "Ms. Appleton did NOT earn that capital 'A' on her throat, as some pilgrim Quaker or Separatists have suggested: by dancing too close with the Deacon down in Dorchester."

These American fathers would be turned on by puffery like perverted soldiers parroting an order to "Charge!" as they ramp-up to take the enemy's *hill* and take a bullet or axe to the head. The same tone could be heard when these fathers talked to us children about sex. The Puritan feeds, cleans, and oils his women and children like his rifle or mules. Their heroic monogamy is hollowed out and overshadows the men they once were as they repeat their chorus to us — getting excited about declaring an accepted lie, passing on a scam or a heroic death.

"Skyler did not dance with the deacon in Dorchester. Let me say it again — Skyler did not dance with the deacon in

Dorchester; it's just her last name — Appleton. Your good teacher would never dance with the good deacon. And most certainly would not be doing it down, down in... well, you know what I mean... doing it down in Dorchester."

Brad Pining in the front row next to Laura says to the class, "Dither not about my dry mutton-chop with a side of blood. All I need is some marshmallows to toast while the bitch burneth."

Ms. Appleton is a corroded damsel not in her own distress, but in society's duress. She wears her silver embroidery as a steel anchor around her neck in order to drown slowly — in order to drown monumentally — in order to die quietly. As students, we are Ms. Appleton's foundlings — we are a siren's child, an orphan — we are pearls in Boston harbor. By and by, Ms. Appleton still has her cute pug nose up in the air as she looks down at me. Ms. Appleton's sinful adulterous life of doing the *deed* down in Dorchester wasn't as bad as my blasphemous blood in the Judeo / Christian Q and A catechism blame-game prayer. The prayer is called "Love, Law, and God," or perhaps it's the Jewish and Catholic old ditty entitled "To Hell with You Because I'm Better Than You."

Ms. Appleton hisses quietly and deliberately as she floats slowly towards Brad Pining as if in a private conversation. "Well, I hate to disappoint you, Brad, but I believe they will be hanging Mary Dyer, not burning her."

Brad says, "Damn," and stomps his boot for violent animal effect.

Here in this Boston classroom, I take my damned soul and live in free-grace *because* of my family's disgrace. Their divorce and death have set me free even though I'm now back in a constant state of war and defense against "Civilized" society in order to protect my sovereignty — my truth. My only relief is prayer; yet I don't know whom I pray to anymore. I pray to "Nothing" but what the hell is *Nothing*? Here I stand, so close to the edge that I can smell my end and I want more! Hand in Hand? Suicidal — no. With a guardian angel?

Maybe... bored? Yes. *Karma, qi,* or *chi?* Fuck yeah! Awakened now, my fictional facade is dissolving into an honest autobiography.

Elizabeth Winterest speaks up, looking at Brad: "Your greedy mettle wilts and withers you from the inside. Pray again fool, pray the prayer of kindness."

My mother Annie wasn't just close to the edge — she was the edge. Annie was also the rasp and file that sharpened and shined the knife that cut the edge so people could see clearly. Praying to this precipice, praying to Nothing, praying to our free-grace church in the dirt was tough on us all. Alas, I think my mother died a Divine rebel, unsure who was her Maker. Anne certainly knew it wasn't the Elders or Elect from the control-fraud Courts of Boston or London with their Black Law and negative life. This shadowy despot Black Law helps spread the same hypocrisies as the old white-devil newspaper called the Bible.

The Brother Bible or Bro-Bible newspaper supports a religious pyramid scheme of salvation though the selling of subscriptions to your neighbor for that myth. And the new Biblical subscriptions never stop, even here in 1650. Their sixteen-hundred-and-fifty-year-old spiritual newspaper is still trusted as the "Truth?" Even though I cannot trust my neighbor with the *truth*... whether a Puritan neighbor, a Separatist neighbor, an Indian neighbor, or any neighbor in between. Neighbors are hell!

CHAPTER 5

Spread the Bro-Word — At Home with Hate — Devil's Divorce Island — Homeroom Inspection

SPREAD THE BRO-WORD

s. Appleton sits down slowly at her desk after being unable to say, "'It's all for the best,'" and says, "Meseemeth weak, children. Pleaseth me and give me a couple of minutes here for me to get my plans together. We'll start homeroom inspection in just a moment when you will *all* explain to our class your *good-work*." She over emphasizes "All" and "Good-work."

William leans back to me and starts to whisper with an all-knowing altar boy grin and his new King James Bible in hand.

He blurts out, "I bet you that is Mary Dyer's Execution Order. Wow, I told you they had her! Well, appropriately, would you care to start this Monday morning filled with machismo the color of shit on a shingle, or, with our Lord Savior brought to you by our one-and-only King James?"

William the paperboy hawker, or perhaps Bill the barker, begins his disingenuous elephant dance and says, "Here is my new King James Bible, the almost two-thousand-year-old newspaper quoted as case law, our 'Word' or our 'Truth.' This

95

truth or just *following the money* regrettably defines and iden-
tifies our Bible as a false flag, a false God. A false God for the
self-dealing synagogue and state conspirators. These treasonous traitors, these pork-barreling Zionistas, along with
the colluding Catholic *conspiradoras*, define and dictate their
Judeo-Roman fascism into our politics as an authoritarian —
as an Elder or the Elect. These are the royal tyrants who leg-
islate for *the haves*, hoping to keep on "Having" versus those
politicking for *the have nots* in order to stop "Not having."
Hell is here on earth for these tired souls, which includes the
Separatist, the Baptist, the Quaker, the native Indian, or any
other "Non-believer" and/or terrorist living under Christian
Zionista love, law, and God!"

I ask Billy-Boston, "Feeling spritely this morning? Where
is that emergency shut-off switch for your diarrhea of the
mouth?"

Billy takes a breath and reminisces: "Just yesterday in
church Minister Winthrop, that priestly legalist, defied our
spirituality, defied our Anglo, Celtic, Norman, and Saxon
forefathers. Our fathers told us that those who say they 'Knew
God' were usurpers of grace — they were 'Smears on humanity.' What's that old Norman ditty? 'Respect the rock, don't
compete with the rock.' Minister Winthrop is that wife-beat-
ing lackey of religious law whose absence of self-abnegation
allows him to control-fraud his own monetary self-interests
right in our face, in front of our common sense. The Judeo-
Christian act of redemption is not a moral justice, but a monetary justice."

Billy from Boston, with Monday morning will, is now
William and he howls and cries like a tom-cat on the prowl.
With a spiked dick swagger and a song similar to that of a
half-dead baby, Billy is looking for a tit to suck while a pope's
pear is expanding slowly in his ass.

Billy continues, "Did you hear preacher Winthrop's cher-
ry-on-top sermon yesterday? The Minister screamed, 'Attack

to protect, attack to protect, attack to protect!' but it's really attack to enrich, attack to enrich, attack to enrich!"

William continues with his *en vogue* Separatist prose: "You know Providence and Roger Williams are right: The Bible is a false God and only a catechism for misogynist capitalism and imperialism written by soul murderers. When you think about it, the Bible is the cause of more debt, killing, torture, maiming, and genocidal war than any other book or disease known to mankind. The Bible is the Scripture of debt, debt is a malignant disease which leads to not just psychological debt, emotional debt, student debt, and spiritual debt, but obviously — financial debt. Debt is written into our "Law" in our "Courts" and prescribed as medicine by our ivy-league lawyers and doctors of doom and gloom."

I say, "Billy, wouldst please tell me something I don't know, or shut up?" I put my finger to my mouth like Ms. Appleton, but it doesn't work — I have no power as a freak. I'm not trendy or chic; I'm frumpy and *passé*, just like my very unfashionable friend Mary Dyer — who will be probably be executed this morning. The ugly, the old-fashioned, and the forgotten are easily killed / sacrificed within patriarchy. I suppose life feels re-born and cleaner after playing "God" after playing "Creator" even though civilization seems to be more a destroyer.

Billy-Boston continues talking to himself, practicing his own self-absorbed toast of me at my wake, a better friend in the afterlife than in the here and now.

I whisper in a faux-concerned manner to Billy in order to egg him on, hopefully tiring barking Billy out: "Billy, you're singing to the choir. Calm down.... You're an active disorder and Ms. Appleton is looking over here."

Ms. Appleton is looking at us, but seems distant or somewhere else. She looks up over us and out the windows, looking for something else. I look out the window expecting to see something interesting, but there is nothing there. No birds, no clouds, no neighbors — nothing.... I look back at Ms. Appleton, who is far off, having a lively and deep conversation with... Nothing.

Billy the Catholic worker hostess, or William as anarchist lite, is a married geisha — a dreamy oriental dinner date with bulimia and a bucket for her after-dinner pig-slop nervosa. He continues his soft-ball rant: "The cruel Bible or today's newspaper in 1650 being hawked down on State Street, like all newspapers sold around the world, this morning, that I, and everyone holds onto so dearly has no *truth*. Everyone still seems to hang on to the spurious newspaper all day as some solid barometer for the *truth*, but today's newspaper, like the Bible, is only solicitation, propaganda, and then solicitation again, and again, and again.... As Thomas Paine taught us in *The Age of Reason*, the Bible is not a revelation, it is hearsay upon hearsay. It speaks to no one, hears no one, and addresses no one. The Bible is written not in the third person, the second person, nor the first person. What person wrote this and for what person? The Old Testament is a legal testimony — a bad deposition for the Sumerian truth, a hostile witness to the Egyptian truth. The Biblicality of life depends on human's bribability. The Bible — the Puritan bad joke as the truth is now the new government that steals your rights. It spirals endlessly down into humans' incivility — which is bottomless."

Billy inhales deeply, flicks his pompadour back and continues in a hushed tone as if he is letting me in on a secret: "Why does God hawk miracles / the *truth* only to the Elected Elder — the reporter / the unidentified author of the Bible? A Biblical blooper serves as a miracle, and a dirty dish-rag is a revelation of the *truth*. This is similar to the way I the American paper boy hawk my *truth*. It's the same way a Catholic Jew hawks his or her truth. I say as Billy the paperboy, 'That's two pence, thank you, come again,' selling *my* truth. The rabbi or priest says, 'That will be two prayers and five pence, thank you, come again,' as you leave after buying *his* truth.*"*

I think to myself, *I wish there were more truths for sale...* before I interrupt William and say, "Hold on, Billy. In the spirit of a fair-play debate, and on behalf of all innocent Ace Carrier paper-boys out there just doing their job, let me say that today's newspaper down on State Street is fifty percent the truth, and fifty percent material solicitation and spiritual propaganda. What do you say to that?"

William, excited by my taking his bait, within his debate, with himself, in the mirror, well-rehearsed, and without missing a beat, continues: "Okay, well, dear Susan, pray that means the Bible is at least fifty percent a capitalist control-fraud used to profit from the meek. Wouldst that fifty-fifty split of truth and capitalism in a newspaper or the Bible be any different five years ago? Ten years ago? Thirty years ago? Fifty years ago? What about one hundred or two hundred years ago? Would you still say a newspaper from 1550 is fifty percent garbage? Fifty percent lies? What about one thousand years ago? Or what about today in the spring of 1650? Why would you believe fifty percent of a newspaper (the Bible) one thousand, six hundred and fifty (1650) years old is telling you the truth?"

Billy takes a breath, looks around, cunning as a mischievous mouse with his nervous hunger for popularity rather than results, and continues: "Have Jewish royalty and their standing-army lightened-up? Have the apostles and disciples of the Bro-Bible and the God of debt given the common man or common woman a financial or spiritual bone? Has the Jewish and Catholic God of debt with pomp and revenue and/ or pump-and-dump revenue *laws* been reined in by common sense? By the common man on Main Street? No, absolutely not... and the common people know this — this disingenuous truth, this disgusting truth, this vainglory truth sanctifies Divine Debt, Divine Love, and/or original sin."

Billy continues.

"The half-dead Jews, Christians, and Muslim faithful are taught to contemplate themselves as THE outlaw, as the debtor, as the outcast beggar, and at a great distance from their Maker or Creator. Abe-Bros and Abe-Babes must make approaches and introductions by only creeping and bribing the Elect and Elders. The religionists with their Big-Daddy personal Gods are not real. Their Abrahamic religions are reproaches of our natural life and reality. The religionists' humility is ingratitude and their reason is self-doubt. The Jews' and Christians' treason is doubting life and/or themselves — doubting reason given to us by our Creator! These Puritan sinners trade Divine indulgences here in 1650 as if greed is good or treason is the truth. The treason of couturiers will be the only global currency until we strike back for freedom's sake as protestors, as Protestants, as Separatists and as Americans."

I say cunningly, teasing, pulling Billy-Boston's leg, "Be reasonable, Billy, but just to be on the safe side — how much is a Divine indulgence going for behind the State House this morning? I'll give you one if you buy me three!"

Billy, not a market maker but a blue-dog investor on a binge-purge, ignores me and continues his last-call karaoke.

"Come on, Susan, you and your family know that —"

I interrupt Billy and say firmly, "I have no family — the earth is my family and my mother, father, and relatives are... my family is celestial."

Billy still facing me says, "Come on, you know what I mean — let me run!"

Admitting that he is not on a laugh track, but high on his hate track, Billy continues: "You know that you and the common people are trickle-down trash with the money-changer's hand in your pockets. Nevertheless, you and your family send out your greeting cards celebrating Hanukah's imperialist move and Christmas plagiarism, wishing your neighbors good tidings as your moral ship lists and sinks because all you're doing is enabling holidays against humanity.

I said, "Holidays against humanity... I like that."

Billy takes a breath and rages on, parroting the tough kids in the barn or his grandpa after his medicinal whiskey shot. "Religion is a standing-army. Religion is control-fraud war. Religion is vanity, religion is low self-esteem. Religion is the root of all corruption. Religion and its holidays have nothing to do with love or respect for humanity or its Creator. It's about increasing human market share. Religion is a human invention of power, wealth, and revenge. Religion is war!"

I say, "Religion is revenge... catchy, dear Billy, you should be a pamphleteer!"

Billy doubles back and then charges, "And as far as your suggesting for me to be 'Reasonable' with all the mixing of synagogue and state — well, I'm sorry to tell you, but that *reasonable* person is not reasonable — he or she is a coward. And if an Englishman or an American — that man is a selfish, treacherous traitor, guilty of high treason because these cowards know better, but pay-to-play religiously deaf and dumb. These *reasonable* globalist courtiers have no consciousness and no state. These squealers only learn about their life at their demise."

I keep nodding my head in a slow approving way, thinking only to myself in order to not excite easily-excitable Billy Boston, who used to be William, but is now quickly turning into Bill the Butcher. But, I also think to myself... why would Billy's newspaper and Bible truth analogy be wrong? It might not be, because if we shine a light on the capitalist wolves hiding as angelic sheep behind the Jewish and Catholic Bible for their profits, we will be called anti-Semitic or evil.

In a hushed voice, as the devil's advocate, I say to William, "You're being anti-Semitic and evil."

William, turned around and still facing me, snaps to attention with eyes all aglow. He sinks away from me, but holds his position, like a cat drawing a target and sharpening its claws. The hair on Billy's neck and spine is straight up, his eyes are still locked on me as he rolls his shoulders forward just as a crazed cat arches its back before it leaps.

AT HOME WITH HATE

William lunges and says, "Oh, please... I'm not anti-Semitic — I'm anti-synagogue and state just as ferociously as I am anti-church and state!" This is not true, but William rattles on: "I'm not anti-Semitic — I'm anti-collusion. I'm not anti-Semitic — I'm anti-extortion. I'm not anti-Semitic — I'm anti- predatory lending. I'm not anti-Semitic — I'm anti- being hated because I don't agree with or want to pay off the Bible-Maker who only prays for vengeance and/or riches only for his *chosen* people. I'm not anti-Semitic — I'm anti-England-and-America legislating for, paying for, and/or doing the racist Jew's dirty-work after our father's warned us not to."

Billy Boston is the anti-Semitic Catholic who sounds like and says he is William the Protestant, but Billy doesn't have the testosterone to be a William.

He concludes, "I'm not anti-Semitic – I'm anti the monetary and political lobby of synagogue and State colluding in order to falsely prove the Jew's Bible is true at the world's expense. The Bible-Maker is now a world-maker at the expense of everyone in the world, except of course the political 'Friends of Israel.' I'm not anti-Semitic — I'm anti- the Jew and his or her 'Friends' hating, torturing, and killing all their neighbors in order to feel at peace, at home. Holy?

Chosen? Resurrection-Ready! Jews are Armageddon-Ready — at home with hate... on Mt. *Sinai* hating, or in their Hebrew language: on Mt. Hate hating. Market makers, King makers, world-makers, Bible makers as haters, accusing the world of both hating and being hated! But perhaps? *Oy vey?*... the Jew is the real hater! An Alpha-Moron? The real problem? Naaay, of course not, Susan... I'm just being anti-Semitic, right? Nay to the end of space and nay to the end of time because history will judge us as religious murderers or co-conspirator murderers. Which sin is worse, Susan?"

Billy starts turning around and is facing front, still red with his raving red neck all aglow — a cable-guy almost out of breath, a forgotten man, a Catholic deer-hunter about to pee in his pants.

William concludes, looking over his left shoulder, not at me but out the window, in a stern whisper, "And most important, Ms. Hutchinson, "Let me also be *evil!* Jesus was as benevolent as Confucius and the Greeks, so he hated freely and was 'Evil' when he called the Jewish high priests of King David 'money-changers.' That was one thousand six hundred and fifty years ago and I want to be a hater and as *evil* as Jesus was, today. Don't forget what Jesus said about haters:

> *If any man come to me, and hate not his father, and*
> *mother, and wife, and children, and brethren, and sisters,*
> *— yes and even hate his own life he cannot be my disciple.*

I say condescendingly with a smirk, shaking my head, "Damn, Jesus was a hater? Damn Christian Zionista haters — always hating."

Billy replies, "When you crucify me as a hater or anti-Semitic for telling the truth about Zionistic Christianity, you will slice your own soul's throat and the cross you nail me to will be *YOUR* cross. You will carry the cross you bear or wear on your breast as a murderer — not as a healer, and certainly not as a Christian. Your rosy cross is plagiarism stolen from man's shadow as he leaves Plato's cave, arms up and open, facing the sun. This Roman and Jewish cross is not, nor will it ever be, my cross, or my false flag. Jesus, in his own words, hates your organized and orthodox religions and civilizations! Jesus Christ hates Judaism and Jesus Christ hates Jews! Jesus Christ hates Christianity and Jesus Christ hates Christians!"

Billy continues, "And how can you blame Jesus for looking at these dead people with their dead language and their dead letters? Conjurors of spirit and royalty with *Kings* representing his father God — our Creator, our Maker? Come, on... really? I mean, Susan, can you really believe Jonah is meditating in the whale? Is it Jupiter and Europa or Adam and Eve? Is it Jupiter in the mountain or Satan in the pit? These Zionistas, like magicians, say, 'Presto, let there be light!' and we're supposed to believe them? Skulking rabbis move the sublime to the ridiculous and then the ridiculous to the sublime. If I was Jesus, the son of God or our Creator, I'd be pissed also!"

"And then the New Testament is no better a freaky stooge. If Mathew speaks *this* — Luke speaks *that*...? *Lo heres, Lo theres* — pick up your breeches! Look here, look there, and Christ says nothing — not even pick up your britches? Then down the road when Mo or Moses speaks this — Larry the rabbi speaks that and Curly the priest says pull down your breeches! Are the Scriptures a punch-line or alibi for Curly and Christ? It seems the Bro-Bible is a mythical musical satire written by poets as a Divine comedy. Unfortunately, the Bro-Bible was translated into a Divine Order written by God. Its authorship suddenly changed from gypsy poets on skid-row to royal prophets and saints in the sky. Mind you, Susan, I still look *here* and *there*... all day and all night long... and no one picks up their breeches."

I give William a slow, somewhat agreeing and non-obligatory, "Aaanhh huunnh," feigning that I'm nonchalantly paying attention to him in order to not egg him on during this frightening Monday morning. Ms. Appleton, the aesthete, is looking over at us again, keeping a wary eye on us whispering by the windows in her classroom's cheap seats for hooligans.

I say to Billy, "Hanging with thy ruffians at the water pump again, Billy? Well, I'm wondering, with all that said, is Mary Dyer anti-Semitic?"

"Why, of course — she's being executed / sacrificed within the hour for disagreeing with the orthodox Jews. If that isn't a Kosher sacrifice then what is?"

I say, "That's ridiculous — she is a Quaker."

"Exactly. Anti-Semitism is just code for anyone who is not Jewish. Actually, scratch that; the smartest and funniest Jews are the most anti-Semitic, starting with Jesus, so therefore anti-Semitic is really not voting Jewish, nor paying the Jews off before oneself. Anti-semitism is the white-hot yin dot in the middle of dark yang. It's reverse-psychology extortion, or passive-aggressive bribery by the little red religionists who have cried wolf since they opened their traps. Haven't you read Benedito the Jew from Amsterdam? He's like your Lenape Indian friends who believe God is nature. Benedito de Spinoza is howling with relativity and his beasty boys that he doesn't feel 'Chosen' either. Those Jewish poets / prophets really have fun blowing up their Elect and Elders with their hypocrisies. And Susan, listen to me here and now: we as English thinking humans must shine the same bright and crass light on our Elect and Elders... we must!"

I think to myself some more, as barking Billy is often close to correct in his forgotten-man tirades with no bite. I know these white-devil wankers who wrote the Bro-Bible also prophesized that the earth does not spin on an axis and that the sun revolves around the earth, as opposed to us revolving around the sun. These capitalist desperados posing as medical professionals also tell us we should drill holes in our head for headaches and allow leeches to suck our "Stagnant" blood to cure us of our "Evils." These subjugators of sin and profiteers of spin are "Spreading the bro-word" that a woman who cannot conceive a child is evil, and if a mother or her child dies, or a child is deformed at birth, that woman and her mutilated child are evil, wicked, and foul. A Monster!

I think how is a common man or a common woman in England or America armed with, maybe, common sense, supposed to believe these Bro-Bible belchers, with their fictitious "Loves, laws, and God?" The English and American commonwealth cannot be bribed because of courageous souls like Mary Dyer, my grandfather, and my mother, yet these wine-sipping democrat dogs like William Demopheare posing as the common people don't have the balls or ovaries to speak the truth. They are Protestants without a protest, common people without common sense, and sub-humans without a soul.

Anew, I lean forward not as Autumn Leaf, but as sweet Susanna Hutchinson and whisper succinctly and with a breathy resonance into William's pricked ear, accompanied with gasoline and a match, "Billy, after your resurrection and with my stitched-up throat perhaps we could start a new religion? I've designed a really good religious marketing strategy and a totally awesome logo. It's called *Later...* Our religious motto will be "*Later* will be *Greater!*" All religionists have to do is sit around, pay us "Laterers" high priests and politicians a cut of their earnings and wait around for *Later...* by a dead tree... with a friend (who is also *a believer* and/or psychotic) because we all know, *our revelation,* will be here sooner... rather than *Later!*

Billy was lit up again, off and running again, on fire again with my wise-ass remark, so he shifted his weight around, ready to entertain, and faced me like a baby bull pawing the ground, about to charge: "Exactly, Susan, that is what I'm talking about. That is why the apostles of pump and the disciples of dump for the 'New Holy Land' franchise are coming to a town near you. They will terrorize us with their crypto-fascist laws, their crypto-fascist police force, their crypto-fascist love, and their crypto-fascist God called *original sin* or *original debt*. These Range-Rover rabbis and Porsche-priests bully our common sense and say that they are the 'Chosen people,' and that they are 'Too big to fail,' which belies and insults the common sense of humanity, the commonwealth, and all those who have and will protect the common man / the forgotten man."

Billy up-shifted, gaining speed: "And moving beyond my drugged-down *rated-G* happy-clapper hypothesis that today's newspaper and the Bible are both truthful and propaganda on a fifty-fifty split, let me speak frankly and say that I think this morning's newspaper hawked around the world and the Bible have only an infinitesimal amount of integrity / truth. The only truthful fact perhaps in today's morning newspaper printed around the globe, or in the Bible, is possibly the page numbers on the bottom of each page, but I wouldn't bet on it. So, in my humble Monday morning Autumn Leaf Treatise, or my Ms. Leaf Thesis, 00.01% of today's newspaper and the Bro-Bible is possibly truth, and the remaining 99.99% of the Bro-Bible is toilet paper."

I say, "Billy, are you applying for Minister Winthrop's job?"

Billy is now Barking-Bill, and he contorts his face, grunting and snorting. " Just like my American father, Thomas Paine, I have chopped through the Bible like a man chops through three or four trees blocking the road after a storm. I have taken my sharpened axe and turned this Bible — big and clumsy — blocking my way with shady reasons, into a cord of wood that fits into my woodstove! The Bible is now a four-by-four-by-eight-foot wood block — shards of a tree, split apart with mathesis. Now the tree is logs upon logs or graphs stacked upon graphs. Tic-tac-toe to the sky — I built a wood thicket, a wood block! The Bible is brutally axed apart, split apart as the trees with words are tickled in places they never knew! Today the trees are tanning, shrinking, drying, seasoning with the sun for years from which they were born. Under many years in the sun the trees have grown in ringlets stretching to the sky in an orbit like our earth and galaxy. My cord of wood / my wood-block has stored the sun's energy in its growth and I will harvest that sunshine in my woodstove! So, as I wait for the winter of my life with my oiled and polished wood stove, and with seasoned wood — that burns like the sun because it is the sun, I'm just asking: what happened to the common man here in 1650? The common woman or common sense? How can the deceived deceive others with self-dealing Bro-Biblical quotes? How can parents do this to children? How can these self-idolizing Abe-Babe lackeys of love sell the bullshit and lies of a newspaper from one thousand six hundred and fifty (1650) years ago when today's newspaper on State Street is 99.99% pope Moses propaganda?"

"Calm down, you little free-Willy friar," I say. "Ms. Appleton is looking at us again."

Ms. Appleton is looking at us, uninterested, thinking about something far away, and then she speaks gravely to the class.

"Before we start Homeroom Inspection, I've got some very important and very sad news, children. I was informed this morning by our Minister Winthrop, who is also our Governor, that we are to report at 9:00 a.m. a half mile south from Swampscott Street at the old Elm by the swamp for the execution of Mary Dyer. All of us, of course, have heard the rumors for the last few weeks that she was in our jail, just two doors down from this schoolhouse, once again for pushing and selling her freaky Shaker-Quaker voodoo Gods. Well, now we shall all see firsthand that the Boston Puritan's might is right. I'm sorry, children, but this execution is part of our Boston civilization — destruction, exploitation, and killing are a major part of our God-fearing Christian life."

Jonathon Every starts singing / whispering that Mary Dyer nursery rhyme and some in class join in, quietly humming, harmonizing, and whistling off-key that melodic and noxious rhyme. Ms. Appleton looks down, then walks towards the front window of the class. She is helpless, as we all are — King Mob is moving! Ms. Appleton swallows hard and tears up silently as the children sing the nursery rhyme chorus with a new verse about our Monday morning Judeo-Christian sacrifice.

Mary the Monster, Mary the Monster, where are you now? Where are you now?

Hanging in the swamp? Hanging in the swamp?

Mary the Monster, Mary the monster...

Away, away, away! Away, away, away!

I am in a daze and still thinking about William's question of how parents street-walk their innocent child into religion, just the way a pimp displays his sellable goods. Why do Jewish, Catholic, and Muslim parents, why do religionist parents sell, then incarcerate their children? Besmirched, I think because they raised us to win for them, but that vanity fails, which raises us to passively aggressively hate them. Society says that a sucker is born every minute, but a parasitic parent says a sucker / winner is born every one one-thousandth of a second. And as a breeding / sucking parent betting on a winner, you can bank on that sucker / winner: that feeder, that follower — especially if that sucker / winner you give birth to (and brainwash) is your own dumb-fuck child. The classroom children continue to sing together:

Hanging in the swamp, Hanging in the swamp.

Mary the Monster, Mary the Monster, where are you now? Where are you now?

Hanging in the swamp, Hanging in the swamp.

"Banking it" as a good religious Abe-Babe parent, you can now love and torture your dumb-fuck child with gift-love (that is, brainwash your Jewish child, Christian child, or Muslim child) with only applause from your religious neighbors. These irresponsible parents or religionists can birth their active disorders! Perverted Abe-Babe parents go around in circles bingeing and then purging, bingeing and then purging, at the end of a dead-end religious cul-de-sac called Armageddon Court.

Ms. Appleton puts up her hand and said, "Children, for the grace of God please stop your song. For the grace of God... please stop!"

Some verse and humming about the Monster drifts away reluctantly. *"Where are you now? Where are you now?"* as I think about how I agree with Billy and his parental hypothesis.

These parental child-changers (analogous to money-changers) are not in it for the child, or the money, but for the rub of the dirty deal. The family love deal is painted as a great bargain, a fire-sale, but the math equates a crime, the gossip shows deterioration, and the egos scream for adoration within the poverty of "Family love." These brokers, changers, dealers, traders, and/or parents are in it only for the high of a hypergamy-whammy. Parents don't believe in the laws of Moses or the words of Christ. The Catholic Jew or Jewish Catholic parents only pray in fear to their fairy-tale "Debt-God" and/or "Guilt-God." Patriarchal parents pay and pray to their white-devil lawyers, politicians, and accountants (the crypto-debt police) for a Divine indulgence of gift-love that protects the "Family" control-fraud. Neurotic "Family love" and children are not selfless charity, or altruism — *family love* is tribal narcissism. *Family love* and children are financed imperialism for the tribe on the go! Breeding and *family love* are the birth of predatory lending and imperialism for the tribe that likes to eat its young.

My classmate monsters continue humming and buzzing the Mary Dyer rhyme like blood-thirsty mosquitos in the dark.... Diana Mallouston in the back of the first row, looking right through Ms. Appleton, deliberately repeats the new verse of the cruel Mary Dyer sing-song and mockingly serenades Ms. Appleton in a slow, airy, icy, and condescending falsetto:

Hanging in the marsh. Away, away, away.

In comparison to this malicious harmony called patriarchal civilization — where a weak neighbor's problem or a child's problem is profit — I evolved to pray to only what I know living in the woods. I pray now only to what I can trust. As I wove feathers, porcupine quills, and wampum shells into deerskin for my Indian tribe for the last five years, I prayed to the sun and its Creator, which gives me life, and the moon that gives me a natural peace. That is natural peace, compared to the Judeo-Christian's unnatural state of no-peace that is child abuse for the innocent and captive children. These children are educated with endless family and parental wars, but they successfully graduate to become Abe-Babe soldiers that continue fighting very similar tribal wars. For the patriarchal soldier, there is no peace within the depraved state as fallen humans. There is no tranquil sunset, there is no nice dinner as fallen sub-humans.

Family love, "Holy War" taxes, and creative destruction economies of the parochial white-devil tribe confuse the Indians because they do not have *a priori* knowledge of guilt or ancestral debt. The birth of a child within the Lenape tribe is a gift — the birth of a child within the Puritan tribe is a work order or an account in arrears. The Indians did not comprehend sub-human qualities until they met the Walofang white-devil. The Lenape Indians and I hunted and gathered, living respectfully with nature and the other surrounding Indian tribes of New Netherland.

This peaceful life I led in the woods is worlds away from Boston's threatening life. The constant threat to the child in default or the colony in default is a Puritan Police State in which no happiness or profit can be earned unless it is stolen at a weak neighbor's expense, or a child's expense! "Civilization" becomes harassment — the tribe becomes a savage civilization that perverts, diffuses, and destroys not only the child's future, but the tribe's future.

Ms. Appleton walks over to the far row by the exit door and says "Ms. Mallouston, please don't be so cheap."

Diana Mallouston the white ghost turns red like bloody murder on a fresh winter snow and the class snickers that such a simple and succinct observation can befuddle and blush Ms. Mallouston the iceberg.

Ms. Appleton strolls back over to our windows and intensifies her gaze out to Nothing. I can smell the wainscoted oil slowly seeping into the wood floor pores. I can see dust molecules, reflecting / floating in the morning sun, slowly falling onto our oak floor as if our classroom is moving underwater. Billy looks at me as if to console me silently in a clownish derogatory manner, as if he knows and enjoys the very dark and ominous waters that follow a smeared woman. A stained and sullied woman like myself, like Ms. Appleton, like Mary Dyer, like my mother, and like... like all Abe-Babe women draped into a corner, wigged into an occupied zone, or, impossibly made possible. The second sex! The Other — the woman and her meteorologist forecast offer a one-hundred-percent chance of hard rain, many downpours, gale-force headwinds, and, after dark, temperatures that will fall, creating black ice and blizzard-like conditions. Accumulations of black sleet and black snow with white-out conditions will freeze and bury femininity for the rest of a woman's life.

Ms. Appleton turns away from the window again and walks down the aisle towards the front of the class. Billy from Boston beams, turns back around to me and says, "See, Susan,

I was right about Mary Dyer. Doff those Indian moccasins and trust me!"

Here in Boston, these dark clouds and rain follow me around no matter how much French poodle lace and Parisian perfume I put on my petticoat. William, Billy, or, correctly, Bill With No Will looks away with a blind eye to my inevitable future. William always predicted to me the sun would eventually come out for my garden. William, a fair weatherman, a young pious preacher, or any subjugating man forecasting the physical or spiritual weather, only talks about the goodness coming, about everything *being for the best*... even though the dark clouds all around are an enemy of all women and all life.

Diana Mollouston, red in the face, sings back to Ms. Appleton and our class the Dyer chorus, "Away! Away! Away!" as if she is releasing arrows and/or armies!

Samuel Payneson says to the class, "I bet five pence Mary Dyer craps her pants on the hangman's scaffold." Israel Wilkinson adds, "I'll take that bet and raise your five to ten."

There is no negotiating with the delusional religionists betting their life away. The only escape is free-grace — with no standing-army, and no debt, which, if even spoken of will have you exiled into an anti-Semitic and/or an evil-doers debtor jail. The debtor jail is a suburban shark tank, where the white-devil wolves of this endless human race will eat you alive. These jackal cops will devour you ass-first, as your *brother-ass* (or in my female case: my *sister-ass*) is our only true patriarchal asset. Your *hot ass* is your covenant of material works for the ass-sniffing Catholics and Jews policing their control-frauds of love, law, God, and family. The jackal cops in this suburban debtors' jail collect your loyalist money in legal codes as gate-keepers when you pass through their easy-pass toll booths.

The loyalist, "Royal" enough / working hard enough to be in "Love" with their family filled with "Family Love" — works hard for the toll-booth money! The "Working life" is a tribal web of ancestral debt, original sin, and crypto-debt that has been woven around the world by the English white-devil in St. Petersburg, Africa, India, Hong Kong, and now here in America. Boston is just another colony-child subject. The deceived continue to deceive others — nothing new with humanity these days in 1650.

Ms. Appleton says quietly to the class, "Your bets and wages on sins will be the loss of your souls."

I think to myself that in all these loyalist-royalist economies, the cash cow is still existential fear and death. One must work the fear-market or milk the death-market. The death-market for war and redemption has blossomed in years branching out to religious war, to economic war, to breeding children for war, to class war, to race war, to trade war, cyber war, gender war, drug war, and, of course, always escalating beyond our infinite hyper-tension into real war.

Samuel Payneson says, "Oh, wouldst Ms. Appleton be a preacher — nay, she is a teacher. Ms. Appleton, please teach us something we don't know!"

The fear- and death-markets derive from the market maker — the existential damnation market. The threat of punishment after our death is *the* market. Existential damnation is annually worth trillions in gold and zillions in souls.... Since the beginning of time who, or what Nation, tribe, pygmy or pilgrim in their right mind would not work their ass to the bone stealing from and killing their neighbors in order not to be thrown into an eternal damnation? Which selfish gene wouldn't steal and kill for that eternal win?

Ms. Appleton, a little frazzled, is on a warpath and says to Samuel and Israel's wager, "I'll take that ten-bit bet, Israel, and double it to twenty pence. Mary Dyer will go out like an Easter candle — no waste, clean, no bending, and she will leave behind the smell and taste of warm honey in your nose and on your lips — she will be effervescent, burning bright for eternity, and most important, boys — I will collect my winnings, I will collect my debt!"

Our class is shocked, but inspired, by Ms. Appleton's gambled play as Samuel and Israel both suddenly look a little worried, uncomfortable, and adjust themselves in their seats.

Aaagh, dear reader, the good ole Neg-Am Jam life... the double-negative life — the NAJ life, the negative proof life — when you think you're going to get ahead, when you think you're smarter than the bank, smarter than the Kings. It is a wagered life — the indebted life, the borrowed life on borrowed time, lived large on floating islands around the world. These imperialized floating islands are known as Devil's Island and they have been franchised, and thus indebted and incarcerated around the world by the English. The English and now the American Alpha-Morons call it "Charity," "Democracy," and/or "Freedom," but everyone else who still does math the correct way knows it as the negative amortized life, aka the NAJ life. The NAJ life pumps up *working* positions that profit only the royal Moby-Dicks trading junk in London.

DEVIL'S DIVORCE ISLAND

Ms. Appleton organizes some papers on her desk and then picks up her favorite twelve-inch golden ruler made of brass. She passes the ruler from hand to hand, enjoying its weight. Then she cradles it like a baby.... Then Ms. Appleton clutches and strong-arms the golden ruler like a Christian missionary holding the cross as a shield in order to keep away devil-worshiping cannibals. Ms. Appleton cradles her golden ruler like a baby again and is frozen there in that trance-like state, completely phased-out metaphysically and whittling her finger nails into the golden notches every eighth of an inch, moving up and down the ruler. Ms. Appleton blinds herself, yet she climbs, scratches, and inches her way along, slowly finding her way subconsciously with her golden ruler. Meditating on the golden rule, she would relax like a cat in between strokes while it paws and scratches a post, a deep, penetrating time-out performed in public. Ms. Appleton is a cougar: cocky, sharp, condescending, and luxurious. She indulges the Other.

Ms. Appleton looks up and out to our class and states, "We must stay focused and continue our good-work here in Boston."

I continued to think about the Neg-Am Jam — the NAJ life and how no one is *working* in the NAJ life whether in Hong Kong, India, St. Petersburg, or Boston. The altruistic NAJ life is about getting or not getting ahead financially or spiritually for our Lord, our God, or our Country. You can put sin in front of your soul and sell your soul to the highest bidder, but you'd be earning trickle-down blood money on borrowed time. That's because your Devil's Island neighbors are soulless barbarians who will torture and kill you for the Elect and the Elder at the jingle of a coin. And that's how the "Intelligent" Elect and Elders purposely "Designed" the Puritan civilization which evolves on the axis of parasites and fashion.

"Amen to good-work, Ms. Appleton, amen to good-work!" Laura Kraven says from the front seat in the front row by the door. Laura, diligent and determined, over emphasizes "Good-work," agreeing with our teacher, Ms. Appleton, as if they both know what *good-work* is.

Bob Testaigne, right behind Laura in everything she does, exclaims, "Awesome God of good-work — beautiful and fair God, one and only God, awesome God, please forgive us and show us the light because our good-work is the only true way and the only true light!"

I think to myself how original sin guilt is sometimes referred to as a paternal or patriotic "Love" for family, father,

Country, or God. For the Jewish jackasses and conniving Catholics on Devil's Island, the beautiful sea is not a beautiful sea anymore, nor our neighbor — anymore our neighbor. When you work on Devil's Island, you trust no one as a self-righteous Jew or a cunty Catholic. You pray and communicate to no one on our earth, this again being no Elect's nor Elder's *intelligent-designer* error. Then we and our Range-Rover rabbis and Porsche priests convince ourselves that we're actually communicating to fairies and angels working for our psychotic imaginary *personal God* — right, fairy-friends from the Bro-Bible newspaper that Fido the foodle shat on one thousand six hundred and fifty years ago.

Lawrence Randison, my cousin from the market, is the son of a successful arms dealer, and he lobs back to Bob Testaigne a rebuttal striking Bob's "Light" description: "Ah, yes, Bobby, your awesome God with your *good-work* and Divine light... is it right that you Christian Zionistas are the light and also the might? Because everyone else is a dirtbag? Is that right, Bobby? A loser? A shiska, Bobby? An Infidel? Right? Little Bobby, I would respect your 'God,' but your God is nothing without my family's swords and guns, so that means your God and you are nothing without me. Right, Bobby?"

I think to myself... the earth and our neighbors are our enemies now, everything is a threat on Devil's Island America — a threat that the truth will escape! The rations are cut and the windows are nailed shut as we naturally assimilate closer to the solipsistic white-devil Abe-Babe lawyers representing abstract franchised Gods undermining our happiness and humanity. We warm up and network with bounty hunters and military police imprisoning our friends and family. We politically go off the commonwealth road as we "Like" and vote for potato-salad politicians whose cunty creditors and macaroni mercenaries murder our family and neighbors for financial profit.

Bob looks back over to Lawrence, who sits up in front of

the class, closer to the windows, and says, "God will temper your fuming soul."

Ms. Appleton answers Bob Testaigne, ignoring Lawrence, and uses her golden ruler as a sort of pointer or whip. "Yes, good idea, Bob, let us pause for a moment this morning in silence and think about the light." Ms. Appleton then goes to the center of our darkly wainscoted square classroom and reaches up to our nautical brass lantern. As she says every morning, "This Mayflower lantern, children, has carried the *light* over the Atlantic Ocean from Leiden, in the Netherlands. Back there, the *light* was to have NO Kings, and therefore, NO wars. These Dutchy Protestants, along with the Lutherans, Calvinists, Congregationalists, Unitarians, and all common people / all forgotten people who want NO religious war, let us light this candle, children, and think about the *light*, and more important — let us imagine life without war."

On Devil's Island, the beautiful open sea is now only a jailer with hungry religious sharks thrashing about and homosexual perverts going door-to-door as salesmen selling sub-prime student loan salvation from their sinking ships. These loan sharks live as priestly metro-sexual white-devils calling themselves "Town Fathers," or magistrates pretending to guard our royal and Divine city on the hill. These lawyers / these courtiers have taken an oath to quarrel as theater; these lawyers have taken an oath to loot and plunder the playhouse as royal and Divine soldiers acting in the play called "The Law."

I leave the theater and think to myself how my soul's solitary confinement with free-grace leaves me counting the waves in the sea, hoping to drown or escape this Devil's Island show business. I'm a happy and hopeful leper floating away on a homemade raft, no daughter of Zion. I'm Autumn Leaf — a floating red flash under the fall equinox sun. I am surfing on top of a jade-colored cold-plankton current. I am transposed into a briny, salty, Atlantic Ocean sea-spray. And, then again, salty and white — I blow away. I float with no debt nor regrets, destined to meet my Maker the sea again with spiritually clean hands on top of those Buzzard Bay whitecaps.

Ms. Appleton lights the golden Dutch and Moroccan glass candle lamp she calls her Mayflower. The lantern is the shape of a one-story pagoda with a wicker door that has a motif in perforated tin. The brass-framed door is made of orange copper and has those undeniable markings of an African craftsman, at once both rhythmic and symbolic, unknown to the English craftsman. African craft, expressions, and art are filled with light and happiness, while English art and crafts seem all too much about royalty, regiment, and heredity. The Mayflower candle lamp has a brass roof, base, and four glass panes. With the candle lit, the luminescent brass structure pulses and flickers with geometric musical scribblings etched into this small metal house. The nautical lamp's protective bands of brass that run around this house of worship are also peppered with mosaics, which make the lantern utilitarian and safe in case of a spill in the ship's cabin while crossing the Atlantic or whilst hanging in our classroom.

When Ms. Appleton lit her Mayflower candle lamp and closed the little copper door, the brass glowed and complemented the frosty white panes of glass — slumped and bubbly. The Mayflower looked like a golden honeycomb cloud. The Mayflower felt like a wet, warm, and electric cloud filled with lightning floating mischievously in our dark brown wainscoted matrix. Worker bees and honey bees worked side by side in their honeycomb home. The Mayflower candle lamp was a busy fourth-dimension honeycomb hypersphere and it was at origin (x_2, y_2) in our classroom, but really the light floated around of its own free will. The Mayflower candle was an unruly orthoplex honeycomb.

Our class, in synchronized obedience, clasped our hands and lowered our heads to think about the *light*. The silent *light* was dark, joyless, and sinister for me in this classroom. All I could hear was the Puritan time machine "Tick-tock, tick-tock, tick-tock." I could only think about Mary Dyer, my second mother, being hanged in an hour by my "Civilization," by my neighbors, killed, murdered, and sacrificed ceremoniously by my own tribe. "Tick-tock, tick-tock, tick-tock!"

Capital punishment? I remember how ludicrous, unreasonable, and bizarre the Lenape Indian thought us white-devils were for hanging and burning our own tribe. They never could figure out the white-devil obsession with mass incarceration and killing people with their Bible in their hands — nor did the Indians care to understand after witnessing one of our public executions.

I tried to explain capital punishment to Wampy my Lenape Chief numerous times. I explained the eye-for-an-eye (white-devil mentality) tooth-for-a-tooth Biblical reality, but Wampy would only look down his nose at me and point to a tree, a cloud, or the seaside, and cry, "No maxitasu "(No respect), to insinuate that he shouldn't be asked such a silly question with nature all around, and that I should take up my query with the spirit world. Wampy answered, "Walofang, no maxitasu. Walofang no respect water, Walonfang no respect thunder, Walonfang no respect!"

Later one day, very alone, down in New Netherland or New Nothing-land, and with a sense of respect sitting on the Devil's Belt seaside, I'd tried to ask the blonde and rocky seaside a question. The seaside is filled with golden sand, pink rocks, yellow shells, and green, scratchy, tough cedars the color of blue spruce seaweed. I sat down for a conversation with one windswept cedar that looked like a giant *bonsai tree*. It was nibbled on by deer, nested in by blue jays, and growing sideways between a boulder and the eroded seashore. The pruned juniper with deadwood as furniture and jays in its hair was drunk, vivacious, and alive. I asked this *Juniper Virginia*, "Can I... can I kill?" The cedar tree said nothing. I waited and some blue jays came and went. I asked the green fire tree — prickly, wiry, and strong, filled with a mean gin — again in a louder voice, "Can I kill?" The *Juniper Virginia* still didn't answer me, so I got mad and sat on its bench-like trunk. It said nothing back to me as I nibbled on some of its fatwood and then I broke off some dead branches and lit them on fire for incense. The smoke danced around us as the cranky blue birds returned in an angry mood and squawked at me three times as if to wake me up like Wampy, saying, "No respect — No respect — No respect. The blue jays' squawk was not a rusty pump, but a mad pump — bold and aggressive. I was awake now as the cedar incense smoke billowed around me and the bluebirds flew away shaking their heads at me and reporting to all the animals and clouds on our horizon that I had "No respect — No respect — No respect...."

My *kill question* seemed ridiculous — forsaken, as vivacious waves the color of jade, from the Long Island Sound, slowly kept on crashing into the sandy and rocky beach shore at my feet. My asinine *kill question* was crushed with its egotistical insignificance as purple and grey berries dropped from the cedar onto my shoulder and lap as the blue jays left their home. Other seeds sailed with the brackish sea breeze into the dirty sand with Momma Earth. Other seeds fell into the rocky tidal pool a few feet away. These seeds — in good faith and in good spirits continued to search and swim for a temporary foundation, a temporary earthbound home — in order to team-up with Big-Daddy sun and then blossom like green emerald fire. These seeds on fire, growing and alive, green with no envy and sprouting in order to not to kill, profit, or pay a debt, but for the hell of it — for the *life* of it.

Numerous times Wampy pointed to our macabre white-devil tradition of public executions as clear evidence of our delusional and self-destructive soul. He elaborated one time by saying, "Do you remember Walking Leech? Walking Leech now good shell weaver — Leechy good wampum boy."

Chief Wampy was referring to when my sister-clan at one

of their monthly meetings had to deal with a disturbed Lenape man called Walking Leech who had sexually assaulted numerous women and then attacked a male mate of one of these women. During the hunts there would always be *accidents* that the sister clan would coordinate with Chief Wampy in order to clean the warrior tribe, but Walking Leech couldn't ride a horse, much less slay a slug. My sister-clan, instead of banishing Walking Leech or killing him — neutered him. The emasculated Indian was sent to work with the other *adopted* Lenape slaves. The after-school art class all day long was for me, two Iroquois Indians who seemed ashamed and never spoke, an Oneida Indian called Skenandoa, and a Dutch marine officer: Captain Graaf van Barvooets (the Lenape called him Captain Barefoot). He refused to speak English to me, continuing our Anglo-Dutch Wars, but the Captain seemed extremely happy, and at home, living in the woods barefoot with everyone making art. There were also three Shinnecock Indians from Long Island, who argued bitterly and constantly among themselves, and one very angry Seneca Indian from the Southern Tier — out near Lake Erie — who sullenly isolated himself. Me and these art school misfits were the Lenapes' weavers of their tribe's wampum shell currency, their wampum treaty belts, and their wampum living art.

My Indian sister Happiness came past our motley crew working on wampum belts a few weeks after Walking Leech's dressing down and she said, looking at the comatose male Indian, "See he grow good now. No more blood-sucking leech. Turtle God is good to the Lenape — he show us the light."

Back in my Boston class I continue to wonder for a juvenile moment what my other classmates are picturing as their *light*. Low self-esteem and anxiety are all I feel... dread and woe are my light.

The gravitas of the *light* is unbearable and I am sweating and twitching. Within this horrible darkness called "Divine Love or Divine Light," Lawrence Randison comes to the rescue and growls back, answering Bob Testaigne's bet that God is an avenger: "Hey, Bobby, nothing will temper me except a better swordsman — God is my anvil, you worm, and I hammer all day."

I like *the light* now as I picture wriggling worms on an anvil and my cousin smiling. Then *the light* suddenly casts a strange shadow this Monday morning as Billy in a sudden huff leans back over his left shoulder towards me and starts to whisper and stutter, "Su, Sus, Susan, are we, we, we, fri, frien, friends?"

But Ms. Appleton sees him and says, "Think about the *light*, Billy, and not how cute you are... because you're not that cute."

Billy stutters, "So, sor, sorry, Ms. Appleton. Okay, thanks," as he farts lightly in between words in a sighing manner like a small pony neighing with a whinny, as the pony is whipped and thus now relieved, relaxing, and stuttering out of both oral openings. Billy really expresses himself phonetically: "Sor, (ppfrrantt) sor, sorry (phrant), Ms. Appleton (phrant). Okay, thanks (ppfrrantt)."

Larry Randison and Nancy St. Clair to our right look over in disbelief and shake their heads, giggling and wincing in dismay. They both in a wispy and solid harmony sing, "Billy butt-puff, Billy butt-puff, Billy butt-puff."

On Devil Divorce Island the child is always worked for and seen, but never really heard, and told vehemently all the while to "Never remember." Weighing on my mind constantly is this disorganized attachment, this cognitive dissonance, and this cerebral discord to *never remember* that I and all orphaned or divorced children slink away with. This primal parental terror occurs after a divorcing violation of the child's trust. This white-devil divorcing disease mutates into false guilt because the child does not speak up or express himself or herself.

When I was a child growing up in Boston and Providence, I had a cuckolded father who was always at work, or hurrying to and fro work, to and fro the barn; to and fro.... My wounded father, my Big-Daddy, in a sad and silent manner skulked around, not just to and fro, but chore to chore. My parochial Big-Daddy was really my "Little-Daddy." He scurried around — shadow to shadow, with our eyes (a father's toward a daughter's) never meeting again. To be fair, my parents had a shadowy wedding and their first child within nine months of first meeting, and a forced shotgun-wedding or musket-marriage is not a good foundation. In any case, after the third or fourth time that I saw my mother Annie adjusting her bonnet and pulling up her petticoat coming out of the hayloft with Henry Vane or Roger Williams in tow, I nailed this letter or thesis to my parents' church-like bedroom door:

Dear Mom and Dad,

1 - *Your "Marriage" problems are not my problems — don't involve your children with YOUR problems.*

2 - *Be responsible for your irresponsibility — I will not be ashamed.*

3 - *Your failed marriage and failed attempt at a "Family" are DEATHS that must be acknowledged, mourned, buried, and respected as such.*

4 - *Don't expect, or even ask me to call you "Mother" or "Father."*

5 - *Don't send me a birthday card because I'm not coming "Home" for Christmas.*

6 - *I'm the black tulip art of your failed family. Please water me when I'm dry.*

Thank you, sincerely,

Susan

My parents never replied.... And still, after both my parents have long been dead and buried, my only identity is still as a divorcee child, a teen-age spinster, a child-hag, a senile teenager, a demented teenager, a sad teenager — abandoned, the limping freak of divorce. Me, the child, a dried and pressed flower, distorted, pressed, flattened into a book, a frame, a legal divorce settlement. I am flat and abstract... I am a work order, I am a debt to be collected. I'm not real — I'm a native, a colony, a colony-child caught in between parents, Nations, and tribes fighting with parental tribal tariffs and/ or wifey trade-wars. Or maybe I'm a friendly-fire casualty of fatherly embargoes, husbandry being seduced instead of seducing, and/or Big-Daddy hypergamy-whammies of course *for the family and for the children.* These sub-human parents are "Trading-up" or "Trading-down" within *their* own narcissistic race and NOT our human race.

The Abe-babe child abuse occurs within civilization before you are born. The chanting and droning rally-cry to "Burn the freaky witch" and/or "Hang the divorced bastard" echoes out from the first building always built in the white-devil colony — the prison. The prison is the foundation and church of the Neg-Am Jam, the negative life. The NAJ church is a maximum-security prison, where the threat of physical or financial pain keeps you subhuman and "In line." The prison's foundation hums "Billy in the Darbies" in a wavering octave while the white-devil glitch-rhyme grinds and resonates musically, a saw-tooth soundwave that has never lost its beat or bite against those living within free-grace.

My polite friends and family say my mother was not an adulterous witch, yet at the same time I'm manically propped, fashioned, and brainwashed into also forgetting my family. I'm lobbied to "Move on" after being rescued and/or decommissioned? Maybe bought? Sold? Or just traded — a hypergamy-whammy fashion accessory? And then I'm dragged back here to Boston by my new captors / by my new parents, traded for some metal pots and pans that the Lenape Indians still can't understand how to make, even after I explained metallurgy to them for five years. Beforehand, I was also told by

Happiness, my Lenape sister for years, beyond intimately and endlessly, that I was her sister, but that was a lie. That aboriginal daydream ended at the drop of a feather when Hap's eye caught a glimpse of some of that new shiny kitchenware Jan Throgg was teasing my sister-clan with. Happiness, my Indian sister, said, "You should leave... leave for the good of my family," never taking her eyes off the silver crockery.

What Happiness didn't say was that she was given a choice between caring for me — keeping her word to me — and a Tupperware party. Happiness chose the Tupperware party and said good-bye to me. At birth, I was a Separatist child — an Awakened Christian at birth, then, as fate would have it, an orphan — a Brit gone Native and then a Native Indian reject in New Netherland. I am now in Boston, not a born-again Christian, but a bought-again Christian — lightly refurbished — "As-is" with no scratches or dents (visible).

Friends and family expect me to forget and bury without respect or acknowledgment my mother and father and all they did or all they did not do for me. Then I'm to borrow a family name or a tribe's name and/or identity in order to not feel deficient, unwanted, or unfinished. The more popular the lipstick and fashion I put on wearing fine English clothes, trying to be *normal* with the white-devil savage on the Boston cobblestone streets, the more lost and abandoned I feel. Even after wearing deerskin and my Lenape wampum belt, and running naked with the Indian savages in the woods, I felt the facade of that savage survivor game become humiliating, painful, and obvious when my sister-clan traded me for some kitchen-ware.

Both the Indians' and Puritans' tribes are based on whispers, secrecy, dishonesty, evasions, and exploitation. The Indian and the Englishman both teach me that *their* tribes with *their* "Love, Laws, Gods, and Family" will build me a foundation I can live on. But both societies are equally preposterous and built upon a cracked foundation or in a bad flood zone that the town carpenter, or the town idiot from either tribe, would realize was a swampy land deal.

Ms. Appleton is lightly slapping / bouncing her golden ruler against the fat of her palm and says, "Pleaseth me, children, and calm down, focus on the Divine light and the light will lead the way."

Billy turns around again, more desperate than ever, as his eyes try to refocus on me as opposed to staring at himself, praying and panting about his *light*, and says, "Susan, I'm not a butt-puff, am I? We're friends, right? Right?"

Billy has the selfish gene stare, the million-mile Republican elephant-stare and the vaselined million-mile Democratic donkey-stare that all white-devil courtiers are masters of. Both gazes are consciously vacant and in collusion with each other as these price-fixing politicians realize that capital or power will be asked of them. The two-party scam system, the poison and the remedy, both the bad cop and the good cop, feign "Forgiveness," and "Reservations," for not comprehending the language of charity or commonsense — the way of free-grace. It's just as difficult for the white-devil to comprehend free-grace as it is for the Indian to comprehend executions.

These apostles of pump for flying elephants and disciples of dump for talking donkeys only know "The normal way," "God's way," the Neg-Am Jam way, or "Their way." William looks at me with his new Federalist composure, satisfied with his trickle-down politics, just after burying alive my body-politic.

I say curtly, "Billy, you know that is not my name anymore. Why are you living in the past?"

Billy, punching down confidently, rejoices at home with need-love questions to those weaker than he. The two-party control-fraud gives Billy a pink bounce in his breath and red color in his cheeks as he lightly whispers to me, "Aaww, come on, Susan, lighten-up." Billy snivels and adjusts his weight in his seat, making small piggy noises, huffing and puffing, concluding after a moment of silence in a tight cadence, "I hate Ms. Appleton — don't you?"

The sunny forecast is believable and I'm warmed with Billy's blue-state radon heat as it poisons my truthful red blood. My stomach turns and I struggle to keep my bloody stomach acid from spilling out of my mouth, which smells like cavities. I look over to Billy, and it tastes like bits of my stomach, tailbone, and gums are in my mouth after retching all night from the bottom of my sour gut. I wince and say, "I do, too, Billy."

This opens the flood gates for William Demopheare, the bard of Boston, the royal Sir Hypo to the fat courts, the Billy Budd suspended / floating in the muddy homosocial political pond. Billy and his merry mutineers splash and swim around like children, as the voting multitude — the mob of alligators, piranhas, snakes, and scum chomp on their bits — and on each other, waiting, writhing, and circling just below the *truth* waiting for Captain Querelle and his first mate.

The watery truth. The consensus is an opaque dark pool with male bonding and voting scams controlled by black magic officers above the surface. The depraved rabble are on deck and at work on time, but subconsciously and financially they are under water, swimming, circling, and staring at William's fair young man's meaty legs dangling below the truthful surface as he salutes his Captain before he walks the plank. Billy's lamb-chop legs continue to float in the watery reptilian world and they look similar to butchered butter-chunks of red meat, or maybe there in the back... it's the silhouette of a hung man... swinging in the the wind at the end of a noose off a galleon's mast. The truth is that Billy is skewered and hung on a butcher's hook, twitting with flies, for sale at the market.

Homeroom Inspection

Our homeroom inspection starts graphically at the first desk closest to the classroom door and travels vertically for each of the four columns on some days and then horizontally across every row on other days, depending upon Ms. Appleton's moods. Homeroom Inspection is never arbitrary or capricious; it's always lineal and filled with mathesis. Through a Cartesian coordinate system, the homeroom inspection travels through multiple dimensions to me — the farthest point from origin O of the X, Y, and Z axes. The O origin of the schoolroom grid is at the threshold of our classroom door, and then down and out the door to Euclidean planes with lower dimensions into negativity. I'm in the back of the geometric classroom (coordinate - x4, y4), a higher dimension next to the window — an imaginary unit with no X, Y, or Z interceptions and almost off the classroom grid. Dear reader, I must admit I'm in a hyperplane and I'm good with that.

The homeroom inspection routine is rote with the comedy and tragedy of male and female sins predictable, similar, and preachy. The drama of yawning and stretching with cheerleader classmates sinfully celebrating our early morning ass-sniffing is broken only with emotional frailty and nervous breakdowns. This candid and frank oral exam for my classmates and me here in the guts of our Boston education is called, alternatively by us students, far from Ms. Appleton's ears, "The Dutch Oven Inspection," and my cheeky favorite, "My Zionista shit don't smell!"

Ms. Appleton is more than a check and balance. She is a floating concrete room in a dunk tank. Ms. Appleton is a cement floor, walls, and concrete ceiling that materialize and solidify around you as she tells you — and you agree, it's just powder and a little water, no worries. Ms. Appleton says, "Now children slowly, come back from the light now... slowly now, trust me... let the light go, it's always there when you need it. Come back from the light now, okay, slowly open your eyes."

The class comes to attention, and, as we do every day, we have homeroom inspection. The check-and-balance oral exam volley is on one's agenda, on one's purpose, a debate on one's *good-work*. Apple polishers beware!

My classmates and I usually tie the knot on our concrete shoes while talking, blabbering, gasping for air as we ceremoniously drown because our *good-work* (our lies and bullshit) is just sin with lipstick and cologne. Our silly super-ball agendas ricochet around our classroom and off Ms. Appleton's cement wall reality check at increasing, convoluted, and chaotic speeds. This abusive entertainment transpires only after we lightly pitch or serve our bouncy-bottom agendas to Ms. Appleton and our classroom. My classmates are far surpassing homework and grade requirements and thus everyone is building and volunteering time in vainglory charity or giftlove. These gift-love extracurricular activities only tease, heighten, and strengthen the ignorant and impenetrable walls of white-devil tribal society.

Ms. Appleton says, "Aaaagh, yes, the inner light. I hope everyone clearly saw the light. My light was especially dark today, a flickering candle light in a cold shanty somewhere with no heat and no wood."

Out of nowhere, Jen Patak blurts, "My light was warm and buttery like pancakes."

There were some snickers and rolling of eyes about Jen's comment, then Ms. Laura Kraven, by the door, sticks her neck up like a blue heron on tall legs — way above the waterline — and says, "Well, my light is always the holiest," looking around nervously at the class behind her with yellow and black birdeyes — glaring at us and daring us to contest her *holy* light.

And then Harold Answhich from the front of my row, along the windows, speaks like a rook — horizontally from across the front of the classroom — and puts *the light* matter to rest. Harold speaks like the lonely high court judge he will eventually become and says slowly and as romantically as possible for a despot dandy, "My light is Divine."

I think, yes, the walls of low self-esteem and egomania are high here in Boston. They compete for the "I'm better than you" carrot on a stick. This is a Boston 1650 education, an unsaid ivy-league education with class-warfare as a divider for the haves and have-nots, a poison ivy education of kissing the rod, paid for with indulgences for ministers-in-training to learn how to kill life, liberty, and the pursuit of happiness for the common man. These Harvard and ivy-league priests and rabbis are British redcoats in hiding; they perpetuate and solidify the royal chess end game. This Boston education creates Minister Winthrops and Governor Winthrops in order to keep America infiltrated, indebted, and led by wanna-be royal red-queens.

It's always very entertaining, yet terrifying, to listen to your classmates' mission in life. The fate of our *good-work* or our soul, with no words and only a look, Ms. Appleton will unceremoniously shatter and allow to slip through the thin ice of her small, but unfathomably deep lake called "The Truth."

Ms. Appleton, the lady of the lake, knows the truth and it did not set her free — it destroyed her; and so, she set out to warn or else destroy others with that same truth. Ms. Appleton knows she "Knew," but tells herself and the world around her she did not "Know." Just as all teachers teach because they cannot "Do," Ms. Appleton teaches us about the "Truth" because she had already been "Done," and can "Do" no more. She could not "Know," so therefore, in perfect Jewish / Catholic *modus operandi*, Ms. Appleton taught us about something she cannot *know, do,* and/or *understand.* Ms. Appleton is an impressed educator or a conscripted soldier with amnesia, marching in reverse against her own army, joyfully massacring her home, her family, and her students, forgetting completely what or for whom she's been teaching and killing.

Ms. Appleton is an eradicator. Her American steely silence is deadlier than the silver shimmer of moonlight reflected on the stalking Mohican's tomahawk on a snowy night. Just a look out the sides of Ms. Appleton's eyes would send my classmates into a blubbering, back peddling politician's path to the stockades in a tarred-and-feathered suit. Our Boston homeroom inspection with Ms. Appleton and my fifteen classmates is very amusing until the black tar is poured over one's own head.

I imagine the black hot tar flowing down my face into my mouth and down my shoulders. Black oil slowly pours down my breasts, back, and torso, over my powerful ass, down my thunder-thigh legs, calves, and ankles, and slowly covers my feet, puddling around me. I gag on the noxious black petroleum as the oil soaks up the white feathers dumped over my head. The feathers mingle with the oil the way a fly struggles and fights, stuck to fly-tape. My black and white feathers and boa will die similarly, fighting to look smart and alive but already dead.

Ms. Appleton, looking over to the door, says, "Good morning, Ms. Laura Kraven. Can you please explain to us this first day of June, 1650, your good-work here in America?"

I say to myself, I'll never laugh at another person's pain, I'll never forget this brilliant lie of mine. This lie allows me to catwalk to the stockades in my black-tar dress with white-feathered boa. Blinded by hot tar, with black gooey white feathers flying around and the taste of oil resin in my mouth, I skip along having fun with my feathery fashion, slipping in and out of poison-ivy style. I'm walking to the stockades, spitting feathers out of my mouth, wondering why this is Boston's "Civilized" Common Square. Then I imagine I'm chained to the stockades and a Providence classmate of mine, Catherine Laud, who once toasted our friendship "Separatists

Autumn Leaf Tarred and Feathered with a Boa

forever!" and "Have-Nots till Death!" comes along eating a large red apple.

Catherine recognizes me and says nothing. She stops before me and stares with a high-church attitude. She glares down on me sucking, spinning, and stripping the red skinned fruit from its white-core similarly to the way a wood lathe eats a block of wood. Catherine's ferocious machine-like sculpting of her apple crescendos and then she throws her gnawed-on, drooled-on, fruitless apple-core at me and says, "Hey, bad seed, why can't you conform?"

As I stretch my neck out scrambling, licking, and chomping at the apple-core scrap with my hands shackled behind my back, I'm now spitting out ants and cockroaches and kicking away rats, which are now my competition in this human race.

Within Puritan life here in Ms. Appleton's homeroom inspection, honesty is not the best policy. Loyalist-royalist performances that powder and perfume the truth to a pleasant degree always pass Ms. Appleton's ass-sniffer quite easily. These classmates of mine that are puffed-up with puffery: these lies, these sins of mine, that shade their *good-work* are sunk quickly to the bottom of her cold, cold, lake.

For me, my mother, Mary Dyer, and other Americans, this orthodox and graphed schoolroom is not where we will shine. With our undefined space, our natural and undefended hearts, and with our truth... our truth that we find it very hard to NOT tell... tell the sunny American truth.

CHAPTER 6

Black Knight Daughter — Religion is War

BLACK KNIGHT DAUGHTER

ront row and next to the door sits Ms. Laura Kraven. The white and bluish sharp heron rises up, feathers up — pleased in her flouncy French attire that was a fresh kill for her father.

Laura Kraven speaks, clearing her throat first: "Ahem, ahem. Good morning, Ms. Appleton, good morning, class. Unfortunately, my good-work with the needy Pequot Indian is put on hold today. For today Mary Dyer will perish and we need to pray that Mary repents! We must pray that we save her wicked soul before it is too late!"

Out on a falling limb and always lecturing, Laura this morning is tethered and tarped in a scaly light blue blouse with leg-of-mutton sleeves and an inverted fleur-de-lis collar. The shifty blue ribbon on top of her head is blowfish bait to lure the slow, stupid, and unimpressed loyalist to become the poisoned and impressed royalist. Ms. Kraven's bloody-brown satin petticoat perfectly matches her drawn-down eyes and gives her an undergrowth guidance she learns from the dark woods late at night.

Israel Wilkinson, who sits to the right of William and catty-corner to me, answers Laura's plea to save Mary's soul and

Laura Kraven

in a deep, cryptic tone says to the class, "Souls, my dear, cost money."

Laura, like most white-devil women, would never admit to, but often dreams of, visiting the woods in the obscurity of night. There is Laura, wandering around in the dark, deep in the woods, so she can maybe write her name with her thirsty blood in the wild man's large, hard, black, and leathery book. The large black book, with a skull and bones embossed on the cover, is clasped together with large iron rings. This warlock book contains all the names of men and women written in their own blood throughout time who desire to discuss art, anarchy, and adultery during the hour of the wolf. Conversely, these bourgeois slaves of the wild-man in the woods profess the opposite with a masonic oath during sunlight. This secret service for the orthodox and honorable Puritan is aplomb and soulless, their arrogance and confidence is their Achilles heel.

Laura clears her pious dry throat again, but doesn't need to speak because her father is on the Massachusetts Governor's Council and her performance is an inherited drudgery. Laura is a pledge of allegiance that everyone has to politely agree with because who in their right mind would cross the King, his black knights, or their black knight daughters?

Ms. Appleton is awkwardly no different and nods in vague approval as Laura continues, "Yes, Israel, souls do cost money, but they also need love!"

Israel and some others scoff and laugh in her lovely, very loving, incredibly lovely face, calling her out on her gift-love bait.

Laura Kraven continues, "I'm loving and working very hard with the Church of Boston's Pequot Indian mission. We are saving souls!"

Laura was conceived within the assembly line of procreating parents penny-pinching for cheap labor and the "Kraven Family Shield." The *nouveau riche* family shield that her parents proclaimed must not be tarnished or insulted — never really existed. Laura is an English privateer's daughter whose bread-and-margarine life was stolen from the unforgiving grim and treacherous waters along the American coast. Under British laws of inducement, Laura's father, Captain Kraven, is a government-licensed pirate and plunderer. Captain Kraven is pimping to be a shiny knight at the round table, but Captain Kraven and his whorish family appear too good to be true.

Through English law, the Captain is able to steal and loot ships and farms from the Dutch and French in America. Based out of Newport, Rhode Island and of, course, "Off-shore" in Bermuda, Captain Kraven sails his ship, *The Divine Drone*, and terrorizes the eastern seaboard of America from Boston down to swampy Virginia. He is a merry mercenary who carelessly steals and pillages on the hot-air winds of King Charles I and his charter to "Protect America, protect the King, and protect our family." These fraudulent winds fills Captain Kraven's sails and pockets.

With bribed blessings and heroic gift-love for the King, the Kravens enjoy the carefree and delightful spoils and booty of England's perpetual religious and economic social wars, wars the English ignited and continue to fan around the world in over thirty colonies. But most important historically is the Kravens' false god-love branded upon their shocked and awed victims. For the Kravens, the *The Divine Drone*'s victims deserved to be threatened and killed, even though Captain Kraven, with extremely advanced naval and military technology, is shooting fish in a barrel. This Kraven sin, this guilt made them germophobes. Clean Puritans look at everyone not playing their Jewish royalty games of King-craft and women-craft, and think those are Gentile germs or bugs to be bleached or stepped on. Captain Kraven, like his daughter Laura, would swing into a fiery rage to "Scrub the decks!" when fishy thoughts or bloody bug-splats landed on the Captain's ship deck, his mind, and/or any shiny Kraven boot.

Captain Kraven's excessive discipline and cleanliness are there to mask his guilt over so many easy wins, after so many easy lies, after so many easy kills. Captain Kraven and his way of life are immoral, ignoble, and he knows he and his family are living a fraud on borrowed time. Eventually this lie will drive the Captain, Laura, and all the Kravens mad.

Laura Kraven is a loyalist royalist's daughter and, just like Captain Kraven's wife, his property, his prostitute. Laura's hair is bleached a lemon-daisy bright yellow. It is curled and bowed in a baby-blue ribbon cut from swollen bodies in the darbies. Laura's eyes are cat-house quick and the color of water-logged dark oak. They are watery and brown like a sunken treasure chest that gets your attention, but on closer inspection hoping for a treasure — one encounters only a skull and crossbones crudely painted at the bottom of her looted and empty trunk. Laura, like her father, is a government-contracted mercenary. Ms. Kraven was conscripted to the standing-army known as family.

The grandfather clock ticked and tocked with its time and the Mayflower candle slowly floated over to Laura as she, with infinite futility, continued, "I'm teaching and educating the praying Indians at their re-education camp, at their concentrating camp, how to concentrate on our one true God, on our true capitalist God! The Pequots aren't used to being judged and God-fearing, but I've taught them how to play musical chairs (originally known as 'Going to Jerusalem'). The Indians were very confused because of the chairs (which they're not used to sitting on) and the sudden stopping of the music. They would yell, 'Tepahatu! Tepahatu! Tepahatu!' which means Stupid! Stupid! Stupid! after not being able to sit down.... This game didn't register with the Indians, so they kept on saying, 'Stupid! Stupid! Stupid!' We decided to not play music so my friend Robert (she motioned to her neighbor behind her,

Robert Testaigne) and I sang and then stopped the music / the lyrics suddenly — scrambling everyone to find a seat. We did the little J-Town ditty like a sweet duet! I think the musical chairs game 'Going to Jerusalem,' is a super way to teach the native terrorist about white-devil heaven, hell, and our God's true Divinity. Hit it, Robby:

Tickets... tickets everyone. Tickets....

Roly-poly - don't lose your seat! Roly-poly, don't lose your seat!

Cause we're going to Jerusalem! Cause we're going to Jerusalem!

Who's not a royal? Who's not holy? Who's disloyal? Who's unholy?

Roly-poly, don't lose your seat!

Who's not a Jewish royal? Who's not a holy Christian? Who's not part of our royal-holy family?

Someone's gonna die... someone's gonna lose... someone's going to hell....

Cause we're going to Jerusalem! Not just anywhere — next stop Galilee!

Does the devil dare? Does the devil see? You think this ride is free?

Someone's gonna die... someone's gonna lose... someone's going to hell....

Cause we're going to Jerusalem! It's our destiny!

Who's not a royal? Who's not holy? Who's disloyal? Who's unholy?

Roly-poly, don't lose your seat!

Tickets... tickets everyone! Tickets....

Laura and Robert finish their little limerick and Laura happily continues, "And we'd stop the music capriciously and arbitrarily and the Indians grabbed their seats; sometimes.... Well, rarely did the Indians grab their... actually the Indians never really grabbed the chairs, but I've taught the Indians they need to NOT shuffle their feet because they will LOSE their seat!"

Elizabeth Winterest, sitting next to me, asks, "Maybe the Indians don't want a white-devil moving target?"

Ms. Appleton speaks over Elizabeth and, in a blithe manner, asks, "Laura, how many Indians' souls have you saved from their terrorist ways by playing musical chairs on your way to Jerusalem?"

Laura answers with confidence, "Well, Ms. Appleton, after our musical trip to Jerusalem, my mother and I have a new family member called Nathaniel, who used to go by his Pequot Indian name of Sapan, which means Corn Mush. After Nathaniel's baptism and his musical-chairs christening he has chosen to go from Corn Mush to a gift from God for our chosen family!"

Laura's mother, Mrs. Katherine Kraven is loudly introduced in quiet parlors with whispers of Brahmin blood. However, Katherine, or "Catherine" as she was baptized, is really a French Catholic trying to be a German Anabaptist and has no idea what State, Colony, or Country she stands on. Mrs. Kraven semi-privately talks in tongues with her looking glass while dancing with snakes in her opulent townhouse on Beacon Hill that she never leaves. This Puritan circus is on view for all those Bostonians brave enough to keep their chins up in the middle of the night. These Boston night owls dare stand in the Common with their jaws down to their bellies watching Katherine Kraven writhing, chanting, and dancing with snakes. Standing there in the dark Common, innocent Bostonians are liable as witnesses or criminal, dependent upon the Kravens' business and political tides ebbing and flowing down at the docks, and, more important, in closed-door meetings at the State House.

Laura Kraven's lust for love is canonized as charity. The Kraven drones, including Laura, are in search of lovely profit from any commodities, such as real estate, sugar, coffee, chocolate, a white slave (an indentured servant), an African slave, an American Indian slave, or anything that can be bought and/or indebted, mastered, collared, taxed, "Loved," and/or chastised.

Laura continues, "Those Pequots can sure be problematic and persnickety! In fact, my father, the brave and heroic Captain Kraven, used to say, 'Why bother, Laura? There is no such thing as a praying Indian. Only the white English blood can understand the truths of the world and our one true God.' I'd say, 'Ohhh, Big-Daddy, you have to give love a chance.'"

The praying Indian who used to be the American Pequot Indian, the savage that found God, came to his Divine senses around 1640, after what has been called *The Pequot War for Freedom*, or the *Mystic Massacre*, dependent upon whether you're talking to the Pequot tribe or the Puritan tribe. I'll take a word from each tribe, so let's call it the *Freedom Massacre*. At the *Freedom Massacre* along the charming, mystic, and majestic Connecticut coast, five hundred Pequot Indians were surrounded and entrapped by the Boston Colony's Continental Army. They were given a multiple-choice question by General DeNamicks and his Minutemen. The General asked the Pequots to choose:

A- Concentrate at your camp on learning and practicing Judeo-Christian laws.

B- Be burned alive. Or,

C- Become a Bermuda or Bahaman sugar-cane slave.

Approximately four hundred and ninety-five Pequot Indians chose B, appreciating the sermon of the flame.... The Indians were toasted to a crisp, trapped in their longhouse. Burned alive, scorched alive rather than being forced to listen to the Christian Zionistas with their Jewish real estate pitch and their Catholic pay-to-play pitch. Of the five Pequots who did not go to the gospel of the eternal flame, one Indian accepted Laura Kraven's Puritan Christ, two Indians decided to be sent to Bermuda to pick sugar, and the last two Indians went on a hunger strike protesting their genocide, their holocaust at the hands of the white-devil. Laura lovingly continues to slither and hiss, concluding, "Converting the Pequots was mission accomplished, as we won over the terrorists' hearts and minds."

Despite the Kraven point of view, the rumor around Boston was that after General DeNamicks gave the Pequot Indians their multiple-choice "No Indian left behind" question, most Indians wanted to go back to the concentration camp in order to concentrate on being a Walofang capitalist and imperialist. The problem was that the Indians didn't understand they had to sign their names. The Indians had no written language before the English anglicized their unwritten language, so being told to "Sign your name" freaked the Indians out as something evil and against their spiritual religion.... The Indians had no idea what they were signing away, but knew they were probably being robbed. Debt was and always will be a deal with the devil. In good faith and in good spirit the Indians looked at the predatory white-devil telling them to "Sign your name on the dotted line." An incredible stalemate: because taking responsibility for a debt and/or a contract, and its legal leverage was either left far behind by the Pequot Indian (maybe centuries ago) or perhaps never learned. Like a yelled at and abused child, like a beaten child, like an ashamed and angry child the Indian rightfully ran away.

The General declared, "Burn them all!" but the second in charge, Lieutenant Rand, consulted with General DeNamicks and suggested the Indians only "Touch the pen" next to the "X" that the lieutenant wrote for each Indian. That sounded great in a win-win, white-devil, Walofang world, but after lining up almost five hundred Indians in front of a crude table along the enigmatic cliffs and stately shores of the Mystic River as it rushes into the Long Island Sound, only five Indians "Touched the pen." Four hundred and ninety-five of the Pequot Indians refused or were too frightened to dis-respect their Pequot world and their Turtle God laws. Four hundred and ninety-five Pequots in white-devil hell ran back into their longhouse hot-box and were torched and scorched alive by the first American Army.

Laura said, "My conversion of the Pequot Indians at their concentration and reservation camp is working miracles for freedom and democracy."

Elizabeth Winterst, to my right and a creep like me in the last row, sends out a truth-seeking missile and says, "Dear Laura, my vegetable garden is more of miracle than your *democracy* or *freedom*. My brussels sprouts and tomatoes are my Lord and Savior... my vegetables make your democracy and freedom look like a man-made scam."

Laura averts the botanical missile following her around our classroom by dancing around and blessing us more with man-made miracles "Nathan is a real Pequot hot-dog, and his four praying Indian friends at the 'Rez' are coming around to their senses by renouncing their terrorist ways and are going to be christened into our new Jerusalem on the hill any day now." Laura concludes her presentation of her good-works with a biological, chemical, and psychological attack. Laura says, "Can I hear an 'Amen'?"

Jen Patacki as usual pops up, then speaks up — chittering like a clueless chipmunk saying the worst thing at the worst time. Jen is in the last row of the second column and she has her back up against the wall like Elizabeth Winterest, Diana Molluston, and myself.

Jen sings out, "Amun, amun, amun! Laura, I agree, Amun to my Egyptian Big-Daddy! Amun, to my hot Sun-Ra man God! Amun, amun, amun!"

Everyone ignores Jen and shakes his or her head in disbelief at her incoherent sense of reality and civilization. The class mumbles an "Amen" that sounds like a long, hesitant lie or a tired and broken yawn. This break-beat "Amen" is because everyone in class knows that two Pequot Indians had already been sent to Bermuda as sugar cane slaves the week before and the other three Pequots were on a hunger strike, not eating in protest of being incarcerated. The Pequots claimed they were imprisoned on their own land, jailed in their occupied-zone, incarcerated in their Jerusalem, interned and caged in their America.

Brad Pining, sitting to the left of Laura in the first row, second column, turns, and over his shoulder says, "Class, ye enrage me. Are you kidding me with that Amen? Pray thee dear God, for you people are pathetic."

Continuing in lullaby tones, Laura lustfully eulogizes, "We are the chosen people! Written into the Bible, we are too big to fail / too proud to fail because we are doing the King's and God's Divine work. Please let us love our one and only true God, our one and only awesome God. Oh, awesome God, thank you for your light. Please, God, bless my classmates and save them with your light! Please save yourselves, classmates, and give me an Amen!"

Laura, the seducer, with gift-love just tried to inoculate the white-devil politicians, magistrates, high priests, rabbis, and lawyers from ever being charged with crimes against humanity in this material world. The Kravens and the parasites that troll these despots as their service industry or subject industry may have a "Covenant of works" (money, family, power) here in this world, but it could be their eternal damnation in the next.

Brad Pining, revved up, inspired, and, looking deep into Laura's eyes, says, "Amen, lovely Laura, Amen! And so be it, awesome God! So be it, with the great wind. So be it, great invisible one! So be it verily to our dying day. Amen, lovely Ms. Kraven! Amen."

I think about Laura's new family member, Nathaniel, who has a lot of leftover food and rum because the two remaining Indians' hunger strike allowed Nathaniel, or Mr. Corn Mush (as the boys called him) to gobble up the scraps of his Indian nobility, dignity, and ancestry. Corn Mush's doggy-bag life after three glasses of rum is Puritan puree or Abrahamic slop. Nathaniel, rightfully so, is now a born-again Mass-hole, a cannibalizing Christian on his way to Jerusalem, a Jew wailing at his wall, a Muslim on his way to Mecca, an apostle of pump or perhaps even a dead deacon of dump. Mr. Corn Mush of course, like all orthodox Puritans, has gotten quite priestly, proud, and porky.

All the while, William is beaming and nodding in approval at Laura Kraven's Parisian performance from his cheap seat in front of me. William respects Roman Catholic pomp and circumstance, but knows of a more pure, purer (not Puritan) but simpler pilgrim way. Regardless, Billy from Boston, the loyalist whipping boy, is too scared and intimidated to say or do anything about the horror of society's two-faced religious control-frauds. He is too scared, too much a coward to fight, so there is Bill with no will applauding — playing monkey-see, monkey-do. He tries to smile, but his face is upside down. Billy is canned, metallic, formed, and only slightly thawed enough to bleed or cry for help with lame jokes and excuses. Billy hangs there, lifeless, on our classroom applause track.

I lean over toward Billy and ask, "Oh, Billy, you're not falling for a Kraven, are you?"

Billy double-deals back, leaning backwards, and says, "You gotta be in it to win it!" as he practically falls out of his sadomasochistic school desk. The domineering wood and metal school desk and seat is bondage designed only to cripple, demean, or chastise the child. The iron and wood school desk is designed to enforce discipline and never educate us, yet Billy not only seems to enjoy being constrained inside his desk, but he submits emotionally and erotically to playing and posing within it.

Ms. Appleton's response isn't as applauding as Billy's. She asks, "Ms. Kraven, are you creating a *New Jamestown* for America? Didn't the English in 1610 learn that those Virginia Cavaliers are not in the 'Old Dominion,' or the *New Dominion*, but in the *New Reservation*? Is Corn Mush your new Pocahontas? Is Corn Mush part of our promised Jerusalem city on the hill for us? Are the Separatist pilgrims in Plymouth part of our promised Jerusalem city on the hill? Are the Separatists' children protected by your Puritan orthodox God?"

Laura is not ready to go skating on the thin ice of defining the difference between a Puritan pilgrim and a Separatist pilgrim in America, but there is Laura Kraven starting to spin and slide out of control — a sloppy pirouette of paranoia. Laura folds her arms in front of her in defense, but she suddenly gives in to the earth and gravity beneath her again and she has to give; she has to swirl and twirl with it, not against it. Instead, Laura fights the twirl and swirl of the earth and she is sent flailing, waving her arms around, trying to get her balance. Ms. Appleton has pushed Laura off the safe shore of religious delusion and psychosis and onto the slushy, lightly frozen lake of water called The Truth.

"I, I, I, I don't know," Laura bleats and pleads.

Ms. Appleton questions Laura, our class, and the world: "Are we not all children of God seeking salvation?"

Ms. Appleton's lake expands into a frozen tundra and there

is Laura in the middle of it, still lecturing, index finger always pointing the way to the bottom of the *Truth*.... The frozen lake thaws and cracks aloud with Laura Kraven's weighty *good-work* that has the weight of lead. Gaps of black water appear between ice floes. Laura's ice starts to splash below the surface as she is seesawing up and down and about to capsize. Laura Kraven tries to fill the black religious gaps that are expanding and fragmenting around her — Laura's good-work is an icy puzzle coming undone! Black watery holes spread open molecularly in jagged fashion across the shattered white lake called The Truth. Laura, still seesawing on her iceberg float, looks down in fear at the black holes all around her. These holes, as big as new galaxies, open Laura up to new universes.

Ignoring reality, a terrified Laura exclaims, "Yes, Yes, Ms. Appleton, but those terrorists are blasphemous heretics — they lost their seats, the music stopped — they don't count — they are losers now."

Ms. Appleton, feigning confusion, asks, "What terrorists are you talking about? The Pequot Indians? The Powatans? The Palashtus? The Paugusetts? Or maybe, Laura, you're talking about the feared wolf people — the Mohegans? No, not that terrorist? Oh... maybe the French terrorist or your Quaker neighbor Mary Dyer, whom we will hang in less than an hour or two? Ms. Kraven, please enlighten us — is everyone who disagrees with your Jewish and Catholic imperialism as religion a terrorist?"

Ms. Kraven bleats and stutters like a sheep being dragged to slaughter: "Bu, bu, but, the, they, they, but they have no allegiance to our King, our God, and they mock our bi, bib, bibl, Bible."

Ms. Appleton laughs to herself and mutters very quietly, "That sounds like salvation to me. And then in a louder voice, she counters, "Isn't it so that we are all children of God and he that judgeth will be judged, Ms. Kraven?"

Laura is now a shivering poodle with a pink tutu clinging to a floating ice raft. She was at first dancing, maybe skating, and is definitely now sinking into the frigid and watery cold truth. Laura's blood is frozen: she has gone out too far out on the thin ice of religion, loving the Other for profit. Ms. Kraven, with the sun setting behind her, has become a French poodle silhouette. Laura is an overdue bill not paid, with an extraordinary high interest rate and penalties. Laura is being enveloped beneath the cracked ice like an old debt, a sacrifice that needs to be paid in order for our homeroom tribe to move on. Laura is now a tongue-tied red-neck — she is an ice house sitting half-sunk in the frozen lake. A "No Trespassing" sign in her eyes and on the front door of the ice house states the obvious as empty liquor bottles float around, clinking together around her sinking and morose ice house. Laura and her good-work were once a good house in which she walked on water and fished for the truth. It was built upon ice and water and now is suddenly useless — just as useless, silent, and silly as walking on water.

Laura looks around nervously, secretly hoping the ice float she sits on will melt quickly in order for her to drown quietly. On the contrary, there isn't enough sun in Laura Kraven's mind, heart, or soul to melt anything. It is always longing and stormy in Ms. Kraven's mind. Laura imagines her coming drowning is not by consumption, but by intelligent design. My class and I are safely on the dry lakeshore, glowing and gawking. We only hear the sound of Laura Kraven's bones, like the ice, slowly cracking, moving, and going glacial. It is lovely — for us on the dry shore. Ms. Kraven is eternally stuck in The Truth — night to day and day to night: Kraven is thawing and splintering, cracking, thawing, and then dripping.... Ms. Kraven night to day and day to night is melting, dripping, running, then freezing again. Day to night — night to day: melting, cracking, expanding, stretching again, then freezing again... Laura Kraven is an icy fruition.

Brad Pining clears his throat and throws a life preserver to Laura and says, "Pardon me, Ms. Appleton, the London Company doesn't have time for terrorists, heretics, pygmies, and pagans. Please stop your blasphemy and finish Laura's prayer with an Amen, as a good teacher should."

Ms. Appleton is looking down at her desk, allowing time and silence to do her heavy lifting, but she is physically and mentally incapacitated by Brad's threat. After a long moment of stillness, with a mixture of pity and disgust, she raises her head and, and in a slight drawl, with a very tired blues rhythm gives Laura Kraven what she has asked for.

She says, "Aaaaaameeeaaaeennnnn"

Religion is War

I look out at the view through my classroom window, which faces south over Corn Hill and down towards Boston Common. On top of the hill there is a weeping willow where my mother used to have her prayer meetings with the other free-grace Separatist pilgrims. As rumored, those sisters of mercy, those *friends*, those freaks, those brothers and sisters of free-grace still meet there to this day in the dark of night and are supposedly starting again to separate from Minister Winthrop's Church of Boston and the Bank of England. I cannot get involved anymore; it's too much — and I'm tired. As I said earlier, maybe American men will have a Great Awakening and start to listen to enlightened women in a hundred years or so.

Unceremonious, there is Boston out my window, foreboding as a pile of ash — an American gothic backdrop supplanted by the weeping willow that sways like a careless rainbow. The green jellyfish willow tree with finger-like spring leaves sways like tentacles of sea-grass underwater. Pea-green leaves with bamboo stems the color of a sharp mustard cut this Puritan grey humid morning to reveal a possible *laissez-faire* (hands-off) life. A crying drum tree, the weeping willow breathing rhythmically to and fro, marching in a slow dirge to its own drum song.

The crying drummer. Chilly, frosty for a moment; warm, then hot and thoughtful — a breeze that exposes the underside of the willow's tentacles. Leaves silver, green, purple, and sincere with peppermint sage crystals. The weeping willow, lively again — funny and whimsical! Always detached — always in the air — floating... then suddenly icy and aloof again. This American rhythm keeps one moving and entranced around the weeping willow no matter the sunlight, moonlight, or massacre of the month. The weeping willow on Corn Hill is a meeting house for those united under one natural religion with the most beautiful church steeple and frescoes in our universe — the constantly changing sky! Our ever-changing sky painted endlessly with cerulean blues, violets, and purple blacks that tirelessly debate infinite wisps and swaths of white cotton clouds that our Creator paints all day and all night just to keep us on our toes.

The homeroom inspection starts to roll down Sin Boulevard... picking up speed. Behind Ms. Kraven is Robert Testaigne, commonly called Bob because there is certainly not a Robert nor Bobby in his soul — just a bob. Bob has courted Laura Kraven since they were childhood sweethearts. Like Laura, he comes from a French family with heavy Catholic loyalist leanings even though they are supposedly Huguenot emigrants. William and the boys call him "Father Bob, missionary spy for the papist devil," or "Choir-boy for State St." Bob and his family were the runt of the tribe that couldn't decide how to achieve power here in America and instead incessantly sang everyone an American patriotic gift-love song in order to prove, or, possibly disprove, their loyalty. Bob Testaigne's patriotism, vain hubris, and ignoble status are based on stepping on and treating all neighbors on the boulevard poorly. I think sin and its seven deadly felonies are obnoxious and obvious — they are unnatural and come from an irrational animal.

Bob Testaigne's coffee-colored eyes are glossy puddles that fit well with his twitching lips at the bottom of his chin. His nose, which he talks through, is like a large piece of pie slovenly thrown on his face. Bob stands up in a feeble manner and straightens his burgundy French-cut suit that would look better with Father Bob not in it.

Father Bob minces no words and cuts to the chase. "Dear classmates, my friend Paul was a Pequot Indian warrior who has buried his hatchet!"

Bob is shrunken and lost within his fine suit... the lightly striped trouser suit outshines, upstages, and overshadows Bob. The inanimate, soulless, and winey suit looks smarter and more alive than gumshoe-boy Bob. He has the aesthetic and spiritual presence of a chewed-up corn husk in the bottom of an empty garbage can. Bob has a vacant strange smell, like that of a coffin or an unused front door: built, but not utilized — lonely, awkward, yearning to be used, but abandoned and locked. Bob smells like the dead-air vestibule behind this locked front door. Bob is nevermore a boy or man within intelligent design — nevermore a home within a dead house. If Bob were just standing there buck-naked he would be more honorable and believable. Bob's suit fits, but it is as if he can't or shouldn't even try to fashion and work that outfit. Bob, the lost shepherd, is shrunken and drowning in French collars, French pleats, and French cuffs that dwarf him. Watching Bob is reminiscent of viewing from a distance a lost man walking in the swampy Fens, or maybe a climber in the foggy French Alps — a speck on the side of a mountain.

Bob continues, "Paul is now a born-again Christian and family member of our 'Fresh-Air Family' cultural exchange with the Pequots."

Robert Testaigne

In truth the "Cultural exchange" is an English imperialist visa-for-cheap-labor exchange that has transformed a Pequot Indian called "Irak" in his Pequot language and turned him into "Paul," an intern or a Gal-Friday grocery clerk for Bob's parents at their General Store.

Bob Testaigne and Laura Kraven are apostles and disciples of the existential pump-and-dump. They are hypergamy-whammies who envy their poison, their downfall, their employee, their interns, and their Master / King more than themselves. Respecting the new interns as "New friends," Bob and Laura have to "Friend down," punch-down and/or hypogamy-slammy down in order to elevate the interns up. It is reverse psychology friendship, predatory friending, and/or gift-love in order to be liked or loved — and therefore elevated once again. But, most important, at the same time that Bob and Laura are conveniently being masked as noble sprigs filled with charity and compassion, they are truthfully and subconsciously un-masked as trolling pariahs.

Bob's new *friend*, Paul, is also a native or a local with influence and many other low-caste *friends* that could potentially increase Bob's imperialist *friend* network. Bob *likes* this fashionable viral disease as a manic-depressive slave likes being beaten down emotionally and/or physically by their Master. For Bob, Laura, and all white-devil predatory *followers*, these interned *friends*, these concentrating *friends*, enable them to orchestrate a slow-motion holocaust or a handicapped genocide. For fashionable leeches and lovable parasites like Testaigne and Kraven with their gift-love addiction, the hypergamy-whammy high is the sweetest fix.

Bob continues sliding around like a spastic scaredy-cat meowing. "Our new *friends* are learning the English language and are becoming a valuable part of our God-fearing civilization."

Bob's ill-conceived fashion is solidified and accessorized when Father Bob opens his mouth. A tinny, brittle voice filled with sarcastic malice and pious commandments sings with a French lilt and blinking, light brown, boggy eyes. His passion is rarely if ever seen and at its most bloodthirsty — bringing up the rear of Catholic-like religious pageants, holding up priests' garments as an altar boy.

Parroting Laura from a few moments earlier, Bob expounds on the pacifying of the Pequot Indians out of their wampum belts and into America's chastity belt. He says, "The Pequots can be a valuable part of our civilization and the Fresh Air Visa exchange program is just the way these adorable primates should integrate into our community!"

The sun pops into our classroom and Bob's calico cat eyes became a muddy yellow. The colors contrast nicely with his thick mane of black and brownish streaked hair like that of a dirty little dog just woken up. His body is short and squat like a piglet hamster. Bob holds his hands close to his chest or heart and scratches, massages, and sharpens his claws constantly within his Huguenot hovel. Bob's work-shoe paws ground him well and give away his pouncing and stalking qualities. Bob, like all cats, never looks at others with any respect and with disdain, a pink, turned-up Quebecois nose, and curt teeth, Bob is a French feral pussy.

Bob is working and hoping one of his Catholic brown-nosing bets will run through and pay off with Divine interest. Bob's good-work is a boy soprano, a polyphony soliloquy, a choir boy sonnet lamenting the missed opportunity for the Catholic church, Ms. Kraven, and Pappa Pope to go on a *ménage a trois* picnic without the threat of mosquitos, ants, or venereal diseases. This trembling lost French puppy is usually slapped shut by Ms. Appleton, especially when Bob's blubbering and drooling hit Ms. Appleton's wide-plank wooden floor — a red-oak floor — wide and hard with frozen dark knots that are well sanded, oiled, and dust-free.

In counterpoint to Bob's blubbering, Laura Kraven appreciates Bob's tithing, tooting, and rooting from her rear. She pleasantly grinds against his nasally French flute voice as Bob bumbles along: "The savages in the woods, and the questioning monsters in the trees, with their unholy thoughts, have been washed away with our love and the Fresh-Air work exchange program!"

Lawrence Randison slips in sarcastically, asking Bob, "Where's Mr. Corn Mush, Bob? Where's your pygmy pal? Where's Paul Irak, the grocery clerk? Mushy and Pippy sleeping it off?"

Harold Answhich says to the class like an omnipresent God, "Follow the rum!"

Paul the Indian Pequot, or Pip as he is sometimes called by the soda-jerks in town, used to be called Irak in his native language, but his new Christian name is Paul. Bob Testaigne had been a "Baptismal sponsor" to Irak, helping him turn from a peaceful Indian into Paul — the angry Christian drunk. Paul sits behind Bob when he is "Presentable" and nods obediently with vacant eyes, never speaking a word. Pip just keeps his nose in his Bible, as if he could read English, but the Indian can't read English nor speak English. Paul, Irak, or Pip, the American control-fraud, can only laboriously, yet sometimes eloquently and with tremendous fanfare, grunt a yes or no, which turns Bob and Laura into hyper children over-clapping at a staged and lame magic show.

Ms. Appleton, speaking mostly to Lawrence and Harold, says, "Oh please, hecklers, can we at least be original?"

Then acting slightly annoyed, Ms. Appleton looks over our class and then looks over to Bob and asks, "Where is Paul, Bob? Wouldn't it be nice if Paul Irak could tell us these wonderful things about himself? How are your English lessons with him? I've never heard him speak a sentence of English."

Bob says, "My father is working this week specifically on teaching him to speak."

Elizabeth Winterest, sitting next to me in the bleacher

seats, snips in brightly, "That's funny, Bob. I saw Pip and your
father's other slaves clearing land and fencing for more pig-
pens around your General Store a little after dawn this morning." In a faux royal tone, she adds, "Nice to see the early birds
digging at dawn for their worms, ain't it, Bobby?"

Bob moans and growls slowly over at Elizabeth in a tired
tone, "We've all got chores to do, Ms. Winterest, especially
those of us that don't have servants like you do."

I realize the Boston Elders and Elect always keep a few
able-bodied friends. Interns? Employees? Independent
Contractors? Or possibly just polite slaves earning an un-liv-
able wage from the white-devil high priestesses who need a
little extra help in the kitchen or with the landscaping. Paul
and the other Pequots are told to be excited they were born
again, alive, and earning a livable white-devil wage. The
Pequots can't or won't understand math nor English, but
they understand they are surreptitiously being attacked and
robbed and they don't know what to do.

Bob describes Paul's christening and the baptized new
life of Irak as if he were "*God*," or, insidiously, as if he has an
inside angle with *God* or a monopoly on *God*. Bob's lust for his
"Personal God" isn't religious faith; it is mommy-issues-bur-
ied-under-puppy-love psychosis and then wrapped in tribal
mass delusion. I comprehend again here with Bob's *good-work*
that religion is lust for power, religion is spiritual bullying
— religion is a heavenly hypergamy-whammy. Religion is
revenge on the unhappy past you cannot change, and religion
is war on your unhappy future you refuse to see because you
know you're too idle, lethargic, and slothful to ever change.

Bob concludes with determination: "The light is with us!
God is with us! Feel the light!" He turns our classroom and our
life into a patriotic wake and a garish witch-hunt that all Jews
and Catholics excel at. The Mayflower candle floats away from
Bob — the candle seems scared of Bob. Bob's good-work is a
crass and feminine fairy tale for an unknown, abstract God,

yet Bob has the most dazzling French collar and French cuffs that prove my first point.

Bob says in a louder, sterner voice, "The light is with us classmates! God is with us! Can I get an Amen?"

In between the ticks and tocks of Puritan time a few "Aaammeenns" fall from the sun-shower Boston sky, approximating icy hail bouncing around on the summertime street, looking for their oli-poly God. The hail sounds like Mexican jumping beans popping around sporadically with no rhythm or point — bouncing, clinking, clunking, and melting away as alien thoughts or meteors coming from a thundering Nothing in outer space. These icy, freak-of-nature *Amens* melt on the hot big-science blacktop before the *Amen* raindrops become self-aware and realize that they are only frozen water — and not angels from heaven. These beautiful *Amens*, these jumping beans hailing from the sky, hauling electricity and water! The small lonely *Amen* pee-puddles from hysterical, delusional, and cloudy people evaporate quickly as the dashing and bright Massachusetts sun peeks through for a moment or so.

Ms. Appleton is looking down, not paying attention. She then looks up past Bob with the million-mile stare all happily incarcerated hypocrites have. Skyler Appleton, the angry librarian, vacantly consoles Bob by saying, "Thank you, Bob, for turning on the lights! Amen."

With the fashionable *lights* now on from multiple dimensions in our classroom, I think of the third letter I got from Mary Dyer also describing her new *light*. Her second letter was from Providence, Rhode Island, about sing-songs and plans to leave Providence, but this third letter was from northern England in 1648. I was living with the Indians in New Netherland and the Dutch trader Jan Van Throgg had brought it to our Lenape tribe. It is amazing how horrible, yet homey and sincere, America can be.

Mary Dyer wrote that she was once again hanging with

Henry Vane in Lincolnshire and also crossing through Leeds on the northern flipside, getting high on shaking and quaking with George Fox and friends in Lancashire. Prominent in those Lancashire hills of England there's a castle called Swathmore Hall. It was an enlightened hotspot in the Lake district where people went further into free-grace and their *inner light*. Mary, Henry, and George were friends. From that free-grace friendship an *inner light* was created. Their *inner light* became a guiding light, a society, a civilization — their *inner light* became the Quaker religion.

In her letter, Mary explained her new strange religion:

"Women can be ministers and there is absolute doctrine about NO church / synagogue and State self-dealing." Mary explained also that Quakers held onto our original Protestant position of NO standing-armies. This Separatist and Quaker political position was in staunch opposition to the Puritans raping and pillaging the New England countryside with their might making right. The Puritans' arms race in Boston and Hartford, Connecticut — which was being run by Governor Winthrop and his son — was quickly replacing the human race. The Quakers wanted nothing to do with the Puritans' hyper-tension manifesto of "Kill, or be killed." Mary wrote that "Quakers believe there are NO Elect and NO Elders; everyone can talk to and be saved by their Quaker God. Everyone has free-grace; everyone is respected as a society of friends! "

Mary, in the letter, ranted, "Puritans in Massachusetts tormented the Quakers by cutting off their noses and ears to spite their faces." Mary wanted to come back to Boston and "Force their bloody Puritan hand." She wanted to fight the orthodox Elders and Elect just the way my mother, Anne, had. They both civilly disobeyed and planted civil disobedience in America. Mary wrote:

The inner light or free-grace Awakening was blinding and/ or disturbing to some, but for us (the Quakers) this striking,

*shaking, or quaking disturbance is our keel — anarchy and then
an Awakening is the foundation of our meeting-house. Quakers
also reject organized religion and state, they reject hierarchy and
monarchy — and underneath it all: Quakers are just hardwork-
ing spiritual folks waiting for a Revelation.*

It seemed the more Mary described the Quakers the more
she described the Lenape Indian tribe I had just been ransomed from.

Mary wrote eloquently about the shaking and quaking
chaotic dancing and singing at their Quaker meetings. She
also deeply meditated about the Quakers' quiet conversations around Jesus the troublemaker, Jesus the bastard, Jesus
the hater. These lesser-known Scriptures reminded Mary of
meetings my mother had as a mid-wife and preacher before
she was exiled from Boston. Mary wrote how she continued
my mother's opening line and mantra of "Well, folks, I'd like
to say first off I don't know about you, but I ain't never met an
Elder here... Have you?" Mary wrote that this ice-breaker to
open her meetings — this "*Elder*" devaluation — was a major
foundation of her new Quaker religion. This disrespect for
the unnatural Puritan and their authority was Mary's guiding light or *inner light* now.

I was kind of getting mad and still do sometimes when I
read this third letter. I think, "Wow, good for Mary and her
royal la-di-da friends going *hippy* back in the safe northern
hills of our motherland... how adorably bourgeois! Hallelujah
and Amen for these lonely clouds dancing with the daffodils!"
Nevertheless, far from the romantic Lakeland, back here in
the back-wash of another English colony gone wild — America
is *the* royalist's / loyalist's and religionist's pay-to-play Puritan
playground.

Mary signed this third letter as if this were the zenith of
her life, and she wrote:

Don't fear the past; your mother's good-work and your family's tragedy was not in vain.

Joyfully I go!

Sincerely,

Mary Dyer

CHAPTER 7

Is Your Daddy a Wounded Warrior or a Wounded Murderer? — Because God Told Me

IS YOUR DADDY A WOUNDED WARRIOR OR A WOUNDED MURDERER?

t is hard to be joyful in the classroom as the shifty homeroom inspection morning moves on to a decrepit and mean-spirited boy. Outside the schoolhouse, the morning spring wind has blown away the sun and the wind is now gusting and blowing itself out. The harsh spring breeze of New England rattles the wooden windows in unison and a thin ghostlike draft whistles for a long lithe moment. Samuel Payneson stands slowly, as if about to start a dance routine. Samuel enjoys the Puritan time; the tick-tock cadence gives him an anxious rhythm as he moves like a well-oiled pendulum cranked up with gears locked into gears. Within this long warlock silence, Samuel's geared-up robotic arms remain rigid and crossed against his boxy body. His feet, one resting on a heel, the other on his toes, are relaxed, as if he is a puppet about to dance a jig.

Samuel, in a slow earthy baritone, says "Good Morning, class," as a blackbird flies into the window next to me drunk on spring fever. The feathery sad thud smashing into a glass wall perfects Samuel's dire "Good morning." Samuel never

Samuel Payneson

acknowledges the dead or dying blackbird, even though Julianne Bequeath and Nancy St. Clair nearby yelp in fright. Elizabeth Winterest, seated next to me, chuckles at the weak-hearted ladies and looks over at me.

The class also looks around back towards me and not at the feathery blood-splat high on the pane of glass; everyone assumed I was making a break for it out the window. Ms. Appleton says to Julianne and Nancy, "Don't be such scaredy-cats; it's just nature running its course."

I think about nature's course as I watch red blood, pink guts and bird-brains mixed with black feathers slowly running / sliding down the window next to me.

Samuel Payneson is the son of Admiral Payneson, who lives up north near Salem. Admiral Payneson was one of the leaders of the Freedom Massacre in Mystic, Connecticutt. He is a merchant marine who helped capture and burn the non-combatant Pequots in retribution for being in the way of the white-devil's *Manifest Destiny*. Admiral Payneson's capitalist delight and pleasure in killing come from his royal Bible. Within this capitalist control-fraud that lacks any sense of humanity, Admiral Payneson and now his son Samuel Payneson live as *Divine* murderers. They were Divine social warriors here in 1650 on the new "Holy crusade," which is the same as the old holy crusade.

I remember Samuel from pre-school days; long ago in Boston 1638, he was a dangerous ricochet rocket from day one. Samuel picked apart Daddy-long-legs spiders, and then put the still-moving legs on boys' and girls' necks or down their pants — that was our pre-school education and initiation to the "Payneson" world. Samuel, or just "Payneson," as he was often called, would be laughing in our faces, holding the dismembered legs as they still writhed and twitched. He would try to kiss and lick the moving spider legs, thrilling himself into an ecstatic frenzy.

Perhaps because of these psychological problems, Samuel the inquisitor and torturer got hit with the ugly stick. Aesthetically, Samuel could have been ugly Catholic or ugly Jewish. Catholicism is Jewish lite for those not that spiritually violent and for those not that metaphysically ugly. Catholicism is evolved Judaic dread and guilt, yet it is still dreadful and guilty. Samuel the holy crusader can barely hide his decrepit spirit one or two parasitic chromosomes above a vulture — Payneson is a grievous blob on the go.

Samuel starts as he does every morning: "My name is Samuel Payneson, son of Admiral Payneson, the great and brave wounded warrior of The Pequot War for Freedom who has served our Country, our King, and our God."

Samuel looks like a balding banker at sixteen or perhaps an indignant antique dealer looking over his shoulder for that antiquity or penny that got away. Samuel never got over that loss, never got over being a son, a brother, a human. He is a commanding five-feet nine or ten inches tall, but is cut down to size and discounted because of his dark grey frog-like eyes that are always rolling around in opposite orbits. The dark-star windows to his soul could have resulted in his mother's lack of nurturing and/or his scratched-and-dented DNA. Regardless, Samuel cannot stay in control. Samuel smells like holystone and exploded gunpowder because he devotes so much time scrubbing his father's decks and practicing his cannon aim on his father's warships. Samuel's fingernails are always dirty from scraping his loose cannon down to the bone as he smolders and aims about. Samuel's round pink head, pointy nose, and frog-like jaw mix well with his dirty grey Mandarin attire made of Chinese linen. Dear reader, trust me that I will draw out this stiff linen suit because I can feel the encrusted canon blast and it feels like rough duck cloth on bare skin. This suited Samuel well because when he gets uncomfortable he will twitch, fidget, and dance about with his arms crossed and with that god-forsaken Payneson grin.

Samuel does not have an agenda — he has his father's agenda. Samuel's homeless voice was out of tune, angry and dying, as he continues, "The Indians do not need to be converted to Christianity, they do not need cultural exchanges — the Indians need to be wiped off the face of the earth. You cannot get blood from a stone, nor civilize the terrorist savage."

Brad Pining, in the first row of the second column, speaks up, sounding like a metal rake scraping on a rock in the quiet mist as he slowly drawls out, "Ammeeeeaan Payneson, Ammmeeeeeaaann!"

Samuel voraciously loses control of himself when he stands in front of our class and tries to communicate. His bitter contempt for humanity is a watered-down madness that speaks so quickly, so thoughtlessly, that most of our class would rather see Samuel draw his rapier blade and do battle with his school-desk — which he sometimes does. I imagine that's what my classmates are visualizing as we listen to Samuel, because paying attention to him and/or trying to communicate humanely with Samuel is too painful to watch or experience. When Samuel opens his mouth, his voice sounds as if a young man is fencing with a metal can in a lonely alley. Samuel's chattering voice is sharp and argumentative. When the spent gunpowder smell dissipates, a whiff of Samuel feels like garbage juice up your nose and in between your toes on a hot summer day. Samuel's echo chamber is a violent smirk and his quickly dissipating blond hair is an old yellow broom. His desperate voice sang sideways because Samuel knew we didn't want to listen to him. This homeroom humiliation was a homeroom inspection that only boiled his vexed bile at a faster roll.

Ms. Appleton, in faraway thought, says "Amen for the savage!" as if wanting to understand the "Savage," and perhaps furthermore is still in awe of the savage.

Samuel, as usual, disrespectfully disagrees with Ms. Kraven and Bob Testaigne in front of him, who believe the back door to Jerusalem heaven in Massachusetts is the conversion of the savage terrorist with the Bible. Samuel Payneson, on the other American hand, believes in the other Jewish and Catholic white-devil conversion tool: the axe. The combination of the two — the Bible with psychological and financial debt and the axe with bloody heads rolling around — are the two faces of English and American theater. The good cop / bad cop with pump-and-dump betrayal is pure white-devil kabuki worthy of the Globe back on the Thames.

Samuel continues his war dance. "This week, we march on the Iroquois Nation, which has been terrorizing our Hartford, Connecticutt, brothers and sisters. The Pequot Indians are savage terrorists and we put them in their place. God has shown us who is pure — who is right. Now the Iroquois Nation must continue to feel the wrath of God. With your prayers and blessings, we will destroy these terrorists. The Continental Army will drive these terrorists from our promised land as the Bible has foretold."

Samuel rests and recesses with his litigating axe and takes off his white lawyer's wig, using the *law* as a weapon. The tick-tock gears of the clock inflate Samuel into a religious inquisitor, as he puts on his skull cap and starts to eulogize, quoting Biblical tick-tock case law. Before Samuel speaks the murderer prayer he slowly and majestically lights an imaginary holy candle in his church or synagogue that is more of a fuse to an explosion or the countdown to a detonation than a prayer to a *God.* Tick-tock, tick-tock, tick-tock... the Mayflower candle slowly flickers and starts to suffocate as if there is a sudden lack of oxygen in our classroom as Samuel opens his mouth and starts to speak:

> *"From the Book of Numbers, they put every male to death.... The sons of Israel took the Midianite women captive with their young children, and plundered all their cattle, all their flocks and all their goods. They set fire to*

the towns where they lived and all their encampments...
Then, when they took the captives, spoil and booty to
Moses..., Moses was enraged.... 'Why have you spared the
life of all the women? So kill all the male children. Kill also
all the women who have slept with a man. Spare the lives
only of the young girls who have not slept with a man, and
take them for yourselves.'"

Payneson is very proud of himself with his Judeo-Christian case-law prayer for neighbors, enemies, new mommies, and, inadvertently, their very own children. This is the Biblical Attack, Divide, Starve, and Profit (ADSP) Prayer for Abrahamic assholes around the world. Back in New England, Samuel obviously has some virgin Seneca squaws and colorful Cayuga wampum beads in his own gun sight. Nothing is better for a standing-army's *esprit de corps* than *spoils* and *booty!*

Tell angry men that there is hot dinner and bitches just beyond that *hill* and they will kill to take that hill. The Bible, or Jewish and Catholic Imperialism for Dummies, is a clear read: Go, go, go! The military science and the big green light to go rape and pillage your neighbors, their children, and, in poetic justice, your own children, are crystal clear — it's Biblical. If this text was written anywhere besides the Bible, it would be an admission of a hate crime, a genocide, a holocaust, and crimes against humanity; but in 1650, it is a religious and patriotic pretext and incentive to be the Elect and/or an Elder.

The forbearance and subterfuge to scheme as a religionist or capitalist are identical. All Abrahamic religions are Neg-Am Jams: premeditated, predatory, and punitive. Alas, to Divide, and Starve... after the Attack, is the most duplicitous and religious of the white-devil traits within ADSP. The hidden interest, the pork-barrel tax, the concealed penalty, the speed-trap, the mysterious tariff, the capricious fine, the shrouded blackmail, and/or a triple-tap funeral Attack are all premeditated, predatory, punitive, and Biblical.

I thought about how Profit is easily plucked from these half-dead and low-hanging enemies or humans. The Jewish, Catholic, Muslim, or Christian convert is prey? Victim? Traded commodity? Saved? A new customer? A new continent? A new income stream? Or perhaps born again — converted and full of life: raped into being saved?

Samuel concludes his pro-synagogue and state / pro-church and state's standing-army rant as the classroom starts to glow in a sunny early morning moment again. Samuel takes the sun as a sign from *God* and says, "The sun warms us this morning because America loves our awesome God! Thank you, God."

The new natural light no longer works with his sideways mouth and now shades him correctly as an unnatural lover in a diseased state, a fallen man. Samuel has no affection, so he can never love — he survives only on need-love and hate-love. Samuel, a righteous boy to match his inerrant Bible, sits down in a huff like a loose bag of bricks.

Unusual for Ms. Appleton, perhaps because of the sudden flash of morning sun, thinking it, possibly as Samuel did, as a sign from her personal God, Maker or maybe even a Goddess, asks Samuel in a pleasant manner, "Yes, Amen for the savage and Amen for Mary Dyer, but, Samuel, please explain how I can give you an 'Amen' for your spoils and virgins, and how, oh, dear Lord, Samuel, is your booty related to the very helpful and innocent sun?"

Everyone knows Ms. Appleton is a victim of the Zionist axe because of her "Impure" relations with her Minister, so it is obvious she likes to turn the tables on *pure* Samuel and the Puritans when she can. Ms. Appleton is a creator and a destroyer, an artist and anarchist; she enjoys deconstructing baseless and self-indulgent lives. Ms. Appleton is the market maker, but she is up against well-armed royal mercenaries in these insecure times. It wasn't just the Elders' standing-armies with their perverted police, but she was scorned publicly by the low-class mob, and so she burns with an inner light for revenge. Ms. Appleton likes to *get* some satire when the satire is good, and a march on the Iroquois terrorist in western New England is just that tragic comedy.

Ms. Appleton the prophetess comes alive, her skin, still white as grandma's doily, only accentuates her brown sparkling Spanish-Irish eyes — like the walnut wood furniture beneath the white needlework. She stands up at her desk glaring at Samuel with a new mask of red, tan and brown freckles that come to light as her snow-white skin quietly recedes and she quickly blossoms into a blushing white rose on fire. Ms. Appleton slaps her golden ruler on the fat of her palm, and she continues slapping the ruler on her palm, keeping time in a menacing way. She becomes exposed and awakened with thousands of freckles that are now her mask — her war paint is her freckles and her golden rule is her axe and they expose a savage on the warpath.

Ms. Appleton says, "Well, Samuel, that's very courageous of you to kill American Natives with muskets and cannons while they have bows and arrows. Is that war or murder?"

Samuel replies in a shrunken and aghast voice, as if to hush what Ms. Appleton said before anyone could possibly hear such an unpatriotic thought. "Ms. Appleton, you cannot insult our honorable soldiers and my father like that."

Ms. Appleton raises her golden ruler like a slow guillotine clicking / ratcheting into its position of execution. Somewhere in the distance, I can hear a drum roll... a rat-a-tat-tat! Or maybe it is the tick-tock, tick, tick, tick-tock of the Big-Daddy time clock. It is both! I hear a drum roll nicely mixed with Puritan time: a rat-a-tat — tick-tock! A rat-a-tat — tick-tock! A rat-a-tat — tick-tock!

Ms. Appleton cocks her head back, looks down her Celtic nose, steadies herself and slices Samuel down the middle with her axe: "Is your Daddy a wounded warrior or a wounded murderer? You still have a spiritual choice, Samuel.... Admit it and your nightmares will stop. Admit that you're a murderer and you'll stop wanting to commit suicide. Ask your *hero* Admiral father if it would be nice to go to bed one night and not want to kill himself. Ask Big-Daddy about the truth of a standing-army soldier!"

Samuel babbles, "What, wha, wha, wa, wa are you saying?" as he starts shuffling his feet, trying to back up while still seated in his school desk.

Ms. Appleton starts to walk towards him as she drives in hard to Samuel's cave by saying, "Don't you believe in the sixth commandment, Samuel: Thou shall not kill? Can't you read — have you gone Native?"

As usual, Samuel turns green with confused resentment and he looks as if he is going to puke, cry, or storm out of the classroom — which he sometimes does. As I wrote earlier, he is a large, slow boy so on some days, Samuel will forget he is still seated in our crippling school desk-chairs.

"I kill because I love my Country, I kill for my God, I kill for my family. I'm going to tell my Father on you!" Samuel declares in desperation.

He tries to exit the very old Ten-Commandment problem and exit the classroom door: exit stage alt-right.

Ms. Appleton speaks to our class and not to Samuel: "Class, you are witnessing post-traumatic stress disorder and/or the crippling and suicidal guilt of a murderer. Why these useless standing-army despots don't just fall on their swords before they come home, I'll never know."

Samuel tries to stand up in the little desk-chair, forgetting there is a metal desk wrapped around his rib cage and hip. The black iron desk is floating bondage that becomes elevated off the floor as he is transformed / disciplined into a crippled lima bean. His back is being strained and arched over like that of an armadillo. The desk keeps him hunched over as he tries to move forward. Samuel the sociopath is the Aesop fable turtle with his S and M home now on his back after not being affectionate and social.

Samuel is sweating profusely and I can smell the salty-sailor low-tide oil bubble out of him. His musk is a proud grime that turns arrogant as it mixes with the dust of a weighty iron desk on his back. He stumbles and sways about in a drunk manner. Samuel waddles and drags himself towards the exit door, grunting and scraping himself along. It is sad and voyeuristically cruel for my class and me to sit there and watch him sway back and forth, struggling to not break his back and get to the door to complain to his Big-Daddy about the "Meany" teacher at school, but this, dear reader, is an education in Boston.

Ms. Appleton jumps up and stands in the doorway, blocking his way. Samuel, clearly exasperated with no peripheral view of humanity or history here in 1650, pleads like an abused child and then quotes *Capitalism for Dummies* and says, "Please, Ms. Appleton, please, I'm scared...." Then after a moment of fresh silence his mantra returns. "I work for my family, I work for my Country, my one God! God is awesome! My father is awesome — I love God."

Ms. Appleton stays focused and says, "Listen, Payneson, you may love God, but you DON'T obey his commandments. I think God wants you to obey him rather than *love* / abuse him with your depraved neurosis you call love. Do you know the difference between discipline and the poison of gift-love? Your diseased *love* is an excuse to hate. Your love is a front to abuse. Your love is a front to kill."

Samuel is retreating and most likely going to drag or salt the debate into a Bible bitch-slapping "Case-law" fest that eventually drives these law slappers — like all lawyers and couturiers: insane, mad, and grizzled. Ms. Appleton and my peers are petrified in a sunny peaceful sun-shower smirk as the hypocrisy of patriarchal religion is laid bare and raw. Religion is constant economic and social war and Samuel Payneson is the deformed living and breathing smoking-gun son of that war.

The silence in the classroom is deafening. Payneson is stopped in our classroom doorway and starts mumbling, confused and thinking about defending his God, his city on the hill, his Daddy, his occupied-zone, his royal dreams of imperialism. But before he can form a thought or sentence, Ms. Appleton metaphysically picks up her golden rule axe and strolls back to her desk, flipping the axe in the air and catching it handle-side rapidly three times in a row, showing off her axe-throwing skills. She then kisses the axe blade and lobs it end-over-end over to Samuel, saying, "Here, my little King Hero, catch this!"

In reality Ms. Appleton says, "Hey, Payneson, remember this, little sailor boy — Jesus never played it safe, and hiding behind your Big-Daddy is *safe*, and safe is all you play. Jesus saw and heard everything. Jesus lived hard and fast and was present fearlessly. Jesus risked everything openly even as he was slowly tortured and died, nailed to a cross by Romans and Jews. And as I said earlier: that execution, that cross you bear — that's so 'In' and 'Cool' now, that's not *my bad* — that's not my sin. Your soft-core Jesus assassination-gone-bad turns up as a souvenir cross over your black heart — and that is not a Christian cross, but a cross made, raised, and fashioned by crusading Jews and imperializing Romans."

Without missing a beat following her sun, Ms. Appleton barks in a nasally New England tenor, "Dear Maker! I declare that I won't pay for other people's crimes. The cruising Jew's crimes and the metrosexual Roman Catholic's crimes against humanity are not my crimes." Ms. Appleton stands in front of her desk, clutching and swinging her brass ruler like a sword and pointer and says desperately in a pleading voice to a higher power, "Neexxttt! Someone, please, nneexxt!"

Samuel, demoted to moral correctional-custody by Ms. Appleton's truthful and risk-averse Jesus from the Geneva Bible, drags his double-wide school desk back to his rented lot in our classroom, twitching and fidgeting, reluctantly keeping his mouth shut and paying his homeroom inspection dues.

Because God Told Me

Ms. Appleton takes out a hanky to clean and polish her brass ruler. She seems distracted for a moment, then looks up and over to Diana Mallouston, soundlessly and sternly instructing her to tell us about her good-work.

Diana's origin is similar to mine — like me, she is in the last seat in her column. She is a creepy hunter with a bow and arrow that are her tool and her curse. Diana stands up slowly and confidently behind Samuel and makes a motion in support of getting Jesus Christ's Swiss Alps sworn deposition thrown out of our homeroom inspection court. Diana, like Samuel, is an old schoolmate of mine from long-ago Boston. Her red, blue, and purple coif has the varied color of harvest corn, and it acts as a convenient halo that covers all of her head so none of her shaved hair is visible. Diana cuts off her jet-black hair daily in order to have less distractions, alas — to have less femininity in her life. Diana's golden sunshine shift is more of a relaxed cartwheel ruff over her shoulders and chest, looking appropriately like a medieval hatchet. The sickle shape at her neck accentuates the glow of Diana's hostile halo. This ruff is a silver platter around her fat, round, pink-piggy face. Diana's charcoal pencil-like frame is straight and black to the core. Her genie eyes are two black moles on a small pig's ass and her mouth accordingly is a squiggly, curlicue pigtail. Diana is a mean little squealer. In the moonlight, her silk cassock dress is as cold, tight, and fluid as a small, steamy mountain stream on a hot summer's night. Ms. Mallouston is a petrified auburn log with icicle limbs and early frost fingers. Diana Mallouston is an archer with quiver hands and arrows as fingers — she is the embodiment of chastised Divine love and moves like a slippery pine stream.

Diana, with the choler of a sable cat in late autumn, speaks aloud: "America needs a strong defense to be safe and the only way to have that is to remove the dangerous terrorist. We need to attack to protect. Attack to protect! The Church of Boston is our Biblical destiny and God will not be happy with us if we shy away from fighting for our promised land. Attack to protect. Attack to protect!"

Diana is a much better speaker and performer than Samuel Payneson, even if that performance is still alien, otherworldly, and disenchanted. Her pugnacious animosity is checked and balanced with a wicked female vindictiveness that Ms. Appleton is delightfully challenged by, respects, and can easily relate to.

Ms. Appleton says, "Diana, why don't we leave the Iroquois Indians alone? Why are we stealing and occupying their land as the Puritan imperialists did to the Pequots and the Narraganset?"

Diana retorts, "We're not stealing their land. We're creating a democratic America where freedom reigns."

Ms. Appleton declares musically, "Nay, oohhh, nay, nye, nye — nay... we have taken advantage of and stolen the primates', the pygmies', the natives', the enemies', the friends', and the under-dogs' land around the world because the English, and now the Americans, are the greediest, sleaziest, nastiest bullies out there — congrats to *the* gaudy and greedy male, blessings to the nastiest louse — congrats to the white cockroach!"

Diana retorts with her back stiff as a board, "No, no, we

Diana Mallouston

are liberating the savage terrorists and saving their damned souls," as she cradles and pets the white onyx charm on her silver necklace. The white, outer-space stone seems to get darker the more irritated Diana becomes.

Ms. Appleton, in a snarky tone, asks, "How can you be so sure we're saving souls, Ms. Mallouston? Seems like we're just going further into a debtors' jail with a debt we cannot pay to unknown Elders and Elect."

Some classmate up front chirps in, "Ask Pip the Pequot!

Israel Wilkinson, nearby, in front of Elizabeth Winterest, says, "Maybe Laura's Mushy-boy can stand up?

Diana, an orb of purity, is beaming from her sprite eyes and thin red wet lips. She wags her holy spear tongue for a moment in her mouth as if she is an animal on a wild hunt licking the air for the scent of prey, searching for a target. She looks directly into Ms. Appleton's black pond-like eyes, and then says softly, letting her arrow fly, "Because God told me."

Here we go again into Biblical case law quotes — the psychotic steel cage Bro-Bible bitch-slapping match for the last sixteen hundred and fifty years! The ultimate fighting *Court*, where psychotic religionists quarrel and loot with their lawyerly fascist friends, quoting sixteen-hundred-year-old newspapers.

Ms. Appleton says sarcastically with a faux surprised Spanish accent, "Oh, you know God, Diana? How's Jesus doing? Is he helping you with your carpentry work? Please tell Jesus and his mother Maria to stop by if they can — I need a little help with my landscaping and house cleaning!" Countering hard in another voice, Ms. Appleton continues: "Do you know, in our enlightened and educated mother country back home in England, your personal psychotic God and religion is a mental disorder, a mental disease? It's called psychosis or the Jerusalem Syndrome. Are you feeling okay, Ms. Mallouston?"

Diana's white onyx charm is the color of black coal.

Ms. Appleton isn't strong enough to reveal the Bible as an existential pooper-scooper for the moveable shell-game called the *Truth*. Like a compass slowly, and perfectly, encircling its pinpointed target, Ms. Appleton asks, "Diana, do you covet your neighbor's property, do you covet your neighbor's soul and life if they don't believe in your *hill* or your *God*? Are you a religious glutton?"

Hotheaded and flabbergasted now, Ms. Mallouston says, "We are saving and liberating the damned terrorists from their Godless ways as we spread the word."

I think about the Jewish and Catholic Trojan horse marketing and branding of "Spreading the word" as an imperialistic smoke screen or false flag. The Trojan horse marketing is a lovely overdose and painless death for need-lovers needing love and colonists needing to colonize. These reasonable addicts of sin and/or victims with low self-esteem spread the word that *it's all for the best*. Faux appreciation and glee from the need-love victim opens up to reveal the truthful *hate* from the gift-lovers gifting. Low self-esteem enables the kill.

Whether it's the Indian totem pole, the Jewish golden calf, or the Catholic holy-grail — the patriotic patronage on the outside celebrates the weakness of God-love as gift-love. These tribes' prayers are for others' pain and not for their enlightenment — there is no individual self-love, God-love, or affection with any tribe. And we know how this Trojan horse analogy goes because, whether it's the Judeo-Christian tribe or the Lenape tribe, the common denominator in humanity is the selfish-gene tribe. Regardless of where that gene is — in the synagogue, under that steeple, or in that hunting territory — the gene is always in the gift-horse, and it is always filled with the same poisonous arrows.

Tribes are loyal only to *their* gaudiest male — their "Governor Winthrop," their "Chief Wampy." A leader of what, when only the fattest and nastiest male cockroach — the *macho gordas cucaracha* — is your Elder? Fat vermin as your Elders and Elect! I think about looking into the eyes of this cockroach Elder. The white male Elder and Elect with their blackness and stillness... it make me shudder as I imagine the male antennae rubbing silently, looking at me quietly and pure — gazing at me, sizing me up — judging me.... This ancient *macho cucaracha* is a timeless male creature — he is a fat bitch, he is King Artist that all con-artists look up to! The steady and infinite Y chromosome, the Big-Daddy Y of genetics made me miserable and I feel my heart wrench, for I am looking at myself.

Ms. Appleton asks Diana, "Did we covet the Pequot Indian's property? Have we given the Pequots salvation by roasting them alive or selling them as slaves to slave-traders in Bermuda?" Ms. Appleton, who knows the answers and doesn't wait around for painful excuses from Diana, barks out, "Next."

My class and I sit with this moral hazard in silence as Ms. Appleton is dancing a witchy waltz. Diana is out of steam, unable to keep even a square dance going with Ms. Appleton: The Lady of the Lake, who, by the way, is still rumored to tango and rumba down in Roxbury on the weekends. Diana, morally bankrupt now, actually seems calm for a psychotic zealot moment as she starts to fall. My class and I silently enjoy this automatic stay — this Nothing. It is an enjoyable tranquility that our class soaks up with respectful stillness and silence.

During this quietude, I recall skinning, gutting, eating, and working a large deer for the first time when I was with my Lenape family in New Netherland. Just as the feisty cat drops a dead mouse, a dead bird — a fresh kill, at its owner's door, Wampy, the Lenape Indian Chief, had brought a large deer back from the hunt and dropped it at my teepee threshold. It was maybe a ten-point buck and my sister Happiness walked over to me with a cleaver in one hand and a scythe in the other. I had never butchered a buck this size and Happiness, assuming this fact correctly, was grinning ear to ear. There was no debating that I needed to respect this dead bloody gift from the chief of our tribe. Spiritually, I needed to respect the deer and butcher him completely and cleanly. I went past the venison meat, seasoned and salted to feed us through the winter, down to the antler tools and buttons. Then working it further, I contained the deer blood for dye and the skin for tee-pees, skirts, pants, and ponchos for my Lenape family. For the Lenape, everything in nature needs to be respected — never forgetting Nothing, never disrespecting Nothing, never abandoning Nothing. The simplicity of the Indian is their beauty.

A dead deer as religion, a dead deer respected as the *truth*. I can still imagine my hands inside the rotting warm deer. It was filled with maggots and buzzing with flies as I gutted it, but regardless of the natural stench and blood I still felt the deer's good-work. It was majestically and spiritually redeeming compared to Neg-Am Jam America redemption. A dead deer compared to the police-state nature of the Jewish Catholic plague. A dead deer compared to the Biblical law and the axe — a rational animal's evolution compared to the good cop and the bad cop death. The respect of a dead deer compared to the torture of Mary and Eve.

Diana Molluston sneers confidently back at Ms. Appleton and rattles off, "You're an atheist! A pagan! A heretic. A loose hussy... A feminist!"

These religious problems and solutions are sold as one to invoke capitalist confusion where the high priests, lawyers, and politicians horde their "Booty and spoil," attempting to validate their "Prophesized" Jewish and Roman Catholic domination. They lobby and legislate their self-destructive Armageddon-Ready and Rapture-Ready agendas. Puritans can't wait to kill or commit suicide because the orthodox hate life and freedom. Henceforth, the Judeo-Christian "Word," or cruel hell on earth, has spread to our free-grace spirits. The religionist's sociopathic behavior devolves and ejects humanity from nature because nature or Nothing would never be as cruel or ugly as the human race or civilization.

Ms. Appleton, answers Ms. Mallouston's accusations with "I'll be all those things and more, Diana, but, more important, I won't be insatiable and guilty like you!"

I think to myself, guilty? Guilty like the Jewish apostles of pump and Christian disciples of dump? Greedy neighbors who will rip out the heart of their neighbor to the east in order to sell that neighbor's heart to their other neighbor to the west. These Range-Rover rabbis' and Porsche Priests' heartless wars and sin are also our sin because we enable the religious orthodox to abuse us. And even more cowardly than our white-devil civilizations' self-destructive behavior is that besides not stopping the crimes and debt against ourselves, we allow, encourage, and profit from seducing our children and the children of other tribes weaker than we are. Vulnerable children, refugees, and immigrants who cannot defend themselves are molested and abused by us, the religious white-devil. Roving rabbis and turbo-charged priests abuse our children, our State, our budgets, our liberty, and our future. The Jews' and Catholics' capital sin of self-idolatry, false Gods, and debt deflates our life, allowing the subjective and abstract to reign over the objective. We lose our life, liberty, and pursuit of happiness when the religionist is the Elect and Elder. Or in my mother Anne's nicer words, "The Puritans' covenant of material works (working for money, family, power) reigns over our covenant of spiritual works (working for equality, grace, and charity)."

The lack of equality, charity, or philanthropy in the Catholic or Jew white-devil heart is dumbfounding and evolves them below a sub-human. The Abe-Bro buys the Abe-Babe and both consumers become irrational and desperate animals: overrun by consumption itself. The religious are mad dogs with worms.

Diana Mallouston concludes with worldly superiority in

a cold and clipped tone: "Well, Ms. Appleton, I pray easily the Elders will hear about this happenstance of heresy, and I know one thing for sure — your oily fat will bubble and burn swiftly and brightly at the stake."

As Diana finishes this very Christian thought, her silver necklace comes unhinged and she struggles, reaching up around her neck as if she is suddenly being strangled or scratching for a bug deep in her clothes. She wriggles like a dolphin in the sea or perhaps someone on fire, grasping at her silky and slippery shift. Lost within this hatchet habit, her necklace shimmies down her cassock dress. Diana shivers, dances, and shakes as her charm falls onto the floor under her religious habit. Everyone in class hears her charm and poise fall. Diana looks around desperately at us as the class acknowledges, with our silence and holding our breath, that her next step could be fatal — fatal to her light, fatal to her personal, pliable, and amenable God. Diana steps to the side as she tries to untangle and balance herself, then she steps back, and to the side again — it is a two-step dance with a crushing finale. Her side step crushes her onyx charm, and the stone crunching and breaking under her boot sounds like shattering glass and devastated youth. Our class gasps in unison — some smirking, others feeling empathy. Regardless, Ms. Mallouston's defeated white charm — her white privilege, her white sin — physically and intellectually hurts us all.

Diana's little white-devil heart and its petty acts of contrition or reconciliation for its disrespectful crimes against humanity are control-frauds and purposely futile. The white-devil heart is incomparable to the Indian warrior heart, eaten by the Indian victors after battle out of respect for each other, not disrespect.

Wampy, my Indian Chief, ate my mother's heart and he said, "Aun Huckson heart was sweet and sour. Like a funny little white chicken — colorful and peppery!" He said, "She still live with me" as he wet and smacked his lips with his tongue.

Wampy concluded in a proud manner, "An ancient, unforgettable, and everlasting taste — timeless!"

Of the two murderers in my mother's life, Wampy's cannibalistic poetry sits kindly with me compared to the Puritan's *invisible hand* lynching. Those white-devil soul murderers and ivy-league smile-fuckers with parlor room politeness and two-faced deceit are either femme-fatale rabbis or priests with big dicks.

CHAPTER 8

Multiple-Choice Imperialism — Do the Pequots Understand Profit-Sharing?

MULTIPLE-CHOICE IMPERIALISM

he ridiculous thought of materialistic salvation or capitalist salvation being charming makes my heart ache some more, especially after Ms. Mallouston sits down, unable to answer Ms. Appleton's coveting questions. Diana can only swear to get Big-Daddy patriarchy after our slutty teacher. The mutating monotone of silence that lingers is eerie and bloodsucking. A syncopated tone: skipping, electrified, crackling, staccato-like. This is the silence of poisoned archers sitting in the Trojan horse. A Trojan tenor: using generosity and gift-love to drum-up greed and wash back need-love. This insipid intonation is a nice segue to Brad Pining, seated in the front row of the second column: a Hessian mercenary on paid-holiday in America.

Brad Pining, the German knucklehead, stands up, and, even if he doesn't have a musket and bayonet on his shoulder, they are still there, figuratively speaking. He is the son of a holy magistrate from London and a German wench from the Rhineland. Brad had stock of the imperialist London Company coursing through his blood before he even saw the light of day. Brad was pawned from the London Company womb on

King's Road in London, which was selling, financing, and raf-
fling off holy crusades or savage vacations around the globe.
Depending upon your imperialist dreams, you could, "Kill a
Zulu on Safari!" or "Conquer the American Wilderness!" and/
or "Learn an Ancient Chinese Secret!" Multiple-choice imperialism took hold in the English Empire, and no sucker, no
moral debt, and no child on safari would be left behind.

Brad Pining has a broad forehead with a tuft of short
dirty-blond hair, large, blurry green insect eyes (magni-
fied by his glasses) and thin bloodless lips. His beak turns up
naturally to define his permanent snarky smirk and lizard
stare. Brad Pining's imperial predatory gaze and judgment
are lifeless, because they are death itself, which is part of life.
Pining is pure Yang with no Ying; Pining is the primal male
cockroach with no affection. He has no feeling or care for a
warm kitchen filled with the smell of fresh corn bread and
the sight of a content dog wagging its tail, snuggled up to the
woodstove. Pining's wasp-like eyes are not "Eye to eye" but a
window to his soulless imagination of how he's going to eat
you. Like religion, his eyes have a parasitoid stare, a masculine colonial gaze: discordant to you and your tribe's survival
strategy. Brad Pining's male gaze is not at you or at your soul,
but *about* you — about the "Other."

Brad, the roach with his gregarious gaze, debates debt,
work quotas, profit plans, and power exchanges as he sizes you
up and down with his domineering gaze. Brad Pining is an
unruly guest, a crashing parasite within humanity that kills
instinctually and maniacally by inviting and birthing more
cockroaches (their sub-human children) into your home and
gut. The roaches' parasitical gentrification crowds out your
survival from within you. Cockroaches are swarming now,
eating you alive, eating and killing you from the inside with an
ancient gaze and cycle of need-love. Need-love is an emotional
need and it masks the real biological need of need-money /
need-food. Over and over the cockroaches' "Love" is a need

Brad Pining

when they should be saying," Can you spare me a buck?" Over and over our needing of love is a gaze of need-money / need-food. Holiday to holiday, birth day to birthday: need-money / need-food, need-money/ need food — need-love.

Pining's swinish smirk is thrown over his red cloak as he always turns his back on you, dumping you, always winning and executing the deal. Brad's lazy bespectacled smirk always seems to foreshadow him licking his lips, sucking in a wriggling worm or two just pecked out of thin air, struggling to get free. Brad sees opportunity when there is none.

Brad Pining's seat is in the front row, second column, and his body is marsupial in stature. His brain cage rattles with incisors because of the indigestion in his gassy belly and large ass. Brad's chin is pronounced like that of a large-mouth bass, which works well with his nervous mechanical movements and screechy voice. When Brad talks, the snake oil seeps, sweats, and oozes out of his pores — the fat cockroach glistens — and, to my horror, I want a taste!

Brad clears his throat and speaks with a chipper London tone: "A glorious good morning to you, my dear Ms. Appleton."

Brad's father, John Pining, is a relative of the Deacon down in Dorchester and he had a heavy hand in smearing, condemning, and almost banishing Ms. Appleton at her adultery inquisition. John Pining was also business partners with the late John Harvard, who founded the white-devil minister school (Harvard University). The school is for Puritans and their couturiers to learn how to loot and persecute the common folk. Therefore, Brad has a twinkle in his frat-boy eyes as he squeezes and presses this unspoken leverage against Ms. Appleton. She is scared of Brad and closes her legs under her desk and grinds her teeth unconsciously. Ms. Appleton, as well as the entire class, feels Brad's lawless eyes move up her petticoat in a hostile, unnatural, and deformed manner.

Ms. Appleton sheepishly says, "Good morning, Brad."

Brad, the gaudy male tourist, ignores Ms. Appleton but continues to look her up and down, licking his lips slowly. After a very long awkward silence in which our class can only hear Pining's heavy breathing, Brad looks around the classroom and addresses us. "And good morning to you, children of God; you soldiers of the Church, in God we trust! Let us take a moment to pray, to pledge an allegiance with our all-powerful and awesome God. Let us thank him together this morning for our lives, his kindness, and, of course, let us thank God for the new Navigation Act tax!"

After a moment of dreadful capitalistic silence in which each in the classroom either writhes, pontificates, or at least fidgets in their seats, Brad declares, "God save the King!" not out of desperation, but as a threat and as a rebuttal to anyone thinking about speaking up about another tax.

We all passively and aggressively answer in proper English, "God save the King," as the mealy and tasteless mantra rots our white and strong American teeth.

Brad was raping and pillaging us with trust, God, and King in our homeroom inspection this morning and every morning. Suddenly our classroom was back in London Square with drawn-and-quartered bodies hanging from chains. But it isn't the London tower keeping time — it is our grandfather clock! "Tick-tock, tick-tock, tick-tock... E, G#, F#, B — E, F#, G#, E... tick-tock, tick-tock, tick-tock." I want to scream, imagining London's Big Ben surrounded by decomposing heads on spikes. Fleas with malaria and rats with the bubonic plague hop and scurry between our feet in playful merriment as we sit in line, in class, or at the pub, waiting for more financial and moral debt over a pint of ale. Tick-tock, tick-tock, tick-tock... E, G#, F#, B — E, F#, G#, E...

Brad brushes off his expensive and exquisite waistcoat cape the color of a red delicious apple and holds onto his finely embroidered and fabricated lapels as he disapprovingly looks around the class. Brad Pining, the sneaky possum, arrogantly starts into his usually short and succulent speech — swinging for the bleachers, desperately trying to be the frat-boy homeroom hero.

"Fellow Puritans, King Charles the First will be rightfully put back on his Divine throne, but until then we must not disappoint or slacken our gross domestic product. The London Company Charter is dependent on the economy and your good behavior in this American Promised Land. Just because the King has been dethroned and there is no royal monarchy in London anymore doesn't mean your Contract or your debt with the financiers of the London Company is null and void!"

Elizabeth Winterest, our only classmate with the highborn nobility to even try to take down Brad Pining within our civilization's chess game, says, "Brad, are we beholden to the Kings, Queens, knights, bishops, and pawns trading and legislating indulgences? Are we yet again beholden to the royal dead and their heirs? How bloody boring you are, Brad... you are a sad, sad clown and with such a tiresome game, circus, and the very stalest of bread."

Brad ignores her and continues, "The American colony is too childlike to succeed alone without the London Company. The Massachusetts colony is not worthy enough to understand the new Navigation Act tax and tariff that God and the London Company have blessed you to pay! Those of you that grumble about these taxes, tariffs, or the selling of 'Indulgences,' as some of you Separatists or Dissenters call them, will be found out and punished!"

The American bountifulness of life, liberty, and the pursuit of happiness are being stripped naked and tied to a whipping post by Brad Pining. "You and your families should be so lucky as to be downstream from the Divining London Company's trickle-down salvation. In God we trust and God save the King."

Elizabeth Winterest, who sits next to me, turns toward me

and silently shakes her head in dismay about Brad's demands. Then she says to the class, "Let's move on, Sir Nasty! Everyone knows Parliament rules us, you Divine fool. The King is dead — the Queen is dead! Lord Nasty is dead and King Mob now rules us, you porky little redcoat!"

Listening to Brad's voice about his good-work is like listening to a possum or raccoon fight in the black of night. The wild monkey vocals and attacks are nerve-rackingly shrill, scratchy, and rabid, as the fight sounds primal and/or pre-historic in the dark woods. This dark fight or fear of judgment is the *Nothing*, it is a primal scream within one's own blindness or helplessness in the obscure, cold, and dark woods. A *Nothing* in the woods that is also a spot at the back of your head. This spot of Nothing, this spot of mankind will never be seen. I feel vulnerable as the bloody screams from Nothing, equate horror, death, and animalistic victories where might does make right. Screams echoing from the blackness continue — I wonder, am I losing or winning this fight alone in the woods? Fighting alone in the dark when I close my eyes? The crooning Nothing song from the silent darkness continues and the chorus is a terrifying and deafening universal reply: "You are losing! You are losing! You are losing!" This is the key Brad Pining and his ivy-league acapella group sing in. Consequently, listening to and looking into Brad's eyes is similar to looking into those dark woods at night, hearing and imagining the animals' fight / your fight, for raw survival. Within this darkness, within the cold, purple-black early hours, the mammal fight goes on even as you close the window, lock your door again, get a glass of water, and tuck yourself under another warm blanket. Warm and snuggly now in bed you still hear the mammal flesh being ripped. You feel the teeth and nails ripping you down to the bone and you doze off thinking, "Please not now... don't take me to the woods to fight it out! Someday yes, but not now, for God's sake — not now! Your confrontation with the woods or Nothing can be postponed, but here at homeroom inspection, without doors, locks, and blankets, one has to listen and look *into* Brad Pining — a walking, opaque Nothing.

Brad faces Elizabeth and says, "Hey, Lizzy, mark my words — royalty dost not wither so fast — you are worn more than your wont and we will be back in power in less than five, maybe ten, years."

Brad, the antithesis of humanity or the humane life, is a rabid rat dog who plays royal savior with pursed lips and a grinding London accent in order to relax and impress his prey by not exposing his foaming glands and jagged teeth. Pining is a grinning date rape the morning after with fresh flowers, breakfast, and plans for afternoon tea with his royal family. After connecting with the Brad Pinings of the world, and having your pockets picked and your soul emptied, you willingly humiliate and drown yourself in patriotic police-state limbo in order to not be abused anymore. This low self-esteem is sub-human and certainly not American.

That's because America is violent and it should be embraced! Perhaps violence will be written into our Bill of Rights or our American Constitution someday. Imagine having the Constitutional right to bear arms against an oppressive and corrupt Elder, the criminal Elect, or a conspiring State that abuses you! Imagine our founding fathers of America as proud murderers, terrorists, and throat slicers of these royalist pigs, courtiers, and the bourgeois? Well, America can hope; we Walofang white-devils can have a dream....

Until then, I, the sub-human American colony-child, nod my head, sign on the dotted line, and mouth the words "God save the King." I, and, many other subjects and servants, wish our police or tax collectors in this debt limbo a "Thanks" or a "Good day" after they give us this ticket or tax bill that will steal our week's or month's pay, our pride, and our American souls. We tip our hats to our royal master, thanking our abusive Big-Daddy; this tip of the hat then matures into a rude slap across our faces when the un-American despot leaves and Appalachian silence falls on us like an icy and steely rain.

Sometimes I say to myself silently, "God save the King," because it feels good to give up and be a European troll. I then theorize like a French philosopher reasoning: *I think, there-fore, I am... aaggh? Confused?* No, that's not it, the European philosopher in me thinks: I don't work for America, I work for the male gaze, I work for the *Other*! I fantasize that I am not human and not American, which is so depressing and so pathetic that I stop thinking and I just do it today like a wild-man, like a wild good American — violently, immediately, and with no regard for yesterday or tomorrow.

Brad returns to not being happy with our musical tempo, measure, or intonation, and says again much more loudly, as if we are his children or soldiers not carrying out his order, "God Save the King! Do you all want to hang like Mary Dyer in an hour because you're too proud to respect the royal Elect and Elders of Boston? Are you too proud to say your pledge of allegiance?"

The classroom's contentment is a social shell-game of pol-ished and waxed contempt. Classmates adjust themselves and look at their neighbors rolling their eyes, but are too cowardly to stand up for the truth against Brad Pining and the London Company, who is their financier, their bank — their *God.* This self-depreciating guilt, desire, or envy for money and power is an orthodox sin that coaxes through all our American veins now.

Elizabeth continues her *good ole cause* and says to Brad, "Mary just wants equality and..."

Brad cuts her off, looking directly through her, and says, "Nay, Mary is a heretic who asks too many questions and she will hang within the hour." Then, turning to the class, in an evangelical tone, he says, "Trust me, class" and then pauses for dramatic effect and concludes by pointing at us all and says,

"The Boston ballet is coming to a town near you. God sees you and God is coming for you!"

The gaze, the revelation, the judgment, the hanging, the burning, the redemption, and/or the raping of a neighbor for power and money could happen at any moment in musical chairs America. The Brad Pinings and his Christian Zionistas of America play *On Our Way to Jerusalem* 24/7/365. These capitalists / imperialists posing as religionists agree silently that, if crimes against humanity brought more food to their own family's dinner table, or to their own tribe's dinner table, then it was NOT a crime to Starve and Divide the common man into the forgotten man. Stealing from the common man became a Zionista rite of passage, a Biblical right, a Divine right, in order for the fashionable criminal to be ready for the Rapture-Ready Ball!

Brad says, "Do we not pledge ourselves this glorious morning to our King? Do we not trust in God?" Brad Pining says again louder and slower, over-pronouncing and questioning every word as if our class are disobedient dumb dogs or children not following his command. "Okay, people, one more time, God... save... the... King!"

Brad Pining and his family have a Divine right to find their place on this earth because his personal *God*, the King, and the London Company have sent them on their high-holy holiday crusade. The King's Cross flag flies in of all of England's poor colonies (including America), signifying that the colonies' pump-and-dump scam-economy of Club Dread is in the house. Club Dread is where Lord Nasty and Lord Fancy-Pants on safari have "A jolly old time of it," setting up the NAJ life! The negative amortized life in third world countries is then incorporated / humanized into a control-fraud humanity and an off-shore Bermuda corporation. English Lords and wanna-be Sir Nasties around the globe to this very moment are sending back to London the "Booty and spoils" from these colonial cons. America has quickly become the new Club Dread colony here in 1650.

The English Colonies or Club Dreads (over thirty) are sprinkled strategically around the globe. These Neg-Am Jam colonies, and now especially America, are stacked, staged, and slobbered with debt — with ADSP. The original or ancestral sin of debt and its fractional interest is an Attack on a child and on humanity. "A" within ADSP is for Attack and the diseases it releases as the Club Dread colony children and natives are then Divided and Starved to death. "P" is for Profit, which is the only thing left standing as the colony and her royal children teeter along as control-fraud citizens — as royal subjects. Within this trickle-down economy the only thing trickling down is abuse because as the Queen abuses her subjects — the mother abuses her children.

The Moby Dicks at the London debt-trading desks are the only benefactors of spreading the ADSP word and/or imperializing civilization. The Royal Cross retirement and its pension is a carrot-on-a-stick tease in the diamond mine of Africa, in the exporting harbor of Hong Kong, or in the farm fields of America.

The royal retirement is an existential control-fraud giving hope to the thirsty Jewish, Catholic, or Protestant weekend-warriors living in an ecclesiastical oasis of God delusion. These anxious religionists have a constant threat of either dying, being marooned, or just flat-out rejected in this faux desert because the self-dealing holy crusaders at the debt-trading desk in London are not looking for a prophet or humanity, but for a false profit.

Brad Pining scans the classroom to make sure he has sold and administered his venom this morning. Pining's eyes come to rest on Ms. Appleton as Brad is now coiled, hissing, and sexually aroused with his earthworm panting in his soiled pantaloons. Her eyes are nervously looking up and down and side to side as she swallows deeply. There is nothing Ms. Appleton, or our class, can do while our teacher is disrespected and persecuted by a good ole' boy's son — this is a Boston education.

My class and I all close our eyes, breathe slowly, and try to move on, every day and all day, with the frat-boys in our world. Ms. Appleton opens her eyes and brings up her hands, displaying them like a brain-damaged Virgin Mary, enticing us to come along into her garden for bad girls in order to discuss how to be a good virgin mother without spreading our legs.

After slowly realizing the latter task is impossible, Ms. Appleton grimaces and winces in pain. She again opens her hands, instructing us and pleading with us to be saved from Brad Pining and his God-forsaken King. In a discordant harmony, the tired class regurgitates, "God save the King." Then Ms. Appleton follows up with a quick "Next."

Brad stomps his boot and says, "Nay, no, nay you unwashed commoners, you white indentured servants — you're no better than the stinking pygmies in Africa — say it like you mean it. Say it like you're proud to be trickled on by the royal elite of England and America!" My class and I stiffen up and start to get nervous, we all look at each other, not rolling our eyes and shrugging anymore, but frozen, scared-straight, looking at Nothing, straight ahead. Brad stomps his foot again, saying, "My Dad will turn the screws on you all!"

Our class is being sized up by a coiled London Company snake. We have to carefully and slowly smile, and back away slowly as a remedy to this walking disease. The new Jewish and Catholic commandment of "Thou shall Profit" is still not believed by Separatists, Protestants, Quakers, and other American pilgrims who don't want the orthodox and elite Puritans up their ass — which, of course, is where ass-sniffing Abe-Babe inquisitors like to be. Profit is perhaps a "Moses Addendum" or a contrite act. An *Act of Contrition* with a drop of golden crowns in the donation box in 1650 or anytime is spiritually worthless. Remorse is only financially profitable for the rabbis, priests, and Elect seducing blackmail settle-ments "Admitting no wrong-doing" from their faithful flock of NOT Jews or Christians, but profiteers.

Brad Pining, the plump and noxious little Boston éclair, is stamping his feet now as if he is marching in place. He shakes in fear at our blatant American disrespect of royalty and heredity. He cries his mustard gas order, fogging up his glasses: "God save the King! God save the King! God save the King!"

The open-heartedness of America and the open Atlantic Ocean that we crossed to get here is being constricted, stran-gled, and asphyxiated by loyalist bureaucrats like Brad Pining. Privateering magistrates and lawyers are leading us back to winey and convoluted royal London or bourgeois Europe here in America. In the last fifty years, since 1600, America has become nothing but a latchkey colonial-child to Mother England and her civil war divorce from mummy monarch. The American pilgrims, the Separatists, the Puritans, the Baptists, and now the Quakers have become nothing except chess pieces for the monarch. Children pawns, human rooks, tribal knights, and religious bishops are used as commodities and leverage to torture each other for the one and only true patriarchal King — King Profit. Constricting and strangling for the one and only true English Crown — the Sterling Pound.

Ms. Appleton, getting annoyed and trying to show the semblance of a teacher and not a frightened baby-sitter, says, "Brad, you've had enough time. Next!"

Brad squeals, "Respect the King and the Empire or their wrath will be felt!"

America is a canary in the colony coalmine for the London Company's white indentured servant (white-slave) and the African (black-slave) trade. It is a colony where the *good ole cause* was banished and a poison ivy-league university system was created for white-devil slaves to learn how to police other less-fortunate white-devil slaves.

Brad shows-off his sharp, irregular teeth and foams at the mouth with his plaque-and-tartar-covered tongue wagging and gasping for air or blood. He drools and growls with back-alley threats in his eyes and raises his fists with bloody knuckles to our class and says, "Give me what I want or I will bludgeon you all."

The royal London Jack canary sings a handsome, slightly warbled song of profit every day at the London Company's currency trading desk. The song is kind of like a question unanswered, similar to that of childhood schoolmate Sir Jackass, chirping and taunting everyone with "I know what you want. I know what you want. I know what you want." The canary song is mixed and mashed with a whippoorwill singing the question "Whip-poor-will? Whip-poor-will? Whip-poor-will?" The London Jack canary mash-up sounds more like a statement: "Profit-I-will! Profit-I-will! Profit-I-will!"

The colony's coal mine is stripped bare and the graceful English colonial economy, the "Invisible hand" or providence that once, maybe, existed in English gentlemen, is emasculated. London Jack is a girly-boy, a Jacky-boy, a virgin Mary, or perhaps Eve the whore, dependent upon on the Bank of England's income stream and their interest rates. Sir Nasty, the metro-sexual at the London Company, sits in a cave with yellow-bellied finches, feigning artistic sensibilities and financial intelligence as these mobsters pump-and-dump free-range ravioli. Between bites of pasta, wagging tongues, cheap port wine, greasy chins, and expanding waist lines, fashionable tales are woven in succulent and sycophant terms about London Jack's rotating and ever-changing profit as... a Prophet!

In a manner one would use to capture a rabid animal or a demented child Ms. Appleton says, "Okay, okay, Brad, now let's calm down. Class, let's work with Brad." She consoles the class with her English passive aggression and reluctantly says, "God save the Kiiinnngg," as she lets the "-ing," run, and ends it condescendingly — stabbing and sticking it to Brad Pining the only way she can.

Brad the cockroach slowly sinks into his seat, ducking his head first into his shoulders and then settling low into his red bloody cape. Pining, the receding goon, is a ghost shying away into the nightmares of America. Brad swivels around in his desk one last time and glares at us all as he dissolves into his cape — a headless male cockroach still gazing — a headless Hessian horseman still riding.

Do the Pequots Understand Profit Sharing?

If Brad Pining's good-work doesn't undermine patriarchal morality, well, next up is Margaret Sheriden, who surely will. No one can put a temporary shine on female immorality more than an Irish lass trying to be an English woman — the conquered emulating her conqueror. Margaret Sheridan, or Marge as she is frequently called, sits behind Brad Pining, and constantly whispers Cavalier poems into his pointed and rat-like ears. The Irish Tiger, as she liked to call herself, is actually deflated more frequently with Marge "The Barge." She is a rambler with a razor blade tucked in her petticoat and a gold cross dangling and dancing in her voluptuous Jesus cleavage. Marge the Barge's groundless high spirits smell like cheap perfume masking dirty diapers, flea-bag pets, lame games, rotten food, and uncomfortable sex. Marge's moral poverty, compared to real financial poverty within a civilization that lives downstream, on the wrong side of the shipping port, the levee, or in the slum, cannot be hidden with perfumed politics. Marge and those within civilization that can afford to hide their moral poverty with a covenant of material works

Margaret Sheridan

escape the physical stench, but it rots these upstanding creepers from the inside.

Ms. Appleton says, "Ms. Sheridan, prithee, child, let us hear about your good-work."

Margaret, the apple-polisher, says, "Ms. Appleton, that shawl is lovely, it looks great on you today!"

Ms. Appleton gets up and walks over to the front window and, for the class to enjoy, she raises her eyebrows and is about to speak, but then thinks better of it as she picks up a corner of her shawl and looks at it in an eschewing and wondering manner with a scrunched nose and dumbfounded eyes, saying to herself and our class with silent body-language, "Why is this girl is complimenting my grandma's cow shawl?"

Marge is a gregarious and bombastic monkey-man of a woman with a convoluted and frizzed-out mind and hairdo to match. Marge's russet constitution is a forgotten dusty sack of potatoes: grey, bruised, moldy, and mushy. Marge the Barge is a Belfast babe with blue/grey eyes playing both sides of the fence. She's the blonde vicar of Bray with dead Jesus break-dancing, popping, getting mellow and doing the moonwalk across her virgin mountains. Marge is a flat-footed mutt who comes on as a loitering linebacker or a hesitant haranguer. In Margaret's company, the best one can feel is knocked down, unable to see the sun, and annoyed with her over-bearing presence.

Ms. Appleton looks out the window and says, in a slow, dejected tone, "Share your good-work with us, Margaret, and, dear Lord, please don't attempt to seduce me."

Margaret, like all social ladder climbers, parrots the poet, priest, and/or politician, depending upon the political winds blowing through the Common at that hour. Marge is a cheerleader for the ever-changing wind, a paper boy who tells and sells people what he thinks we want. She is a whistling jester, regurgitating what is needed in order to get the chump change, the easy-pass at ANY tollbooth. She is the happy widow inheriting a fortune faking tears at the wake. Marge, with a mournful black and blue outfit, a maroon coif and jagged white lace symmetrically placed on her cuffs and hem, thirstfully rises, speaking more to her imagined *Irish Tiger* than to anyone in our class:

"I'm volunteering with the Massachusetts Agriculture Commission (MAC) teaching the Pequot Indians to farm correctly."

The MAC attack (or McAttack as the anti-Irish English folks are calling it) is really an after-school-special ruse for Adverse Possession or Eminent Domain (white-devil theft via their "Law") over the Pequot Indian's farmlands.

With glassed-over eyes talking to perhaps her imagined personal God, Marge the Barge says, "The Pequots are really learning a lot from us good Christian folk."

The *Walking Agreement* control-fraud education of the Pequot Indians that their farmland should be used year after year and that the Puritans need to build barns and homesteads around these farmlands, is a bait-and-switch real estate scam. A scheme of Jewish smoke-and-mirrors entertainment, then cleaned and pillaged to the bone by maggots posing as Catholic charity. The nomadic Pequot people were livid when they were told they couldn't return to their farmlands, but, in Margaret Sheridan's Irish farmers' world, the Indian terrorist is a rock that needs to be plowed out of their American field — identical to the Irish rock plowed out of the English field. The English field or the English garden isn't far from *Eve's* garden, and in fact the two are connected with a small bridge over a pond. This gently rolling garden is green, symmetrical, and the formal garden of science — it is the painted mind of Atlantis.

Marge's family is migrating north towards New Hampshire and paying wampum pennies on the royal sterling Crown for

acres and acres of Indian farmland. Marge the Barge continues: "We're educating the Pequots about how to separate the
wheat from the chaff. We're going to teach the Indians how to
build a bigger canoe."

Marge's Puritan lightning is insurance fraud or a charity fronting for extortion. Marge is "Saving" the Pequots into
debt, into religion, into sadness... Like all gift-lovers, gifting
"Love," she blackmails and brainwashes the looted and ran-
sacked Indian into a "Love Reservation," the Neg-Am Jam
Reservation.

Marge speaks like sour–dough bread rising above the class
in a patronizing manner to the starved. She looks down her
broken nose at us while delivering a positive piece of news.

"We're having a Thanksgiving dinner with the Pequot
Indians in order to celebrate the autumn harvest!"

Our anti-social very English class all look at each other
in purebred Anglo, Norman, Celtic, and Saxon disgust.
Grumbling, huffing, and hooting aloud disrupt our class. My
classmates and I imagine the same horrific future — a London
Company Holiday party in the bosom bush of America with its
Elders, its Elected, its subjugated, its tortured, and its enslaved
pretending to love and/or respect each other!

Laura Kraven speaks up incredulously: "A sit-down with
the savage?"

This "Thanksgiving Holiday" is very sad, sad just like Paul
Irak the Pequot, or Pip the "Saved" Indian, who cannot read
English yet holds his Bible like a mother holds her dead stillborn baby. This patriarchal holiday called *Thanksgiving* is just
like Pip's and Mary Dyer's stillborn — *A Monster* from another
world. Now you are like the stillborn baby Monster: cursed,
deformed and better off buried alive and tamped down. Baby
Monster's hand is smacked down with the shovel again as it
reaches up and out of the dark soil for oxygen; the monstrosity
is beaten down, squashed for a third time quickly before your

fence-watching neighbor peeks over and sees you planting baby monsters in your garden.

I can imagine Pip getting ready for the Thanksgiving Dinner. Pip, with an incarcerated future, feels elated momentarily looking in the mirror after greasing back his Indian black hair with religious snake oil. Pip dons a fashionable Walofang topcoat and pouts with a kissy-face in the looking-glass mirror like a wino whore. The next morning, hungover Irak feels sad and haunted, not wondering, but positive he should have died nobly fighting as opposed to dying comfortably sad and fat — white-devil style. Paul Irak should have died gracefully and not despondent and maudlin. He should have died with a yelp, a holler, and a fearless charge protecting his lands. Pip should have died with his tomahawk still in his clutched hand, dangling from his dead body. Paul Irak should have died, because living wounded, indebted, and hijacked in the Walofang world is not really living... it's desolate, dejected, and depressing.

Nancy St. Clair props up the Thanksgiving Holiday idea by exclaiming, "I'll bring muffins!"

Marge the Barge continues to try to convince our class that "We will all be thankful to God, thankful to Country, thankful to the London Company, and thankful to the King on this new holiday appropriately called 'Thanksgiving Day!'"

I think to myself, wondering if Wampy and Gela from my old Lenape tribe would like to come to Boston and be "Thankful." I speak up to Marge and the class and ask, "Can I bring my Lenape friends from New Netherland?"

Everyone laughs at me, but I didn't know why.... Depressed and unthankful now, I debate in my mind who would breed depressed children into a depressing world with gift-love and expect those children to be "Thankful." This unanswerable question and malignant sadness is a spiritual tax to the father and mother first. This post-mortem depression or buyer's remorse always befalls the Biblical parent, the rabbi, the priest, or the Bible salesman tenfold. The Abe-Babe salesman is in the hayloft with secret Scriptures of booze and porno for his VIP customers. The salesman / the lo-man can't stop raping the handicapped for his profit. This abstract "Profit" or tax comes from the mischief of treason, which is in all social ladder climbers, sales people, and brokers trading hypergamy-whammy love. The Abe-Babe salesman thinks about Nothing, wonders about Nothing, and bellows like a drunk southern hound-dog to his personal God, "Tell me when it ends, tell me when it ends, tell me when it ends!" Consequently, Ms. Sheriden the saleswoman is also voraciously inadequate and beautifully ill-fated. Marge the Barge and all Abe-Babes are dismembered and unnatural members of humanity.

Samuel Payneson declares, "Nay. Over my English dead body will I be thankful! Don't tread on my hill, you sassy lass!"

Elizabeth Winterest answers, "Perfect! We'll put Payneson the pig on the barbecue spit and have a real Thanksgiving!"

Margaret's white-devil method to madness is her ADSP — Attack with gift-love charity, enflame divisions and Divide with tribal greed, and then Starve with kindness.... The new American spice or Profit here in New England is the Native Indian's three sisters of corn, beans, and squash. The old English spice — the monopoly of fear — was laid bare due to a real agricultural discovery. All three American commodities are being ferociously exported back to England and Europe, creating small fortunes for the London Company and the royalist bourgeois in America, London, and Europe. This financial treason or circumvention has disemboweled and emasculated the American Pequot Indian forever. Marge and her MAC Attack Profit is building up homesteads, barns, feudal manors, and Boston itself. America is built upon the Starved, the Divided, and the shallow mass grave of Pequot Profit.

Ms. Appleton asks, "Margaret, do you think Thanksgiving dinner will bring us closer to the savage terrorist or the savage terrorist closer to the new white America?" The Irish Tiger is now the Irish kitty and she thinks for a moment and seems confused, as all of us are, by Ms. Appleton's stealthy Taoist question.

The Irish Tiger meows like a spoiled kitty, "We have shown the Pequot Indian the way toward salvation and the light!"

At this moment the Dutch Moroccan Mayflower glows brighter as it hovers back above x2, y2, right above Marge and her golden Jesus cross dancing on her breasts — he is b-boying and top-rocking. The candle-lamp seems to be flashing a message. All I can hear is the Puritan time machine called Grandpa snoring away, "Tick-tock, tick-tock, tick-tock." The class starts to snicker at Margaret with the candle-light blinking above her so she looks up at the orthoplex honeycomb like a cat and, making sure Ms. Appleton isn't looking, swats at the Mayflower as if it is a swooping mocking bird. The Irish Tiger misses and the Moroccan mocking bird barrages her with a strobe of twittering lights that are so sweet and savage at the same time it makes our classroom seem fair.

Ms. Appleton, still looking out the window, asks quietly not to just Marge, but anyone listening, "Are you whole?"

Our class becomes silent — as if suddenly found guilty, as most of my classmate are confused by Ms. Appleton's witchy metaphysical question. My classmates instead, after an awkward silence, continue mumbling and grumbling to themselves and nearby neighbors about the hypocritical horror of a holiday-inn dinner scam called "Thanksgiving."

We all struggle with Ms. Sheriden's meaty farce and repugnant fruits displayed as the *The Irish Tiger* continues, "Under a Divine light we will sit at an open Thanksgiving table celebrating the harvest for all of the converted terrorists and pure Pilgrims to share!"

As Marge the Barge crudely paints her picture of the disingenuous *Thanksgiving* dinner date with the emasculated

Pip and his third-world crew, it makes our whole white-devil class cringe. Marge the Barge concludes, seducing each syllable of the word with sultry satisfaction; "I cannot waiiit till Thaaaankss ggggiiiivviing!"

Our class gasps, winces, and struggles in unison, moving backwards in our desks, scratching the floor in a synchronized dance style. Ms. Appleton turns from the window, strolling pleasantly, slowly, thinking in front of the class.

She then asks suddenly, "Marge, have you shown the Pequot Indian the way towards profit sharing? Have you explained to the Pequot Indian during their parasitic 'American education' that 'Teaching' the Indians agriculture techniques they already know is creating huge fortunes for some of the Elect, Elders, and the London Company? Have you explained to the Pequots, the Narragansett, or the Mohicans that the weighted-down ships in Boston Harbor are setting sail for foreign ports, drafting low as a skiff, and that these ships receive four Crowns for every pound of corn, beans and squash? What percentage of the Profit are the Pequot Indians receiving for their use of their American lands and the *education* they have given to the Englishman? What percentage of your Profit have you given them? And most importantly, Margaret, why do you abuse the American Indian as WE were abused in Ireland, in England, and in Europe by the royal bourgeois and their standing-army?"

Margaret's commercial cravings start babbling religious catechisms in order to not answer this buck-shot of important questions. Margaret brings up Ms. Appleton's witchy past and how her questions and words against the Elect and Elders are blasphemous and heresy. Ms. Appleton yawns in Marge's face because she is parroting the other sinful children who promised Big-Daddy retribution and revenge. Ms. Appleton is getting tired and reckless in her homeroom inspection.... Our teacher is starting not to care anymore, which is heartbreaking.

Marge the Barge contemptuously sits down like a tug boat bumping into a dock, concluding and offering eternal redemption at a charity price to Ms. Appleton: "May God have pity on your soul!"

Brad Pining's ears are pricked, hearing his own tired language being aped by Marge the Barge behind him. Brad, being on the ball, jumps up to defend Marge — his lackey-loo, realizing that her psychotic God-love pity or psychotic God-love threats are last season's newspaper headline and no one in our class is buying yesterday's potato-eater newspaper.

Brad says, "Ms. Appleton, please be professional and polite, as I'm sure it's a fair compromise."

Ms. Appleton, feeling feisty with the truth spread-eagle on our imagined *Thanksgiving* dinner table, again in a louder voice says to Brad Pining, "Do the Pequots, do the Narragansetts, do the American Indians understand Profit sharing? Do the Pequots understand our fiduciary duty to them under English common law? Do the Pequots understand that the three-sister discovery in agriculture they handed us in good-faith is revolutionizing agriculture and humanity not just in England, but in Europe, and around the world? Do American Indians understand Profit? Does the American Indian want to profit-share the millions in revenue from their three-sister diet that the Indians just casually and unassumingly — with no malice and no thought of Profit or capitalism — just gave to us? How greedy are you, Pining?"

Brad, with musket and bayonet now drawn, stabs back at Ms. Appleton: "America has brought the savage terrorist democracy and freedom. We have won their hearts and minds. They will be thankful."

Ms. Appleton, a true American lady, magnanimously continuing the *good* ole *fight*, answers Brad Pining, the moral and physical bully. "We shall see, Brad... we shall see...."

Brad retorts, "I know the American native savage will be

as free and happy as the English have made the African native savage."

Ms. Appleton makes the doubtful, questioning, rolling and disapproving "MmMmMmmmm?" noise followed with, "So you think so, Brad?"

The class is silent as death, caught in a teacher and student cat-and-mouse standstill.... The black birds flutter outside the window again and pitter-patter on the roof. From the back of the classroom and to my right, Jen Patack honestly scoffs, giggles, and questions Brad's absurd statement, blurting out, "Happy African?" The class bursts into laughter as the absurd thought of a "Happy African" slave is laid raw as a Walofang delusion, a tragicomic play — a white-devil sarcastic dream, an American nightmare.

Brad, who sits in the front row in the second column, looks around cluelessly, quickly, and violently at the class, trying to pinpoint the questioning rabble, the laughing mob.

Ms. Appleton says confidently, "Aghh, pray thee, Brad, pray thee for the Happy African, yes, indeed — pray thee...." motioning to our next classmate to speak.

Brad continues to stretch his neck behind him looking for the hecklers and/or the *truth* as the swarm of cold blackbirds outside continue to scratch and peck at our schoolhouse outside. The birds flutter, flicker, and cast abstract funny shadows into our warm wooden classroom. These shadows seem to be laughing with us and the Mayflower candle-lamp as it hovers, glows and twinkles like a Moroccan star.

CHAPTER 9

I Don't Have a Boat — Sunday Painter

I DON'T HAVE A BOAT

 am enjoying the natural light-show and notice that William in front of me is still looking down at his desk, not paying attention, a million miles away, still thinking about Ms. Appleton's lady-of-the-lake questions. Billy, within William, is so easily depressed, triggered, and/or so easily thrown. I kick William's desk leg to wake him up as Jonathon Every also comes to attention in a lazy aplomb fashion.

The blackbirds disappear as misty morning clouds and the sun fight it out for who is going to be the dominant male within our sappy and turbulent blue spring sky. White clouds roll along hither and thither — sugaring off within an icy New England bluster. The small rural schoolhouse with my classmates in it seems like a small ship's cabin during some stormy voyage, or maybe a dark cabin in the middle of a blizzard? It is frightening to look outside as our classroom berth is rolling and rocking around with a carpenter's heavy silver square, a golden level plane, and a never-ending smell of curled wood shavings. We are in the hands of our carpenters as our hull creaks and sighs as the earth tirelessly and perfectly spins round and round, or is it the Atlantic Ocean washing us around and around?

Jonathon Every, Jr., stands up with profits already spent and speaks to our class on "The Lighthouse Bond Act," which is going to a vote next week in the Massachusetts Legislature.

Johnny caws and belches like a bloated seagull down at the seashore fish market with his fat fingers perched in his fancy vest: "The Lighthouse Bond Act will help the Boston economy, so you and your families MUST vote yes if you are TRUE patriotic Americans!"

Johnny casually takes his hand out of his pocket and silver coins scatter and roll about Ms. Appleton's soulful red oak floor. In this underworld there is no graph — under our school desks, in-between chairs, around skirts, around muddy shoes, boots, and pants — coins roll like anarchy, with no regard for order or hierarchy. One coin in particular keeps on rolling on the hollow wooden floor, jacking up Johnny's potential loss. Johnny scrambles this way and that as our class giggles at this rabid money-changer.

Samuel Payneson, by the far wall near the back, says, "Oh, hey, Johnny, here's a coin."

Just as Johnny tries to scramble back towards Payneson, Lawrence Randison, on the opposite side of the class by the front window, says, "Wow, looky here?! Finders keepers — losers weepers. Thanks, Johnny!" These remarks whirl Johnny into a tailspin and a charge across the classroom towards Lawrence.

Johnny Junior, when not chasing loose change, is thinking of his father's mercantile business. He is sure to lobby us to build a lighthouse out on the watery peninsula the Boston City Council had given to the Pequots last year as their *Club Dread Rez.* The Town Fathers set up a "Reservation," or some type of "Concentrating Country Club," so the Indians could "Re-educate or concentrate" on converting from savage terrorists to good, God-fearing Christians. But now the Continental Army and the Chamber of Commerce wanted to move the Pequot's Rez using "Eminent Domain" or their "Divine Right." This Lighthouse Bond isn't just about a lighthouse; it is about genocide, might-makes-right, and the Town Elders and Elect using the common man's money to profit.

The Everys and Johnny Junior care only about the volume of goods imported to Boston when the ships from the East India Trading Company arrive from the other side of the world. Johnny Junior (J.J.), Johnny "E," and/or Sir Every are a few of his aliases. From England's West Country, Johnny Junior is almost as slick as his white-devil father — Lord Every. Johnny Junior is expecting that the Far-East's spices, tea, and opium will bring a nice profit for both HIS and his father's business.

Johnny Junior has a large oval pumpkin head that is way out of proportion with his fashionista body. Johnny Junior's luxurious sherwani pajama party in contrasting black silk and yellow satin is a jeweled uniform for a fuzzy bumble bee. His reddish-brown jew-fro is a buzzing antenna that frames his pale blue eyes and pollinating tongue. Sir Every always seems to be hiding something and this suits him well — he is a wader and a skimmer. Johnny Junior's bowtie tries to conceal the fact that Junior is a fancy pirate, or maybe a gregarious Jew. Johnny Junior's eyes are murky, so after a moment in his gaze you are lost, slipping, falling off a cliff into a trance.

Johnny has a small, angry mouth that is always opened, sucking in the plankton of the world around him. Johnny Junior will dance on high-heeled French boots, waving around his arms, blade in hand, with embroidered white lace cuffs accentuating his clipped-wing tantrums. Sir Every, Jr., wears a tri-corn hat that is too small for his butter-chunk head, making his hat look like the cherry on top of a sloppy Sir Sundae boy from the sticks.

Sir Every, like Margaret, is under the constant glow of the Mayflower lamp in our Cartesian-coordinate classroom. The candle-lamp is the only source of heat and light within our

Jonathan McEvery

brown wainscoted graph. And after the Mayflower's blinky performance with Margaret, the golden honeycomb seems to burn. The Mayflower axiom flashes an SOS with a violent, jealous, and thrashing rhythm; it becomes a talking light as Johnny continues, flapping and squawking with puffery: "Dear patriots, the new Boston lighthouse will be our triumph on the hill. We will be a beacon to welcome and warn the newcomers of the dangerous sirens and reefs along our prophesied city on *the* hill. We must build to protect! Build to protect! Build to protect!"

Elizabeth Winterest scratches at Sir Every, saying, "Dear Sir, you're a vile Indian giver — a bully!"

Sir Every, quick on the draw, returns rhythmically in a slightly lighter, but more confident and sarcastic voice, "And you're an Indian-lover."

Ms. Appleton steps in and says, "We're all guilty here on Earth, children — all guilty."

Elizabeth blurts, "Dost not know the Everys' slave-trade, Ms. Appleton? Johnny Junior is a pork-barreling fraud just like his Big-Daddy."

"Maybe we're trying to grow our Boston economy here, Elizabeth," Ms. Appleton answers. "This Bond debt is part of our growing pains and will possibly benefit us."

The nautical candle-lamp's distress signal of Save Our Souls (SOS) slowly fades away like a missed lighthouse beckoning on the shore or a sinking ship's Morse code — doomed, rudderless, and lost at sea. Elizabeth mutters something about shipping companies paying for the lighthouse, as she is always biting and kicking for something or someone besides herself. The under-dog, the overwhelmed, and the ugly — everything Elizabeth is not — is her guiding-light in life. Elizabeth reminds me of Mary Dyer: some people seem so bored or put off with their own soul they have to worry about everyone else's soul. Most of these wanna-be martyrs want credit, not just during their lives, but before they break a sweat.

But Elizabeth is right: the Lighthouse Bond Act or debt would only help the Elect, the Elders and, of course, the Everys. Johnny Junior has little concern for his sloth because his real business is beyond indolence. Sir Every discarded the "Unclaimed cargo" that arrived "Damaged" from the East India Company and he was reimbursed with insurance claims and late-night flea markets in dark alleys. Johnny Junior, or J.J. after midnight, sold the black-market spice and opium in a gold-lording manner to the highest bidder within darkened Boston shadows. J.J. was just like Lord Big-Daddy — a Sir criminal! Sir Every, Sr., a profitable man, and his spoiled and polluted son are an American evolution.

The ambition and vitality of Johnny's father was displaced with John Junior's loafing and lolling around. J.J. was not just lounging around with pilfered goods in high heels and Parisian haute couture — he was stealing from his employer and his Big-Daddy! It would only be a short time before John Every, Sr., heard of someone undercutting his services of vice and spice in the secondary market. And like a smart Walofang white-devil, Lord Every would know the competition will have to be a close relative or friend under-cutting him.

Wanting only to get back to his simony ways, Johnny Junior absently and in a hurried manner squawks to the class, "Please vote yes for the Lighthouse Bond Act, which will be an economic beacon to lead our Biblical future." Johnny quickly sits down exhausted with his maritime martyrdom service and the tick-tock, tick-tock, tick-tock of Puritan time chasing a criminal.

Ms. Appleton rapidly instructs Johnny on how to be a better politician by saying, "Dear Jonathon, are you heedful to your good-work? Why are you such a brute? Please explain politely how the class will benefit from the new Lighthouse Bond Act."

Bouncing up off his seat, Johnny Junior rolls his eyes and balls around, looking at us classmates for the first time in a while; the more he looks at us, the more he silently realizes... no one in the classroom will benefit from the new lighthouse.

Johnny Junior's belabored grunts of, "Uuugghhh..." "Weeeellll...." and "Uuummm..." answer Ms. Appleton's and Elizabeth's question quite honestly, truthfully, and poetically in the Lenape American Indian language, but, in the forked English tongue, Jonathon Every, Jr., has just buried himself alive.

Johnny Junior spits and lobs out a knuckle-ball with his Big-Daddy's bullshit pitch and says, "Well, Ms. Appleton, the Lighthouse Bond Act will raise the tide and when the tide rises, ALL boats will rise."

Mrs. Appleton says dryly and unsympathetically, "I don't have a boat, Johnny, but thank you for your tidal update. You can sit down now. Next."

Sunday Painter

Right behind Jonathon Every is Jen Patacki or Jen Patack, as her family, from Eastern Europe, dropped the "i" when coming across the Atlantic Ocean. Her father is a dock builder and fisherman, so she is also the cheerleader child for her family business and the Lighthouse Bond Act. Jen is a haggard, pudgy little field mouse hanging off a limb, hanging in there — till Friday. Her brunette bangs are etched into her forehead by a ruddy coif wrapped too tightly around her head. Jen is a blind mole or chipmunk with large cheeks, but she sits in the back row of the second column like Diana, Elizabeth, and myself, so there is a camaraderie or a social status we share — Jen and all of us in the back are freaky creeps.

Jen Patack is insincere with her large, much-too-honest,

brown mousy eyes that belie any enthusiasm for life. Tirelessly, all day, the snotty aardvark is diligently apathetic in her nocturnal quest for vision and power. With her worm-like cheerleading one feels exhausted quickly when looking at and/or listening to Jen Patack. She is a visionless, unrepentant, hairy little anteater with a flouncy shift in the shape of a very large bow. With not even a peppering of politeness, consciousness, or honest cheer, Jen Patack sells herself as having vision, but she is a liability on a limb that has nothing except a Philistine's shrill voice and a young, sticky-like-shit soul.

Jen jumps up like an eager beaver early in the morning, and says exuberantly and overly politely, "Good evening, I, ugghh, aahh..." Jen realizes mid-sentence that it is 7:30 in the morning and that she misspoke, and tries to revive her sloppy momentum: "Pardon me, my wont is endless. I mean, uauagghh, I mean, Good morning, class! Happy to be here!"

Jen uses her cheers, mantras, and communication tools backwards. Last week in physics class, Jen and I were partners. She placed the screwdriver tool backwards into the screw and wondered why the tool didn't work. Jen yelled and scolded the tool, saying in her native Eastern European tongue, "Tupoy vilka, Topoy vilka!" which means "Dumb fork." But Jen was jabbing, missing, missing, sticking, stabbing the "Fork" backwards... Jen sat there in a trance, whispering — wondering, "Tupoy vilka, tupoy vilka." All I can picture when thinking about Jen Patack now is her thrusting, stabbing the handle of the screw-driver into the screw head and crying, "Dumb fork!" The depth, reason, and lack of geometric, mathematic, spatial, and general common sense in Jen are so unknown that it hurts me. It hurts me because I was once as helpless as Jen. Unable, or deliberately abandoned, the English and European woman is lost without masculine tools being cranked, hammered, and screwed by the male and his mantra of "Righty-tighty — lefty-loosey." And yes, it's a given that I had to run, hunt, and kill with the Lenape, but I was taught by the Indians

Jennifer Patack

to use tools. I wasn't kept, marginalized, and/or handicapped like Jen is.

On good days, Jen happily cheers, chants, and canonizes anthems. She acts clueless or dumb when people don't agree with what the hollow parrot did not understand. Jen will get confused and switch the words while singing harmony to the heavens at church. She will belt out "Love sin," instead of "Hate sin!"

Jen baffles most right off the bat, but the bewilderment comes in stronger waves if one tries to understand her by spending time with her.

Mental or biological defects or syndromes such as hysteria, dyslexia, Asperger's, autism, and/or your attention span at a deficit disorder level (ADD) can get you banished or burned here at the stake in 1650. For that reason, Jen's mental flip-flops are quite dangerous on one hand; but on the other ironic hand, her flip-flops very successfully take the wind out of the patriarchal conversation and/or mission, which is usually pretty funny, unless you are partners in physics class.

Strange, different, and/or angry women like myself swim like slow humpback whales in a small school. We are poorly defending ourselves from Puritan great white sharks (both male and female) as they repetitively hit, rip and tear off chunks of our fat blubber. The sharks' attacks divide us, killing off the weak and slow females first, not because the Puritans are hungry, but because their sin is animalistic, hereditary, and instinctual.

Jen Patack does not fathom civilization. Some say it is her genes, but the Patacki parents should have known better than to raise their children like flags on a pole. "American" children in their parents' eyes, but immigrants to everyone else, are tethered to a flagpole, flap in their parent's tribal wars, and wear out quickly in these icy and stony New England civilizations.

Looking pleasant, yet slightly nervous, Jen stands up to Ms. Appleton's boat-less life. Jen thinks to herself for a polite, common sense second, then she is lost. I can tell she reasons quietly and incorrectly, "I should talk about something besides the Lighthouse Bond Act."

The Lighthouse Bond Act stresses Jen out big time. All conflict and tension freak Jen Patack out into some type of high-anxiety or hyper-tension. But Johnny Junior cautiously looks over his shoulder at our class, and then at the distribution-of-wealth life preservers floating around us that Ms. Appleton has figuratively thrown to our class. Johnny Junior, an East-India man and with the ways and means of cooked books from Amsterdam's finest accountants, German mercenaries on twenty-four-hour guard, and crooked English judges in his eyes, glares at Jen with a disappointed gaze. Johnny Junior clears his throat, which freezes and petrifies the blind bat Jen Patack. It immobilizes her for only for an animalistic moment, as Puritan time does not stand still in Boston — every moment is murdered in its due time. The Puritan *time* machine or Big-Daddy clock rings out its cadence and chime again — tick-tock, tick-tock, tick tock — E, G#, F#, B — E, F#, G#, E. The Big-Daddy grandfather clock rings out eight times. It is 8:00 a.m. and orthodox Puritan time marches on, "Tick-tock, tick-tock, tick-tock."

With Puritan time now on her side, Jen revels loudly and suddenly, "I'm working for the Lighthouse Bond Act because it will make us safer! The harbor needs to be dredged and developed for our economy and security." Jen, in a feeble falsetto like a spazzing chick-a-dee, continues, "The Bond Act will protect. We need the Act in order to protect! Act to protect! Act to protect! Act to protect!"

In describing Jen Patack I'm reminded of the fourth letter I received from Mary Dyer. In it, Mary explained how

Simple-minded Puritans in Boston are torturing innocent

Quakers by cutting off their noses if they don't swear a pledge of allegiance to their imagined and abstract Puritan God. She explained, These free-spirits lose their nose in order to spite their face, which titillates the violent and perverted Puritan.

This fourth letter from Mary was written about a year ago, in 1649, from the Boston jail two buildings down from this very schoolhouse in which I sit today. I was surprised then, and still always think how Mary the heroine was really following through on her good-work. Mary wrote that she was now back in Boston after her little time-out party in northern England with Fox and friends, shaking and quaking with a new religion. The letter was written two days before Mary Dyer was to be hanged alongside two Quaker men. In the letter, Mary explained the callous disregard by Providence, Rhode Island, for *Boston's puritanical bloody laws and their cowardly bourgeois attitude.* She shared the cowardly Baptist excuse of *Can't see those Puritans from my house,* and the lazy democratic defense of *History will not repeat itself — man needs to be trusted.* Providence Separatists took the low road, saying, *The Boston Puritans will not create a new corrupt royal monarchy mixing church / synagogue and state with a zombie standing-army here in America. Not after England's Civil War ironed that good ole cause out. Don't you worry!*

Mary continued: *With wicked hands, simple mind, and simple heart, the Puritans torture humanity, but I do forgive them. However, my life is not accepted in America so I'd rather choose to die.* Mary continued confidently about her inner light, and the joy of being a Quaker. She also explained, *Two Quakers had their noses cut off to spite their face by the Boston Puritans and now I have been told by Governor Winthrop that "You shall go the great elm in the swamp, to this place of execution, and there be hanged till dead."*

Mary said she replied to Winthrop's Execution Order as she had in her third letter, *Yea, and joyfully I go!* Mary signed this fourth letter differently than her last joyful letter, but before signing off, she playfully questioned me: *Autumn, will you still respect me without a nose and with a stretched neck? I hope so!* Mary always had such a great sense of humor and humility. I remember my mother's trial and how supportive Mary was, not just to Annie, but to us children. My sisters and brother would have been lost if no one, at least another woman, didn't stand up with our mother against Boston's misogynist patriarchy. Mary signed the letter with my mother's thesis and epithet.

Still, Never Met An Elder Here.

Sincerely,

Mary Dyer.

Ms. Appleton, looking over at her grandfather clock, says, "Thitherward, class, we have to speed this homeroom inspection up in order to get to the 9:00 a.m. execution."

In a gullible tone Ms. Appleton asks Jen Patack, "If we build a lighthouse, wouldn't the Atlantic Ocean pirates or the Dutch Navy know where we are?"

This common-sense remark throws Jen Patack's inertia off track and she stands there in the panicky silence of being a defenseless human lost in capitalistic America. Instead of being a comfortable sloth hanging upside down, Jen is now an upright and evolved marsupial. She is barely hanging on, and getting panicky on a spring branch with the most adorable buds of nature blooming.

Jen looks down at Johnny Junior for guidance; he turns away, shaking his head, muttering something derogatory about "Dumb fucking Pollacks," and ignores her.

This indolent tag team of Johnny and Jenny, filled with a disinclination of drive, and an idle listlessness, is lazy-fraud on top of control-fraud. This is trickle-down economics. Jen

Patack is very slowly reading Johnny's angry body language and starts shuffling her feet.

Jen gives up, grimacing and burrowing, and then explosively says to our class and not to Ms. Appleton with relief and glee, "Don't you think the lighthouse will be pretty?"

The class, relieved and caught off-guard with this bright, yet brain-dead, assessment of the Lighthouse Bond Act, look around and honestly agree it would be pretty indeed. Diana Mallouston, who sits next to Jen, feels Jen's creepy camaraderie and says, "We could have picnics on Sunday!" Laura Kraven, in the front row by the door, says, "It would be a terrorist act if we didn't build the Lighthouse!"

I think to myself— *Picnics if you do and terror if you don't!* This is why I enjoy my sleeping sub-consciousness; this is why I close my eyes and imagine.

Ms. Appleton says sardonically in a faux-jubilant hyper tone, "Yes, the rich and drunk seashore Sunday painters will be delighted! They will paint our lighthouse, filled with an *inner light*, high on the city hill, and that will make us safe; well, actually... uumm, it will at least look safe! The lighthouse will be a real eye-catcher and make us safe... I guess... in our minds, and, and, and in the painting.... A safe space, for a moment or so — I guess."

Ms. Appleton, looking to pack it up with lifeless Jen, who seems to be an orphaned anchor in Boston harbor, left behind by the ghost ship called *The Gratefully Dead*, says, "Good luck with your Sunday paintings and your pretty vacant lighthouse, Ms. Patacki... I mean Patack. Sorry... next."

CHAPTER 10

This Is Child Abuse — Capitalist Perverts

THIS IS CHILD ABUSE

y pen and ink will slice and swirl with Lawrence Randison. His eyes, like Ms. Appleton's are sometimes crystals, but here the fashion is tight and masculine with a slight flare. And mark my word dear readers, proportions are correct. Lawrence Randison thoughtfully rises from his seat as smoldering orange and white frankincense rises from black burning coal. Lawrence, like burning rocks of honey, stands there bristling, billowing and flowering, forming his silence, his presence. Never Larry and always Lawrence, his sexy hazel eyes are a strange and turbulent mix of Spanish siesta and Norman Conquest. Like the Mayflower candle-lamp, he is mysterious, strong, and wise as the Bay of Gibraltar. The brass and glass facade of the lamp complements his skin, which is translucent Waterford white china. The Welsh lad rules from under a black stallion mane of hair, a raven crown or crest that cools his noble spirit. Lawrence's sporty doublet silhouette in a velvet mahogany is cut close to his dark-horse body. A Highland grandee with black lace Piccadilly wing tips on his shoulders that perfectly match his web-like peplums on his ox-blood jacket and breeches. His rapier sword never leaves his pelvis unguarded and is the sword of might in America.

With one hand? Two hands? With a shield or without, hand-to-hand combat quenches hardened Lawrence Randison and our American tribe with violence till the end of time. Lawrence's black leather sheath hides his long foible, but his elaborately displayed hilt and pommel are his pronounced manhood. The golden Mayflower candle knows this, so it always pulls back from Lawrence — wisely not trusting my cousin. Lawrence Randison's eyes are a dark Milky Way and he stands at attention, yet at ease. He clasps his hands behind him in a respectful and dutiful manner, making his fencer's Cheshire grin all the more dangerous and delectable.

Lawrence is in the front seat of the third of four columns. He gets up, looking at his neighbor Nancy behind him with a smirk first, and then looks around to all of us and in a lithe, Scottish baritone says, "My father and I are starting to teach blacksmithing classes, as the colony needs more blacksmiths for the booming business of steel weapons in America."

Lawrence's family is related to my own, but being away from Boston civilization for seven years, since I was eleven years old, I've lost track of my meaningless bloodlines. Lawrence, or "The Law" as he was nicknamed, is the nephew of Henry Vane. Henry, or Sir Vane, came to America as a young English aristocrat excited about the Separatist breaks from the English royal monarch and the Bank of England. He was Awakened about the Bible being a false God, existing and prevailing only to prop up royal or monarchal law that favors *the haves* — instead of the *have-nots*. Henry Vane, with a soft spot for the under-dog, was Awakened by a Reformation from the Catholic Church and the Jewish synagogue manipulating our Massachusetts Commonwealth. Philosophically, Lawrence's Uncle Vane, as well as other English aristocrats, wanted the monarchy of King Charles and the Church of England to forge on ahead of the Catholic cro-mags, but the oligarchy of royalty turned against him, so he did likewise and joined the Parliamentarians and their *good ole cause.*

Lawrence Randison

Like Henry Vane the Elder, Lawrence Randison has a wild side — a zest for life, a rocket in his pocket that doesn't always prioritize Puritan Boston, Separatist Plymouth, or Baptist Providence. Both men are more libertarian playboy, more feminine then statesman; both are narcissists. Henry Vane, very much like my mother, may have conceived and consummated the contrarian bastard / bitch union of 1638 when Sir Vane had his savage holiday here in Boston's Club Dread. Annie and Henry? These fashionable fascists posing as Democrats? Tories? Republicans? Separatists? These two political noisy assholes were as boring and predictable as swinging monkeys in heat.

Bastards like Henry Vane and nasty bitches like my mother are also always "For the people," and for the underdog, for the silent-majority, for the Commonwealth, but in reality, aren't for anything except their own megalomania. Politicians always selfishly lean toward the dastardly. They are only *for* themselves deep within a small union of ego supply. Their power to lead as the sexy son or Big- Daddy's little girl sooner or later turns our stomachs and souls wicked. And when these political hounds abuse their power just a smidge with some smutty lickerishness, it becomes their severed Achilles heel. The altruistic slick-willy politician, the homeless intellectual, and/or any oxymoron's wandering eye is the smoking gun that arrests them.

The American rabble, as it is with all those who are unfashionable, ugly, or on the wrong side, never receives its just pay or royalties. Unfortunately, the silent majority and/ or the forgotten lie to themselves, their children, and anyone they can bully, tax, and/or imperialize. They lie that they will attain royalty (and royalties) through hard work for the King, for their Country, and for God. This humane lie, as old as humanity, is the carrot on a stick for human jackasses. It is the spine of American moral poverty; it is the truth's demise. It is a calling for the common man to be a loyalist royalist coward.

It's a calling to blow-off our fathers', devalue our grandfathers' and disrespect our American forefathers' "Good-work" and VERY lives for you. We are not warriors, we are not engineers, and we are certainly not poets. Consequently, we are barren bitches and numb nuts dragging innocent children down, going further into circles of debt rather than facing our own cowardly grave. If history is not kind, these Bostonians in 1650, including myself, are taxable jerk-offs. If history is kind, we are... well, history is never kind.

Lawrence Randison addresses our class and explains further: "This Saturday morning, we will offer a class to men on how to make nails and musket balls. There will be blacksmithing demonstrations with tea, coffee, crumpets, and Ms. St. Clair's beautiful English muffins."

Our muffin-lover class giggles and steams up as everyone looks over at Nancy St. Clair, who turns as red as a May rose set against a white sugar snow. William looks around at me with a wink, and I see Bob Testaigne blow lightly on Laura Kraven's neck, simulating a spider and causing her to shiver and fluster. Lawrence also quickly loses his composure, looking flustered, holding Ms. St. Clair's muffins, and then gets back on track after flashing his Waterford smile, melting the young ladies' petticoats.

Lawrence *the Law*, continues: "Doff my silly words. I, I mean, of course, beautiful Ms. St. Clair AND her muffins."

Lawrence Randison and his family are very active in the Minute Men Continental Army and their blacksmithing is needed to supply this New England army. With all their militaristic hammering and keeping the cannons and blades hot came a natural eagerness for power and/or an itch to control others with a musket, a sword, or their lame wit. Lawrence's wit comes from his father's side and is as sharp and profound as a Celtic cudgel. Soon after this short-lived randy humor ran out and their petite intellectual drubbing was done, the Randisons brought out the omnipresent threat of guns and steel, which quickly silenced the bully's small talk and the victim's forced laughter, as might makes right!

Lawrence and his family lived northwest of Cambridge on the Mohican Trail and have a lovely manor that they built off the brisk gun and sword trade with the Continental Army. The funny thing about Lawrence and his uncle Henry Vane is that they are more salesmen than soldiers and therefore more interested in molesting the terrorist socially than raping and pillaging the terrorist physically. Lawrence and his uncle Sir Vane, like my mother, think it beneath them to enslave or abuse the native pygmies or Indians. All three dogged fighters complained endlessly that it isn't a fair fight with the natives, which most Americans appreciate. Regardless, this Antinomian controversy, this free-grace controversy, is an English controversy, not an American colony-child trophy. It is an English gut-check, a check-and-balance on your soul that tests whether you're a royal tool or a royal whore. A Mary or an Eve? Are you a fucker or are you getting fucked? Infertile? Impotent? On the sidelines? Meaningless? Lawrence the lusty *Law* likes a fair fight, in the flesh, with hand-to-hand and tongue-to-tongue combat, otherwise known as fucking.

Brad Pining speaks up in his gravelly voice: "Sounds good, Lawrence. I wanna bang some steel!"

Laura Kraven, a front-trading female, high strung and with her eye on the prize, questions, "Oh, hither / thither, who's gonna make me a candle-holder?"

Samuel Payneson, from the depths of the wrong side, slowly asks, "Can I make a cannon?"

I think how the Antinomian controversy or the free-grace controversy is such an affront and is akin to an attack against patriarchy. Free-grace is an intervention against patriarchy's loves, laws, and Gods. My mother's and Mary Dyer's free-grace are individually different, but still a subtext to the English Civil War, the Protestant Reformation and/or *the good ole cause.* Free-grace started out as women fucking who they want, where they want, when they want. And that's on Monday, Wednesday, and Friday.... On Tuesday, Thursday, and Saturday, these emancipated women fucked how they wanted and why they wanted.

One hundred and fifteen years ago in 1535, Muenster, Germany, that's exactly what Protestant women did and they called it free-love. On Sunday in Muenster the women rested, living free of debt, free of love — free of marriage and free of children — they celebrated! Nonetheless, on Monday morning the Roman Catholics from the Vatican raided their town and all the women were buried alive as their male lovers were castrated, disemboweled, and then imprisoned in little cages. These half-dead Muenster men dingled and dangled, they were a jing-a-linging and a jang-a-langing fifty to seventy feet off the ground, crudely caged and hanging off the steeple of the church. The men were starving Christmas balls on a church tree — Catholic ornaments of civilization and sex education gone bad. That was one hundred and fifteen years ago and the cages are still there, a jang-a-linging and a dang-a-ling in Germany. The black crows pecked away all the men's meaty bones, but the free-love ghosts and the empty cages with the skeletons of some fine Franks are still rattling above your head as you enter a German Catholic house of God.

Thinking about this historic lesson of women's rights being suppressed, I raise my hand to speak. Lawrence silently nods towards me and I say, "Oh, dear Lawrence, will you please show me how to make a rock?

Everyone in class laughs at my freaky question, but they are cut off when Diana Mollouston in the back of the first column gravely says, "Knowest thou thy Bible, fools? Knowest David slayed Goliath with a rock?"

I jump in and say, "Yes, thank you, Diana — accuracy and timing is everything." Turning back to Lawrence, I add, "I have a hemp sling made from my days in the woods with the

Lenape, but I need a new type of rock... a rock disc made of steel. But I want my steel discs to have holes, grooves, and wings that I can fill with cargo and messages. I also want my rocks to sing, warble, and whistle like a demon bird."

Lawrence is smiling ear to ear, bewitching everybody in the class. He cheerfully congratulates me and the class on our murderous intentions. "Whistling demon birds! That's the kind of American spirit I like!"

Contemplating my theory on women's emancipation is tough because our mother England is still in the middle of a Civil War over her women's shaggy rights. The tribes of England: the Tories, the Separatists, the Puritans, the Parliamentarians, the Cavaliers, the Welsh, the Rumps, Labor, the Scots, the Roundheads, the Levelers, the Whigs, the Irish, the Diggers, etc., etc. — all jockey to own women, but not in America! My mother and possibly Mary Dyer here in 1650 are the first and second martyrs of fucking in America! Free-grace, I believe, is when women discovered it was a blessing, not a curse, to be a woman! Women became unashamed women. Not butchy: masculine and materialistic, but feminine — artistic, spiritual, and mysterious.

Even numb-nut Sir Henry Vane, knowing this truth, but too much a scoundrel coward to speak up, split back to England to help Parliament rule after planting his demon seeds here in Boston. Back in merry-old England, Sir Vane may lose his head to King Charles II if the royal monarchy bubbles back into *depeche mode* (fashionable news) after the northern Roundheads in due course lose their *je ne sais quoi* (inexplicable positive quality).

However, Lawrence, unlike his uncle Sir Vane, has a very disciplined and playful passion, so Lawrence *the Law* will never cause his own demise. Regardless, Lawrence is a playful pilgrim compared to a passionate pilgrim like William Demopheare or my Grandpa Frank, who vicariously turned my mother Annie into his Protestant soldier. Instead of Annie being a solid, well-behaved, Christian child, Grandpa Frank created a feminist, which is a polite word for an adulteress and/or an anarchist in a dress. And, perchance, self-actualized, these savages in skirts will evolve into grand prophetesses or profound artists.

My mother was born a suppressed woman, just as all Jewish and Catholic women are born, and then they are divorced from their bodies once again at the first site of their own blood between their legs as young teenagers. My hysterical mother and all women are then taught to live in the white-devil society as a bleeding, smelly, and overall a nasty and replaceable subordinate — an "Eve." *Eve* is a *damsel in distress* waiting to be let back in the Garden after she was bad. This is parental child abuse and a crime against humanity. This is no Abe-Babe mistake; this is religion.

The Catholic-lite mother Mary and Jewish-lite mother Eve assassinate my feminine soul and all women's souls with their Judeo-Christian duality. The bilinear vector spaces of *Mary* and/or *Eve* are a theorem of dual vectors in which duality is a truth that works off both negative female facades, creating a whole; it is a double bind. It is two complementary extremes that play against each other: good cop vs. bad cop, and Mary the good obedient virgin mommy vs. bad Eve, the questioning whore mommy. Neither abstract entity could exist without the other, proving it's a crime, a scam, a trap — a patriarchal control-fraud.

Then after the assassination and hysterectomy are completed, my mother, motherhood, and all women stand alone. They are frozen sculptures made of cheap plaster, hollowed out as a Virgin Mary statue in order to keep costs down. Each is a cheap statue at a dead house in front of dead shrubbery with a dead front door. Dead-letter newspapers filled with a dead language litter this path to nowhere. The nowhere path that leads to the Virgin statue is lined with artificial Negroes and pink flamingos. The statue is a grotesque liability, a crime against women and our Creator. Similarly, my mother, a ghost of womanhood, a Jezebel goblin, was liquidated to cover up society's and my Grandpa Frank's white-devil tracks. Patriarchal Abe-Babe women are buried alive and thrice removed.

The black birds are back at our windows as they enjoyed sunning themselves on our school, church, and Town Hall roof lines. The black birds are now chasing a crow up on Corn Hill. The crow was continually swooping down towards their unhatched eggs, sitting like delicious teal-colored *hors d'oeuvres* (appetizers) on a silver tray nest. The crow was looking for breakfast, but the black birds swarmed and trailed the crow in mass like a mob of mosquitos in a bog during a summer night. The blackbirds have become the crow's large shadow — these shadows fight other shadows in flight, but the hunted fight the hunter with these shadows.

Ms. Appleton raises her hand as if she has been reduced to a student amongst us. She asks gingerly, in a slightly sultry manner, "Well, Lawrence, can I bang your anvil?"

The class immediately laughs at the ridiculous idea of a woman blacksmith, but I know Ms. Appleton isn't joking. She continues, "Women need to work with tools, they need to take back their tools to help the commonwealth, and more importantly (speaking louder and looking deep into my confused eyes), women need not be so clueless and helpless."

Ms. Appleton, as usual, cracks the thin ice / my ice beneath my delusional world with her dark humor. Everyone in class laughs for a moment or so. Except me....

My world becomes quiet, I am even deaf to the tick-tock, tick-tock, tick-tock of Puritan time. I instinctually looked away from Ms. Appleton and out the window past the alarmed blackbirds, past the weeping willow, and beyond towards the executioner's swamp. Out there in my shitty future, out there in Boston I thought about my *Other*, and my *Nothing* and I started to cry. Never before had I felt such dread and disgust with my Boston tribe. Even in the woods with the Lenape, with a people whose language I couldn't even speak I felt more at home with myself and my world than here in Boston with my new family and friends. My nose became tingly, my forehead turned light and feathery, the muted June spring colors outside the window of yellow, green and sandy tan turned into a Chinese watercolor. The early morning yellow sun, the lime green new growth on the trees and bushes, and the sandy brown scrub brush dirt slowly turned into a Taoist watercolor — a creamy, milky and gentle jade watercolor in which sea-green strength, reality, and materialism are inverted into a misty spiritual Nothing. My tears quench a thirst on my lips, my tears are warm, thick, and salty like they mean something. It's relaxing to cry in the white-devil world; my tears, all tears, are an Awakening to teach or show me something. The truth as minimalist lines, scratches, and puddles of ink frames my Boston Nothing with seashores and emerald oceans.

Tears run down my cheeks softly. I think to myself... fuck... I'm still alive. I'm still alive even though I'm an incarcerated orphan in a Boston classroom cage. I'm still alive and breathing even though Mary Dyer is going be executed in an hour. It's all becoming too dismal and shocking. Startled by my tears, I wipe them away quickly and think: damn... Ms. Appleton... a wanna-be adulteress, a wanna-be anarchist, and a wanna-be artist teaching me something! Granting all this, I concede Ms. Appleton and womanhood are forevermore a red-hot ember floating up towards the midnight-blue hour, a glowing coal that will never freeze, that would never go out. Ms. Appleton and her tools burn bright and deep in the starry night, Ms. A, buried deep in our earth's soul.

Capitalist Perverts

I think there is a slight applause as Lawrence Randison takes his seat, silently nodding a sly "Yes" to Ms. Appleton's banging anvil question. Their eyes are still locked on each other's as Nancy St. Clair eagerly jumps to attention, seeking to end her teacher's and her boyfriend's hammering for Thor.

Ms. St. Clair starts her homeroom cheer-tease in a quiet, unassuming voice: "Please do come to the blacksmithing class. I'm baking and juggling my English muffins as usual, so everyone should merry-over for a patriotic time!"

Her Norman yoke family was also active with the Confederation Army, but as a shipping and storage contractor. The St. Clairs maintained and supplied the endless Indian wars and imperialism with horse-drawn carriages and booze. Like the majority of humans, the St. Clairs delight in others' pain, but they are also now making quite a pretty penny off of pain: militaristic pain and addicted pain.

While relishing, gossiping about, or profiting from another human's sorrow or demise, otherwise known as capitalism, it's best to be greased and liquored-up. Capitalism, like alcoholism, is an addictive drug, and best run analogous and parallel to drug addiction because capitalism properly shows off and/or stomachs your deformed life. Alcoholism or any drug addiction is a solid defense against ever attaining common sense in society. The Elders, Elect, Nancy, and the St. Clairs, realizing this, sell pints of fruit-gone-bad nonsense from one of their very popular cider wagons. This allows the St. Clairs to get rich and their civilization to get drunk on the blurred pursuit of life, liberty, and hard-cider happiness.

Nancy St. Clair is a lumpy lemon climber left too long on the limb, a sumptuous golden tiara clematis, beautiful in her vain ardor, but sour, a tart with poisonous vines and fashionable fruit flies that smother growth and spoil the drink. Nancy's fair hair is furious and the buttonholes on her hunter-green blouse are stretched open as her lewd and las-civious breasts demand constant fresh air and daily manhan-dling. Ms. St. Clair's body is bountiful / hungry, and divided by a large leather belt the color of port wine. A large brass buckle, tarnished but buttery, covers her warm belly.

Ms. St. Clair's origin O (x3, y2) writhes and steams under-neath her sage-colored petticoat and crisp white apron. The Mayflower candle-lamp above her showers down radiation as the sun tans a snake, or, from the perspective of an eagle's eyes, — a snack in the spotlight! Nancy's gin-rummy eyes are the color of a far-off grey fox, always busy looking for the next tip, twit, or foxy deal. Nancy is a muffin-marm with a bouncy butt and dirty boots. She is a lustful vine, a barmaid siren, a bully maiden — a bar-maiden, who introduces herself as "*Eve*" in a sexy voice in a snaky-basement garden-bar. Ms. St. Clair is a Viking seducer who pretends she wants to be seduced, but she would never allow herself to be so vulnerable — so honest.

Nancy was not a wanna-be virgin mother or a bully-mom, but a "Mother" too far. Nancy tries to be a fun woman — a funny woman, a "Fun-to-be-with" woman, a masculine woman, all of which is impossible. Nancy is a happy prisoner turned grim prison guard within gender jail and is now dis-pleased with freedom. Nancy's now an escaped prison guard on a raft slowly floating to nowhere, dehydrating as a bar-tender serving drinks under the bright sky on a patriarchy warpath. She is emotionally beside herself, a thorny and thirsty cheerleader cactus, perfect for the dead Salton Sea of American womanhood.

Back in class, everyone is still thinking or dreaming about Lawrence "The Law" Randison, and Nancy can sense this dis-traction.

She pretends to fall forward and kicks Lawrence's chair in front of her and says again in a shrill, panicked voice, jug-gling her muffins, trying to get everyone to forget her lovely Lawrence, "No, really, my muffins are the best! Grandma St.

Nancy St. Clair

Clair's relatives stole the recipe from Louis X - The Quarreler himself!"

Both Nancy and Lawrence are hot-tempered, child-hood sweethearts with wandering eyes and the likelihood of an eye-gouging if either catches the other coveting or eyeing-balling a sexy neighbor. Nancy is a voluptuous mer-maid in training, or, more correctly, a barmaid in training. Regardless, she is drowning, but her motherly mammary glands and saloon-sally style is a wet-dream for every male Puritan and Pilgrim from Providence down south all the way up north to Exeter, in New Hampshire.

This wet dream keeps American men alive. They dream of rescuing their siren-on-the-rocks and then dragging her home — making and then breaking that bitch into an *honest woman*. Nancy and Lawrence's patriarcal "Love" cannot be compared to that of the Lenape because the Indians have no shady or ambiguous word such as "Love."

They have a word for respect: "Kitahala." Respect comes from a matriarchal woman's point of view, in which sexuality and passion are embraced by not just a woman's gaze, but her rolling ideology of respect and, most important — her judg-ment! It is similar to the ancient gaze of the female cockroach to her male partner when she thinks about breeding and "Loving." Not the *eros* of a roach, but the friendship, the *philia* and charity of a cockroach! This feminine respect, compared to Lawrence and Nancy's *love*, makes the young Americans seem to be rabid animals competing for hunting grounds rather than respecting or *loving* one another.

Lustful English and American teenagers with bayonets drawn at the drop of a petticoat seem confused, possessive, and insanely violent. These sexless and sadistic children are the poisoned flower of capitalism as religion. Lawrence Randison and Nancy St. Clair are the *eros* and erotica of impe-rialism. Compared sexually to the red-skinned terrorist in the woods, Lawrence and Nancy and all American lovers don't seem loving, humane, sexy, or honest at all. The Americans

seem meticulously apathetic, bitterly frigid, and, overall —
cruel. These perversions of affection, these perverts of civilization working and milking need-love and gift-love, have
no respect for themselves or their lovers; Americans are not
lovers — Americans are capitalist perverts.

Everyone in class seems to slowly agree with Nancy's
good-time invitation; this includes William, who leans back
and says to me, "I bet you could mold metal with your mind."

I look deep into his flirtatious wanton eyes and say, "The
only metal I mold is human mettle." William, or Billy in
fourth gear, was turned on by my ratcheting up of his flirtatious advance into a truly religious homophone conversation.

He asks me, "Can you mold my mettle?"

I said, "I will gladly when your mettle starts to get warm."

William, shunned and humiliated, says, "I will go to the
blacksmith breakfast and prove my mettle is filled with hot
fire by hammering metal until the God of thunder doth hear
me." William speaks up to the class and Nancy St. Clair and
says, "Count me in."

Nancy says, "Aww, wouldst thou, Billy? You're the cutest...."

I say with a smirk, "Why, William, blacksmithing and
muffins sound dangerous! Shouldn't you check with your
Mum first?"

William, shocked with eyes wide open, sighs, pouts, and
then looks out the window. Billy is just a weak-kneed fence
sitter, a bartering butterfly with diamonds up his ass, slowly
negotiating his fair-youth plan as he sinks beneath the quick-
sand surface of political life. Billy is grasping for any truth or
a reason to live, and he can't find any.

Ms. Appleton strokes her golden brass ruler gently, notch-
ing-up at her desk, still looking up and over at Lawrence peri-
odically, and after a moment or so says dismissively, "Thank
you, Ms. St. Clair, for that enlightening muffin-marm party
memo.... Next."

CHAPTER 11

Israel Didn't Just Squirm, Our Entire World Squirms — Good Morning Elizabeth

ISRAEL DIDN'T JUST SQUIRM, OUR ENTIRE WORLD SQUIRMS

s. Appleton looks over to Israel Wilkinson and says, "Let us not dawdle, Mr. Wilkinson, we have a hanging to go to this Monday morning. Please tell us about your good-work."

Israel stands up gracefully and says, "I agree, Ms. Appleton, today is a great and valuable day, a gift from our one true God."

Sitting behind the St. Clair muffin militia is the curmudgeon of Cambridge. Israel Wilkinson is the sunken son of a Captain Wilkinson, who smoothly sailed from the Royal Navy into the insurance business after realizing risk traders were the only people making money in the shipping business. This realization came to Captain Wilkinson after he was ship-wrecked for the twelfth time within twenty-four transatlantic trips. Seasick and delirious, floating lost in some dinghies tethered together in the horse latitudes, Captain Wilkinson realized that a *loss* isn't always a *loss*. Life is too risky to actually *do* anything, but life is worth betting on because dead men are worth money, especially if you take the short side,

the Neg-Am Jam side, because, within this NAJ world of capitalism, eighty-five percent of everything is mathematically
wrong, unless it's not....

Israel Wilkinson wears the customary tall- and wide-brimmed
English hat cocked forward and worn on the top of his head for a
Puritan God, not a pilgrim savior. Shadowed by his hat, Israel's
furry brown eyebrows and crucifying eyes match the shades
and obscurities of his stalking cape. Israel has a crooked nose
and his mouth seems to be smiling and frowning at the same
time. Israel's facial features run around his face. His eyebrows
scrunch down into a furrowed brown brow, then they go up
in surprise! The fury rollercoasters smile up and frown down
within milliseconds. Israel's eyes are mud-slicks and sharp as
crosses made of diamonds with a high-gloss glow. The disingenuous nature of Israel flows from his mouth, which is shaped
like busy crab legs running in circles. Israel's forked tongue is
always selling, scheming, wagging, and howling along with the
wolves at night off in the Blue Hill hillocks, chasing their tails
because they cannot sleep.

Israel stands up at his desk and says, "Dear class, my family
business was born to help. Please help me — help you. I want
to protect you, I want to serve you, I want to insure you!"

Captain Wilkinson, and now his son Israel, sells insurance
policies. The Wilkinsons are making money no matter the
outcome. They are option-trading on both the positive side
and the negative side of life. Making money on the tragedy
side and on the NAJ side. Just like all insurance men who sell
fear and risk as a charitable front or gift-love, the Wilkinsons'
angle or edge is their underwriting as graveyard investors.
Death and sin stick to the Wilkinsons because they put policy
premiums and money above their souls.

Negotiations with the floating dead, the sunken half-dead,
and the desperate heirs of the *maybe* dead are always profitable. Do nothing, be Nothing and trade / control everything

Israel Wilkinson

was Wilkinson's *modus operandi*. Why go win-lose, when you can go win-win-win?!

Whatever commodity, whether it be coffee, corn, currency, passengers, and/or slaves, that ran aground, that float away, something valuable (an insurance policy?) could also float away... maybe; maybe not? Or that insurance policy could wash up on the beach! Perhaps it could be tucked away — deeply, warmly, and alphabetically in the widow's files under "I" for insurance. Or, perhaps, lost? Misplaced? Maybe; maybe not? Or maybe the insurance policy is half burnt and discarded in someone's fire pit or ash can? Maybe; maybe not? The only thing left for the insurance Claim is the Adjuster's math, calculating the loss... maybe; maybe not? And then the policy pay-out with Mr. Wilkinson's signature... maybe; maybe not?

Regardless that humans are slowly sinking to the bottom of the Atlantic Ocean, Captain Wilkinson is going to collect on his rising premiums and countersue that Claim. The Captain and Israel love their *short*, their negative bet, the NAJ life more than they enjoy a positive life because it's easier and more profitable to be negative.

The Wilkinsons, in their leathery and wood-paneled Beacon Hill offices, wave around fancy quilled pens and compare Italian *machismo* colognes as they cherry-pick clients, policies, premiums, distressed debt, and commodities out of the shipwreck. They cherry-pick passengers, cargo, and slaves out of the dark, cold water at night. They cherry-pick humans and backdated policies out of the biting, bottomless Atlantic Ocean. Because there you are: a good insurance customer, swimming for it late at night after your boat goes down....

As I gasp for air and the black ocean fills my mouth and lungs with wet cement I think, where is my insurance policy? I'm sleepy now, drowning now, submerged again, upside down and tired, flutter-kicking now, shivering, doing the doggy-paddle into a black wet infinity. All I can hear is that Puritan music box, their time ticking away, adding weights to my feet with every tick and tock: Tick-tock, tick-tock, tick-tock! It all becomes clear as my shipmates disappear beneath the surface. It's getting quiet again. I yell aloud to the beautiful moon above, "Hey, diddle diddle!" wondering if I am swimming east back to England, west to America, perhaps on the horizon that is Africa? Or maybe I'm swimming north to Greenland? Then I refocus: clueless, directionless and totally in control! I'm hoping, wondering, whether I will be able to take a gasp of air after this twenty-foot black wave in my face passes?

Now submerged, underwater, where it's quite peaceful as the cat plays the fiddle. I wonder, is this it? Is my life over? So quickly? Just like that? So easily transpired. No warning, and not really that big of a deal. Kind of funny: not really funny, but *funny*.

Unfortunately, I rise up out of the water and gasp into the wrong murky wave, at the wrong time, with the wrong insurance policy, and again I suck black cement into my saturated body. Tick-tock, tick-tock, tick-tock. Water pours into my lungs, down to my tailbone, and squirts out of my ears, fingernails, and toenails. I'm a water bag in the Atlantic night with heavy black chains draped around me I used to call my favorite dress — *haute couture*. The sound of fashion — tick-tock, tick-tock, tick-tock.

High fashion is water-to-water osmosis, floating for a moment in style, then, in an instant — concretized, out of fashion and sinking fast to the bottom of another world. Unfashionable now, I breathe again, I hope, gag, and wriggle for my dinner date with Captain Neptune. I gasp and wheeze while I do the doggy paddle to Atlantis, just like the fat cow that didn't make it over the moon.

I wonder if that darkness was a shadow or a shark that just swam along my leg. I wonder about surviving, being eaten alive and/or drowning. I think about giving up.... I, the swimming sow, I, the blubbering humpback — giving up and bowing to the black lava ocean with her sharks. This wet swim and starry darkness with no horizons is the blackheart of the NAJ life.

Israel points with the purple tassel that he uses to keep his place in his fashion-accessory Bible and says, "Now, I know you classmates of mine don't have a home, business, or life you want to protect, but tell your parents: Israel wants to help." He says again, "No, really, don't be embarrassed. Who here needs help? Everyone needs help. I'm here to help you achieve your dreams! Who here is smart enough to insure their dreams?" Israel's Bible bookmark is a stiff, purple, morose satin bar that has black tassels. When he waves the tassels around when speaking he creates a troubled yet frisky lavender haze. When not holding his Bible, he will use his purple tassel bar as a pointer during his policy pitches. The tassel is an Indian reminder for me that Israel is an insurance salesman and an insurance dancer. He did his black-crow feather dance not monthly, but all-day long. Israel sold purple policies from his underwriter God — dancing in vain for his life.

Israel says, "I'd like to talk about a valuable customer of mine who insured his African slaves and" but he was interrupted by Jen Patack.

"Bring back 'Two-for-One African slave Mondays!'" she yells out.

Numerous "Yeahs!" "Hhmmhhhms!" and "Ooohh yeahs" percolate up from the class, agreeing with Jen.

Israel always carried and quoted the Bible in order to convince people he was NOT a graveyard investor or money-changer, but I think the Bible did the reverse. The Mayflower lamp, our orthoplex honeycomb, nervously inched closer to Israel as he spoke, as if keeping a wary eye on him.

It only takes a quick look into Israel's religionist eyes to feel the cottonmouth poison hemmed throughout his small-print salvation. The snake oil Israel is merchandising and trading is a quick-fix remedy and an insurance plan for a religious itch, an existential itch. It is the X-itch, wherein you wonder: Why am I here? And, more important, why are these white-devil vipers like Israel Wilkinson selling me dreams and controlling me?

To not answer or to mask these questions, Israel Wilkinson and other money-changer merchandisers legislate and police Americans into an expensive Puritan insurance plan that covers their original sin and "All Judeo-Christian religious *good-work* without liability for their actions, damages, and/or genocides now and/or in the future."

Englishmen and Americans pay on time, if not beforehand, for their original sin umbrella policy. I hear Puritan time now: tick-tock, write a check — tick-tock, write another check. Tick-check — tock-check. Tick-check — tock-check, total insanity... I think Puritan time is, besides being unhealthy — very expensive.

But insurance against absolute liability married to being "God-fearing" makes Jews and Christians feel good and immortal even though they know the small print says "No Refund. No Guarantees." I imagine in the afterlife these reasonable and religious Abe-Babe people will argue with their Maker — showing their cancelled checks to the synagogue, church, and insurance company, as proof of payment, which will only show proof of guilt.

Ms. Appleton says, "Jen, mind your manners speaking about Monday like"

"No insult was taken, Ms. Appleton," Israel cuts her off proudly. "The 'Two-for-One African Monday' slavery sale day was valuable to the community, and my father is lobbying with the Minister... aaggh... I mean Governor and the City Councilor members to smooth out the conflict."

The "Conflict" was that the Boston Elect said more taxes

were owed, as the Wilkinsons were paying tax on one African slave sold, not two on Mondays.

Israel continues, "Silly us! 'We admitted NO wrongdoing' with the State and we're happy to give Governor Winthrop his tax."

In all fairness to Israel, growing up the only son of Captain Wilkinson he had little choice but to be a trade or commodity himself. He was born and doomed to be the insurance man, trader, and/or salesman bully who in poetic consequence insures, trades, and sells-out all those weaker than himself: his family, friends, children, and community.

Israel could have become a runaway son / a runaway slave; a loss — a claim? But that would be a strong genetic move. Israel did not possess this gene; therefore, like his mother, he was merchandised, brokered, traded, and enslaved. The enmity Israel has for his Abrahamic father is unleashed on everyone except his Big-Daddy. Israel's ill will and spitefulness burned brightly in every intonation he blathered and in every thread, he worked. He was hammered hard not by a father, but by a wounded murderer — a Big-Daddy trading not just risk, humans, and debt, but trading and enabling paternal suicide. Because Israel grew up running around musical-chairs America and singing "Going to Jerusalem," he deeply understood another human's market / commodity price at the insurance claim department or at the auction block.

Tickets... tickets everyone. Tickets....

Roly-poly - don't lose your seat! Roly-poly, don't lose your seat!

Who's not a royal? Who's not holy? Who's disloyal? Who's unholy?

Who's not a Jewish royal? Who's not a holy Christian? Who's not part of our royal-holy family?

Someone's gonna die... someone's gonna lose... someone's going to hell....

Cause we're going to Jerusalem! Not just anywhere — next stop Galilee!

Does the devil dare? Does the devil see? You think this ride is free?

Someone's gonna die... someone's gonna lose... someone's going to hell....

Cause we're going to Jerusalem! It's our destiny!

Ms. Appleton says in a jovial and sarcastic tone, "We understand, Israel... the State is always fashionable... I'm sorry — I mean negotiable. Unless, of course, the State is not fashionable — I mean negotiable."

Because kidnapping and ransoming are still a noble political practice here in 1650 and a kissing-cousin of slavery, I, like many, was taken hostage five years ago. Other Indian tribe members and English and European nobleman and their families are often taken hostage and then ransomed back to their invested family or tribe. I'm sure the Dutch trader and broker from New Netherland (Jan Throgg) who brokered and merchandised the end of my five-year fresh-air summer vacation in New Netherland got a fat bag of English Crowns for my Boston ass.

Israel asks once again, "I want to insure you — I want to help you. I'm serious; who needs help here? Don't be ashamed, I won't bite — I want to help you with your American dreams!"

I think to myself... maybe this "Insurance" racket could help Mary Dyer or even me. I need help and so does Mary... I raise my hand gingerly and Ms. Appleton nods for me to speak. I ask, "Israel, can I buy a life insurance policy for Mary Dyer?"

Everyone laughs joyfully and I don't know why.... I am serious! Mary needs this insurance help, but my classmates are still laughing as I suppose they think I can joke about this execution / murder of a woman we were about to commit within the hour. Yes, I was out in the woods of America for seven years — a year in Providence, a year in New Netherland, and then five years with the Lenape and I don't understand the pump-and-dump tactics of insurance men yet. The class continues to laugh and then, slowly, one by one my class-mates and Ms. Appleton realize I wasn't joking as I sit there in an uninsurable and half-dead manner.... The Atlantic tide of reality slowly returns and covers my buried body and protruding head in the tidal surf. It is depressing to drown here — watching my classmates' expressions go from, "She's funny!" and "Wow, she's finally really one of us — thank God!" to "Wow, Autumn Leaf is fucking gone... just toast...."

It is as if I suddenly died yet again, and I was at a Viking ship burial along the shore at night. The problem is that I am the dead person on the burial ship and I was just pushed off shore and the ship I floated in was set on fire. My classmates looked generally relieved to see me on fire and floating away. Some looked sad as the flames around me grew and sparkled off the water. Flames lit their proud and contorted faces. I saw compassion in some of their eyes — Ms. Appleton's, Elizabeth's, but mostly I saw bitterness and envy from my classmates that I was dead! Even William seemed pissed and panicky that I was going to the afterlife, leaving him behind — alive and not dead. The afterlife is a place William and my classmates have no idea (despite their Bible) how to imagine. My peers are both scared and jealous of my finding out first what happens upon our death. This jealousy and resentment makes them cry, not in sadness, but in spite. My sinful class will now have to find another punching-bag freak, another scapegoat to torture. My Puritan mourners are begrudged by my death.

Israel gives me a low-man answer and says, "I'm sorry, Ms. Leaf, but there's no value in Mary Dyer."

Having gone American "Native" from thirteen to eighteen

years old I don't exactly understand that everyone has a monetary value. It seems that your value is determined not by you, but by your friend's and/or family's *loss*, and how much they're willing to pay for you and your life. If you have no friends and family with money, or money they're willing to spend on you, then you are not worth being taken hostage. You are an orphan... yours is a devalued life... you are worth nothing... which isn't that bad if you're an orphan of sorts, because that puts orphans closer to *Nothing* and their Maker or Creator. But be on guard, foundling, because the Puritan points to you only as a negative life, with a Neg-Am Jam soul — a lost soul. As the foundling with "No value," you are first thrown overboard or burned at the stake for a sacrifice — a Billy Budd / a Mary Dyer. You are the forgotten, the silent service industry and/or an organ donor for the rich or, perchance if you're lucky — a lonely composting water balloon lazily leaking and loitering your way through life.

I ask Israel, "There is no *value* in Mary Dyer?"

Happy water balloons — red, yellow, and green, colorful balloons dancing — blue and orange water balloons pissing. Brown, pink, and white balloons killing and fucking all over the earth until... pop! You return to the watery Nothing, you return to the existential mistake and evaporating pee-puddle that you fear you are.

The human value is not in the hostage or the slave, but in how much perceived *"Value"* the merchandiser, the master, the bidder will pay at market during an auction for that human life. The market's 'Bid,' 'Ask,' and 'Offer' determine my white-devil auction price, the African slave's price, and pray, dear reader — your eventual price.

Israel says, "The risk / reward of Mary Dyer is not investable. Mary has no value."

Israel Wilkinson looks at me and everyone in the classroom with disdain and knows only our commodity value: our risk-loss value, our ransom / blue-book value. For me, my bid / ask / offer / confirmation of trade, price, and value was only paid a few months ago by Aunt Alexandra to Jan Throgg, which makes me a comparative sale or a "Comp" at the very least! I started to become self-aware and know my patriarchal value in Boston — I was a comp! Out of respect for Aunt Alexandra I still don't know or want to know the Boston pretty price or *value* in English crowns for white good girls gone *Native*, but at least Israel has a solid comp to leverage his victims, I mean customers.

I ask, "Am I investable, Israel? What's my risk? What's my reward? Please do tell!"

As I say this I think about Jan Throgg down in New Netherland, who, as a Tupperware sales consultant, said he traded the Lenape Indians: 1- cook-n-serve, 3- popsicle freezy molds (1 cracked), 1- cereal container, 2 - dirty red tumblers, and 1- Jello-rama servy-time tray for my white-devil savage ass. So, I suppose I also know my Tupper-ware value coming from Jan Throgg's little Tupperware party down at Hell's Gate. Jan said the Lenape only took the red kitchen-ware as they thought it was part of the sun and kept calling it "Wipecko-ware." Jan said they were thrilled holding it up to the sun and watching it glow while repeating over and over, "We want wipecko-ware; wipecko-ware piece of sun!"

Israel says, "Susan, you are too much of a risk. I cannot insure you. You have no reward."

As I wrote, the price is always dependent on perceived *value* in the market. The price is also controlled by the social fashion of the church, synagogue and state. But have no doubt, Israel Wilkinson knows everyone's value and he knew fashion. Israel was the market maker of "It" — Israel is fashion.

Israel is getting tired of trying to get rid of me, the rabble — the uninsurable, the forgotten, the deplorable with no *value*. Israel says, "Susan, you're sub-prime. I'll have to talk to my cousin in the sub-human market... I mean sub-prime market." Israel continues looking away from me, "Okay class, you shall have the American dream with enemies and leverage. Um... excuse me, I'm sorry, I mean, you should have the American dream with FRIENDS and INSURANCE! Insurance is American!" Israel proclaims and concludes, "Trust me, you cannot afford to NOT take my help."

The disturbing truth or the cancer eating away at Israel Wilkinson is that, like me, he doesn't know or trust his own value, his own ransomed, blue-book, commodity value. This is because Israel doesn't know or trust anybody, including himself. Yes, his Big-Daddy would most likely pay anything to get him back (for face or book value), but, just as all pirates and those with no value know, the indebtedness to the hostage investor — Israel's Admiral father, my Aunt Alexandra, and/ or the local loan-shark, only increases our indebtedness. This hostage investment supplants the natural evolution of those with no value. The ransom, or more correctly the *rub of the deal* interrupts the peace and tranquility of a watery orphan grave.

In 1650, the son or daughter of a bastard or bitch goes down to the same watery grave in America as the one for pirates and orphans. Angst and lack of trust always have been, and always will be, a problem for the children with an inherited sinful itch. The lack of sympathy in Israel is hard to fault, just as my kindness and sense of humor are hard to believe.

Ms. Appleton says sardonically, "God is not enough, children; the world is a jungle with savages and it needs insurance men like Mr. Wilkinson who really know VALUE."

Israel is a parasite, a bloodsucking flea or tick that burrows into your skin and life with physical, psychological, and biological warfare. Israel and all white-devils use one's own fashion, business, life, or risk to conceal and insure themselves as a host. Israel, the white-devil salesman, is more a reincarnation of death, or an affirmation of death, than a fulfillment of life.

"I'm also working with the Pequot Indians" he continues. "We've given them a new chance for salvation by giving them jobs in Bermuda and Barbados." Washing himself in his own excrement, Israel boasts, "There in the bosom of our God's lovely earth, the Pequots are enjoying gainful employment in the garden of Eden." In reality, the American Pequots are scattered around the West Indies, sold and merchandised into slavery on sugar plantations that the Wilkinsons own.

Israel continues, "The Pequots found gainful employment that has saved their savage terrorist lives and we have brought them freedom and democracy!" In reality, the Pequots are dropping like flies due to the West Indies climate change. If the white-devil slave driver doesn't kill the exported American Indian slave, then the sugar cane rum the Indians are harvesting, distilling, and drinking to ease their agony surely would.

Following an awkward few moments of silence after Israel speaks the words "Freedom and Democracy," the sun goes behind a cloud and the wind begins to blow outside as the classroom clock slowly ticks and tocks loudly again. I can smell a fireplace log still smoldering, leftover from a chilly spring night, as a breeze rattles the wooden window frame again. The wind and the window create a break beat with the "Tick-tock, tick-tock, tick-tock" from the time machine music box; it gives me a chill and goose bumps, for some reason.

Ms. Appleton, okay with white-collar crime, but not okay with blue-collar slavery, begrudgingly looks at Israel's rising premium and says, "Are you sure these Pequots want to leave? Maybe the Pequots don't want to be forced out of their homeland for you. Have you really ever talked to the Pequots, Israel? Do the Pequots really want to go to Bermuda, Syria, or wherever you're sending them? Maybe the Pequots would like to go to New Hampshire or New Netherland. Did you ever ask the Pequots where they want to go, Israel? Have you ever respected the Pequots, Israel? Have you respected your natural neighbors without your unnatural Bible? Is your *help*, your original-sin, or your *insurance* going to cover these claims and losses?"

The thought of a sincere conversation for Israel with anyone besides his Big-Daddy, including himself, is not possible. Israel is eighteen, but he is emotionally an unsteady and feeble senior citizen. He is a resentful ghost of a boy hawking, haunting, and bullying those who live around him. Israel's neighbors enjoy celebrating life, but Israel enjoys pulverizing life, perverting life, policing and insuring the Neg-Am Jam life.

Ms. Appleton continues with a smirk: "Israel, honestly, is your leverage... um, I'm sorry, is your insurance really worth it to anyone besides your underwriting department?"

Israel sits down silently and ashamed, making lists and taking mental notes, as he allows his vaporous resentment to fog our classroom with Ms. Appleton's unanswered questions. Everyone knows the answers to Ms. Appleton's questions and allows Israel to painfully grow closer to death. This is Israel's only positive direction, his only good will, quiet enjoyment, and/or good-faith direction in life. Bad shit makes great compost. Israel is just like Walking Leech back in the woods with the Lenape — Israel needs to be neutered and taught to weave colorful wampum beads all day.

Ms. Appleton does not say, "Next," but lets the classroom silence twist a knife in everyone. We are all just as evil as Israel for letting him get away with his crimes. We are scared of Israel because we are cowards, because we are scared of ourselves — because we are scared of our value.... We are at a tipping-point and Ms. Appleton our teacher knows this, and Israel knows this.... Israel didn't just squirm, our entire world squirms.

Good Morning, Elizabeth

Ms. Appleton, pleased as apple pie with her early-bird squirming worm class, silently segues to Elizabeth Winterest, who sits next to me and behind Israel. Ms. Appleton says in a questioning tone, "Ms. Winterest?"

Elizabeth, or Lizzy as she is sometimes called, is the daughter of haughty Separatist pilgrims. They moved here from Plymouth and either couldn't or wouldn't adapt easily to Puritan Boston.

Elizabeth picked up the setting of a silent classroom perfectly. I can faintly smell old-lady body perfumes or oils as Elizabeth stands up next to me. She is a pleasant-looking young lady who acts sometimes like a senior citizen with slight dementia, or perhaps a handicapped ballerina named "Edwina."

This *Edwina*, an alter ego of hers, can't stop talking about her old ballerina injury from long ago. Elizabeth has kind of lost track of the dancing accident, so now the injury is more important than the dance — any dance. Elizabeth's mother, who was the real accident, made sure that Elizabeth, her walking neurosis, never forgot about her injury.

Elizabeth is a beat-up actress who starts her soliloquy with stillness, with reticence. Elizabeth does not brush off the cat hair, crumbs or dandruff from her clothes. Her eyes rise, downcast, from underneath her scratchy dark brown wool coif, coat, and skirt, as if the creepy rag-doll clothes weigh on her. She wears a wool melton outfit — the color of a foul and turbulent brown Atlantic Ocean. Her ocean seems to be foaming from under her coif, as her wavy dark hair is prematurely grey. The storm around Ms. Winterest is insatiable in its desire to grip, to swallow up, the shore, the docks, the seashore homes, and Elizabeth herself. The Mayflower lamp seems to navigate around or with Elizabeth. The candle-lamp flares up casting strange African shadows that seem to steer her. Unbeknownst to Elizabeth, the lamp is weathering the storm with her, but her eyes are not open. The brass Moroccan candle-lamp is navigating the waves and stars — the Mayflower is rolling and sailing with Lizzy.

Elizabeth says, "Good morning, class" in a tinny falsetto that comes from her head and escapes barely through her slurry overbite. The weight on Elizabeth's back is not really her Salvation-Army clothes, but her mother, Victoria Winterest, who is pushing her daughter on all available Boston bachelors in an unforgiving manner. The Winterests come from Tudor wealth dating back to Roman times. Elizabeth doesn't need to act or audition; she can afford to not perform. Elizabeth is enlightened, yet she is also asexual and her freedom has been replaced with maternal worrying, which makes her intellectually arthritic.

Elizabeth is being hawked by her mother as the best hoagie-honey south of New Hampshire. Victoria's red-queen crassness and passion for power are balanced by Elizabeth's passive aggressiveness and her passion for the underdog. Elizabeth continues, "I'd like everyone to know that the Plymouth Separatists should NOT be attacked for their blasphemous and heretical ways. The Puritans' self-dealing and co-mingling of church and state make politics dirty and sinful for the true Christian."

Elizabeth is young morally and philosophically and resembles a newborn fawn stumbling for solid footing. She has thin legs and a body frame that looks sometimes as if she would crumble and collapse if the classroom window were opened. Her hands are like mitts, her face like a catcher, and she wears large, heavy shoes. Elizabeth raises her Godzilla-like eyes and looks angrily at Ms. Appleton and the class with pan and broom in hand because she does not know what here good-work is. Elizabeth's resentful housewife, "Lady in waiting," and/or housekeeper demeanor is hung by her white virgin shift and tied like a noose around her neck, giving her a hang-man's stretched neck for a crime she did not commit.

Elizabeth reminds me sometimes of Mary Dyer at an opium den with mommy issues. Elizabeth is just another dazed debutante, an intellectual addict, an angry librarian who reads viciously and studiously, but lives saintly and safely. Elizabeth sees everything, but says only what is fashionably crass — Lizzy is a compassionate and liberal bloody Mary, Lizzy is a horny virgin Queen. Lizzy is a devalued patriarchal woman — a *Mary* prophetess or an *Eve* artist with analysis paralysis.

The last letter I got from Mary Dyer, who has no Mommy issues, was from Long Island, just north of the Southampton Separatist pilgrims who defected from Boston in 1642. Mary wrote, "I'm on a small island in between the fish tails of Long Island and that a friend of mine, Nathan Sylvester jokingly called it "Shelter Island." I didn't know what Mary meant and thought she was snacking on some of those psychedelic Shinnecock Indian mushrooms all the Lenape used to rave about, but, apparently, instead she had a wonderful winter commiserating, but not really communicating, with the many orthodox misfits on Shelter Island.

Elizabeth continues, parroting her parents' lame political propaganda: "Our Puritan Fathers are not right in attacking our Separatist Plymouth neighbors to the south. Forget the moral drunks who ape and harangue, 'Attack to protect — attack to protect, attack to protect!' and let them drown as I praise my God! Let them drown, let the wind blow, and away they will scatter."

Elizabeth sounds like a tired preacher, a drunken, com-placent sailor singing an out-of-tune and off-key "Spanish Lady":

A maid so fair, a maid so sweet.... Whack for the too-ra, loo-ra, laddy.

Elizabeth Winterest

Whack for the too-ra, loo-ra, lady-lee.

Ms. Appleton interrupts: "Slow down, Elizabeth, you're going to hurt yourself, just tell us about YOUR good-work."

Elizabeth is a vengeful nervous-nelly, a hands-in-pockets actress, an overly sensitive artiste. She doesn't breathe life into her words; she sucks the life out of them. Everything Elizabeth Winterest wears, speaks of, and/or touches is a successful and spiteful act to hide and to slum. She hides the truth, she suppresses the truth with animosity. Elizabeth's salt and pepper greasy hair is barely contained under her grubby wool coif, which lies on her head like a heavy oil rag. She is slow, gummy, and clingy. Elizabeth is at home with humidity and the smell of wet, moldy wool. Elizabeth Winterest tries her best to be hinged desire, but her mother drags her anchor along the bottom of the Boston Harbor hoping to get stuck. Elizabeth is the bitter sailor who slid desperately from Elizabeth, to Elly, to El, to Nell, to Nell the cunt. One-note Nelly would get upset if you didn't applaud her parents' ancestral sin and then Nell the knee-breaker would burst in — breaking knee-caps. Nowhere was Elizabeth El, Elly, Liz, Lizzy, or a nice Nell.... There was only Elizabeth — unhinged, sexless, and abused because of heredity.

Back in class Elizabeth looks left, right, and then down again. Here in her emotional wasteland, Elizabeth lives, plotting slowly a royal escape from her mother /from life.

Nancy St. Clair, sitting two seats in front of her, turns around in her seat and encouragingly invites her, saying, "Elizabeth, come bang some heavy metal with us on Saturday!"

Elizabeth shuffles her feet anxiously and starts to speak, stuttering excuses. "I, I need to help my, my mo... moth... moth... mother."

The wind continues to blow outside and the grey cloud-cover continues to shade our classroom. There are no black-birds, just the clock ticking: tick-tock, tick-tock, tick-tock towards Mary's execution. The loose window next to me shudders within its frame again with a spring fever chill and sounds like a washboard melody mixed with a jug band counter-rhythm.

With Elizabeth's homeroom inspection, I'm reminded of Mary Dyer's fifth and last letter to me. Elizabeth is an antonym of Mary Dyer, because most of the time Elizabeth was just another dazed debutante — envious of the poor as the grass is always greener on the other side of the moat. Also, slumming as a royal intellectual addict or a virgin librarian was quite fashionable for the *nouve riche* Puritan at the time. Elizabeth and Mary, because of their wealth, saw everything, but Lizzy did nothing, and fought only that which was popular or the prevailing easy prey. Mary Dyer in contrast went for the throat — always.

Mary Dyer's last letter, from Shelter Island, explained how she realized or awoke to her free-grace faith and moved beyond death. In this fifth and final letter, Mary radicalizes herself while on safe and serene Shelter Island. Mary wrote that the Quaker and Separatist pilgrims were negotiating a land purchase with the local Shinnecock Indian tribe and that the Indians walked away from the negotiating table writing:

The Pilgrims are disrespecting our Indian land and our tribe. I taught the Shelter Island Elders and Elect how to value their partnership with the Indians.

Mary described how the Shelter Island pilgrims and the Indians came up with "The Mashomack Accord" at a place called "Conscience Point," which valued each partner's strengths and weaknesses in a complementary way, not a competitive, way. Mary wrote:

The Mashomack Accord was the closest the white American came to respecting the American Indian. Wisely, Mary still had her reservations about: *The English and American bait-and-switch bastards and bitches I was borne amongst.* Mary continued in her last letter: *Never trust a white person — all is low-self-esteem*. She wrote about her last winter on Shelter Island, describing it as: *An oasis for snow-birds, snowflakes, and the grandparent bird-watchers that envy them*. Mary wrote: *These Shelter Island Shakers and Quakers are really just bed-wetters, they talk MORE about human-watching than human DOING. I'm going stir-crazy here... I think I'm getting island fever!*

Mary wrote those word as she planned her: *American Spring with the orthodox Puritans in Boston*. The other misfits on Shelter Island pleaded: *Don't play chicken with those animals, don't be a martyr — Boston will kill you. Boston will hang you!"* Mary's answer to the Long Island bird-watchers was: *I'm just smoking them out — you get 'em as they come for me!* With that answer Mary wrote that: *The misfits flitted away like waddling little piping plovers back into their sandy caves.*

Mary saw herself as a sniper's sandbag: a dead body martyr for the next patriot fighting the good ole fight to hide behind. Mary thought that behind this sniper's sand-bag, David, or anyone, could launch his rock at their Goliath. Mary was right and playfully recognized the problem of loyalists on Long Island as she ended her final letter to me:

> *I scared those red-coats posing as Separatists. Those life-watchers and those bed-wetters were more scared than myself at my plans for my American spring in Boston. The vicious circle is that reasonable misfits here seeking shelter on Shelter Island don't leave their cave because that is unreasonable, and if they do — well, they ain't a good shot!*
>
> *Still Never Met an Elder,*
>
> *Mary Dyer*

Nancy St. Clair continues to prod Elizabeth, "Awww, come on Lizzy, no excuses!"

But Elizabeth cuts her off: "M, my mother sa, sai, said..."

Dead silence and suspense fill the classroom waiting for

the end of Elizabeth's thought just as a heavy silver coin drops from Jonathon Every's pocket again. It rolls across the wooden floor, slowly echoing in our wooden speaker-box classroom. It rolls in gradual circles as the class listens, ears perked, eyes glancing nonchalantly at the floor. This silver spiraling crescendo fills our class with financial bubbles, yet the coin concludes with only the heavy flop of money and everyone looking at each other to see who will lean down first — no one moves.

Ms. Appleton doesn't hear the coin as she gets up and strolls over to Elizabeth and our row by the windows, which makes Elizabeth shift her weight again while she unconsciously steps back and dilates her pupils. Elizabeth is caught in the crosshairs of a hungry hunter.

For no apparent reason, Elizabeth again bleats begrudgingly, "My mother said, I, I, I..."

Ms. Appleton is that hungry hunting nun and she is licking her chops, closing in on an Elizabethan venison steak chop with chocolate gravy dressing. Ms. Appleton stands down the aisle from Elizabeth. They each have a full-frontal view of the other, about ten feet apart. I think it is going to be a duel as Ms. Appleton just stares at Elizabeth and her downtrodden and translucent emo constitution. Elizabeth, still shoe-gazing, says nothing and paws her feet in place, muttering something no one can understand. Ms. Appleton's eyes turn from throat slicer to humanitarian with a quick thought and a very long meditation on that thought.... She closes her eyes and rocks back and forth to catch that thought and the spin of the earth. She rocks until she surfs with a new life and then Ms. Appleton opens her beaming eyes and silently showers unsaid praise and good wishes on Elizabeth, the jealous downbeat.

Still rocking ever so slightly on her heels, Ms. Appleton says, in a green, mossy, white-and-black birch voice, "Good morning, Elizabeth."

Elizabeth looks up, shocked and confused that Ms.

Appleton, or anyone for that matter, would be so polite and professional with such a large calm air, after her regurgitated Plymouth propaganda that she had no place delivering as a Tudor in hiding. Elizabeth doesn't catch Ms. Appleton's eye before she skates back to the front of the class. Regardless, Elizabeth suddenly glows with hope and humility after only a "Good morning" from our teacher.

Elizabeth Winterest, instead of avoiding eye contact, is now looking around at us in the class, nodding, agreeing, and exclaiming that "It is a good morning!" Tears well up in Elizabeth's eyes and start slowly sliding down her face. She stands at attention and cries as one can imagine she frequently does in her large Tudor house under the reign of her royal parents. Elizabeth's tears don't fall on a frown or a scowl as they often have, but her tears today, like morning dew on a white daisy, water her new radiant white and bright smile. Elizabeth happily exclaims, "Yes, it is a good morning... good morning to you, Ms. Appleton... good morning, class!"

Elizabeth, the shoe-gazing smithereen and/or Nell the cunt, was taught by Ms. Appleton to keep her chin up and eyes open, and most of all to be hopeful and polite. Sometimes teachers do listen and learn and, even more so, sometimes students do learn and listen with just a "Good morning."

Nancy turns around, facing front, and says to the class in general, "That Lizzy lady needs some sunshine!" Nancy St. Clair lets Elizabeth and everyone agree quietly for a moment and then commands, "Lizzy, do hear me now — I'll be picking you up early Saturday morning for the blacksmithing hoedown so we can whack a laddy, whack a laddy-lee!"

And like a fuzzy strawberry chick-a-dee, Elizabeth blushes, chirps, waddles, and blazes anew, nodding yes silently and smiling in spastic new friendship glee.

CHAPTER 12

The English Civil War on American Holiday — Not Real, but for a White-Devil Male: Ideal

THE ENGLISH CIVIL WAR ON AMERICAN HOLIDAY

ext up on the homeroom inspection grid is my column along the two classroom windows. William and I sit in the back of this last column, the cheap seats for hooligans with heredity and a view.

Hooligan number one is Harold Answhich. Harold goes by Ham to his male friends, but is still Harold (or Hammy, but not to his face) to me, other females, and/or his subordinates, which is everybody except his magistrate father. Ham Answhich and his classroom neighbor behind him, Julianne Bequeath, are selling legal Court indulgences through royal legalese this morning and every morning.

Julianne smacks Ham on the back of the neck, snickering sardonically, saying, "Tis your time — speak up, counselor."

Ham stands up briskly and upright as if he has been awakened and questioned by a judge in court. Ms. Appleton then taps her golden ruler on her desk into an escalating climax like an impatient or irate judge banging a gavel in order to calm our class down. Harold says, "Uumm.... Excuse me, yes, good morning, Ms. Appleton and good morning to you, fine classmates."

Ms. Appleton asks Harold, "Is the Ham and Anne comedy show going to take it on the road?" Julianne shrivels her nose at Ms. Appleton and looks down, and noisily shuffles her feet.

Ham happily retorts (he always had the best answers), "Well, Ms. Appleton, we can only hope our holy father will judge us to be so worthy!"

Ham and Julianne are courtier demon twins cut from the same cloth. They were the majestic and manipulative asexual monkey-see son and monkey-do daughter of lawyers. Their parents, devotees / clerks of Judge Cotton, were high-ranking magistrates of *Divinity* and/or the "Law" of our Royal Court. Harold and Jules (as she goes by) look more like brother and sister chimps with white wigs waiting in earnest for their banana court entrance. Ham and Jules competed viciously with each other both consciously and subconsciously about who could conform or press themselves into monkey-see / monkey-do "Puritan Law" in the purest way. Ham and Jules emotionally and religiously tortured and scared themselves in order to feel alive. Ham and Jules were born, fed, and interned to the warm poisoned bosom of royal social engineering and/ or the "Law." Ham and Jules are the walking and talking deformed fruit of infertile rationality and lawful exuberance. There was no silence in their world, only constant Decisions one had to Appeal or argue with Motions using "Case-Law." There was no private and public — everything was fair game! Ham and Jules are the date-rape children eighteen years after our blind-folded American Lady Justice went on a blind date with God from the fraternity "In God We Trust (IGT)." The Ham Answhich and Julianne Bequeath families always had litigious fires burning. If they weren't litigating — then they weren't living.

On the other scale of American justice, on the quiet American side, living with the Lenape Indians for five years taught me how to read faces, which is Indian litigation. The Indians didn't talk much; they enjoyed and respected silence, but that didn't make them stupid. Silence was pure; silence was fair for the Indians; silence was neutrality. It was within this mediation that their future could be seen. The Indians closed their eyes and trusted themselves. The Indians listened and watched the intonations, sound effects of life; intuitive sing-song was the Indian's slow-motion communication. And in case you haven't heard the wise Onondonga Indian sing-song chorus yet:

Kaipu sospe — sospe kshiku, Kaipu sospe — sospe kshiku!

(Slow is smooth and smooth is fast, Slow is smooth and smooth is fast).

Ms. Appleton, getting saucy and surly, says, "Okay, well, give me a good Ham Answhich and spread some Boston on it."

Harold replies from his dark side with a perplexed raised and dropped eye brow, to answer Ms. Appleton's coy request. Then from his bright side, Harold says, "Today, I want to talk about justice and the American Indian."

Ms. Appleton throws out an Asian throwing star: "That's perfect, Mr. Answhich — simply perfect!"

Ham's and Jules's sanctimonious smiles and faces are almost identical. Both of their faces are two-faced — unsymmetrical, divided, and contorted into two faces. On one side, a white prosecuting profile, and, on the other side a black, abstract, and defensive portrait. On each facade is one cracked, dark, defendant eye, and one disfigured, prosecuting, self-important eye. Opposing them, they have one crooked or broken plaintiff smile at any moment, dependent, of course, on who is judging and/or paying for legal representation in Court. There, two black-and-white faces are like spinning yin-yang symbols, lawyers constantly changing shade: black to white, and white to black, dependent on how they can manipulate the *Law* for their personal gain.

These dualists' spirit and character traits are not complementary, but bi-polar and those of an addict. Each fence-watcher has a pompous nose, a broken smile, and a devilish eyebrow that could fall either way the gold coin falls when perched on edge on top of that fence. Hammy and Jules changed position so often they forgot what legal body they are attached to. For lawyers the *who, where, when, why, how,* and *what* positions are career- and monetary-based. With the English's *Black's Law,* one can build a good foundation amongst an insane and rabid civilization, producing great theater and a running a control-fraud Court for the Black Law rich.

The burning white-trash smell one smells in the company of these courtiers is coming from their "Laws" dark side. Their garbage is burning, I can smell it right now smoldering, and it smells like burning hair or melting plastic in a garbage pit. Half their face was a burn pit below their furrowed brows of litigating and scheming plans in and out of court with case law and, more important, cocktail-party law. Their positive side is a white-powdered façade — whole and together, Ham's and Jules's faces are not the balanced scale of blind justice. They are the foul face of American justice as clownish courtiers — grotesque and unbalanced.

Harold, the trusted, politically correct child of the politically corrupt court, continues. Ham climbs skyward into the control-fraud bliss and abyss of litigating *justice* and/or soft-core racism, and says, "Justice and the terrorist is impossible. How can we be equal? Look at the fine English Royal Navy here in 1650 compared to the Indians' canoe. Can the American pygmy make a bigger canoe? With sails? Does the American Indian even want a bigger canoe? Nay, the savage can't even spell his name or create an alphabet — a language! How can the illiterate understand justice and God's Divine law? And more important, should we, the literate, even care?"

Julianne Bequeath, excited, and flush with Ham's thesis, adjusts herself and makes a gospel-reaffirming and/or horsey sound like "Mmmhhm" to elongate Ham's point, as she repositions herself, nodding her head, sitting more up-right and at attention like an anxious mare head-butting her foal.

Harold and Julianne are tag-team winners because they represent and enable both sides of the Court aisle in their blind justice scam. They are both sides of the coin at the same time of the coin toss. For Hammy and Jules, there is always a winning verdict every day, even on the weekends! They are control-fraud winners writing the *Law*. Dependent upon the court's fits and fancies, Ham's and Jules's families and their lawyerly lackeys engineer and design themselves, the *Law*, and civilization.

Ms. Appleton says in a questioning, wanton manner, "Dear Harold, is this blind justice for the Indian?"

Harold quickly twists the knife and says, "Yes, justice... Ms. Appleton. Justice not just given not to the Indians, but also to Mary Dyer, who will be executed in less than an hour. Mary was given due process, but flagrantly disobeyed our Town Elders, who banished her years ago. Mary will hang and justice will be served. Mary Dyer the martyr will dingle and dangle like a pagan-pygmy wind-chime! Alas, Governor Winthrop has judged her correctly and God will reward us. The God we trust in does NOT care about pagans, pygmies, or non-believers."

Ms. Appleton, still holding her ruler like a gavel, linguistically steams in a sultry voice, "Excellent, Hammy. It's delicious — hot, hard and cheesy, just like I like it."

As Ms. Appleton finishes her sarcastic compliment, Jules fluffs up her Julie-curl magistrate wig and gives her white ringlets a pet and some fresh air. Jules is stocky and, like Harold (and all polite liars), keeps her arms behind her like an arrested soldier or a polite bull-shitter. Jules also carries an

Harold Answhich

Juliannne Bequeath

air of charity and kindness, which turns out to be high-interest predatory lending at its friendliest and soft-core genocide at its most militaristic. Jules's lack of dieting is self-evident because she has the shape, decorum, and hygiene of a looting homeless woman.

Jules is a meat-and-potatoes shoplifter loaded up with a week's worth of dinners at the free-for-all grocery. Jules's skin is the color of a coal miner's ashen face and her nose follows her crooked smile trend down to a frown with too much pink lipstick. The windows to her soul are two iridescent oil stains on a large grey face that looks like a cement floor.

Ham's wig, with matching Julie-curl ringlets, is also parted on top of his head, but he keeps his wig in a more rumpled fashion. Hammy is a teenager already acting like a middle-aged man. Hammy's one crazed, jaundiced eye is frightening large and white, and has a tiny pupil. It is a petrified and frozen staring eye within the shadows of his face. His other eye is reptilian and jovial, and runs down his hooked nose into a smirk. A smirk of a known *decision*, before an announced Decision, sits above a fat nest of baby jowls. Ham is bulbous, top heavy and usually has his hands clasped behind his back as if he is addressing the court or accepting an award. Ham would be twiddling and tickling his fingers behind his back the entire time he talks a mile a minute, basking in the spotlight.

Hammy, like all lawyers, likes to hear himself talk, they like to please the Court; lawyers like to *strike* their low self-esteem. Most of all, lawyers dream of judging, writing, and deciding the *Law*! Hammy is no different and his lazy garments are a white aristocratic vest and dark jacket obviously waiting for his true fashionable legal inheritance — the hand-me-down black robe and white band for the "Decider," the judge! In God We Trust? No — In Ham We Trust!

Coming from the woods, I think how love, law, and God are so abstract, so fluid, so fashionable, and ever-changing.

Laws and Gods are created as conceptual art by litigious-legalists and religious fashionistas. Red-in-the-face queeny lawyers, like fashion designers — are Cavalier parasites who manipulate and torture the *Law* and fashion, dependent upon the royal-hem-index and the politically-correct Courtier weather. Before this *Court* was in session, before a Decision was made on the *Law*, the wheels of justice, or the catwalk of justice, have always been and will always be corrupt. Justice is the May-pole dance in front of the cranky Judge that morning. The *Law* is written not by Judges but by their morning lovers, or their absence thereof.

Ham clears his throat and taps his imaginary wand, conducting and transposing this classroom-to-court room, court room to theater. Hammy the gentle mad-dog just charges ahead with his new legal fight of the hour, every hour, on the hour. Ham imagines that the human race has just thrown him legal bones to see Hammy run and chew. Ham, now with a deeper Bath baritone accent, says, "Thy equal protection for our Indian terrorist enemy is unconscionable. The savages must not receive the same Divine rights as a Puritan."

The *Massachusetts Body of Liberties* was being debated both on the back of my dead mother and around the neck of Mary Dyer, who will be hanged this morning. Harold is lobbying us this morning against our American colony, ratifying this landmark legislation. My mother's and our family's tragedy produced this Bill of Rights for the American individual to enjoy the rights of the accused and the rights of free speech. Harold, his family, and their lawyer fraternity are the legalist lackeys that helped lynch my mother with complete and utter disregard for English Common Law.

Back in class, Hammy's climax is, "Tell your parents to vote 'No' on the Equal Protection legislation, or be cast out to eternal damnation."

I suddenly think about Ham's father: John Answhich. He was the assistant prosecutor, a witness, and a judge at my mother's trial. My mother and Defendant — Anne Hutchinson, was not allowed counsel nor attorney because she was an "Enemy combatant" and the American Puritans rejected English Common Law for her trial. My mother was also not allowed to be judged by her peers (a jury) because she was an anarchist, an adulteress, and an artist — a woman. An *Eve* without a right to be let back in to our earthly American garden.

Ms. Appleton, knowing the answer she would get, egged Ham on: "Isn't equal protection or the unequal 'Royal' protection of the Elect, or the Elders, why we left our feudal caste system in England and Europe?"

There was no court appeal allowed for my mother because pressing toward justice, or an Awakening of truth, would destroy the synagogue, the church, and the State. Therefore, my mother's trial was a lord of-the-fleas cluster-fuck in the middle of the English Civil War. The American free-grace controversy was the Protestant Reformation on a savage field trip. It was not an American debate, but an English debate. The free-grace controversy was the English Civil War on an American holiday.

Harold, unfazed, says, "We are not bourgeois or racist because we realize the terrorist will never understand our justice and our God. We are the chosen people — our destiny is Biblical."

The legalese of Biblical case law is a slippery slope with gaps as big as galaxies that my mother, Hammy, and all the Bible bitch slappers eventually fall into. The Judeo-Christian psychosis deepens with more *faith*, more *love*, more *law*, and/or more *God*. Throughout religious time, be it with the Sumerians, Egyptians, Jews, Christians, Muslims, Separatists, and/or the *Anne Hutchinsons* — organized religion rots and spoils. Religion turns into third-rate tribalism, a personal God's abstract ego. Religion is Wampy scaring white-crackers in Connecticutt. Religion and civilization become arbitrary and capricious, sold to the highest bidder. Civilization cheapens and devalues into a religious control-fraud and/or a police-state. Religion always turns into a tithe, a tax, and/or "A Mission," "A Crusade," "A Fatwa," with capitalistic tribal warfare at its core. Religion is soft-core capitalism... religion is soft-core war.

My mother, Anne Hutchinson, had *a mission* and the mission killed her. It happened when seven-eighths through her trial with the help of No English Common Law, my mother, *pro se*, was representing herself and was litigiously and judicially winning in the Boston Puritan Court. My mother was sitting high on her horse not realizing there was a solid and well-tied legal noose around her neck. As always, Grandpa Frank's favorite little anarchist, his little tom-girl, his little squeaky wheel with a big red bow every day, not only bit the *invisible hand* that was feeding her, but Annie the cowgirl drove her spurs right through that hand.

Annie get some anarchy? Annie got some anarchy! Anne Hutchinson stuck her cowgirl boot spurs into the powerful muscles of the horse beneath her and said, "Giddy-up."

The banishment of free-grace and my mother in 1643 institutionalized English royalty in America. This loyalist break with the English Enlightenment retards America. This break of freedom, or snapping of America's neck, was heard around the world when my mother's body politick dropped, twitched, danced, and swayed in the wind. America danced and swayed like the weeping willow on Corn Hill. The free-grace controversy continues ideologically to blow in the American wind. It haunts, vibrates, and awakens people till this very blustery day here in 1650.

My mother and Mary Dyer are American orphans abandoned by genealogy who questioned our Elect and Elders. Annie and Mary were painted as serpents and "A woman" in order to banish them from civilizations' asylum garden. My mother's body and soon enough Mary Dyer's body will hang from that poison ivy tree at Harvard in Cambridge. Per

Minister Winthrop and Hammy, their bodies dance in the wind so all their ivy-league ministers will not forget who their enemy is. For these itchy ministers, free-will, free-grace, and/or a debt-free life are their enemy. In American terms, the Ivy League's mission or enemy is all those pursuing life, liberty, and happiness.

My mother and all other proponents of free-grace were either assassinated, jailed, martyred, and/or idolized by Hippocratic cowards who admonish their religious and social points, but physically and politically do nothing. Satisfying their sinful life, the Christian Zionistas, the Hutchinsons, or any other faithful religious slave too proud for their own good are all shady charlatans who poetically and financially recant their false Gods if you follow the money.

Ms. Appleton realizes she does not want to Biblically argue with a Judeo-Christian master-of-the-universe frat boy and falls back comfortably and confidently with her own God or Goddess as she strolls past the windows to the left of our row.

"Your destiny is Biblical, Ham? I think 'Biblical' is a front for real estate development. Jesus would not want a bigger canoe or a new apartment complex on someone else's land in your 'New Jerusalem.' And I'm sure Jesus would be very happy to float around in a canoe, or on a log, or some raft, just drifting / floating.... Dost thou, you think, Mr. Answhich? Sounds fun, right? Floating...." As she is pulling a U-turn next to me, Ms. Appleton quickly follows with a quick and determined, "Next," which sounds like an annoyed judge saying even more quickly, "Overruled."

NOT REAL, BUT FOR A WHITE-DEVIL MALE: IDEAL

Julianne Bequeath, right behind Harold in my row, is cheerful and jolly, to rise and shine for segregated America. Jules's feminine birth is a patriarchal curse and not a blessing. The professional and polite Abe-Babe is a Jezebel, a virgin Mary, a recanting Eve, a handy-man, a slut, a male soldier, not real, but for a white-devil male — ideal.

Julianne flips back a few strands of her Julie-curl wig, sticks out her overbearing chin and asks our class, "Isn't today a beautiful morning?"

There are some grumbles and muted answers from our class. Samuel Payneson dryly says, "Not if you're Mary Dyer," to a medley of chuckles, snickers, and amens.

Julianne is a control-fraud cheerleader, not really a "Decider," but more of an "Answer-er" — a female who thinks and answers like she was a male *Decider*. Jules, with distinguished legal representation in the royal Court for our religious souls and our interest-earning money in our pockets, repeats the question: "Isn't today a beautiful morning?"

My classroom peers have lost their patience with Samuel's disturbing Mary Dyer joke — not even a protest, just disgust and silence. My classroom and my Boston education becomes a blunder and a perverted disgrace. Ms. Appleton asks Jules, "Thitherward your good-work, Ms. Bequeath?"

Laura Kraven, my first classmate to speak, says in a smarmy, we-all-know tone, "Jules wants to marry Ham so she can divorce him. Jules's good-work is to litigate with love." Jules giggles and then drools in disgust before she launches a little bit of spit out of her mouth when she speaks up to Laura Kraven's Motion on love and says, "My agenda is to give thanks to God for this beautiful day by loving all of you with the word of God: 'Give not that which is holy unto the dogs, neither cast ye your pearls before swine, lest these or the savage terrorists will trample them under their feet, and turn again and rend you.'"

"Thank you, Ms. Bequeath," Ms. Appleton interrupts, and then, speaking to the class, says, "And we should all be thankful because Jules through Biblical case law has just compared poodles and pigs to pygmies and also she doesn't want your dogs or pigs to borrow your pearls. Wow, I honestly don't know why, but very good, Jules. Thank you. Next!"

CHAPTER 13

Why Has Providence Been Outlawed? — God Works in Mysterious Ways

WHY HAS PROVIDENCE BEEN OUTLAWED?

 illiam? Please tell us about your good-work," Ms. Appleton asks. "William, you're next!" she again prods as she wanders back to the front of the classroom.

William is still stuck on my blacksmithing mettle comment after Lawrence told us about Ms. St. Clair's muffins. William is Billy, stuck in a daydream daze about how to get the temperature of his lukewarm mettle past Catholic tit-sucker cordial. William comes to attention with a start, and fumbles some words, thoughts, or the end of a prayer out of his mouth.

It sounds like William says, "I am a passionate pilgrim. I am a passionate pilgrim. I am a passionate pilgrim," but I can't be sure.

Regardless, I say out loud, "Pray, dear God whhhaaatt are you saying?" and start to laugh in his face. I then take my finger like the Puritan time machine hand on top of the Grandfather clock and move it around in a circle — taunting the Puritan boy posing as a Separatist boy with pie pieces of his time. Sequentially, I say, "Tick-tock, tick-tock" moving my finger around like his Puritan time machine does. I tick-off and tock-off slices of his life forming a circle and a song that doesn't end.... I sing along with his Puritan time, "Tick-tock, tick-tock, tick-tock" freaking Billy out. I say, "Got your Jerusalem ticket Billy? Next stop Galilee."

Ms. Appleton is getting angry and impatient, and says, "Susan are you speaking for William today? More comedy and tragedy from the rowdy-lady row?"

William regains his composure, stands up brightly, and says with chipper northern England sunshine, "I'm sorry, Ms. Appleton, I'm working diligently on the Massachusetts Bay Colony Commissioners' delegation to Providence in order to bring peace and good will to the outlawed Quakers and Baptists in Providence, Rhode Island."

Ms. Appleton quickly turns on Billy and says, "Why are the Quakers and Baptists outlawed, William? Why has Providence been outlawed?"

William starts deflecting and dancing around the question in strict silence, doing an interpretive dance that I believe he and other Catholics in hiding called, "The Clueless Act of Contrition." The existential anguish looks similar to the monthly Lenape Indian dance, though Billy's body language is more robotic, his fashion is a drag, and vocally his mumblings are out of tune and lacking harmony. Billy is now Billy your buddy — Billy Budd keeps on pushing back his hair, casually shaking his head, but he is doing it every twenty seconds like a nervous tick mashed with a song-and-dance routine.

Billy Budd babbles and stutters along. "Prov, Prov, Prov, Providence. Ummmm.... Prov, Prov, Prov, Providence," while he taps his foot on the ground like the hoof of a nervous little gelding horse in a small pen.

Annoyed with Billy's contrition dance, Ms. Appleton whips him lightly, saying, "Well, Billy it's because Providence believes Boston prophesizes religious salvation through a covenant of material *works*, such as money, families, politics, and power. On the other hand, Providence prophesizes a more Christian covenant of spiritual *works*, such as charity, happiness, and free-grace (forgiveness) with no debt. Providence puts forth the proposition that free-grace, with no psychological, emotional, or financial debt over your neighbor, is true life. Providence says life should be charitable — not capitalistic."

William finds it very difficult to tell the truth. He was an actor, not a doer, a repressed Catholic Jew or a Jewish Catholic — not an American. And just as it is with all these emotionally and intellectually retarded people with no sense of humor: the joke is very funny — till the joke is on them.

Ms. Appleton enjoys squeezing William in her winch. He is a parentally guided jester, a grape she would crush for a drop of wine, and our class, including myself — loves to watch! For Billy, the bard of Boston, to have his tasty testicles in such a female vise under control of an adulteress like Ms. Appleton is well worth coming back to Boston for. To watch white-devils torture each other is a Judeo-Christian way of life, a low-class English and American way of life. I do not miss this humiliating existence, but then, upon seeing Billy squirm, stutter, and hang, while saluting his executioner... well, I now realize how the patriarchy neurosis of torture has dragged down England, Europe, and America.

My Lenape Indian tribe was so strong, so simple, so pure, that it would not even understand or comprehend hypocrisy. The forked tongue white-devil Englishman and European was a jester, the walking biped definition of hypocrisy. The American Indians say what they mean and means what they say. The white-devils say and do what they have to — just to get by....

Ms. Appleton asks, "Billy, do you think the Quakers hanged last year was justice?"

Billy Budd blubbers. "We, wel, well. I… I, I, I don't know."

Ms. Appleton stretches the rack on Billy and says, "What about the other Quakers last year who got their ears and noses cut off? You look pretty as is, Billy, but without ears, a nose, and/or a stretched neck you'd be puritanically perfect!"

Billy is getting lost in a conversation he can't carry. William dances around like a tenured Harvard professor in his ivory tower only wearing his pajamas, giving abstract definitions, posing unanswerable questions, and giving no solid conclusion to students who don't care. These Ivy League students / these ministers of the Crown and jesters of aristocracy are only interested in *da money* and their heredity. William's politically-correct jokes and glances are snacks, trickle-down thoughts, with no meat or any semblance of a meal that could even start to feed or satisfy common sense. Starved and brittle, Billy's shenanigans are much ado about royalty, power, love, law, and God, in reverse order. Billy's life, like religion, amounts to unbelievable theater, a tragic play perpetuating only tribal despondency, temporary entertainment, and perpetual warfare. And like arms dealers being the only beneficiaries of religion and war, the only beneficiary of perpetuating the passionate pilgrim is the popcorn popper. William Demopheare was a spiritual control-fraud, and a drowned life — a rejected spirit, an insincere life.

Brad Pining, from the front row, second column, near the door turns around and condescendingly interrupts: "Dear Billy, what about Mary Dyer? Your good-works seem very safe and fashionable, but in less than half an hour our God-fearing civilization will hang Mary Dyer because she believes in a different love, law, and God. Mary Dyer respects her life differently and we will hang her for this. Wherest art thou on this, pretty-boy? Are you just a Mary Dyer-crier? Silent and too scared to fight? I'd call you a woman or a pussy, but that would be derogatory to strong women. Billy, you're just the limp-dick favorite — a jerk off."

Billy says to Brad in a shrill and feminine shocked tone, "That's hate-speech!"

"Might makes right Puffy," Brad shoots back and then he starts serenading Billy with "Billy Butt-Puff, Billy Butt-Puff" while making masturbating movements with his hand under his desk.

GOD WORKS IN MYSTERIOUS WAYS

Billy ignores Brad's militaristic and psychological hypothesis, does a little dance with his hands in his pockets, looks frazzled, and begs Ms. Appleton's pardon by saying, "Yes, of course, Ms. Appleton, you're correct. The Boston Commission is trying to persuade Roger Williams and the rest of Providence to come back to our Puritan ways."

Ms. Appleton replies, "I heard Mr. Williams has gone to London to ratify Providence's charter. Is this true? William?"

"Yes, I believe it is," William sheepishly admits.

Ms. Appleton, riled up now, stands up at her desk and begins to slowly keep time with her golden ruler on her other palm and walks around to the front of the class.

She says, "Well, I guess your Bay Colony Commission, sent to Providence, was as good at convincing Providence of her lost ways as headless King Charles was at convincing the English Parliament of his Divine right to rule."

"The King is not dead." Brad Pining shouts! "Long live the King!"

William has a capital "A" (for Appleton) hook in his mouth; he is a fish swimming and dying at the same time. William is pulling Ms. Appleton's line, running hard, diving fast, hopping, and jumping out of the water into unknown worlds.

Ms. Appleton, continues ignoring Brad. "I've heard that

Roger Williams will receive his Providence, Rhode Island, charter and all of your commission's work to smear the 'Heretics and terrorists' in Providence will prove unfounded and foolish. What do you say to this?"

William is a flustered field mouse cornered by a cat. Billy, with his hands still in his pockets, surrenders to his duplicitous ways and throws a *Hail Mary* bomb. Billy is falling back on the *Holy Joe* upstairs while peeing in his pants and says in a questioning, disingenuous, misguided, and slipshod voice, "God works in mysterious ways."

Ms. Appleton plays with Billy, allowing him to run, then she bats him back with her playful paw. Bored, she lets Billy run the other way and then whacks him back for good in a resounding red-oak octave, over-emphasizing the short and simple third word and person she is addressing. "No, Billy YOU work in mysterious ways!"

William / Billy Peeing in His Pants

Chapter 14

Autumn Leaf — Nothing — My Maker

Autumn Leaf

s. Appleton continues along in a brisk manner, looking at the clock as it is about thirty minutes or so till nine o'clock.

"So always last, but certainly not least, Ms. Susan Hutchinson, please grace us with your good-work."

I stand up softly and speak not from my head, but from my diaphragm, from my gut and the back of my spine.

"Good morning, class. Please call me Autumn Leaf, I was re-born Autumn Leaf with the Lenape Indians in the woods of New Netherland. I stand here again today, wholeheartedly explaining that my good-work today and my agenda everyday will always be nameless, faceless, and Godless."

Laura Kraven says, "Aagghh, great... it's homeroom heretic time mmhhmm...."

I continue, "I've worked vigorously at Nothing for many seasons now. My great Nothing is not neutrality, but indifference, balance, and the polar opposite of Something. Nothing is wasting nothing, wanting nothing, and always generally having nothing. Nothing is emptiness and respect. Within my Nothing, I'm out of control: I'm an adulteress, an anarchist,

284

an artist, and this is my home — this is my church. My home is Nothing and it is my imagination, so when I close my eyes I am home. Colors float and twirl as my home in Nothing, my Nothing is alive and wet. This is not the patriarchal Abe-Babe way, this is the new way — which is actually the old way — the oldest way."

I pause for effect and then continue, trying to communicate with my classmates and neighbors — trying to communicate with my thorny sins, searching for a common denominator and a common sense in order to lead us out of dementia.

"Nothing is the negative space in between notes on a piano or cello playing a slow winding nocturne. There I sit in this negative space that is actually the positive space. This positive space negative space, one hundred times bigger than us, actually sculpts and shapes us. Most people design themselves as the main point in life, the NAJ life... when they are not a point or even a force to be reckoned with. We circle the sun — the O origin, the sun does not circle debt."

Laura Kraven makes a snarky snoring noise to numerous chuckles and then says, "Wow, I feel so much different now knowing which way I'm spinning around this very moment.... What was I thinking and feeling beforehand, Ms. Leaf? Silly me. My poodle and garden, who I know were wondering about this 'Science' of yours, will be just as enlightened as I am. It's really life-changing, don't you think so, class? We can just check that one off! Thank you so much, Ms. Leafy!"

"Yes, Laura," I say. "My Nothing is a sleepy, subconscious scientific space — which mathematically is half your life. And, most important, this Nothing sleepy space you mock is a selfless space, it's a free-grace space — a place to rest, a place of dreams. This Nothing is a blank piece of paper, perhaps a blank page inside a book?"

I continue, "What shall you do with this Nothing? Is

Nothing in the table of Contents ? Is there an illustration of Nothing? Do you look up Nothing's page number, excited and thrilled — turning the pages to witness Nothing and then you thumb your way to Nothing, and then your disappointed... wondering why is Nothing nothing? You turn the page hoping there is a back page for Nothing? Some small print, a clue, maybe even an address for Nothing? Could there be linear notes for Nothing? Cliff's Notes for Nothing? Someone's notes, not even a Penny-Saver coupon for Nothing?"

"But Nothing... is nothing... and we think this is another nothing scam. We then pause and think with this thin piece of paper in between our fingers that is Nothing, we think about creating something out of this nothing. Is this the blank page for my greatest poem I will create? Is this blank page left for me to I draw out my masterpiece in charcoals? Or perhaps I just rip this blank page out, this Nothing, I will tear out and fold it up into an origami bird and/or a paper airplane and fly Nothing around? What a wonderful flying and chirping Nothing that would be!"

As I finish saying these words I pretend to be folding up a piece of paper and then I throw my imaginary hyper plane towards the Mayflower candle lamp variable and my class and I watch in amazement as it spins, and circles the Mayflower lamp before slowly flying, flapping, and floating out the door — Origin O.

I continue, "Nothing is that pause or breath between words when singing or reading poetry... Nothing is the space between a painter's strokes of paint that can be anything: a mountain or a mite, anything at all. This is Nothing — this is free-grace."

I roll on, "Nothing is the only flag I can afford to fly. I fly Nothing only for my Maker as thanks. Nothing shows no mischief, no royalty, no airs, no malice, no war, and no competition with *God* and/or *Creation*. There is absolutely no dead cockroach in my white box. My Nothing is clean. Clean

Nothing

as the cockroaches' love — my love, our love, and the oldest eternal love, the love of life, the love of respect and the love of Nothing.... Nothing is my only hope and will that our Maker — not any God, but our artistic Creator and our biological Maker — will recreate the sun tomorrow. My only religion is that I hope and pray that our sun will rise tomorrow morning — beyond that: it's a good day — not to be wasted!"

Ms. Appleton gives me that nasally / questioning New England female noise: "Mmmhhhmmm?" The noise is that condescending down-beat roller-coaster intonation that Yankee and now Appalachian women are notorious for. It connotes not just phonetic and ethical superiority, but a moral hazard warning that the one speaking or blubbering is risking his or her life if he or she dares to move forward or against the unknown known of "Mmmhhhhmm?"

I continue communicating to my classmates, unimpressed with Ms. Appleton's phonetic warning: "I happily surrender to Nothing, to everything except my body and soul given to me by an undiscovered, unidentified power. This *truth*, this unknown known, this nameless and faceless creator — this Nothing is the only truthful force in our world. This Nothing is embodied in nature. Look out this window today at the spring growth: the tulips, the daffodils, the spring grasses, the new cedar and pine sprouts, those obnoxious blue jays squawking, and the busy bees buzzing, struggling and fighting for life... yet this violent chaos is balanced, it is constructive and not destructive."

Someone to my right starts making a buzzing sound, "BbuzzzzZZaazzzZZZ," but I don't look because these sins are not my sins. I look out the window, focusing on my future, then I look down.

Ms. Appleton says encouragingly, "Chin up, you little Digger. Spin, girl — spin!"

I come to attention, look at Ms. Appleton, and then say

to my classmates, "Please remember the red summer moon on your skin during sleepless nights, nights that make you tingle with Nothing. Please recall the bright-white sub-zero February snow in your face, in your nose — freezing your snotty head, as Nothing. Remember the swollen spring rivers in your ears before you turn the bend, hoping the bridge isn't washed out — this is Nothing. Taste the stormy teal harbor kicking up a salty mist on your face and on your lips — this is Nothing. And, class, please remember the cold Autumnal winds of Nothing as I, Autumn Leaf, live and fall, with the other desperate and spiritual leaves out there. We are the color of yellow, red, and orange fire, falling from grace, falling beautifully — composting our earth."

I have the class's attention and continue: "I remember these sensations because they are the most beautiful things I've seen in my first eighteen years alive. These elements have only one thing in common — they have nothing to do with other humans. That's because humans are not real creators or actual doers. We are just visitors on earth and definitely — not a joy to have in class. Humans are NOT good for the animals or the earth, so how could we be complementary for each other? Humanity — brother-asses and sister-asses hiding out. Humans, at best, are water balloons pissing and polluting their way through the world thinking they're *the chosen people* or the *chosen balloon*. It would be funny if people didn't take themselves so seriously — fancying one a rocker. We are cold water — falling balloons filled with hot air waiting to hit the hot rock. Life is falling and waiting to hit *it* and 'Pop!' Some fertilization, some condensation, but mostly pollution.

The class is silent as everyone imagines their last chapter in life — some imagine pain, some imagine convalescence, some imagine drowning into Nothing. Ms. Appleton is looking out the window. I sigh and take a breath in order to calm down. I think to myself, pausing... this is going well, as my sins and classmates imagine themselves dying.

All of a sudden, a large "POP" startles my classmates out of their desperate ways. Lawrence Randison has clapped his hands and shot a cannon ball into my homeroom garden. My classmates jumped as if awakened with nightmares on their deathbeds. My classmates laughed and giggled amongst themselves uncomfortably for being so fearful — for sweating it so hard, for my big, bad, and bold sins are, in-fact: scaredy-cats.

I continue, not wanting to be upstaged by *The Law*, and, in fact, use *The Law*. "Thank you, Lawrence, for your brutal reality, because that quiet desperation we all just experienced — that tragic comedy is Nothing. I yield to Nothing, I respect, and feel inferior to nature and Nothing — that, thankfully, seems alien and far removed from our Abe-Babe civilization. With this existential submission, I live within free-grace without airs. I live gracefully without original sin or Big-Daddy debt."

Ms. Appleton hums like a roller coaster ride from the heavens above down to hell and back with her celestial intonation, "Mmmmmhhhhmmmmm...." She continues condescendingly, "Life without debt... how lovely. Well, Ms. Autumn Leaf, didn't you and your family learn about straying from the flock, not respecting your Elders, and the justice for those that do stray or disobey the *law* of debt?"

I respond, "Thy flock is a control-fraud of sins, thy flock is a pack of mad dogs with worms."

My class gasp and squirm, pretending to be in shock and insulted. Someone up front barks, like a small, annoying mad dog, "Ruff-ruff, ruff-ruff, ruff-ruff."

Ms. Appleton says, "Nay, stop it, you dirty hounds," and slaps her golden ruler down on her desk. The dog barker then whimpers as if running away, "Mm, mmm, mm, mm, m."

I endure and say to my sins, "I will not be arraigned. I'm not a dog with amnesia. I'm a human with reason and knowledge of humanities and history — I understand the rights of man, I understand reason. I'm trying to improve and build off that history by not repeating our mistakes. I will not take part in religiously-correct or politically-correct murder with *love*, *law*, or *God* as my excuse — excuses I honestly believe will not work for my... my... my Creator." I stutter, unable to open wide the large door to the even larger ambiguous space that is NOT the Judeo-Christian God delusion. The left-brain-to-right-brain existential shift where you start to see the world around you is actually more important than you, your family, and your trickle-down tribe.

Ms. Appleton questions slowly, "Your Creator?" as if to demote or demean me.

I continue, "My Creator or Maker is not a man, a book, a flag, or a newspaper from long ago," I declare. "My Maker is not a personal God or Goddess. Nature and Nothing is my Maker."

"From my days as a child in England, we raised the Union Jack flag with trepidation and dissent. Then in Massachusetts, here in Boston, my family and I raised with hope the Bay Colony flag, wanting a democracy and equality, but soon enough we realized we had London's Bank of England and the Church of England running an American banana colony. The Puritan loyalists say they want equality and justice, but these traitorous Americans have the monarch's ministers and magistrates running a royal English colony in America. A control-fraud America on State Street where Church St. and Synagogue St. run-round like moats."

Someone towards my right whispers, "Mischief, mischief — witchy, witchy...."

I dial down. "Nonetheless, moving on and out with my family, still undeterred, in Providence, Rhode Island, my tribe and I raised the flag of American Providence and thought we were finally home. But then the Providence white-devils started splitting the hairs and beans of what providence *is* or what providence *is* not.... How can you argue about providence? Those selfish dogs. In other words, Providence in America was over. We couldn't contain self-dealing, collusion, and the selfish gene! Our English Enlightenment was over in America; Christian original sin, a franchise of Jewish royal debt, had won."

Ms. Appleton is looking out the window again and notching up an eighth at a time on her heavy golden ruler. Aloof and theoretical, she is purring to herself as I can tell my good-work is getting through to her. In a hushed, trailing voice, Ms. Appleton says, "The disrespect of mathesis is the downfall of humanity."

Jen Patack yells out cheerfully to the class, "Oh, joy! I love mathesis! You know Oxford teaches that it inspired Martin Luther's *Ninety-Five Theses*, Spinoza, and that weird rumor that Francis Bacon and Shakespeare wrote the Bible! So much for Moses, Matthew, and Mark!"

I continue as if I don't hear either of them: "We realized then and there in Providence that the monstrous birth or creation of a flag (or a child) begets the destruction and death of that flag or child. Life is cyclical... it's abstract and pointless — it's Nothing. People and flags come and go, so it's best to know yourself first. My grumpy grandpa, my bitchy mom — the Union Jack, this star-spangled, striped American crap, and even Mary Dyer? All meaningless — Nothing. And even in New Netherland my family as polite immigrants flew a Dutchy flag. Then I, alone for the last five years, I pledged my allegiance every morning and evening to the Indian totem pole. But after being traded for some Tupperware by the Lenape Indian, after being bought and/or ransomed and brought back here to Boston, I realized there is only one false flag or false god for me now. I want to fly my good-work flag, the philosophical and ideological invisible flag, the honest flag flying the free-grace colors of 'I don't know,' and vitally — neither do you!'"

I take a quick breath again, and exhale, getting in rhythm, getting soulful, getting comfortable underwater with my eyes open. I settle down to the vastness — just a cell in the ocean — I swim like a wave from afar. I feel both heavy as molten orange lava and cool as light green sea spray, moving in-between and with the waves, and say, "I, in fact, enjoy the lonely sad song of the flag-less flagpole at night. No sheets or sailing tonight — tonight we float rudderless, we drift the leeway, we flow like water. Tonight ropes, pulleys, and lanyards are tethered down hard — tied tight in a figure eight. Clasped in the winds, clinking and clanking ropes and lanyards slapping and drumming the tree-like wooden mast, the wooden drum — the safe harbor at night."

Jonathon Every says, "My Lighthouse Bond Act could make it safer!"

Using his comment as a tool I say, "Well, Sir Every, sorry to pull the plug on you, but the safe harbor home is a false flag — it's untrustworthy and nefarious, yet extremely hard to leave, like your cave and/or home. I'm Nothing — a shutout, a stowaway waiting to be pushed off shore... waiting for the sun, I pray for the wind to blow me further out to sea. When I close my eyes, I hear an imaginary wind and raise my sail. I silently pilot with celestial navigation till the wind is resounding, relaxing, and at my back. I sail and orbit like a star and a sun in the Milky Way, the safe harbor is behind me, and the wild blue yonder is in front of me — this is the free-grace way.

Ms. Appleton, in a dumbfounded, lost type of way, says, "Aaaghh, yes, Ms. Sweet Leaf, safe harbors or safe-spaces are overrated, the real action is out beyond the breakers — dead reckoning outside the meridians in celestial heaven."

I resume describing my good-work: "This wild blue yonder is an exquisite world where no one is asserting authority and picking your pocket while they 'Save' or hijack souls. My free-grace prayer or meditation on this safe harbor home is not going to a Jewish, Catholic, or Lenape God. My prayers and mediation go to Nothing and rely on the intangible, on the unsaid. This free-grace is refreshing — it makes me feel light again, like a child's early thoughts about nothingness... this is Nothing. Born again — alive, Awake again."

Brad Pining yawns obnoxiously loudly and Ms. Appleton says, "Brad, I'm sorry, is Autumn Leaf's good-work boring you?"

He looks up and around, and adjusts his body from somewhere in his pelvis or stomach, looking down, concentrating on his large core, adjusting himself before he speaks. Pining snarls slightly and speaks in his low, grave voice: "Americans don't like sad songs... we like them peppy with some salt and vinegar. These Autumn Leaf sad songs are not American, but European drivel for tit-suckers. This Yankee porcupine sings sad songs best left in the bath tub and outhouse."

Then someone else to my right grades my performance, somewhat successfully with a, "Pppwwaaaaattt," farting noise.

NOTHING

The class roars in congratulatory applause for the anonymous noisemaker, but I continued unabated, telling my class about my good-work.

"Even you, Ms. Appleton, will have to surrender eventually. Everyone will succumb — why not do it now and get your spiritual homework done? I want to pursue life, liberty, and happiness, in a well-armed flagless world. Nothing is talking less and listening more to the melody of singing crickets and fighting opossums at night. Nothing is symmetrical and synchronized to the blue and grey skies with white cotton clouds that are every shape and every shade of white. Nothing is a white-out as the snow piles around the Nothing pole. Rain and snow fly sideways to an important conference and symposium on 'How Nothing is maybe not nothing?' I surrender to the mud, to the ashes, to the dust, to Nothing my Creator — because, from where I've come, I shall return. So please take me to that tidal pool on the New Netherland shore I mention so often, for my only leaving is what I've found: which is that salt-water bath in the sun at Hell's Gate."

Ms. Appleton is slightly taken back, but also energized by this Christian mystic plane of existence I have started to unearth and enliven. My digging has revealed an old foundation that had been purposely buried by the Jews and Catholics. The class was for weeks already talking to friends and family about the crazy Hutchinson girl who went "Native" and stayed *native*, but Ms. Appleton was a chastised and abused woman pioneer, just like my mother, just like Mary Dyer, and just like me.

Ms. Appleton says, "Mmmmhhhmmm... Nothing, you say, is your agenda? Well, I cannot remember *Nothing* be prophesized in the Bible. In fact, I think the Bible says, 'The idle mind is the devil's toy.' Does it not, little Ms. Leaf?"

"I disagree, Ms. Appleton. I believe anything, but *Nothing* is the devil's toys. The demented salute many material objects, including flags and idols, in their Maker's face. A false flag, a false brand, a false idol, or a false God idolized through the selling of indulgences warms only the delusional and shallow. The patriotic flags, States, Bibles, idols, and the killing are the sub human's verification of their ego-mania and self-destructive psychosis. Mathematically, the flags, the State, the Bibles, the idols, and the killing can have nothing to do with love, law, or God, unless love, law, or God *is* the flags, the State, the Bibles, the idols, and the killing."

"The coldest, saddest steps for the examined life are the first few steps on the existential Nothing bridge, with no love, no hate, no beliefs, no ego, and only *a priori* knowledge from your gut. This guttural instinct was my leeway drift as well as the wind in my sails as I crossed this Nothing bridge to the other side. This old transcendental bridge cleanses us of bitterness and betrayal."

I persist with my homeroom inspection: "Here on earth we can try to build that spiritual bridge that combs us out, by not giving or accepting debt, but we will be persecuted for this independence. My mother's and Mary Dyer's independence and dissent against religious hypocrisy and its bloody laws light the Commonwealth and the common people's spirit on fire. An Awakening of common sense from the dismal white-devil malaise. No debt, no standing-army, and free-grace is the American path to freedom in 1650. It is the only path to our American revolution and our continued independence."

MY MAKER

Ms. Appleton says patronizingly, "Okay, little Miss Maple Leaf, so everything is evil besides spiritually surrendering to your Maker?"

"I don't like the word evil," I respond, "but I will say all activities — everything besides life, liberty, and the pursuit of happiness — are all meaningless and surrogate. *Evil* is abstract activities caused by low self-esteem and child abuse. Evil and sin and/or my fifteen classmates' good-work clearly explained this morning — is anything besides life, liberty, and happiness — these cardinal sins are an American treason."

Ms. Appleton questions, "All activities are sinful even if it is for synagogue and State or church and State? Are you saying all activities, even for gross domestic product and economic stability, are meaningless?"

I nod my head yes and say slowly and deliberately, "What is profit, but debt down the road? What is profit, but a crime or an unfair advantage?"

Ms. Appleton teems with a lawyerly roller-coaster response in a sarcastic tone that ends on a surprising good note: "MmmhhmmMM!"

I look for a moment outside the schoolhouse as small grey clouds filter in and sit on top of a sunny horizon. The rain clouds sprinkled showers on our schoolhouse roof, and the rain drops sounded like cat-and-mouse games in the attic, running here all night, running there all night — endless. I look back at my classmates and can only think how they all resembled the sins of the demiurge: the lion-faced serpent of fashion; but I remained focused and continued to fight the good fight for the *good ole cause*.

I look back outside and the sunlight becomes refracted into a washed-out halcyon of sparkling wet showers that look like garland and tinsel on our piney and sandy landscape. I can smell the new sage-colored honeysuckle growing, climbing, struggling to stay alive and develop. Lime-green leaves and buttery honeysuckle flowers, lithe, delicate and pungent — killing themselves with good-work.

I continue: "Yes, that is correct. All is me… me… meaningless…" I hesitated and stalled because my words were a chemical fire on the Judeo-Christian double-negative life. I try hard to pull my already-thrown punch, but my words are a skin-eating disease on my classmates. Unforsaken, I straighten my back, pick up my chin, and walk through the fire. "Ms. Appleton, please understand that these surrogate activities are caused by parental child abuse and low self-esteem. All activity is a surrogate activity. All actions beside non-action are meaningless, all action is low self-esteem."

Ms. Appleton, politely aghast, says, "Well, the London Company, the Church of England, and the Bank of England would not want to hear that…." She continues, "I appreciate your imagination, but isn't *surrendering* or *Nothing* a lonely, dismal, place? What do you live for? What do you work for? Who puts food on the dinner table? Who pays the rent, *et cetera?*

Are you trying to start some rebel Protestant or wild Lutheran free-love cult or tribe here?"

Lawrence the Law quietly slips in like a shadowy tiger shark in the shallows and says, "Hey, Autumn, the Jew tribe pays, the Christian cult pays, and the fascist bureaucrats at the State eagerly *pay to play*. Tribes are playing, praying, and the most successful are paying me for swords, bullets, votes, gentrification, holocausts, and/or a fully catered Mary Dyer execution breakfast this morning. I'm wondering, my dearest and sweetest Ms. Autumn Leaf, is your *Nothing* going to pay to play?"

I ignore Lawrence the Law's *Pay to Play* question, and try to keep the homeroom inspection beat to continue explaining my good-work: "All good questions, Ms. Appleton, but I believe people in America and even people in our mother country England don't want to be told, forced, and/or wormed into believing the Church of England and the Bank of England is not a rigged game. Let me say as no heroine, as a commoner, as the forgotten within not a commonwealth but a common-fraud, let me say that this trickle-down *game* destroys our life. The rigged game or the Neg-Am Jam extinguishes the common man and rescinds our common denominator and our commonwealth. The rigged game or NAJ life clouds individual reason, our free-will, our loves, laws, and Gods. Math and common sense become a control-fraud, and there is no balance or rest. Our self-aware reason, our free-will or free-grace discipline, is the only thing that separates us from the animals. This respect, this reason, this mathesis, is the only thing that separates us from a dog with worms. Instead of worming, Ms. Appleton — I respect."

I persist: "Roger Williams, a.k.a 'Mr. Providence,' said, 'Forced religion is the rape of the soul,' and it is with bold providence that I stand here in class and bring you intangible free-grace. I bring you my surrendering soul with being Nothing and wanting Nothing. I know, class, it may be incomprehensible to you, but this belief of mine is NOT the Lenape spiritual religion. My Maker, whom neither I nor anyone else knows, is my only creditor. My faith is with my Maker and, as always, it will pay for it all. I am not a debtor and my designer certainly is not a financial creditor. Nothing will adapt and Nothing will certainly be the last to die."

Ms. Appleton says, "Well, Ms. Autumn Leaf, *Nothing* can be very threatening to a lot of people. As Lawrence asked you, are you prepared to defend Nothing?"

"I have nothing to take and nothing to defend."

Ms. Appleton says, in a gruff, deep, matter-of-fact way, looking deep into my eyes again this morning, "Well, Autumn Leaf, that's why you are so dangerous."

The class is hushed and looks back at me with trepidation and fright as the Big-Daddy grandfather clock ticks and tocks. Tick-tock, tick-tock, tick-tock. There I was in the far corner, next to the window, floating, next to the green weeping willow on Corn Hill — an outsider, off the grid in a hyperspace. I danced well with my free-grace guardian angel in this golden New England sun shower — my good-work is a glistening, sunny, nourishing, eloquent, and unknown space.

Ms. Appleton, even-keeled, awake, and sailing along now with me at a good clip, says in a sporting tone, "Thank you, Autumn, for your homeroom inspection report, but we've got to get going. I wish you good luck with your free-grace."

I sit down and then Ms. Appleton says to the class, "Thanks to everyone for sharing your good-work — pray thee, dear children, both morning and night, it goes your way!" Ms. Appleton walks over to her Mayflower candle-lamp and extinguishes it with a brushed silver candle-snuffer. She continues, as the smoke billows around her, "Unfortunately, now we must follow Minister Win... I mean Governor Winthrop's Execution Order that our class witness Boston's Puritan justice when it comes to religious civil rights."

Ms. Appleton seems suddenly dazed at her own words and slows down as the candle-lamp smoke wafts and curls above her head. "The Puritan right of our civilization to execute our neighbors for crimes may seem inhumane, children, but for the Jews, Christians, and Muslims, killing is loving — killing is living." The Mayflower cloud shifted above her like a large grey ghost enveloping her and causing her to vanish into the Mayflower cloud as she repeated absentmindedly three times trailing off, "Loving is killing... loving is killing... loving is killing...."

CHAPTER 15

Might Does Make Right — I've Never Met an Elder Here

MIGHT DOES MAKE RIGHT

ur class is now a small litter of kitty cats in a sack on the way to *the* pond. We are stuck in time: bagged and tagged, being pushed and pulled as the sunshine shower turns to a darker steady rain. Low rolling thunder off in the distance trolls around our horizons and my palms start getting sweaty. The small grey clouds lead the way for a new front of large cumulous clouds, the dangerous colors of dirty basements and drowned rats. I swallow hard as the thunder rolls in and encapsulates us. It vibrates not just my own body, but the earth below my feet — the earth shakes beneath our schoolhouse, in our *hill*.

Empowered by the thunder and feeling righteous, Laura Kraven, says to Ms. Appleton and our class, "The executioner is just doing his Divine job; taking an eye for an eye, or a tooth for a tooth. That is just Divine justice."

Elizabeth Winterest asks, with dripping sarcasm, "Whose eye did Mary take? She's being punished as a murderer, but Mary is arguing freedom of speech."

Samuel Payneson answers as if to correct a wrong, "Mary has killed Boston's authority. Mary has spat into our Elder's face and she will pay."

Ms. Appleton says, "Pleaseth me, children, for we can agree that we've all heard the Temptations before, 'An eye for an eye — a tooth for a tooth, vote for me and I'll set you free!' We've all heard all these political excuses for bloodletting before, back in England and Europe. I suppose America will be no different. That's a shame, as America seemed so innocent, so wholesome and honest at first."

I say hopefully to the class, "Happiness is in America." Everyone scoffed at me, the freak in the corner, but I was thinking about Gela / Happiness, my Indian sister.... I'm worlds, galaxies apart from the Boston Puritan and that's the way it shall stay.

Ms. Appleton says, "Okay, class, please line up in alphabetical order by twos outside the schoolhouse. Let's go, children; let's not be late! No hanky-panky. As good Puritans, we can't be late to a date with an executioner, now, can we? She concludes, "We definitely will miss the show so now tally-ho you scally-wag grimalkins," as she starts shepherding and herding us crawling half-dead kitties. Ms. Appleton is waving and moving her arms up and down like a tired humming bird or possibly practicing a sacred Seneca sun dance without her correct costume.

My peers and I started to get out of our desks. This was a class fieldtrip into the real world! Some classmates are excited, and some are indifferent, but most, like me, are in a daze. William leans over to me and asks me, as if he could care, "Are you going to be okay, Susan?"

I don't know what to say. I just keep my sweaty hands on Mary's letters wrapped in my little leather papoose and concentrate on not crying. I am not going to cry for Mary's coming pain and death nor for my complete loss about where Mary's soul is going after she is murdered. I was crying on the inside for having to live in Boston without looking forward to new Mary Dyer letters! Crying for the fact that I should just join Mary and put my neck through that same noose. Might as well get this civilization bullshit over with now, I thought.

This is why I started to cry — because with this execution, with this death, my ridiculous bourgeois powder-puff life will be laid bare. My destiny will open up and it will be a noose and a lonely tree. I can suppress this vision, but all will NOT be for the best. I answer /corner William, and not Billy for the first time today, in a curt know-it-all tone: "Yes, Billy, I'll be fine as soon as the opium cough drops kick in and I learn to live with you unnatural and demented bonobos."

William and I walk out with our classmates to a spring thunderstorm that is starting to gain traction, making me feel claustrophobic. The grassy-green spring leaves and buds are stretching to their sun father from their earth mother. Bushes and trees reach to the steady rain even though their deep roots barely fabricate their dirty home. The green and brown earth smells muddy, fertile, voracious, and on the move. The class, clamoring, form two lines within our bagged life. I line up behind Jonathon Every with his tricorn hat, and he snorts at me like a wild boar. When I slide behind him, tagged, he raises his left shoulder as if to hide or shield himself from me as his sweaty cologne makes me gag. I take out one of the coins he lost earlier during our homeroom inspection, stick it in my eye like a monocle, and tap Sir Every on the shoulder. He turns around, and I say, "Finders keepers — losers weepers."

Jonathon gasps and his jaw drops to the ground, so I opened my eye socket and his silver coin falls into my hand. I then throw it up in the air and watch Sir Every's fat face follow the coin like a dog following a ball to fetch, down to my hand, up into the raining thunder sky, and then down again into the mud. The silver coin rises and twinkles in the grey-cloud camouflage and then slips back into the slippery spring mud. The coin drops like a dead man, or as if the coin belongs to the mud. The mud is the sexy color of a sweaty proud Negress in the rain and the silver has returned to the earth, from where it had come — so I feel good for a moment. Sir Every quickly drops to all fours and digs in the brown mud like a dachshund on the hunt for his currency and then glares at me. Johnny Junior is looking good, covered in chocolate muff... but he burrows out of the dark earth with only a rock in his muddy claw and no silver.

Laura Kraven, the smile-fucker alphabetically behind me, was not impressed with my little see-doggy-boy-run trick. She was waiting patiently and then welcomed me into the line-up with a smirky open-hand gesture, as if she is also waiting to slice my throat. She says kindly, in a whisper, "I know your loss."

I shake my head in disgust at Laura and then I turn my back on her. Israel Wilkinson is to my right and carries his Bible, and he seems to be going to an awards ceremony, not the execution of a woman. Israel refuses to look at me; we are both toward the ends of the two lines of classmates. I am losing focus so I just train my eyes on Sir Jonathon Every's fat neck rolls below his tricorn hat in front of me and continue to gag, becoming nauseous because of his cheap male cologne.

Ms. Appleton says, "Walk silently, children, don't mind the rain, it will wash away our sins — eyes ahead, and no talking. Let the rain fall and wash away our sins! Besides, June's soggy showers bring July's most magnificent flowers."

We slowly lurch forward into a black Sabbath march that quickly turns into a Chinatown dirge in the rain. It seems to be a march to my hanging. Blue jays or catbirds fight and scream to my right amongst the lime green scrub brush just as a bolt of lightning explodes off to the left in the Harbor and shakes us all. We were drowned kitties in a grey bag tingling and mingling with the power of thunder as electricity coaxed through and radiated our fleshy fiber.

We waited for the storm. We counted the seconds — one,

waiting for the thunder, shuffling along to the giant Elm tree. Two, trying to figure out how far away the approaching storm is. Three, the storm and the Elm tree in the swamp make some classmates feel empowered, and, four — others, like myself, feel demoralized and petrified. Five, Laura, in my rear, steps on my heel, and I am just about to whirl around and ring her when — six, the thunderclap shakes our world! I think, six and a half miles away and I — like a heavy bell — ring with thunder! I do nothing except reverberate... my eyes refocus — eyes straight ahead I gag hard, marching forward behind Sir Every — a fat boy with fat rolls in a perfumed blur. I gag and retch again — I'm going to puke.

I reach down to Mary's letters in my leather envelope and then remember suddenly the last time I saw Mary. It was in Boston and I was ten years old and we were going to my mother's trial. My Hutchinson family walked along with the townspeople whispering, taunting us as if the trial were a sporting event, which I now realize American justice is. The mob was not sad but patriotic, as if preparing for a duel or joust with many floats and parties afoot. Gambling, beer, whores, and hotdogs were being sold on the corners. Vendors had plaques and banners to commemorate the Puritan event. Today, with Mary Dyer's execution, it is no different. Misogynist Bostonians yelp along, scurrying for what seems like a lottery or contest for free land and royal privileges. It isn't a land rush in America, but a sacrificial death rush.

Ms. Appleton straightens us out, and in a motivational tone says, "Look, proud children — YOU are our American future! The Town Elders know what's best."

My class and I meandered down narrow old-growth paths to the salty marshes in the rain that has had become warm, gentle, and serious. The tree canopy is high and brilliant as the eel-grass meadows sway in the distance. The goldenrod and Queen Anne's lace line our path that leads our way to the swamp. Boston is majestic and it looks and smells like anything is possible. We walk down the natural yellow and white alley highlighted on both sides of the path with giant white oaks trees that seem like ancient fathers. I remember playing here as a young child under this ceiling of green that seemed like our alien ancestors. I look towards the coast — the smaller, scrappier, cedars, down low with us, the shape of green fire, the *Juniper Virginias* — these cedars are my only friends!

The low-tide smell of sandy-brown crustacean life washing and dying with the horse-shoe tides can knock you back. Eucalyptus trees mingle with black pines, jellyfish, and huge seagulls with six-foot wing spans who dine like flying sharks. Bogs with bright green reeds sway along the mud-clay coast filled with snapping turtles and steamers. Beach grass neatly trims the harbor whitecaps not far from the shore. The Atlantic Ocean white-caps chop on top with briny teal water the color of jade and cobalt. The Sargasso seaweed smell is delicious and enchanting as it touches my spine and soul. Boston Harbor is commanding and floating in splendid synchronicity with the seashore and her sharky gulls.

The execution crowd at the Elm tree is fairly large for this small colony. Everyone is dressed as if for church or a celebratory dinner with dead rats. Church ladies — Ms. Vassar and Mrs. Radcliffe are selling horse manure balls and rotten fruit out of wicker picnic baskets so the mob can throw them at Mary Dyer as she is led to her execution. Mrs. Holyoke knitted commemorative pink doilies that read: *"Mary the Monster" and "Away, Away, Away — Boston,* 1650.*"* Dear reader, and for those who do not read the English language, I will draw and smudge out these fine linen doilies that looks and feels like a meaningful breath of air. However, the doilies that lay and float like tissues are snowballs of surgical sutures that grow from the inside out like a cancer. The reasonable women says, "A stich in time saves nine," but these doilies that look like wounds with sutures and stiches saves no one. The excited doily customers line up, clamoring and yelling for more because these dead-end doily scars are a memento or war trophy for those happy to get away with killing.

The mob's eyes are black and alien; everyone wears a mask or is unmasked. It is a macabre French opera — top hats with colorful flowers and red lip stick smeared across lips as the powdered white-devil ghosts cackle. Skulls pop into focus on the half-dead; or is it faces and masks on the dead? The charade of civilization is exposed and insanity has taken over. Lovers chew on each other's tongues as poets, priests, and politicians fight for the most votes with cash and loose hips. The diseased dance and sing their way towards a death rush.

The crowd chants, "String her up! String her up! String her up!"

The Elect and Elders of Boston stand at attention under the giant Elm tree conniving how to carve up the Mary Dyer's estate after they "String her up." All is for the best in Puritan America, or so they pray.

At the base of the executioners' Elm tree, eyes dart about, except for the eyes of those who wrote the script to this tragedy. Minister Winthrop, the Governor of this Colony, was at the center of the scrum with the other Elders, Elect, and magistrates. The rain came down steadily now, and in a Puritan's eye this damning rain, this execution, and this female sacrifice would show the Christian Zionist's Divine power. A mighty rain makes right in America.

Governor Winthrop walks over, bows, and tips his hat to Ms. Appleton and our class and says, "Ah, yes, you beautiful, Christian, God-fearing children. The future ministers and Governors of America!

Governor Winthrop is in all his glory during this tributary murder of a troublemaker. Governor Winthrop continues, feigning respect of our class and the common folk gathered for the hanging, which highlights him to be really that type of man, and that bureaucratic despot that actually

Mary the Monster Doily

Flower Doily

enjoys drowning bags of kittens. My class look up to Governor Winthrop as half-dead cats or cockroaches do before they're going to be squashed. Winthrop is the last thing we are going to see before he ties the bag, or brings down his might. But before that happens he says, "Children, this morning you will learn one of the most important lessons in life: Don't ask questions! Don't ask the monster in the trees for the answers to life, and always respect your Mother and Father. Respect your Elders or you, too, will dance a little duet with this Elm tree."

As the sinister Minister says this, he holds up two fingers upside-down, impersonating a person's legs and body kicking and twitching during their execution. Then the Governor and the mob laughed as he puts his hands behind his back, rolls his eyes in back of his head, and starts to twitch and jerk like those who dangle from a hangman's rope. The orthodox Governor mocks those ugly and handicapped souls who are executed at the hands of society. The Divine Governor simulates the executed victim — blinded, muffled, stagnant, forgotten and with useless movements. The patriotic mob roars approval and appreciation as the Puritan Governor continues to mock his many silent victims, simulating a mouth gagged, enabling only mumbled screams for help. Foul, whiny bird-like shrieks dribble out of his mouth: "Annnna, Eewwww.... Annnna, Eeewwww.... Annnna, Eeewwww...."

Winthrop is a royal adagio, a *pas de deux* — a step of two, an adagio between the Bank of England and a Puritan false-God. The Governor's loyal subjects' love, the Governor's laws, and the Governor's God's arms are now tied behind him — love, law, and God, abandoned in Puritan America. America is like a ballerina jumping, falling, squirming, yet still trying and failing with only a one-step *sissone*. The Minister's facial contortions mocking his loves, laws, and God are deep and profound, yet, at the same time, the Governor feels and knows the subject's and victim's sin intimately. Like Winthrop, the future orthodox and Ivy-League Governors and Puritan Ministers of America, they will dance a short dance, but their two-step *sissone* will never land.

The Governor quickly drops his Boston ballet routine and becomes Minister Winthrop again and declares aloud, in a demanding and God-like voice, looking into all of our eyes, "Then, after your little Boston ballet — MmmMmmm... down you shall fall into the devil's inferno of hell! Respect your Elders or you will dance like Mary!"

The class shuddered, our eyes frantic and aglow. We all stepped back aghast at this Boston education, as this Puritan tragic comedy was revved up into a patriotic blood sport. At this very moment, someone in the mob yelled, "Here comes the Monster!"

The crowd went hysterical, throwing bottles, yelping, and a-hollering! Our parents, the Town, the Elect and Elders started singing low and heavy in a dirge, hooligan style, "Mary the Monster, Mary the Monster, Mary the Monster."

Everyone turns around to rubberneck over his or her neighbor and cheer. A small garrison of soldiers escorts what seems like a small tornado rolling, rotating, a dancing devil of people, towards us. Instigators, pundits, and idiots are bouncing along, throwing rotten and moldy fruit at the center of the brigade. Packs of dogs, dancing with the mob, yelp, bark, growl, and bite each other. The roar of the multitude became deafening so I covered my ears, closed my eyes, and huddled with my chin down in my chest.

Israel, to my right, pokes me in the ribcage and says, "Lawrence was right — you and William are Mary Dyer criers. And I thought you were tough — a Separatist."

I look up, hold my chin high, and, with streams of tears coming down my face, I concentrate on Sir Jonathon Every's fat neck roll and his barber's incredible skills of trimming hairy fat rolls.

Mary was unseen as the devil mob around her moved closer. The human hyenas taunted Mary, yelling, "Where's your *God* now? Should have hung you last time! Should have stayed on Shelter Island, loser!" And my favorite, "Providence is for Pussies."

The soldiers pushed this rolling mob towards the Elm tree with their spears as if they were some type of noble discipline, might, or justice on this earth. Whether you're part of a civilization, a universe, or a tribe, jackals and minnows will always feed off the fat cat. Trickle-down economics, survival of the fittest, and/or might-makes-right, keeps the heart dark, and the sharks and vultures fat and happy. I can feel them circling below and circling above — the NAJ life.

I've Never Met An Elder Here

I struggle to look over or around Ms. Appleton as she is now standing in between me and the approaching Mary Dyer dirge. A soldier pushes back at the rolling mob and for a moment I see Mary's face looking up into the sun. The soldier marches at attention again and blocks my view, but the funeral dirge is turning into a rollicking float at Mardi Gras. The garrison soldier rolls with the mob, allowing me to see Mary's content smile for a moment before it is sideswiped by a rotten tomato. The rotten fruit knocks her almost off her feet and produces a downcast frown as she closes her eyes. The soldier steadies Mary and moves her along towards Boston justice as a ball of manure splashes the two of them. In slow motion, Mary closes her eyes, protecting herself from what she doesn't want to see.... Mary, a free-grace friend, smiles again as her face is smeared and drips with compost. Mary's ferocity and passion for changing Boston's bloody laws and moving beyond death are not blocked or thrown by these gluttons of sin.

Just at this moment and within this viewpoint Ms. Appleton turns around and looks directly at me. She takes a few steps towards me and in a low, secretive and advisory tone says, "This will be you if you don't shape up, you crunchy little Autumn Leaf."

I feel violated. All of Boston knows this Shaker, Quaker, free-grace freak hanging could be me next. But why is my teacher — Ms. Appleton — stating the obvious and rubbing salt in my wounds as my only living mentor? My female teacher is cruel and petty. Mary Dyer is about to drink her hemlock poison and my heroine teacher is going to hand it to her! Like this mob, Ms. Appleton became sickly, insane, and stuck in her *warrior* mode; she is a woman and teacher conscribed to the sad circus of breeding soldiers, debt, and the taste for blood.

Ms. Appleton goes to the head of our two lines and says, "Class, please stay together and listen to your wise Governor. Life is not to be examined or questioned." She concludes, with an eye on me, "Stay in line, keep your head down and your mouth shut." She adjusts her bonnet and corset before sashaying over to the other Boston ladies-in-waiting. At that moment, Mary passes my class and we do not look at each other. Mary is proudly focused and present as she is led to the Elm tree and put on a crude stool or a bucket that elevates her slightly above the unruly crowd.

Just at this moment, Israel Wilkinson, to my right, with his Bible now held like an axe in his two hands above his head, slowly starts chanting and chopping, "Mary the Monster, Mary the Monster, Mary the Monster." Israel is pumping and striking with his Bible in time to the anthem "Mary the Monster, Mary the Monster."

The manic mob sing along with Israel, escalating the chorus into a frenzied uplifting hooligan harmony. The soldiers continue to keep the mob back as the Governor motions with his hand to the crowd to calm down as one would pet, pat, or cajole a barking dog to simmer down.

The mob recedes and the Governor clears his throat. "We are here this morning as holy Christians in control of our domain. We will not tolerate blasphemers and heretics here in America."

The crowd cheers!

The Governor continues. "Whether these lost souls are Baptists, free-grace freaks, Quakers, Shakers or whatever voodoo they do — it will not be tolerated in America."

The crowd cheers, "The Monster! The Monster! The Monster!"

The Governor continues. "Mary Dyer was given many chances to repent and respect our one true God and his laws just like her witchy friend Anne Hutchinson. Mary has disrespected our Elect and Elders repeatedly and today she will be punished."

The crowd again roars louder, "String her up! String her up! String her up!"

The Governor asks another magistrate to read the criminal charges, Judgment, and Execution Order. Mary Dyer, tottering on a bucket, seems focused on something else now. The magistrate reads aloud the Puritan laws which are complicated excuses or *legalese* that Christian Zionists use to kill even though Moses and Jesus told them not to kill.

The crowd again roars even louder, "The Monster!!!" This segues nicely into a sloppy and drunk chorus: "Maaaryy the mooonsteerrrr, Maaaryy the mooonsteerrrr, Where are you now? Where are you now?

The Minister bids them to some politeness by saying to the mob, "Dear Americans, I pray you will learn to obey our laws and learn from this justice before you today." The Governor turns to Mary and says, "Serpent woman, dost thou have any last words before we cast you into a fiery eternity?

Dost thou wish us good Divine Christians, us elected Elders of New England, to pray for your cursed and damned soul?"

Mary looks older than I remember and I am ashamed of this thought. She seems to be losing her faith and starts to tear-up slightly.... Mary's dark brown walnut hair used to be that of a noble heiress, but now it looks like a grey tangled fishing net. Compost and manure are streaked down her face and her thin drab grey dress clings to her wet body showing us more than we should see. It is vile to stand here, it is sickening to be part of this mob... it is revolting and nauseating.

Mary was still lost in her despair as she slowly looked at everyone in the crowd, saying nothing.... Her Welsh eyes slid slowly left like heavy black rocks on solid ice. Her eyes slid right, looking for something or someone.... I cannot look anymore and bury my head. I want to run and hide. I know Mary is looking for me — one of her last hopes for New England. Her happy-go-lucky Autumn Leaf!

The main actors in this macabre Boston opera knew whom she is looking for and it is most likely was going to be the next person dangling and dancing from this Elm tree. Minister Winthrop and Ms. Appleton both turn to me in order to hook another Separatist pilgrim during this fishing-expedition execution.

Minister Winthrop says to Mary, "Speak now or forever die an animal."

Mary says nothing... there is the silence of Nothing! These pigs waited in doubt! I look up, chin-up, soul sovereign, filled with nothingness and free-grace, and yell, "Joyfully you go, girl! Joyfully you go!"

Mary's eyes, like a hawk's, catch mine. Not as a predator, but as a solid family hunting together in the woods, we connect! Mary knows I hear her telepathic joy: "There is my sister, there is that little red fire — Ms. Autumn Leaf!"

"Sorry," I say with my eyes as my free-grace sister with a

rope around her neck bids me adieu with a confident and slow nod of respect. I yell, "Joyfully we go, Mary! Joyfully we go!"

The Governor is livid and clears this throat in the direction of the Boston Court Clerk, who has been volunteered to kick the bucket Mary is teetering upon. Time starts to skip and glitch, it collapses into a silent slow-motion horror. My now-manic teacher Ms. Appleton runs away from the ladies in waiting and starts to charge me silently and slowly with a clenched fist above her head and her index finger on her lips insinuating that I must keep quiet. My world is languidly and wordlessly falling apart.

Mary Dyer almost falls off the bucket and the crowd gasps! The Clerk steadies her and the mob breathes a sigh of relief as no one wants to spoil a good religious sacrifice. The quiet relief with awkward chuckles and smirks slowly and painfully turns into introspective horror as the orthodox Puritans slowly realize within this quietude how truly guilty, pathetic, and deeply horrible they are. The silence around the Elm tree screams the truth and justice is lost. Everyone here under this tree, from all walks of life, from high-born royals to those cast as unholy look at each other uncomfortably in dumbfounded silence.... We all look at Mary Dyer, a women with her arms tied behind her back and drenched with slop and spit. The obscene Puritan mob is Awakened to the fact that they are unaware of what justice is.... We are perverted murderers killing a half-naked women. Here is civilization falling apart — here is Nothing.

The Governor growls back, "The Elected Elders in the Boston Church and State are willing to give you justice and pardon you, Ms. Dyer! Do you want justice, are you willing to repent?"

Mary chuckles to herself, taking in her last bit of air, and replants *the good ole cause* firmly in America. She looks directly into John Winthrop's eyes with an American honky-tonk accent and says, "Well, sorry to disappoint you, Johnny-boy, but I've never really met an Elder here in America." She slowly looks around at all of us in the crowd. The Boston mob with its mouth down to the ground is damned and witnessed by Mary and then she repeats even more confidently, "Nope, definitely never met an Elder here."

The Governor and crowd are speechless. I laugh heartedly.

Then Mary turns to me, concluding her own homeroom inspection and good-work in an upbeat style with an experienced and wise tone in her voice. Mary looks up and over the mob of the Elders, Elect, lawyers, and their courtiers, and says, "And yes, my lovely Autumn, yes, indeed — joyfully we go!"

Governor Winthrop, disgusted with Mary's last words, snorts and shakes his head in order to rid himself of that blasphemy, which gets in his face and mouth, and up his nose. The Governor shakes his head like a neighing, sneezing horse trying to rid himself of Mary's free-grace happiness.

The Minister, before he kills Mary, spits in her face and repeats the Mary Dyer nursery rhyme back to her like a bratty child: "Mary the Monster, where are you now? Hunhh?" And then in an escalating sinister Governor tone he declares, "Away with the witch. Away, away, away!" flicking his right hand towards the Court Clerk to kick the bucket, as if he is removing lint from his pant leg.

Mary drops laughing and then dances her last dance. I look away... the crowd cheers as Mary dies — dancing the Boston ballet.

The mob starts up again with the Mary the Monster nursery rhyme, but now amazingly and obediently, the demented religious civilization sings the new chorus already transposed and parroted from the Minister's lips just a few moments ago! I think, wow, the rabble learns quickly when it wants to. All I can hear over and over is the new rhyme: "Away with the witch. Away, away, away!"

Alone now within this witch-hunt, the Minster and the

mob's murder party sized me up as the next female sacrifice. Scheming eyes all around me tightened the noose around my neck. Or is it my mother's hands around my neck — tightening and strangling? Or is it Ms. Appleton's hands? That someone or something that was holding my hand earlier in the morning is gone. The hands on my neck squeeze tighter. My guardian angel is dead and my imagination is playing tricks on me. For all I can hear is the Puritan grand-father clock beating like a heart. The Puritan time does not: tick-tock, tick-tock, but the clock beats like an Indian drum in the woods: drum, drum, drum, drum. The hands on my neck squeeze tighter. The clock's heart beat slows as a fire on the inside of the clock smokes and spreads like wild fire. The clock cabinet door slowly swings open. Flames lick the face of Puritan time as the gears, pulleys and weights melt and crumble. The heart beat stops. The hands on my neck squeeze tighter.

Waking me up from this dazed strangulation is Ms. Appleton shaking me by both arms, yelling, and screaming incoherently at me. Dear reader pray, I can't understand what she is saying — I am going somewhere else now. I think to myself, now I know — I *know*, as I become unfocused and stare at Mary's dead silhouette looking back at me, swinging from the elm tree.

My mouth becomes metallic and bloody. I gag, swallow... no use — I heave, sweating a cold sweat — I swallow hard again. I start to taste the biscuit I ate earlier this morning... I heave, I retch... I droop over puking on Ms. Appleton and the new shoes Aunt Alexandra bought for me. I think how sad this reading is... I heave again and spit up some bloody bile. I beg your pardon, dear reader, for sharing so much during these last four hours, but hear me pray and see my drawings from this fine spring day. For all I can see are women dancing and all I can hear is America singing, "Away with the witch. Away, away, away!"

The Boston Ballet

www.ingramcontent.com/pod-product-compliance
Lightning Source LLC
Chambersburg PA
CBHW051135030726
47504CB00004B/885